D0469194

TOR BOOKS BY R. A. SALVATORE

The Highwayman
The Ancient
The Dame
The Bear*

*forthcoming

THE DAME

R. A. SALVATORE

TOR®
fantasy

A TOM DOHERTY ASSOCIATES BOOK
NEW YORK

THE DAME

Map by Joseph Mirabello
Chapter opening illustrations by Shelly Wan

A Tor Book
Published by Tom Doherty Associates, LLC
175 Fifth Avenue
New York, NY 10010

www.tor-forge.com

Tor® is a registered trademark of Tom Doherty Associates, LLC.

ISBN 978-0-7653-5745-8

First Edition: August 2009
First Mass Market Edition: July 2010

Printed in the United States of America

0 9 8 7 6 5 4 3 2 1

The Turghar Glacier · Mithranidoon · ALPINADOR

VANGUARD
● CHAPEL PELLINOR
TANADOON ● ● PIRETH VANGUARD
PORT VANGUARD
GULF OF CORONA

MIRIANIC OCEAN

PALMARISTOWN
● CHAPEL ABELLE
POLLCREE

DE LAVAL CITY · HONCE
● ESKALD

BELT-AND-BUCKLE
PRYD TOWN
YANSINCHESTER
FELIDAN BAY
ETHELBERT DOS ENTEL

THE MANTIS ARM
THE BROKEN COAST

BEHR

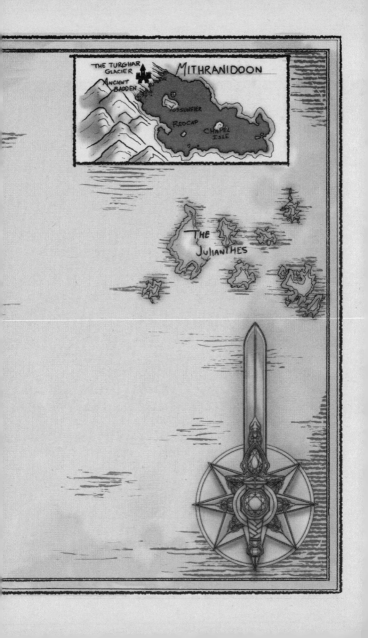

THE DAME

PROLOGUE

Brother Pinower hooked a finger inside the collar of his brown woolen robe and jerked it back and forth, suddenly feeling uncomfortably warm. And itchy, so itchy, as if a thousand little insects were crawling across his skin. But it wasn't the sun or the wind that had this young and healthy rising voice in the Abellican Church squirming. He knew that he should leave the wall immediately to report the dramatic and troubling sight before him, but he found that his legs would not answer his call. He couldn't turn away but was mesmerized, as were the other brothers of Chapel Abelle who were working on the main wall this day, by the long lines of ghastly wounded men.

Ghastly wounded and with many dead along the road behind the lines, no doubt.

"Someone inform Father," another dumbfounded monk managed to remark.

The sound seemed to break Pinower's paralysis. "Set them up in the courtyard," he instructed his many juniors. "Gather servants with blankets and fresh water and brothers with all the soul stones we can muster." He cast a pensive glance down the long slope to the southeast, to the seemingly endless line of casualties. He tried not to think about the many excruciating deaths he would witness that night.

When he climbed down from the wall, the horrible vision mercifully lost to him, Pinower found his footing and his purpose, and he sprinted across the wide courtyard, past the lower buildings of the gigantic chapel complex to the main keep and the office of Father Yurkris Artolivan, the oldest man in the Order of Abelle.

Artolivan looked every bit of his more than eighty years that day, slumped behind his desk, his skin sagging, his eyes dull and weary. Even his sparse, white hair seemed thinner and lifeless. He glanced up, as did his attendants, when Pinower rushed in unannounced.

"Wounded arrive from the battles," Pinower said, gasping for breath. "Many."

Artolivan exchanged concerned looks with his attendants.

"The rumors of the fighting in Pollcree?" one of those younger brothers remarked, for indeed they had heard only a few days before that two great forces were closing in on the small village from opposite ends and were sure to meet in bloody battle. Pollcree wasn't far from Chapel Abelle, barely a day's hard ride, and if these reports were to be confirmed by the arrival of the wounded this day it would mark by far the closest any of the heavy fighting had come to Chapel Abelle.

"Many?" Father Artolivan asked.

"More than all of those wounded we have seen cumulatively," Brother Pinower replied. He could not be certain if that was technically true, but it certainly seemed so from the view on the wall.

The old man rubbed a hand across his weathered and wrinkled face and with great effort pulled himself up from his chair. The nearest attendant brother offered an arm of support, but the proud Artolivan brushed it away and moved from around his desk.

"If there are men of Pollcree among their ranks, it would not do to keep them here," Brother Pinower reasoned. "I know our agreement, but they are too close to home. I would fear retribution or attempts at escape."

Artolivan paused and nodded, flashing a yellow smile at young Pinower. "You look better since you were put in charge of handling the prisoners," he said, a rare compliment from the man known as the father of the Order of Abelle. "Some of that paleness is at last retreating from your cheeks."

Pinower shifted uneasily from foot to foot, not even beginning to know how to respond.

"So, too, have you realized a confidence to speak of such policy in a room full of your superiors," said Artolivan.

Brother Pinower's shoulders slumped, fearing that he had overstepped his authority here. He glanced around at the older monks, all of whom were staring at him.

"We need such confidence in these dark times, Brother Pinower," said Artolivan, and several of the others cracked smiles that put Pinower at ease. "I have watched you grow beyond my expectations through this time of crisis."

Pinower felt his face blush fiercely.

"Crisis," Artolivan repeated, suddenly sounding like he was tired. So very tired. Artolivan and the warring lairds had worked out a compromise to allow the various chapels of the Order of Abelle, particularly the immense Chapel Abelle, to be used by both sides in the ongoing and escalating war between Laird Delaval and Laird Ethelbert as a neutral repository for the many prisoners taken on the field and, of course, as a point of medical care for all the wounded of either side. That was the best role for the Order of Abelle, Artolivan had rightly decided, a way to bring some manner of order and peace to a land ravaged by continuing war.

Thus, Chapel Abelle had become a dumping ground for prisoners from both the warring lairds, Ethelbert of the southeasternmost Holding of Honce, Ethelbert dos Entel, and Delaval, the most prominent and powerful laird in all the land, who ruled the strategic and fortified city at the southernmost navigable spot on the great river, the Masur Delaval. Scores of prisoners, hundreds even, had come into the increasingly vast complex of Chapel Abelle over the last months.

Brother Pinower had been the one assigned to oversee them, to heal their wounds, to put them to work, and to ensure that this encampment of opposing sides had remained secure and peaceful. His work had earned him praise from Artolivan and many of the other older brothers, and the young Pinower had felt as if his contribution here had been in the truest spirit of the tenets of Abelle. He used those thoughts to bolster his courage at that moment, for he knew that this day would be different. Of the prisoners who had come in before today, few had been seriously wounded. The battles had been so far-off that any soldiers grievously injured had not survived the long and arduous journey. Thus, before today, most coming to Chapel Abelle had suffered only minor wounds or no wounds at all. They were simply prisoners, who, in return for their lives, had taken an oath that their stake in the fighting had ended and they would serve out the end of the war in hard labor. Instead of killing their Honce brothers who happened to be fighting on the side of the other laird, Delaval's men would toil for the monks and their never-ending construction on this, the greatest chapel, perhaps the greatest complex, in the known world.

"Which banner, Ethelbert or Delaval?" Artolivan asked, his voice slurring, as if he had been drinking. He had not.

"I could not discern, Father. But likely both, I believe, by the sheer number of men involved."

Artolivan and the senior brothers exchanged looks again, but this time of doubt. Someone had won and someone had lost, and while many of the wounded would no doubt be men of both lairds, the prisoners who would remain behind in civil captivity would be of one faction or another.

O n the ball of one foot, the small and lithe brown-skinned woman slowly pivoted. She stayed in perfect balance, ultimate grace, as she brought her other leg up teasingly, knee bent at first, but then straightening to become perpendicular with her body.

At the same time, the soft, silken robe she wore slid away from her smooth flesh, revealing her delicate foot and calf, her smooth thigh all the way to her hip.

Though deeply entranced in her dance, moving with the precision of a warrior and the discipline of a Jhesta Tu mystic, Affwin Wi still managed to glance from the corner of her large, dark eyes at the old man sitting and watching.

The septuagenarian, Laird Ethelbert of the southeast-ernmost Holding of Honce, gave a great sigh at that al-luring turn and revealing movement of the woman's soft clothing.

Affwin Wi smiled a little bit outwardly and a great deal inwardly. She heard the longing and the love in the old laird's sigh, the wistful dreaminess in his still sharp eye. She entertained him, but she was no harem piece, no subservient or helpless creature.

She was, or had been, Jhesta Tu. She could outfight any man or woman in Ethelbert's army, and he knew it. She carried great power and great independence, and she was here, dancing before him, because she chose to be and not because he had ordered her.

And that gave her power.

She danced on and on, to one sigh after another from the man who wanted to consume her in passion but no longer could.

Gradually, Ethelbert's eyes closed, a look of great contentment on his face. Affwin Wi danced over to him and slid down onto the arm of his throne beside him, hugging his face against her small breasts until he began breathing in the deep rhythms of pleasant sleep.

Smiling still, Affwin Wi left the room, to find Merwal Yahna, young and strong, his virility shown in his hardened warrior muscles and exaggerated by the imposing profile of his shaven head. He wasn't large and bulky like so many of the greatest Honce warriors, who required such brawn to swing their gigantic swords and axes, but lithe and taut, a warrior of the desert and the fighting arts favored there, where speed and precision overcame bulk.

"I do not like that you dance for him," said the man, whom she had trained in the ways of the Jhesta Tu, her finest student.

She laughed dismissively.

"He loves you!"

"He cannot make love *to* me," Affwin Wi reminded as she reached up her hand and gently stroked Merwal Yahna's chiseled shoulder and upper arm. "He desires it but is too old."

"But you would let him if he could," the man accused.

"Your jealousy flatters me," Affwin Wi replied playfully. "And excites me." She moved toward the man alluringly, but he grabbed her by the upper arms and pulled her back to arm's length.

"You would!" Merwal Yahna growled.

With a subtle roll of her arms, Affwin Wi brought her

hands up, under, and then back out over Merwal Yahna's grasp, her elbows breaking his hold. She caught a grip on his forearm as she pressed his arms wide, and let her hands slide up until she had him firmly by the wrists.

A movement subtle, gentle, and effective, as was Affwin Wi.

"We are here to fight," Merwal Yahna reminded her. "We are paid as mercenaries, not whores!"

Affwin Wi laughed disarmingly. "We are employed by Ethelbert."

"To fight!"

"And so we have and so we will. His warriors look upon us with awe," said Affwin Wi. "He pays us well, but is there nothing more?"

Her conniving grin gave Merwal Yahna pause, and he stared at her curiously.

"Ethelbert is the ruler of a great city and land with wealth to rival the sheiks of Jacintha," she said. "He has no heir."

Merwal Yahna, not even fighting her hold, could only sigh at the ever-pragmatic attitude of his lover. Affwin Wi had no shame about her body or about lovemaking. To her, all of her physical being was merely a conduit to help her attain the emotional and spiritual goals—or in this case, the simple power offered by her alliance and dalliances with Ethelbert.

She had never pretended to be anything other than a woman who would have her way. No man—not Ethelbert, not even Merwal Yahna—could ever possess her.

"I grow warm and hungry when I dance," she purred, her voice suddenly husky. "Are you going to disappoint me?"

Merwal Yahna tugged his hands free and pulled Affwin Wi in for a crushing hug and passionate kiss. He tried to bend her backward to slow-drop her to the thick pillows spread about their room, but with an easy step and a twist of her pretty feet it was he, not she, who went down on his back.

Merwal Yahna was not disappointed.

Two banners preceded the lines into Chapel Abelle's courtyard soon after, one of Laird Delaval and the other of the third great city of Honce, the port of Palmaristown. The pennants came in side by side, a curious arrangement in these times, when the arrogant Laird Delaval was claiming unequivocal kingship of the whole of the land. But when Father Artolivan, no stranger to Palmaristown, noted the man riding the armored chestnut stallion before the banners, he surely understood.

The large warrior held up his hand to stop his entourage, then trotted the chestnut stallion over to the group of monks and dismounted with great ease, a man obviously accustomed to riding in full and decorated bronze armor.

"Prince Milwellis," one of the brothers greeted when it became apparent that Father Artolivan was struggling to recall the young warrior's name. "How fares your father, Laird Panlamaris of Palmaristown?"

"Well, Brother . . ." the man replied and motioned as if he, too, could not remember a name.

"Jurgyen," the monk explained.

"Indeed, and I do recall seeing you at my father's court."

"And this is Father . . . ?"

"Artolivan, yes, that name is known to me," said Milwellis. "A fine day to be in such company, Father." He bowed low in respect.

"A fine day?" Father Artolivan replied. "You have many outside who might not agree with your description."

"The battle was won, and that is no bad thing."

"Won at great cost."

"Pollcree?" Brother Pinower asked, and Milwellis snorted.

"It once was," the warrior replied. He pulled off his helm and shook his great shock of red hair, which bounced thick about his shoulders.

The flippant response brought a sour look to the faces of some of the brothers, Artolivan included, but that only made Milwellis snicker even more. Brother Pinower decided then and there that he didn't much care for this one.

"I did not know that Palmaristown had joined in the fighting," said Father Artolivan.

"We threw in with the claims of Laird Delaval long ago."

"Yes, yes, of course, the brothers of the Chapel of Precious Memories so informed us," Artolivan pressed. "But I did not know that your army had marched."

"No choice to it," Milwellis explained. "Laird Ethelbert has procured the allegiance of the many holdings along Felidan Bay and even on the Mantis Arm," he explained, referring to the long stretch of rocky coastland of easternmost Honce. "They had claimed neutrality, but no more. Ethelbert the dog has raised the stakes in this war."

"Many of those same seaside holdings have been sailing for Laird Delaval, have they not?" Father Artolivan interrupted with startling forcefulness, the man clearly tired of all this seemingly pointless warfare.

"They would have been wise to hold with their first choice, then," said Milwellis. "Their march to Pollcree was no more than an act of the deepest desperation by Ethelbert. Laird Delaval has established the center around the Holding of Pryd, commanding a line from that crossroad all the way to the Belt-and-Buckle in the south. Desperate Laird Ethelbert thought to flank that line and strike at Palmaristown, but rest assured that the tactic has failed."

"I will rest assured when this war is at its end, and not before," said Father Artolivan.

"We near that day!"

"So we have been hearing for many months. And yet, the wounded and the prisoners come in at greater pace each week."

"Many wounded today, I fear," said Milwellis, and he turned to glance back at the gate, where his soldiers were bringing in dozens of injured men.

"They will fill the courtyard and more," Brother Pinower dared to interject.

"Nay, that is the lot of them," said Milwellis.

Pinower wore a most curious expression. "Surely there is many times that number! I saw them from the wall."

"Mostly Ethelbert's men," Milwellis explained. "They will not enter the chapel courtyard until all of my men are fully attended. Every scratch."

"Prince Milwellis, that is not the agreement of the church," Father Artolivan reminded, but the man from Palmaristown was hearing none of it. He stepped forward and rose up tall, towering over the old Artolivan and making him seem small indeed in that moment—a realization that did not sit well on poor, shaken Brother Pinower!

"Here is the new agreement, old Father," Milwellis calmly explained. "You are to immediately and fully tend to my men, the men who serve Laird Panlamaris, my father. The dogs that run to Ethelbert's whistle will wait."

"And if Ethelbert's general brings in the wounded and the prisoners next time, are we to follow a reversed edict from him?" Artolivan shrewdly asked.

"No general of Laird Ethelbert will reach Chapel

Abelle, unless as a prisoner," Milwellis assured him. "You will do as I instruct."

"And if we do not?"

The man smiled and lifted an eyebrow, a clear measure of threat in his posture. "That would not be wise."

"Nor would your stubborn and determined effort to drive the Order of Abelle from the side of Laird Delaval, which is surely the end result of your insistence," Father Artolivan replied with an evenness and strength in his voice that those around him had not heard in years, one that impressed and amazed Brother Pinower. "We have remained neutral, to the gain of both warring lairds and, more importantly, to the benefit of the people of Honce. If we are forced to break that neutral posture, I assure you that we will break against the laird applying that pressure. Rethink your position, Prince of Palmaristown, or I expect that Laird Delaval will come to blame Milwellis for the great loss of the brothers and their healing stones!"

The prince seemed almost to deflate at that, albeit slowly, as he gradually rolled back onto his heels. He kept his eyes narrow, though, and his teeth gritted, and he did not blink for many heartbeats.

"Brothers," Father Artolivan went on, "go through our gates and retrieve the wounded Ethelbert soldiers. Prepare the triage in the courtyard, as according to our agreements with both of the warring lairds. And when you do, be sure that there are no indications, on clothing or jewelry, of those poor unfortunates to determine allegiance to either laird. Those most wounded are to be tended first, regardless of allegiance, as is our way."

"These men are my prisoners!" Milwellis roared.

"And when you leave them here, they fall under the protection and responsibility of the Order of Abelle. As was agreed, Prince. Look around you at the nonclergy working on our walls and structures! Nine hundred and more have been sent here, and nearly half are men of Laird Delaval, captured by the forces of Ethelbert! Many came here wounded, many whole but as prisoners. They are out of the fight . . ." He paused as Milwellis whirled away and leaped back up onto his horse.

Without another word, the Prince of Palmaristown spun his mount around and galloped through the gate, his personal guard sweeping up in his wake.

"That one is trouble," one of the brothers remarked.

"It will come to this in the end, I fear," said Father Artolivan. "As the stalemate inevitably deepens and the common folk begin to grumble and stir in revolt, their families decimated by the continuing war, we will be forced into choosing a side."

"And how will we choose?" Brother Pinower dared ask.

Father Artolivan had no answer.

"They break and turn!" came a cry from the wall.

Artolivan led his entourage to the open gate, to look down upon the field, where indeed Prince Milwellis and the bulk of his forces had turned away.

"Abelle save us," Brother Pinower whispered as he sorted through it, for while one group of Palmaristown soldiers hustled the healthy Ethelbert prisoners toward Chapel Abelle, no doubt to hand them off and be rid of them, the main Palmaristown group led by Prince Milwellis took with them the wounded men loyal to their enemy, Laird Ethelbert! They were not going to allow the monks to heal those enemy wounded.

"The fool has just assured that there will never be peace in Honce, whether Ethelbert or Delaval proves victorious," Father Artolivan remarked.

"What will they do to them?" Brother Pinower dared to ask.

"Nothing," Father Artolivan said bitterly. "Prince Mil-wellis will simply let them die of their wounds."

Pinower looked over to another of the brothers, who merely shook his head and shrugged, and in that moment, Brother Pinower came to know the dark truth of Father Artolivan's prediction.

PART ONE

AFTERMATH

What do I owe?

*To myself, to those I love, to my community around me
and to the world, what do I owe? This is the essence of the
question Dame Gwydre put to me when she insisted that
I would not flee her beleaguered Holding of Vanguard in
its time of darkness. Her contention, her belief in me—
not in my fighting abilities but in the essence of who I am
as a person—has shaken me profoundly.*

*Vaughna, Crait, Olconna . . . they're all dead now. And
Brother Jond has been horribly wounded, his eyes taken
by the fine edge of the sword I carry as my own. We five
traveled together, we fought together, and I am alive only
because of their efforts. With my gemstone lost, they all
but carried me the many miles to the glacier, where, if I
had simply fallen to the ground along the way, our troll
captives would have put a painful end to me. When Ancient Badden, that most vile creature, discovered the
truth of my sword, Vaughna claimed the blade as her
own and died horribly in the maw of Badden's monstrous
pet.*

*When Badden tried to kill me, Cormack and his pow-
rie friends, who knew me not at all, rescued me. Cormack
and Milkeila healed my wounds and gave to me a soul
stone, that I might again become this alter-creature they
name the Highwayman.*

What do I owe?

I have been given a great gift from my parents, Abellican monk and Jhesta Tu mystic. I have seen both these respective transformative powers, the wisdom of the book my father penned and my mother practiced and the undeniable strength of the Abellican gemstone magic. Despite my infirmities—nay, because of them!—I have found a deeper truth and a more profound strength.

When I left Pryd Town those months ago, I could fight as well as Laird Prydae's champion, the legendary Bannagran. Now I believe I have only grown stronger. Without the gemstones, I find moments of greater clarity than ever before; I can align my ki-chi-kree for short bursts of tremendous energy and power, as I did when Ancient Badden threw me from the edge of the high glacier. I do not know that any man alive, other than an Abellican monk with the proper stones or perhaps the greatest of the Jhesta Tu mystics, could have survived that fall, but I did, and did so without the crutch that is a soul stone.

I have found the alignment of life energy, the perfect harmony of mind-body union, for those short moments in that highest crisis.

And as I have grown stronger without the soul stone strapped firmly to my forehead, so too have I grown with the stone. We are as one now; I can hold it in my hand and seal the line of life energy in place almost as well as if I had it upon my forehead, the top point of ki-chi-kree. The transformation from Stork to Highwayman, from drooling and staggering cripple to fine warrior, is nearly instantaneous now, and without conscious thought. And that transformation is far deeper and far stronger. Every muscle movement, every swing of the blade, every anticipation of an opponent's strike or parry crystallizes without a moment of consideration, and my appro-

priate response is launched before a thought need be given.

If I battled Bannagran now, I would defeat him, and with little difficulty. I say that with the full humility and understanding that such a truth brings upon me a call for responsibility.

And thus, the ultimate question hangs heavy over my head: What do I owe?

It's always been an easy question for me regarding those I love. I would have died for Garibond and would die now for Cadayle or Callen. I would fight for Jond and must admit that even Cormack and Milkeila and the powrie pair have become beloved companions in the manner of Vaughna, Crait, and Olconna.

I could have parted ways with them on the rocky rise above the glacier, but I did not. No one was more surprised than I when my feet hit that ice, when I rushed down to join in the fray against Ancient Badden's multitude of minions. By all rights, I could have turned south and gone all the way back to Dame Gwydre, and I do not doubt that she would have granted me my freedom for the trials I had already faced.

But I went down and fought, all the way to Badden, beside these companions (dare I hope, these friends?).

I owed them.

Dame Gwydre speaks of responsibility to people she does not even know, to her people across Vanguard. Is it just the truth of being a ruler, I wonder, that demands such a sense of community, or is it that we all owe one another in this greater community?

I have Badden's head in a sack; I will be freed of my indenture when we return to Dame Gwydre in a couple of weeks' time. I can then gather Cadayle and Callen and hold the promise that Gwydre will sail me wherever in the world I want to go. I can go on my way and let the

world go its own, I can forget the battles here in Van-
guard and the continuing strife between the too-proud
lairds Ethelbert and Delaval in the south.
  Or can I?
  What do I owe?

—BRANSEN GARIBOND

ONE

Six Cogs One

S he felt his calloused but gentle touch on her shoulders
and neck, rubbing the stress away with oft-practiced
perfection. Dame Gwydre sat staring out her window in
Castle Pellinor, looking to the cold north. She had cut her
brown hair quite short, but there was nothing mannish
about her appearance, for the cut only accentuated her
fine, thin neck and slender shoulders. And even under all
the duress of the recent months, and even well into middle age, Dame Gwydre's face featured an eternal youth
and vigor and sensuousness that belied the icy strength
and determination ever in her eyes.

Gwydre sighed.

"We'll know soon enough," Dawson McKeege, the only
man in the world who could be massaging Dame Gwydre,
said to her.

She craned her neck to glance back at him, gray stub-
ble prominent on his grizzled leathery face. Dawson was
only a few years Gwydre's senior, but, having spent most
of his life at sea, he looked much older. How well Dawson knew her!

"What makes you believe that I am thinking of them?" Gwydre asked.

"Because ye haven't been thinking of anything else since you sent that band after Ancient Badden," Dawson said with a laugh, and he kneaded Gwydre's shoulder as he spoke, bringing a wince of both pain and pleasure from the woman. "And you're all in knots under your skin."

It was true enough and he had seen right through her attempted dodge. Gwydre led Vanguard, and that vast wilderness holding was enmeshed in a brutal war, one that was taking a terrible toll on Gwydre's hearty subjects. Desperate times had forced a desperate gambit, and so Gwydre had enlisted some of the elite warriors of her land and sent them north to behead the beast that had arisen against her, the priest leader of an ancient and brutal religion.

"Why do we fight, Dawson?" she asked her dear friend.

"I've got no fight with you."

"Not us," Gwydre replied in exasperation. "We, men and women, all of us. Why do we fight?"

"Now or all the time?"

Gwydre half turned as her friend backed away and offered him a shrug.

"Now we fight because Ancient Badden's afraid that his Samhaist Church is being pushed aside, and so it is. He can't let go of that power without a fight, as we're seeing. He'll do anything to hold it."

"And so he has inflicted misery across Vanguard," said Gwydre. "To those loyal to me, and to those loyal to him. Great misery."

"They're calling that 'war,' I'm told," came the sarcastic reply.

"And why is the rest of Honce, all the holdings south of the Gulf of Corona, now in the grips of war?" Gwydre asked.

Dawson chuckled, seeing where this was going and having no answers.

Gwydre, too, gave a helpless laugh. Up here, the folk of Vanguard were embroiled in a brutal war with the monstrous minions Ancient Badden and the Samhaists had enlisted as mercenaries. Down south, across the far more populous holdings of Honce proper, it was brother against brother, laird against neighboring laird, as the two most prominent rulers battled to unite the land under one king for the first time in known history.

"They fight for the same reason we fight," Dawson said quietly, and in all seriousness (which was a rarity for Dawson McKeege). "They fight because one man, or two men, decided they should fight."

"Or one man and one woman?" Gwydre asked, clearly implicating herself in Vanguard's troubles.

"Nah," the sailor said with a shake of his head. "You didn't start this. This is Badden's folly and fury, and you've no choice but to defend."

"Thank you for that," Gwydre replied, and she patted her hand atop Dawson's, which was still on her shoulder. "In the southlands, Laird Delaval and Laird Ethelbert have decided that one and only one should rule over all the holdings, and because of that rivalry, thousands and thousands of men and women have been trampled under the march of armies. So is it just them, Dawson? Just those two men? Or do the armies marching for them want to fight?"

Dawson's face screwed up with puzzlement. "Many are believing in their leader, not to doubt," he said.

"But do they want to go to war?"

"Milady, I doubt any man's looking for more war after he's tasted war. It's an ugly thing, to watch your friend writhing on the muddy ground after his guts have been opened by a sword."

"So it is the pride and ambition of two men driving the insanity," said Gwydre.

Dawson shrugged and nodded. "As up here, it's the pride and ambition and anger of one, Ancient Badden."

With another sigh, Dame Gwydre turned back to stare out her northern window, and Dawson immediately moved nearer to her and began rubbing her neck once more—not because he had to, but because, as a friend, he wanted to.

"My father would not have gone to such a war," Gwydre remarked offhandedly.

"That's why the people of Vanguard loved Laird Gendron," said Dawson. "That's why the whole of Vanguard cried with you when he fell from his horse that day and didn't recover. And Pieter wouldn't have thought to fight such a war, either," he added, referring to Gwydre's husband, whom she had married while still a teenager, after Laird Gendron's death. "You picked a good one there."

"I miss him, Dawson. It's been more than a decade and a half, and still I miss him."

"You miss him more when Ancient Badden's pushing you, I'm thinking."

"I hate this," Gwydre admitted. "The suffering and the blood and the simple worthlessness of it all."

"There's nothing worthless about defending Vanguard against Ancient Badden and his monster hordes."

Gwydre patted his hand again. "And in the south?"

Dawson snorted derisively. "Who can be saying? Tough days in Vanguard, to be sure, but when we win—and we're to do that, don't doubt!—I'll be glad that we're a hundred miles of water or a hundred miles of wilderness away from those armies."

"I pray you are right," Gwydre said softly, and she stared to the north, the empty north.

I ain't a'feared o' fighting," said the tough little powrie Mcwigik. He plopped his bloodred beret on top of his wildly bushy orange hair and rubbed it into place as if he was adjusting a helmet. "In truth, I'm liking it, and likin' it more when we're talking o' fighting trolls. But if ye're asking me and Bikelbrin to go down there to fight that mob, and ye're thinkin' o' keeping one back here to watch over no-eyes there, then ye're thinking wrong. We're just five, ye dopes!"

"Six," corrected Brother Jond, the man Mcwigik had called "no-eyes." Dressed in his brown woolen Abellican robe and weather-beaten sandals with cloth wrapped inside their black straps to keep his feet warm, the monk shifted in his sitting posture to better face the sound of the dwarf's voice. He did nothing to hide his torn face, both eyes and the bridge of his nose lost as a prisoner of the wretched Ancient Badden; indeed, Brother Jond strained his neck to better demonstrate the wound to his companions.

"Bah, ye're a blind fool, and that's not a mix I'm wanting to fight beside," Mcwigik argued.

"I can use gemstones!" Brother Jond retorted.

"And put a lightning bolt up me arse!" roared Bikelbrin, Mcwigik's powrie companion. The two looked like bookends as they stood bobbing side by side. Both were tall for powries, five feet at least, and seemed as solid as the stones upon which they stood. And both had never met a blade suitable for trimming either hair or beard, it seemed, which gave their heads an enormous appearance.

"The soul stone!" Brother Jond argued. "I can send healing energy."

"To the trolls, ye twit!" said Mcwigik.

Similarly dressed in Abellican robes, though he had fallen from the order, and a powrie beret won in a fight with one of Mcwigik's former clan's dwarves, Cormack cast a nervous glance at his wife, Milkeila.

"If you do not lower your voices, the fight will come to us," Milkeila warned them all. The weight of the tall woman's words was not lost on any of the three arguing. She stood as tall as Brother Jond, a foot above the powries;

there was nothing delicate about Milkeila. She had been raised among the shamans of Yan Ossum, a barbarian tribe on the Lake Mithranidoon. She had seen battle both magical and physical since her early days and had lived a life of discipline and dedication—and her defined and strong muscles bore testament to the fact. By any measure, human or powrie, she was handsome, even beautiful, her wide and round face showing a range from feminine wiles to warrior ferocity. The sparkle in her dark eyes promised passion or battle, and anyone engaging in either with this formidable woman would enter the fray tentatively, to be sure. She kept much of her brown hair braided, but it was obvious that she didn't fret with it for the sake of vanity.

All of that—her size, her obvious strength, her sheer intensity—brought gravity to Milkeila's words. Even the stubborn powries lowered their volume as they continued their argument, which again wound along the same path to Bikelbrin claiming emphatically, "Ye'll put a lightning bolt up me arse!"

"No, he won't," said the sixth of the party, a smallish man wearing an exotic outfit of black silk, a wide farmer's hat, and a fabulous and intricately detailed sword on his hip.

"Then he'll heal the damned trolls!" Bikelbrin fumed.

"No, he won't," the man, Bransen Garibond, said with a confident grin and a wink at the blind Jond—a wink that brought a chuckle to the blind brother's lips. What a ragtag group they were, Bransen thought. Outcasts all, except for Jond, they had banded together in common purpose to bring about the end of Ancient Badden. For the others, it had been a personal battle—the powries, Milkeila, and Cormack were defending their, and one another's, communities on the warm Lake Mithranidoon below Ancient Badden's glacier, and Jond had come north with Bransen at the behest of Dame Gwydre of

Vanguard, in an attempt to decapitate the enemy by killing the vile leader. Bransen considered himself the biggest mercenary here, when he thought about it. He was not personally invested in the Mithranidoon communities, or in Vanguard, a land to which he was a stranger, and he had been tricked into the service of Dame Gwydre. He had come hunting Badden to earn freedom, for himself and for his wife and mother-in-law, reparation for his actions as the Highwayman that had outraged many of the Honce lairds. Now they were all traveling south from the defeated Ancient Badden's fortress, back to Dame Gwydre with their gruesome trophy. There was nothing left up here for the powries, Cormack, and Milkeila, and wounded Jond wanted to go home to Chapel Pellinor, and Bransen just wanted to get back to Cadayle and Callen.

Bikelbrin and Mcwigik both started arguing with Bransen, but Milkeila interrupted, and all turned to her to see her looking from Bransen to Jond curiously. "How did you see that?" she asked the blind monk.

"I saw nothing. I see nothing."

"You reacted."

"I agree with Bransen."

"To the wink," Milkeila insisted.

Jond's smile widened. "I felt it."

Both powries, Cormack, and Milkeila stared long and hard at the blind man.

"Ye felt the wink?" Mcwigik said with obvious doubt. "I got a great fart coming—ye feelin' that, are ye?"

Bransen drew his sword suddenly, pulling all attention his way. With a shrug, he poked its fine tip into his palm, drawing blood. "I am wounded!" he said to Jond, and before the monk could react, the agile Bransen silently shifted around to the other side of the group, behind the powries.

Brother Jond lowered his head and lifted a hand from

his pouch, his fist clenched around a small hematite, a soul stone, which Milkeila had given him from her necklace of various magical gems.

Bransen, remaining perfectly silent, held his hand up for all to see, and sure enough, a wave of magical energy from Jond sealed the small wound.

"How is that possible?" asked Cormack, formerly Brother Cormack, who knew well the properties of the Abellican stones. "How did you anticipate his move?"

"We are all joined, connected," Bransen explained.

"Only a great shaman can sense such movements through the earth," Milkeila protested.

"Or a Jhesta Tu," said Bransen. "Brother Jond and I have formed a bond. He can heal me, and will heal me, unerringly, as we do battle with the trolls we spied on the road ahead. He will not heal the trolls by mistake."

"And I'll cast no bolts of lightning, I promise," said Brother Jond.

"And how're ye to keep the trolls off yer torn face?" Mcwigik asked. "I'll not be looking over me shoulder to protect yer arse when I'm fighting for me own!"

"Nor would I ask you to," said Jond.

"We'll find a place for him, near the fighting," said Bransen. "Near enough to throw a healing spell, at me or at any of you who can find a similar bond."

Cormack was nodding with obvious appreciation, and so was Milkeila, and after a moment of looking at each other, both dwarves said, "Well, all's the better then!" and the issue was settled.

"Six cogs one!" Mcwigik proclaimed, an old powrie expression of a team of warriors working in unison toward a single goal. "Now, let's go kill us some trolls, just because it's a fine day and there's no better way in all the world to spend it."

* * *

Bransen held his breath as he watched the approach of the troll mob, some dozen or so of the creatures pushing and shoving and growling as they made their way along the path, windblown free of snow, that served as the main road into Vanguard from southern Alpinador. The young warrior couldn't help but remember the last time he had been in a situation just like this, when he and a few friends had attacked a troll caravan in an attempt to free the humans they held as prisoner. Crait, a warrior of great legend and stature, had died in that fight, and Bransen and the remaining of his band had been taken captive.

The trolls had surprised them with their tenacity and with sudden reinforcements.

That would not happen again, Bransen, the Highwayman, had decided, and so, before he and his new friends had come to this point, he had circumvented the troll mob and ensured that this time there would be no reinforcements following closely along the road.

Still, the Highwayman could not deny the nervous sweat that made his sword less tight in his grip. He glanced back to Brother Jond and Cormack, to see them engaged in the same type of bonding that he and Jond had used to allow the blind monk to sense Bransen's proximity. Milkeila had already done so, but the stubborn powries would have none of it.

Bransen had seen Mcwigik and Bikelbrin in battle. He flashed a much-needed grin their way and figured that those two wouldn't need any help from Brother Jond.

Mcwigik noted his glance with a nod, then held up six fingers, clenched his hands together, and then held up one finger.

Six cogs one.

With an exaggerated wink, Mcwigik slapped Bikelbrin on the shoulder and the pair ran off around a ridgeline to the west.

So much like Crait and Olconna, Bransen thought, for in that earlier tragic battle those two had similarly separated themselves from the main fighting band in a flanking maneuver. This was not the same thing, Bransen reminded himself quickly. Mcwigik and Bikelbrin had concocted this plan and insisted upon it.

"Only to get themselves right in the midst of it," Bransen whispered, trying to lighten his own mood.

Bransen took a deep and steadying breath, falling into the state of the warrior, the state of the Highwayman, as Cormack and Milkeila came up to either side of him, as the trolls below neared the designated spot. All three of them turned to the ridge west of the approaching trolls and sucked in their breath as one when they heard the opening cry of Mcwigik.

Over the ridge came the rambling powries, their short, powerful legs seeming more to roll than to pump, but propelling them surely and rapidly at the surprised trolls below. The dwarves hardly seemed to be paying any attention to their foes, but were looking back and yelling warnings of approaching enemies.

For powries and trolls, though not on the friendliest of terms, were not mortal enemies (outside of Mithranidoon, where all who were not troll did war with trolls) and had often banded together in Badden's assault on the men of Vanguard.

"Great, now they're ready for us," Cormack muttered.

"Ah, but with a pair in their midst," Milkeila said as the dwarves moved into the welcoming troll group.

"And looking the wrong way," added the Highwayman, and he flipped off his farmer hat and pulled his black silk bandanna down into a half mask, holes cut for his eyes. "Be quick!"

Cormack stood a foot taller than the Highwayman, and most of the difference seemed to be in the length of his legs. But he couldn't begin to pace the explosive speed of the silk-clad warrior. Fast as a hunting cat and silent as its shadow, the Highwayman closed the ground to the trolls far ahead of his two charging companions. As he neared, he heard Mcwigik yell, "Here they come!" and smiled as the dwarf pointed at the ridge over which he and Bikelbrin had run.

And the trolls were looking exactly that way when the Highwayman came spinning into their ranks from the other side, his fabulous sword of wrapped silverel, a Jhesta Tu sword crafted by his mother, slicing troll flesh as easily as it would dry parchment.

And the trolls were still looking that way when the two powries pulled stone axes from their belts and began chopping at them with abandon.

And the trolls were still looking that way when Milkeila's shamanistic magic reached out to a nearby tree and coaxed down one of its branches to grab a troll about the neck and hoist it, flailing pitifully, from the ground.

The Highwayman cut through the first rank, took a fast stride at the dwarves, and then kicked off suddenly, throwing himself into a forward-diving somersault. He landed lightly on the other side of the pair, running still, and a slash to the right, a reversed backhand, behind-the-back stab back to the left had two more trolls down.

Cormack came in almost at the same time the bulk of the trolls finally grasped what was happening and tried to form some semblance of defense. Three of them fell into a skirmish line, just hoisting crude spears when the former monk flew at them, turning his body horizontal as he leaped. He beat the spears to the spot and sent all three trolls tumbling.

As the pile unwound, though, one of the beasts managed to re-angle its spear enough to stab at the man, tearing a painful gash on his hip. He squealed in pain but gritted through it and, still on his knees, unloaded a barrage of short and heavy punches into the troll's face, crushing its bones and dropping it to the cold ground.

Milkeila was beside the man, then, and nearly as formidable in melee as in magic, the shaman cracked her staff hard on another troll's head.

"Are you all right?" she called to Cormack as he came up beside her, but when she glanced at him, she found him strangely grinning. He led her incredulous gaze down to his wound, showing her that it was already on the mend—the magical mend.

Brother Jond. Six cogs one.

In a matter of heartbeats, the powries gleefully went about dipping their bloody caps into troll blood, and coaxed Cormack, who understood well that there was powerful and beneficial magic in a powrie cap, to do likewise.

"Not much of a fight," Bikelbrin lamented.

"Yach," Mcwigik agreed. "Someone find me a giant to kneecap!"

"We fight only when they're in our way," Bransen reminded them as he wiped his bloody sword on a troll vest. "Our goal is to the south, to Vanguard and Dame Gwydre."

"To yer lady Cadayle, ye mean," said Mcwigik.

"No less substantial a cause, then," Cormack remarked with a wink at Milkeila.

Bransen cut short the conversation by nodding his chin back to the north, where Brother Jond was making his way along the road, tapping his walking stick before him.

"He healed me from afar," said Cormack.

"Might be that he's worth keepin', then," said Mcwigik. "But I ain't standing watch over him!"

"No one asked you to," Brother Jond answered from afar. "To be blunt, I feel safer knowing that no powries are hovering over me."

That erased a few smiles.

"Six cogs one," Bransen reminded, and he knew in

looking at his mismatched companions that it would be an oft-repeated litany if they were to make it across the miles to the more hospitable reaches of civilized Vanguard.

Of course, once they arrived at the court of Dame Gwydre, a host of other problems would certainly emerge, Bransen knew, and as Cormack and Jond also certainly knew, in trying to explain Mcwigik and Bikelbrin to folk who had never known the bloody-cap dwarves as anything but mortal enemies.

TWO

The Center of Gravity

They were smashed!" cried Yeslnik, the foppish Laird of Pryd and favored nephew of Laird Delaval, who proclaimed himself King Delaval of Honce. He flailed about as he spoke, his voluminous sleeves and leggings flapping and tightening over his limbs just often enough to remind those in the room of how delicate and stick-limbed this excitable man truly was. Not that any would remark on the man's erratic movements, for Yeslnik was also widely rumored to be the heir apparent to Delaval's expanding holdings.

"The son of Laird Panlamaris sent the traitors running back to the Mantis Arm! Oh, but we'll make them regret their decision to take Ethelbert's gold!" As he spoke, he danced around the circular chamber that marked the bottom floor of Pryd Keep, punching his fist into the air and smacking his hands together as if engaging in a battle with some imaginary foe.

His soft skin reddened under the blows.

A few of the men in attendance, Yeslnik's entourage from Delaval City and a pair of young brothers of Chapel Pryd, grinned stupidly and became animated at the less-than-inspired performance, but the true center of weight in the room, a muscular middle-aged warrior with long black hair just beginning to show a bit of salt with its pepper and a face that seemed carved out of stone, showed not a hint of emotion.

He did glance to the side, to exchange looks with Master Reandu of Chapel Pryd, the highest ranking of the village's brothers, who was serving, quietly, as leader of the chapel due to the failing condition of Father Jerak, who was by all reports beyond sensibility. Ever doubtful of the brothers of Abelle, Bannagran had nonetheless found himself growing closer to Reandu over the last few weeks, particularly with Yeslnik and his insufferable wife, Olym, bouncing about incessantly.

Still a young man, barely into his thirties, Reandu had played an important role in the dramatic events of Pryd Holding. He had halted the hand of his superior monk, Master Bathelais, when Bathelais might have struck dead the Highwayman, right before the Highwayman had crashed into Laird Prydae's room, initiating a fight that had cost Prydae his life. Soon after, it was Reandu who had spoken for the Highwayman, and favorably, and had convinced Bannagran to spare the life of Bransen Garibond and allow the outlaw to leave Pryd.

With all the tumult of the growing war, the investigation of Master Bathelais's death by Chapel Abelle had never come, and, indeed, the brothers up north had seen fit to elevate Reandu, the next highest-ranking brother in Pryd, to Master, giving him leadership in Chapel Pryd.

That promotion hadn't bothered Bannagran in the least. To Reandu's credit, by Bannagran's estimation, the monk seemed quite unimpressed by Yeslnik's proclamations and performance. Master Reandu shrugged at Bannagran with obvious resignation, as if to point out that they had to suffer the idiot.

"You do not view this as a great victory?" Yeslnik

shouted at Reandu, his tone full of consternation and indignation.

"The Church of Blessed Abelle is neutral in the conflict,
Laird Yeslnik, per agreement with both lairds Ethelbert
and Delaval," Reandu replied. "Your claims of great battle
mean to us only that we will witness more suffering."

Yeslnik stopped suddenly, as if some marionette strings
had simply fallen limp around him, and his face seemed
indeed to be made of wood or stone.

"The Decree of Neutrality by Chapel Abelle is well-
known to both warring factions," Reandu reminded. "And
accepted, and was even advised by your mentor, Laird
Delaval. We do not ask the allegiance of a wounded man
when we prepare our blessed healing."

Yeslnik gave a little, deprecating snort. "The situation
is changing, Brother," he calmly—too calmly—explained.
"A nimble church survives, while one set in the ways of
the past can easily find itself marginalized."

Bannagran closed his eyes at that and tried to tune out
of the conversation. Rumors had been spreading from
both lines, Ethelbert and Delaval, that as the war had
grown more furious, as the stakes had crystallized, pres-
sures had been exerted on the brothers of Abelle in chapels behind each of the respective lines to tend only to
those wounded supporting that region's ruling faction.
The lairds were playing a dangerous game with the people, Bannagran knew from long and bitter experience, for
the enemy wounded were too often friend and family to
the peasants living about the chapels where they were
brought for healing.

Peasants could be pushed hard—Bannagran had seen
that from his friend and former laird, Prydae. But peasants also had the capacity to strike back hard when pushed
too far.

In his mind, Bannagran saw again his errant throw, his
axe spinning end-over-end, sailing above the wretched

Highwayman and planting itself deep in Laird Prydae's chest. He saw again his friend's blood explode from that wound, saw again Prydae thrown down to his back with such force, the fountain of lifeblood spraying high above his horizontal form. Bannagran shook himself from the awful memory.

"The brothers of Abelle should be aware that Honce is changing," Prince Yeslnik was saying when Bannagran tuned back in. "The shameful Ethelbert has no sense of the community of Honce! He is not worthy of the title of laird, and many of the folk of his rogue holding bear more allegiance to their brethren south of the mountains than to their fellow men of Honce!"

"You speak of Honce as if it is a united kingdom," Bannagran couldn't help but interject.

"And it will be!" Yeslnik barked back at him. "And King Delaval will rule it!"

The answer was perfectly expected, of course, but Bannagran always liked hearing the insistence with which it was pronounced, particularly by this ambitious young man, who had everything in the world to gain if his fantasy came to fruition.

"But it will never be united under Ethelbert, and this the brothers of Abelle must know," Yeslnik went on, and he was flailing his arms again and turning and storming this way and that, as if little bolts of lightning were exploding through his limbs. "Nay, under the wretch Ethelbert, the Holdings of Honce will become subservient to the needs of the desert kingdom of Behr to the south!"

A couple of attendants gasped at that—so perfectly on cue, Bannagran thought.

"Will our women be sent south around the mountains to serve as whores for the sheiks of the desert wastes?" Yeslnik asked. "Will our children be indentured as water-carriers to mule the precious element from the few springs and ponds to the cities?"

Bannagran had followed Prydae into the court of Laird Delaval and thus against Laird Ethelbert, and his loyalties rested there, to be sure, but he could not help but be amused by the rapt expressions on the faces of many in the room. The bigger and more outrageous the tale, the more it intrigued, it seemed. For Bannagran knew Laird Ethelbert, or had known him a decade before, when the men of Pryd and Ethelbert had fought side by side in the east against the powries. On two occasions, Ethelbert had entered a battle in the nick of time to save Prydae, Bannagran, and their men. When war had later broken out between Ethelbert and Delaval, Prydae had initially sided with Ethelbert, in spirit if not in action. Laird Ethelbert, with no living children, had hinted strongly that he would name Prydae as heir. It wasn't until it became apparent that Prydae, because of wounds he had suffered in those previous powrie wars, was also the last of his line that Ethelbert had moved away from that course. He would not name Prydae as his heir, and so Prydae had thrown in with Delaval, who was offering the better deal to the young laird.

Part of that deal, though, had ceded Pryd Holding to Laird Delaval upon the end of Prydae's line, and that end had come prematurely at the end of Bannagran's thrown axe.

Now Bannagran was stuck with little Laird Yeslnik.

He sighed and pushed the frustration away, ever the good soldier, and tuned in to the continuing conversation. To his credit, again, Master Reandu seemed unfazed by the outlandishly dire exaggerations Yeslnik was spinning regarding Ethelbert's relationship with Behr.

"What say you?" Yeslnik finished, rushing right up to within a few fingers of Reandu and staring at him hard.

"I am a servant of Abelle," the Master from Chapel Pryd replied. "My course is determined not by my own emotions, not by the pleasures of a laird or prince, but by the edicts of the father of Chapel Abelle. You appeal to the wrong man, Laird and Prince Yeslnik. Your passion would better serve you in the north, where Father Artolivan's pen proclaims the actions of all in his clergy."

Yeslnik continued to stare at him for many heartbeats, and gradually Yeslnik's face softened into a cold chuckle. "Practiced in the art of diplomacy, I see," he said. "Well done! You have successfully delayed—not avoided, but delayed—the inevitable confrontation. But take heart, for I am certain that your Father Artolivan will choose wisely, when choose he must. Delaval is for Honce, Ethelbert is for Behr, and the beasts of Behr are no friends to the brothers of Abelle. Their gods precede yours and reject yours, and their God-Voice, the father of their religion, has put more than a few of your missionaries to the stake."

It was true enough, Bannagran knew, but remained quiet. Many of the missionary brothers of Abelle, those nagging and unrelenting proselytizing prigs, had indeed ventured into Behr and never returned, by all reports. Bannagran knew one exception, however, a monk from Pryd who had come back from the deepest reaches of the southern desert, along with an exotic wife, no less, when Bannagran was a young man, serving his friend Prydae and Prydae's father, Laird Pryd. The brothers of Chapel Pryd had not treated that monk very well, Bannagran recalled.

The standoff between Yeslnik and Reandu, neither of whom was blinking, ended when a man crashed into the room, huffing and puffing, and breathlessly announced, "They come."

"Ah!" exclaimed Yeslnik, turning to the man. He rubbed his hands together eagerly and flexed his fingers as if he couldn't wait to wrap them around a sword hilt (which amused Bannagran, since he had seen this one in "battle" before).

"So it will begin as we expected right here in Pryd Holding," continued Yeslnik. "Ethelbert's move in the north was crushed by Milwellis of Palmaristown. He knows that Milwellis will now march east and then south along Felidan Bay, then south from there, sweeping up in his wake villages formerly in Ethelbert's pay. Thus, Ethelbert did not retreat—he cannot retreat. Not this time, or he will be pushed into the sea. So he comes with all that he has left to strike at the heart and center of King Delaval's gains."

Yeslnik clenched his fist, his eyes sparkling with diabolical glee. "Never could you have guessed that your humble little hamlet of Pryd would become the center of the world! For all the world is drawn to this place, as if the weight of Pryd Town pulls in the armies, compels them to this place in this time to finally, undeniably decide! Never could you have guessed this, eh, Bannagran?"

Not in my darkest nightmares, the warrior thought but did not say.

Laird Ethelbert slowly sauntered on his mount toward his tent, as if neither he nor the beast could handle a swifter pace. Palfry, his devoted attendant, rushed up to help him dismount. Glancing around to ensure that no one else was watching, the proud old man accepted the helping hand.

He was just into his seventies now, his once bulky frame wilting and thinning about his arms, while thickening about his waist. He was glad for the comfortable robe he wore, a gift from a Jacinthan merchant. The men of Behr were so much more practical in their dress than the men of Honce.

"You must have ridden under a low branch, my laird," Palfry said. He brushed a leafy twig from what remained of Ethelbert's hair. Once thick, black, and curly, now it was thin gray fluff. Ethelbert's eyes, though, were still the steel blue of an ocean under clouds, still hinted at a great depth behind them, and still held the sparkle of a dancing wave.

"Bah, more likely a squirrel threw the branch upon me," Ethelbert replied somewhat churlishly. "Every creature in this part of Honce is against me, I say!"

Palfry smiled, so in love with this man who had become like a father, though Ethelbert had no living heirs. The laird had made it clear to Palfry that, though he was not in line for Ethelbert's title, neither would he be cast from the court of whomever ruled the great holding. Ethelbert had seen to that.

"Where are my commanders?" Laird Ethelbert asked.

Palfry turned and nodded his chin toward a distant clearing, where three warriors sat on logs around a tree stump, a parchment spread upon it. Ethelbert started for them, Palfry at his heels.

"My laird," the three commanders said together, standing as one.

"The soldiers were pleased that you rode their line, no doubt," said Kirren Howen, the senior of the group.

"Huzzah for Laird Ethelbert!" added Myrick the Bold, champion of Entel, the name given to the port regions of the city of Ethelbert.

Ethelbert hushed him with a waving hand and a snicker. "It is the least we owe them and less than they want, I am sure," he said. "They want to be done with this foolishness and go home, as do I."

"Our cause is right," said Tyne, a young and promising leader, a man Ethelbert had attached to his elite guard right before the advent of war.

"Righter than Delaval's, to be sure," the more seasoned Kirren Howen added.

"The claim of a dactyl demon would be more right than that of Delaval," Ethelbert said with a derisive snicker. "And I'd sooner my one daughter, were she still alive, marry the dactyl!"

Ethelbert's joke prompted an uncomfortable laugh around the tree stump, for all knew that Laird Ethelbert spoke only half in jest, revealing his deep wounds over Laird Delaval's treachery. In times past, the two greatest of lairds had worked together to build Honce's network of roads. With those roads connecting the many holdings, marauding powries and goblins had been more easily driven away. Trade had blossomed, and a sense of unity had spread across the land. Citizens thought of the notion and nation of Honce more than a particular holding.

All that changed abruptly when Laird Delaval struck, and struck hard, declaring himself King of Honce.

Laird Ethelbert had lived too long, had fought too many battles, and had worked to bring too many warring lairds to common ground to allow such a thing. And thus the current war began.

"What news of the son of Panlamaris?" Ethelbert asked now.

"He has not turned south," said Kirren Howen.

"To the east, still," said Myrick.

"He will turn," Ethelbert assured them. "Milwellis's win in Pollcree has convinced Delaval that this push to the center is our last, desperate try. And not without reason," he admitted.

"Had that battle turned differently . . ." Kirren Howen started to say, but Ethelbert cut him short.

"It could not have. We did not understand the true strength of Palmaristown or how deeply Laird Panlamaris had entrenched himself with Delaval. Panlamaris is seeking the favor of the man who claims the title of king, no doubt, so that Palmaristown can control all of the sea-borne merchant trade in this new kingdom Delaval proposes. Our friends from the Mantis Arm peninsula could not match Prince Panlamaris's ground forces."

"I do not consider this to be our last and desperate try!" Myrick exclaimed.

Ethelbert's chuckle calmed him. "I am more interested in what our enemies consider it. In recognizing their thoughts may we act appropriately. Fear not, my fearless Myrick"—his joke on the man's title brought a bit of laughter from Palfry, Kirren Howen, and Tyne—"for I am not desperate, I assure you, and while I mourn the loss of so many allies at Pollcree, I have no doubt that the fierce peninsula warriors handed the son of Panlamaris great losses in the battle. He is stung, surely, and his soldiers, who have never marched across the land, are already missing their homes, I am certain. Their legs are built for ship planks, not cobblestones. We are not as wounded as they believe, of course. We have other allies and other methods, and I can only hope that the apparent victory in the north has served to foster a feeling of invulnerability among Delaval and his followers. None fall harder than the confident, after all."

"And no one's fall is more relished than the defeat of he who thinks himself invulnerable," said Tyne, the youngest of the group, to approving nods from Kirren Howen and Laird Ethelbert.

"Young and proud Milwellis will turn south," Ethelbert said. "Delaval and his commanders have come to think this our last stand. The son of Panlamaris, hoping to secure a prominent seat for his father and his town, will not be left out of the victory."

"And when he does turn?" asked Kirren Howen. "How long do we hold?"

"We know the terrain east of Pryd Holding," Ethelbert

explained. "Laird Delaval does not. His generals are not well versed in the eastern reaches of Honce. The same is true, even more so, of Milwellis of Palmaristown."

"As long as we can, then," Kirren Howen replied, and Laird Ethelbert smiled and nodded, fully confident in these men who served him. Kirren Howen would not allow Ethelbert's army to be smashed by the bulk of Delaval's forces here in the middle of Honce; they were not here for that purpose.

"We hold faith that our journey to central Honce will not be in vain," Myrick the Bold asserted, and there was nothing but supreme confidence regarding Laird Ethelbert and these unknown ulterior motives in the old man's words. He bowed low, as did Tyne and Kirren Howen, and Ethelbert took his leave, signaling for Palfry to remain here with the commanders.

In another clearing not so far away, the Laird of Ethelbert dos Entel met with a second group of warriors, a half dozen men and two women of darker skin and black hair and blacker eyes. It was no secret among his ranks, or among his enemies, that Ethelbert had hired mercenaries from the deserts of Behr, but this group was another matter altogether. Their leader was a petite woman with deceptively soft facial features, a disarming wide, white-toothed smile, and dimples that could melt a man's heart at the same time that her sword—or even her bare hands—could dismember him. And, oh, how she could dance, Ethelbert mused, the turning and weaving of those supple limbs enough to melt an old man's heart.

Her name was Affwin Wi, the Eyes of Bursting Sunrise, given to her by her masters at the Walk of Clouds, home of the Jhesta Tu. Affwin Wi had been known among that order not as a creature of introspection or quiet meditation but rather as something akin to the sudden explosion of light when the sun peeked above the eastern horizon, an excitable and impetuous sort. These characteristics had gotten her into trouble among the introspective ascetics who sought to teach her. Jhesta Tu was an art of mind and body: Affwin Wi's masters feared that she possessed too little of the former and an abundance of the latter.

She had left the Walk of Clouds as a young woman, only a few years before. Again, contrary to Jhesta Tu teaching, Wi had taken on the role of teacher for the similarly fiery men and woman standing around her.

"Laird Delaval continues his advance?" she asked Ethelbert now.

"He cannot surrender the center, and Pryd Town is the center," the old laird replied. As Ethelbert spoke Merwal Yahna walked over to stand beside Affwin Wi. Ethelbert noted that the rest of Affwin Wi's disciples, amazing warriors all, shrank back as this one passed. He wasn't a large man, and the loose fit of his soft black silk clothing did not reveal his tightly packed muscles. Only his clean-shaven head could perhaps be construed as imposing—that and his eyes, narrow, small, and intense.

Watching the sureness of the Behrenese man's stride and the pure grace of his movements reminded Ethelbert of the value of this gift of deadly mercenaries the Sheik Kali-kali-si of Jacintha had given to him.

"Laird Delaval intends to meet me on the field with every warrior he can spare, and he can spare them all, so he believes."

"But he has not arrived to join them in this glorious victory?" Merwal Yahna asked, his voice measured. The deference Affwin Wi showed him by allowing him to speak was yet another testament to the man's rank.

"He is not well, by all word, and desires to heap praise and stature upon his buffoon of a nephew. No, my warrior, Delaval will not be on the field."

Merwal Yahna's small eyes lit up, and he gave a slight nod. A quick glance around by Laird Ethelbert told him that he need say nothing more, that the plan was understood and now in action.

Ethelbert bowed to these fearsome disciples of Affwin Wi and took his leave.

He would sleep well that night.

THREE

Out of Their Element

He stumbled through the blinding storm, the cold wind whipping his cloak wide, the persistent snow rushing in around his armor. He stumbled and nearly fell, but knew the group behind him, nearly ninety men, depended on his continuing forward against the harsh elements. He shielded his eyes, futilely, and leaned forward against the wind, driving on.

But the ground gave way before him as he walked right over the edge of a chasm he could not see. His cry diminished as he dropped fifty feet to where the snow and ice cushioned his fall enough so that he did not die immediately. Twisted and broken, unable to draw in enough breath to scream out, he tried to hold faith that his brothers would get to him with their healing stones.

He died alone that night.

"He's gone over!" a monk had cried when Brother Juniper fell. "Ropes! Brothers! A stone of levitation!"

"Turn east and trek the length of the gorge!" Father De Guilbe ordered, his tone accepting no debate. "Brother Juniper is lost to us, and many more will perish if we do not find shelter from this accursed storm! East, I say, and with all haste!"

They did find shelter, meager though it was, amidst a tumble of boulders and a few thin evergreens. With frozen fingers, the servants of the brothers moved about the area, digging out any piece of wood they could find, breaking branches from the trees. Brother Giavno held his hands in front of his face and blew into them, trying to get feeling back into his fingers. He stood at the back of the camp, a wall of rock climbing up high behind him to the north. Before him, the servants dumped their thin loads of kindling.

Giavno waved the next brother in line over to the latest pile and presented him with two gemstones, serpentine and ruby.

The younger brother placed the ruby down and clutched the serpentine close to his chest, offering prayers to Blessed Abelle and reaching into the gemstone magic until an aura of bluish white light glowed about him. Shield in place, he bent and retrieved the ruby, then thrust his hand into the kindling pile and called forth its fiery properties.

The fingers of pine branches exploded to flames, but they didn't last and could not fully take hold on the thicker, wet wood. The brother called upon the ruby again and again until finally the flames caught. Still holding the serpentine shield, he left the ruby for Brother Giavno and carried the burning pile to his appointed section of the encampment.

"There is little shelter for the light of our fires," Brother Giavno warned his only superior among the group, Father Cambelian De Guilbe, a giant of a man, larger than life, standing well over six feet and weighing nearly three hundred pounds. De Guilbe's girth seemed all the more remarkable because the rest of their group had thinned considerably during the years away from Vanguard and Honce. De Guilbe was almost a decade older than the middle-aged Giavno but possessed of no less vitality. Indeed, with Giavno's own head more skin than hair, many who regarded the pair could not be certain which was the older. "The hill behind us blocks a view to the north. The chasm to the south perhaps protects us from attack, but the flames we need to stave off the cold this night will be seen for a long way."

"Yes, yes, I know," an obviously impatient De Guilbe replied, his tone revealing that this decision had weighed heavily upon him. When word had come of Ancient Badden's designs over Mithranidoon, a plan that would have wiped out all the communities living in the many islands scattered about the warm waters, De Guilbe determined that this fight was not his. He turned from the barbarians and powries, long his enemies, and their call for unity against Badden and decided that the time had come for his missionary group to return to the south, to Vanguard and the civilized lands of Honce. Away from the warm waters of Mithranidoon for more than two weeks, with no knowledge of what had happened in the brewing fight with Badden, the band of monks had wandered the rugged and broken terrain of Alpinador without much success. They had expected to be in Vanguard by this point, back in Chapel Pellinor, at least, but more than once they had lost days of travel by wandering in circles.

And worse, they had lost ten men to the elements and to monsters. Brother Giavno's warning recalled a dark night only a week before, when a host of ice trolls had descended upon the band. With magic and fighting skills, the brothers and their servants had driven the foul creatures off but at a cost of three lives and many wounds—so many that the entirety of the next day had been spent using the healing magic of the soul stones.

"Our food stores run low," Giavno said. "When the storm abates, we must form hunting parties and send them out."

"You are a beacon of hope on this miserable night," Father De Guilbe scolded. Brother Giavno went respectfully (and fearfully) silent.

"You still carry the weight of guilt that we did not follow Cormack up the glacier to do battle with the Samhaist ancient," De Guilbe accused him. "Or is it that you still carry the weight of guilt for the flogging you delivered to the traitor?"

"No, Father," Giavno denied, his eyes averted.

"Yes!" De Guilbe shot back. "Let it wash downstream, Brother Giavno. Cormack was condemned by his own actions. Your arm struck not from personal vengeance but from the demands put upon us as brothers of our beloved Abelle. You struck with righteousness."

"He was once my friend," the humble Giavno said simply.

"Of course it pains you, but our road is not easy. Spiritual purity and devotion are oft the harder roads, but it is a course we walk with pride!" He glanced around and gave a helpless little laugh. "Although I admit this Alpinadoran road is at least as confusing! Would that we had an Abelle of a different sort, yes?"

Brother Giavno's eyes widened at the apparent blasphemy, but Father De Guilbe patted him on the shoulder and chuckled his concerns away. "It is not an easy road we have chosen," he repeated, "not in body, not in spirit."

Before Giavno could respond, a brother along the western perimeter of the encampment called out, "Intruders!"

De Guilbe and Giavno rushed down, as did every other member of the group until De Guilbe impatiently waved them back to their posts.

"In the trees!" the monk explained to the leaders when they arrived. He pointed to a small copse of deciduous trees and a few evergreens about twenty yards from the boulder tumble.

De Guilbe stared hard for a short while, believing he

noted a form slip through the trees, though he could hardly identify it. He waved several brothers over and handed each a smooth gray stone, a graphite, the stone of lightning.

"All at once," he explained and held his own hand forward, clenching the largest of the graphite stones. "If it is a troll or goblin scout, then let our barrage ward any others from thinking to come so near. On my count of three."

"Perhaps it is an ally," one of the monks replied. "Brother Cormack, or—"

Father De Guilbe fixed him with a withering stare. He most certainly did not want to hear that name with the reverent word *brother* before it.

De Guilbe looked back to the copse and began counting down. As he finished, ten bolts of lightning reached from the monk line, slashing through the trees, thundering into the snow-covered ground.

"Whoa, now!" came a cry from the north, up the hill below which Giavno and De Guilbe had just been standing. All in the camp turned with a unified gasp to see a man sitting calmly halfway up the rocky, seemingly unclimbable rise. He was dressed in deerskin, a thick brown cloak about his shoulders and upper chest. A tricornered hat, small feather in one side, adorned his head. A stick of some sort, perhaps a bow, rested easily across his lap.

One of the monks near De Guilbe lifted his hand toward the man, as if intending to loose another bolt of lightning.

"Whoa, whoa, young one," the stranger said, waving his hands defensively and wearing a smirk that showed no fear at all, that almost seemed to mock the impetuous man.

Father De Guilbe slapped the monk's hand down and stalked up to the stranger, Giavno in his wake. "Who are you, and what business have you with us?" the leader demanded.

"You boys seem a bit lost," the man replied. "Been

watching you for a couple of days now, and I'm guessing that you haven't any idea where you're going."

Father De Guilbe bristled. "We are on our way to Vanguard and Dame Gwydre," he announced stiffly.

"Oh, I'm not doubting that you know where you want to go," the man replied. He slapped his hand on his knee and stood up, hooking the bow, for it was indeed a bow, over one shoulder. He eyed the decline before him, then skipped down nimbly and sure-footedly across the snowy and icy stones.

He was not a young man, clearly, his short hair and thick mustache long gone gray, but he moved with the grace of a twenty-year-old. He kept his upper body incredibly still while he moved down the broken path, and his legs seemed too long for his body. He was thin but not skinny and exuded an aura of great strength and power. Monks and attendants shied away from him when he got down from the hill.

"I said that you haven't an idea of where you're going," he finished, coming up before De Guilbe.

"I asked you who you were."

"I could be asking the same of yourself, since you're the ones who are out of place here."

"This is your home?" De Guilbe asked, looking about with mocking doubt.

The man shrugged. "As much as any place could be called that, I expect."

"And your name?"

The man laughed. "Jameston Sequin," he replied. "Not that it should mean anything to you."

"I have never heard of you," De Guilbe concurred.

"And that pleases me," Jameston replied. "The fewer of your church who know my name, the happier I am."

De Guilbe's face further tightened. "You are a Samhaist."

"Not in this life, not in the next, if there is a next,"

Jameston said with a snort. "And not in the one after that."

"Then—"

"Then nothing," Jameston said with finality. "I'm a hunter, and I know this land better than any man alive. You say you want to go to Gwydre, and that's where I'm going, so you should be glad to see me."

De Guilbe glanced over at Brother Giavno, who shrugged, unable to deny that they could indeed use some help in navigating their way from this inhospitable land.

"I'll take you, monk," Jameston offered. He looked over at the copse of trees, one of which was still showing small flickers of flame from the lightning barrage. "But only if you promise to stop scarring my home."

Just a few miles to the west of De Guilbe's group, Bransen's band of six unusual characters settled in for the night. They had found a small hollow between two large stones. The two powries of the team had gone to work immediately widening it, mudding and blocking any creases, cracks, and openings. Now the six—three men, a woman, and the powrie pair—settled in quite comfortably. The industrious dwarves had even constructed a chimney of sorts to keep the smoke out of their impromptu chamber.

They had left the glacier above Mithranidoon a full week after the departure of Father De Guilbe and his monks, after the fall of Ancient Badden and the sorting that needed to be done in the aftermath. Little fighting had been required after Badden's fall, for most of his minions, including the many Samhaist priests who had come into his call, had fled at his demise. These six, along with Milkeila's barbarian tribe and the other powries of Mithranidoon, had remained in the ice castle the ancient had constructed, awaiting an attack. No other priests of

Badden's Samhaist order had arrived, however. The trolls, giants, and goblins brought together under the power of the great and evil man had simply dispersed to the mountains with his fall.

Still, there had been much to do. Ancient Badden had constructed his grand ice palace through the earth magic of Mithranidoon, digging a deep well to access that power directly. Day after day after his fall, the shamans of Milkeila's Alpinadoran tribes had worked tirelessly to close that conduit of power, to heal the wound Badden had inflicted upon the glacier, the lake, the earth itself. There also remained the disposition of Badden's prisoners, of which Jond had been one. Of the others, more than fifty in number, some had seemed capable of making the journey south with the winter coming on in full, but others obviously could not have survived.

And so it had been decided that just this one band of outcasts, unaffiliated any longer with the church or the tribe or the clan, would make the arduous and dangerous trip to Dame Gwydre in the hopes of securing a rescue caravan in the spring. Until then, the other survivors of the ancient's insanity would live on Chapel Island, the now vacated land where Cormack's Abellican brethren had built their home.

It fell on this group, now taken to calling themselves Six Cogs One, to relay the tidings to the people of Vanguard and to find the resolution.

"You should return with the caravan in the spring," Bransen said to Milkeila as they discussed the tasks before them again that night in the hollow.

The woman shook her head.

"Don't overestimate the generosity of Yan Ossum," Cormack answered for her, using the proper title of Milkeila's tribe. "They understand that in agreeing to bring the refugees from Vanguard to Chapel Isle they are threatening their very way of life."

"Longer than our memories have we lived on Mithranidoon," Milkeila added. "Only rarely have outsiders come to our shores, as with the brothers of Abelle a few short years ago. Now we have invited strangers to settle upon our waters, perhaps to learn our ways, and then they will be allowed to leave. I am amazed that Teydru and the others agreed to this—I think it an impulsive decision made in the glow of Ancient Badden's fall."

"The fall and, therefore, the salvation of all who dwell on Mithranidoon," Bransen reminded.

"Yach, but that Badden would've washed them all away," Mcwigik put in.

"All true, but there is no doubt in my mind that the shamans and elders will come to recognize the danger of their decision," said Milkeila.

"You do not believe they would hurt the refugees?" Bransen asked.

"No," Cormack insisted before Milkeila could answer. "They are honorable to a fault. They would not bring such dishonor and treachery upon themselves."

"But they will not be pleased at the arrival of the caravan from Vanguard in the spring, should it ever actually arrive," said Milkeila. "And I would not have myself associated with that troubling spectacle any more than I would now. I will not return to Mithranidoon, likely not for the rest of my life."

Bransen, having no argument, simply nodded.

"But me and me friend're going back, and might be in the spring," Mcwigik said. "Soon as we find a place for our kin away from that lake, we'll go and fetch 'em."

"Yach, and hopin' it'll be a place back on the Julianthes," Mcwigik's powrie sidekick Bikelbrin added. "Back to the dark sea, at least."

"Where to, then, for any of us?" Cormack asked, drawing all eyes his way. "You, Bransen, will find your wife, and Gwydre promised you that her Writ of Passage will allow you to go wherever you will, but what's in store for Milkeila and me? What for the powries, whatever their desires? We know where we are going now, to Dame Gwydre, but what about tomorrow's journey?"

"Wherever the Father of Chapel Pellinor tells me to go," Brother Jond said with a little laugh.

Bransen tightened up at the reminder that his friend Jond had ties greater than their road-sewn bonds.

"It is so much easier when you bear no responsibility for your road, true?" Cormack asked playfully. Bransen noted that the former monk was looking directly at him as he spoke.

"Sometimes, Broth . . . Cormack," Jond corrected himself, echoing that helpless laugh. "And sometimes it is a burden, truly."

"Perhaps our roads will stay as one, then," said Milkeila. "I would enjoy that."

"Not mine," Bransen said immediately and definitively. "With the fall of Badden, my indenture is ended and my road is my own to choose."

"And you would not choose to be with us?" asked Jond. "You wound me, friend."

"No, it is not—" Bransen started to explain, but he noted Jond's mischievous grin and knew the blind man was playing him here. "I miss my wife," he finished simply.

"I can understand that, certainly," said Cormack, who was now staring at Milkeila intently, a look Bransen understood, recognizing that he wore that same mask of desire and longing whenever he looked upon Cadayle.

Cadayle! She filled the young man's thoughts then, more fully than any time since his departure for Alpinador. His anticipation grew by the moment as he sat there in the comfortable hollow. All he longed for was to be in Cadayle's arms once more.

Soon, he knew. Soon.

* * *

I left the injured woman with some friends in Alpina-dor," Jameston Sequin explained to Dame Gwydre only four days after he had met with De Guilbe's party. With the scout leading them, the troupe had made great time moving into Vanguard and to Gwydre's castle in Pellinor.

Eager for news from the front, Gwydre had wasted no time in summoning Jameston to her court. When he had arrived, Gwydre had immediately shuffled Father De Guilbe and Brother Giavno, along with the other brothers of Abelle in attendance (including the father of Chapel Pellinor and her own lover, Alandrais), off to the side of the room.

Her smile had drooped with Jameston's every word as the man recounted his short time with her strike force, ending in a disastrous fight with a troll prisoner caravan, when, seemingly, it had all come undone. When, Jameston believed, Bransen and Jond and the others had been fully defeated.

By Jameston's grim account, it seemed certain that Ancient Badden had won.

"I went back toward the glacier, but just a few miles," Jameston explained. "Badden surrounded himself with many powerful minions—giants, even. I couldn't get near the place."

"But you do not know if they are dead?" Gwydre asked, obviously uncomfortably. Beside her, Dawson McKeege put a comforting hand on her shoulder to steady her.

"Only poor old Crait, and a fine fighter he was," said Jameston. "And that strange younger fighter, the one in black."

"Bransen," said Gwydre. "The Highwayman."

Jameston nodded. "Not sure if he's dead, but it seems as if he got hit on the head, and hard. He could hardly walk as the trolls led them off. I doubt he made it alive to the glacier."

"That'd be a terrible loss for us," said Dawson, who had brought Bransen to Vanguard to fight for Gwydre's cause.

"He is alive, or was, when we left Lake Mithranidoon," Father De Guilbe interrupted. It was obvious that the man had been waiting for an opportunity to jump in ever since Jameston had entered the room.

"What do you know of it?" Dame Gwydre asked.

"As I was explaining before we were sent aside," De Guilbe began peevishly, "we left the lake because word came to us of the designs of this very same Ancient Badden. Word from this man, this Highwayman, as you call him. So, yes, Dame Gwydre, he survived to the glacier, at least. If we're to believe the word of our fallen brethren, he also survived a fall from the glacier."

"The Highwayman came to enlist you against Ancient Badden?" Gwydre asked incredulously.

"He came to warn us that Ancient Badden meant to destroy everyone living on the islands across the lake," Father De Guilbe carefully equivocated. "And so we left, as my directives clearly demand."

"You did not go and do battle with Badden?"

De Guilbe bristled. "It is not my place."

"So who or what are we to blame for this new alliance between Abellicans and Samhaists?" Dawson McKeege asked sharply.

"Alliance and enmity have degrees in between, friend," said De Guilbe. "And we were ignorant of your current struggles with Ancient Badden and his followers, or of any edict from Father Premujon of Chapel Pellinor or Father Artolivan of Chapel Abelle decreeing that the Brothers of Abelle were at war with the Samhaists. We have been on the roads of Alpinador for years. It was not my place to go and start such a war."

"Surely you could have found your answers from the Highwayman!" Dawson protested.

"Who came to us with a traitor to our order!" De Guilbe shot right back.

"Who came to you with information enough to send you running to the south!" said Dawson.

"Enough!" Dame Gwydre interrupted.

"Makes me miss the birdsong and chirping toads," Jameston mumbled. Gwydre shot him a sly twinkle to let him know that she didn't disagree, for she, too, would surely have preferred a walk in the forest to this inane bickering.

"So at least we know that the Highwayman survived the ordeal of the troll capture," Gwydre recounted to Jameston. "To your great surprise."

"I'm not arguing."

"And he returned to do battle with Badden?" Gwydre asked De Guilbe.

"As far as I know," he said stiffly.

"Could you elaborate?" There was no missing the sharp edge creeping into Gwydre's tone or her weariness at De Guilbe's annoying verbal dance.

"He went with the traitor to our order and his woman, a barbarian girl," the large monk grudgingly explained.

"Ah, then, not to wonder why you kicked him out of your church," Jameston interjected. Gwydre hushed him with a look.

"Her people were joining in the battle, as were the powries of Mithranidoon," Brother Giavno interjected. Father De Guilbe shot a threatening glare of his own to back the monk down.

"Truly?" asked Gwydre. "Then there is hope."

"They are all dead," De Guilbe stated flatly.

Gwydre arched an eyebrow. "You know this? Or you presume?"

The large monk shrugged impatiently.

Gwydre nodded and turned back to Jameston.

"Any odds for armies going against Badden aren't good odds," the scout reminded.

"But the Highwayman had already been up there, so he knew . . ."

Jameston's laugh cut her short, and she stared at him, seeming less than amused.

"Your pardon," the scout said with a low bow, even bringing his hat down to arm's length to sweep it across the floor. "I'm always enamored of Dame Gwydre's optimism. Sure but you are a warm ray of sunshine on a dark forest trail."

"Take care in how you address the Dame of Vanguard," Father Premujon warned, which only made Jameston chuckle harder.

"Then we can hope," said Gwydre. She put her hand familiarly and warmly on the strong shoulder of tall Jameston Sequin, much to the annoyance of Premujon and every other Abellican brother in the room. "Then we can hope."

"Always that," Jameston replied.

They didn't have to wait long for their hopes to be fulfilled, for word rang out later that same afternoon of more travelers coming down the northern road. The alarms sounded loud and clear long before this second group neared the town, for among its ranks were reportedly at least two powries and a tall man wearing the beret of a bloody-cap dwarf.

Many people went into the streets to await the arrival, and Dame Gwydre and her entourage moved to the front of that throng. Soldiers and scouts slipped out all about the town perimeter, watching, their elm bows drawn and ready.

The approaching band came into view at last, over a rise to the north, and many in the crowd gasped, "powries," at the unusual sight. But Dame Gwydre was not looking at the bloody-cap dwarves. She was smiling, her eyes on Bransen the Highwayman and on Brother Jond beside him. She led the gathering right out of the gates, doing all she could to stop herself from breaking into a full run at the very welcome sight.

"We feared you dead!" she said when she stood before the band of six. Gwydre gasped then, and so did others around her, noting the garish wound on the face of the beloved Jond. Immediately a group rushed from Father Premujon's ranks to attend to the man.

"Yach, but so did we," said one of the dwarves, and he and his fellow laughed.

"Ancient Badden hoped that to be the case, I assure you," said the Highwayman. He rolled his sack off his shoulder and dumped its gruesome contents—the ancient's head—onto the ground before Dame Gwydre.

More gasps arose and several wails of protest.

"Remove that wretched thing!" one man demanded.

But Gwydre held up her hand to silence them. "Truly, I have never seen a more beautiful thing in all my life."

"Let it thaw a bit so ye can enjoy the stink of it, as well," advised the same powrie. Again he and his friend exploded into laughter.

Dame Gwydre looked from one to the other curiously, then stared hard at Bransen.

"We have a lot to talk about," the Highwayman admitted sheepishly.

FOUR

Throwing Down the Torch

Bannagran stood at the top of the main keep of Castle Pryd, staring to the east. He could make out the light of some campfires, seeming to twinkle on and off as the many trees waved in the evening wind. The savvy leader had set the torch on the wall near to him so that any milling about the streets of Pryd would see him up there in his shining bronze breastplate, cut to accentuate his solid and muscular form. He wore no overcoat and his arms were bare, showing the man's powerful muscles. Bannagran leaned forward so that his strong features reflected the torchlight. He kept his visage solid and determined, to direct the gaze of any onlookers to the plumed bronze open-faced helmet he had also set on the stone. How many times had the men and women of Pryd Town seen Bannagran adorned in that helm, his oft-broken nose crookedly protruding from the single line of bronze that ran down the front below his brow? They had seen that inspiring sight not once in the course of defeat, only in victory.

This was his role, he knew, and he had been taught well by his friend Prydae. As mighty as he was in battle, his biggest role was to serve as inspiration. "Better to kill one enemy loudly than ten silently," Prydae once said to him. He had to look and act the part of leader. If the warriors didn't trust in him, they could be routed and turned at the first sign of defeat, leading any one of a battle's ebbs and flows into a self-fulfilling prophecy of disaster.

So Bannagran wore his decorated bronze breastplate on the tower top that night. He was too far up for any below to make out the details of that crafted suit, of course, but just seeing the shine would remind them of the craftsmanship, of the line of carved silver wolves running across the chest and the multitude of jewels inlaid above and below that bas-relief. Bannagran was a simple man and had never been overly fond of such finery but, again, he knew his role. He hadn't come up here simply for appearance, however.

"What are you doing, Ethelbert?" he asked quietly, for something here was not quite right. Laird Delaval's forces were gathering around Bannagran in Pryd Town, with more streaming in every day. Surely Ethelbert knew that. No scout could miss it.

Milwellis had won in the north and was in position to swing to the south and press Ethelbert hard. Surely Ethelbert knew that.

So why hadn't he attacked Pryd a week before, as soon as Milwellis had handed his Northern forces the defeat at Pollcree?

Pryd Town swelled with soldiers. Even now Bannagran had at his command more men than Ethelbert could put on the field. That number only grew in Bannagran's favor with more of Delaval's warriors streaming in every day.

Bannagran looked past Ethelbert's distant camp then swung his gaze to the south, looking for some hint that Ethelbert had another force moving in to support him. The night was dark, unbroken by fires beyond the known encampments. Bannagran had scouts wide and far south and east of Ethelbert. There seemed no reinforcements on the horizon.

So, with the balance obviously shifting day by day to Pryd's favor, why hadn't Ethelbert already attacked?

And now, with the full weight of Delaval congealing around Pryd Town, why hadn't Ethelbert turned and flown the field, back to the east and the south where he could rally more allies?

Bannagran knew Ethelbert and had seen him in battle years before against the powries. He was a capable commander, a fine tactician who knew when to strike.

"A fine night," came a voice behind Bannagran. He couldn't stop his reflexive wince at the familiar nasal whine of Prince Yeslnik. Bannagran leaned more heavily on his hands, his fingers pressing tightly against the stone of the tower crenellations.

Yeslnik walked up beside him and followed his stare to Ethelbert's campfires.

"They are many," Yeslnik said.

"Not so many. Not nearly enough."

"I will defeat them," Yeslnik said, and by "I" he meant "Bannagran."

"If we can catch them and engage them, then we— you—will prove victorious, yes," Bannagran promised. "More so if Prince Milwellis pivots his force to the south."

"I prefer to let Milwellis run to the coast to put those wretched lairds of the Mantis Arm to the fire."

A tactical blunder, both militarily and politically, Bannagran knew, but he also knew that voicing such a concern wouldn't do much to dissuade the stubborn Yeslnik and, indeed, might prompt an even more stupid response from the impetuous and spoiled young man. Let the lairds of the Mantis Arm hold their loyalties to Ethelbert for now, Bannagran silently reasoned, for once this fight was decided and Ethelbert routed, those lairds would quickly realign behind the victor. They had no ideological and deep-felt belief in this war, after all, and were simply trying to figure out which laird's victory—Delaval or Ethelbert—would benefit their respective holdings the most.

"Do I need Milwellis?" Yeslnik asked. "Have I not given you enough to properly deal with this old sot from the south?"

"Yes, my laird, I mean, no, you do not need Milwellis, and, yes, you have more than enough men already gathered in Pryd Town to destroy Ethelbert's force."

"Then why are they not yet destroyed?"

Bannagran summoned his patience. "Because time works against Ethelbert. He is ill-supplied, and our numbers grow daily."

"But I can beat him now."

"A difficult fight."

"So?"

The callousness of that remark was not unexpected by Bannagran. Yeslnik didn't care how many men and women, his own as well as Ethelbert's, he sent to the grave as long as he achieved his victory.

"If Laird Ethelbert comes at us, we hold a defensive posture and he will be utterly destroyed," Bannagran tried to explain. "That would be the sweetest victory for you of all. If we must fight him in the open, then we will still win, though I fear that Ethelbert himself and many of his warriors will escape. If we must find him, we will win more decisively with every passing day. It is not just the victory, Laird, but the extent of the win that is important."

"I grow tired of the waiting," Yeslnik sighed. "March tomorrow morning."

Bannagran managed to avoid Yeslnik's gaze as he rolled his eyes.

"What will Ethelbert do in that event?" Yeslnik pressed. "He will see my strength and know his doom."

"He will likely flee the field," Bannagran replied, thinking it through as he spoke. He started to explain to Yeslnik that Ethelbert assuredly already knew of their strength, but the words caught in his throat and he stared back to the east more intently and with obvious alarm.

"What?" Yeslnik demanded anxiously, and he, too, looked that way. "What do you see?"

"Ethelbert is a shrewd commander. He knows he cannot win this fight," Bannagran pondered, more to himself than to Yeslnik. "He will flee. He seeks no more, perhaps, than to draw us out or to keep us occu—" Bannagran cut himself off and shook his head with slowly blossoming concern.

"That is a good thing, is it not?" the confused Prince Yeslnik asked as Bannagran wheeled away from the wall and started for the ladder leading back into the keep.

"How protected does Delaval City remain?" Bannagran asked.

"Behind her high walls?" the oblivious Prince replied.

"You have emptied her guard?"

"To fight Ethelbert," Yeslnik said, somewhat defensively, without knowing why.

"It is a ruse," Bannagran explained. "A feint of the highest order. He does not sit there intending to fight but only to keep us occupied, to keep us gathering our forces for a decisive battle that will not commence, not here, not soon."

"Then go and get him!" Prince Yeslnik cried, not catching on to the cause of Bannagran's alarm.

"Why is he here?" Bannagran asked.

"What puzzles are these?"

"To bring us here," the general from Pryd answered his own question. "Why does Ethelbert wish us here? Why does a swordsman invite a parry?"

Yeslnik stared at him blankly.

"Because such a parry will not defeat his true intended

attack," Bannagran explained, and when Yeslnik at last seemed to be catching on, he repeated, more grimly, "How protected does Delaval City remain?"

Yeslnik's wail confirmed Bannagran's fears. The seasoned soldier rushed into the keep, Yeslnik dithering in his wake.

Guard Captain Rubert was widely considered the toughest man in the service of Laird Delaval. He had grown up on the streets of Delaval City, literally fighting for his every meal. His knuckles carried the scars of a hundred fights, a hundred crushed faces, and he wore a necklace of teeth he had knocked from the mouths of his opponents.

His reputation served him well, with an appointment to Delaval's own elite guards and a climb to the rank of captain, and in this latest adventure, where most of the soldiers had been sent from the city on the miserable hike to Pryd Holding, Rubert had escaped the call.

He was too tough, too valuable to Laird Delaval, the would-be King of Honce.

"Ah, but there's a cold wind coming down the masur this night," he lamented, tightening his cloak against the frigid breeze rushing down the great river, a harbinger of the approaching wintry season. "And I'm out o' weed for me pipe and got not a striker pad to light it up. Be a good sport," he called to his fellow sentry atop the wall encircling Laird Delaval's main keep. "Put a light up and a pinch."

As he neared, the man stood up and shrugged off the guard cloak. Even in the dim light of the quarter moon Rubert knew at once that this was not his companion. For that moonlight shined off a bald head, where his companion wore a thick mop of black hair, much like Rubert's own.

"Who are you?" Rubert called, his hand going to his finely crafted sword.

The imposter strode calmly toward Rubert. He carried no weapon that Rubert could see, and he was not a large man, certainly not near to Rubert's two-hundred-fifty-pound muscular frame.

"Far enough!" Rubert warned, drawing forth his sword, its dull metal gleaming in the moonlight.

The stranger continued toward him.

"You have been warned!" said Rubert. Heart pounding, he retracted his arm and thrust his blade at the man's chest.

But the man was no longer standing before him, having somehow moved enough to the side so that the blade slipped harmlessly past. Rubert felt a slight thump against his throat. He fell back, slashing his sword at the stranger, who by then had retreated safely out of reach.

"What are you about?" Rubert said, or started to say, or tried futilely to say, for no sound moved past his lips, though he did hear a wheeze a hand's width below them. He brought his free hand up to his throat and moved it before him into the moonlight, feeling the warmth of his own blood on his fingers. He started to protest, to ask the man another question, but again nothing came forth but a wheeze.

Another form scrambled over the wall behind his attacker, then more behind him. The original assailant grinned at Rubert and calmly walked by. Rubert meant to strike at him with his sword. He really did, except that his arm wouldn't heed his command to lift the weapon; indeed, he heard the sword, as if very distantly, clang against the tower's stone roof.

The stranger walked past, along with his companions. Rubert stood there, staring ahead, only vaguely aware that he was perched on the precipice of death's dark pit and falling forward without reprieve.

Only vaguely did Rubert feel his nose and cheekbone shatter against the hard and cold stone of the tower roof. Only vaguely did he hear the shuffle of light footfalls go past him. He didn't think of Laird Delaval, the would-be King of Honce, then. He didn't think of anything at all, just the inviting, irresistible blackness.

L aird Delaval was not a young man, and he surely felt every day of his nearly sixty years that evening. Winter was coming on in full force, with frost every morning and several snow flurries already. Delaval wasn't looking forward to it. He had hurt his knee in battle three decades earlier, thrown from his horse when some impudent peasant had stabbed his mount in the flank. Though the laird's wounds had healed—he was back to fighting form within a few weeks—the knee used every day of inclement weather, whether rain or the constant ache in the cold winters, to remind him of that long-ago fall.

"If my nephew can be rid of that troublesome Ethelbert in the coming battle, I just might winter in Ethelbert dos Entel this year and every year thereafter," Delaval said to Genoffrey and Tademist, his personal attendants and generals. Genoffrey had been with him since the early days, before Delaval had even been named successor to his father, the laird. A large man, his muscles not slackened in the least by the passage of the decades, Genoffrey wielded a claymore of extraordinary weight. More than once had he taken down heavy warhorses on the field of battle with a powerful swipe, and he had one time slain three men with a single swing, a feat that was still much discussed across the holdings of western and central Honce. Tademist, half the age of Delaval and twenty years Genoffrey's junior, had only recently joined the inner circle. Tall and lanky, the young warrior had not yet thickened with age. Where Genoffrey won with sheer power, Tademist was more of a finesse fighter, wielding a short sword and a long dirk, a rare two-handed fighting style, with cunning and unmatched speed.

The two men glanced at each other with obvious skepticism.

"I know, I know!" Laird Delaval said with a wave of his hand and a snicker. "Prince Yeslnik is not known for his martial prowess."

"But he has Bannagran, the Bear of Honce, with him, my king," said Tademist, who, along with Genoffrey and all the others of Delaval's inner circle, had started referring to Delaval by the title all in Castle Delaval considered inevitable.

"You know this one?" Delaval asked.

"I know that his reputation is well earned, by every account," Tademist replied, and Genoffrey nodded. "As is his title. They call him the Bear of Honce because of his great strength and size, and when he enters the field, the enemies flee."

"I have seen him in battle," the elder guard said. "Both when he was beside Pryd's son, Prydae, those many years ago, and in our most recent fighting south of Pryd Holding. If anything, his prowess in battle and in commanding his forces is greater than the whispered huzzahs. The Bear of Honce, indeed, in strength and sheer power, but he is more the fox in cleverness. Prince Yeslnik is well-served by that one and will win every day if he heeds the instincts of Bannagran of Pryd."

"That is good to know," Laird Delaval said, nodding. He started for his armoire, unbuckling his sword belt as he went. He knew that Genoffrey and Tademist were glancing at each other again behind his back, both of them concerned by his pained hobble. "I plan to live a hundred years, my friends."

"You will, my king, of course!" said Tademist.

Delaval laughed. "But these are dangerous times, and I fear that I've abused my body over the decades. Too many battles, too many hunts, too many women, and too much strong drink!"

Tademist started to protest, but Genoffrey cut him short. "I hear no regret in your voice," he said slyly.

Laird Delaval laughed again more heartily. "You were there for much of it," he replied, turning to face his oldest friend. "Do you believe that I should hold regrets?"

"Ah, but if our lives are twenty years shorter for the games of it all, then we'd have lived more than any man deserves!"

Tademist looked at his companion with horror that he would talk to the king so casually, and then both Delaval and Genoffrey laughed.

"You've been here for more than two years, young swordsman," Genoffrey said to Tademist.

"Do you not yet understand?" asked Delaval.

"Understand what, my king?" the poor young man stammered.

"That when it is just we three, you need not call me that," Delaval replied with obvious exasperation.

"But—"

"Oh, shut up," said Delaval, laughing once more, or still, actually. "All the formalities are for those out there," he explained, waving his hand at the closed door of his private chambers.

"And out there, never forget your place or his title," Genoffrey added.

"But in here we are friends," said Delaval. "Genoffrey was by my side when he was just a boy, a groom. As he grew, he trained with me and then became my constant companion in the wars. We saw men die, and often."

"Too often," Genoffrey grumbled.

"Aye, and we've killed men, and goblins and powries, side by side," Delaval continued.

"I am blessed to be here, my king—" Tademist said with a bow.

"Nonsense!" said Delaval. "You earned it with your skills! You remind me of a young Genoffrey, and I assure you, that is no small compliment."

Tademist, who considered himself fortunate in his daily sparring with Genoffrey on those rare occasions he even earned draw, didn't doubt that for a moment. He looked to his companion and smiled.

A knock on the door interrupted the conversation.

"Speak!" Delaval called.

"Your hot towels, my king," came the familiar woman's voice of Maddie Macabee, another of Delaval's personal attendants.

"Hot towels for aching bones," Delaval said with a sigh, and he nodded Tademist toward the door.

But a sudden and sharp cry from outside the closed door froze Tademist in his tracks. "What are you about?" Maddie yelled, followed by a thump and a scream. Not just any scream. Delaval and Genoffrey knew such a keen quite well, the dying shriek, the final wail of a man or woman as death descends.

Tademist knew it, too, and drew his weapons as he rushed to the door. From over his shoulder Genoffrey pulled out Spinebreaker, his legendary claymore, and Delaval slid his fine blade from its scabbard and let the belt fall to the floor.

The door burst open before Tademist got to it. In rushed Maddie Macabee, though not of her own accord. She was already dead, her chest gashed open. She flew forward, tumbling before the dodging Tademist, who did well enough to ignore the shock enough to prepare for the man following Maddie into the room.

Behrenese, judging by the color of his skin, the man held a fine, slightly curved sword in both hands. He en-

tered in a fast and steady walk, perfectly balanced all
the way to Tademist, where he launched a sudden thrust,
then retracted his blade with amazing precision and speed,
launching it into a downward diagonal swipe that would
have taken Tademist from shoulder to hip had he not
been focused solely on defense.

Tademist twisted away from the thrust and backed out
of the downward cut then responded fast with a sudden
thrust of his own sword, a stab of his dagger as he retracted the sword, and a second thrust. He advanced as he
attacked, thinking to drive the man back, for other Behrenese appeared at the doorway.

But the man was suddenly not in front of him. Luck
alone saved Tademist as he happened to turn the correct
way in trying to find his too-quick opponent and happened to have his sword at the proper level to barely deflect another thrust of his opponent's fine blade.

A man went by the combatants to Tademist's right as
he squared back up with his opponent. A woman entered
next, as sounds of fighting erupted in the hallway, the
castle guard rushing to their leader's aid.

Tademist faded right as the woman, a fine sword in her
hand as well, moved to pass him on the left. He wanted to
intercept, but his opponent kept him dancing, kept him
dodging.

As the woman passed, she smiled at him, and such an
awful grin it was! Tademist felt his knees go weak, as if
she had just withered him to his core. In that smile he
knew—somehow—that he and his beloved King Delaval
were surely doomed.

Genoffrey was used to missing with his first swing.
The claymore wasn't wieldy, after all, and Genoffrey never took pains to disguise his first attack. The

blade came lumbering down from on high and the warrior before him easily and gracefully leaped back and to the side.

Genoffrey hid his grin, purposely seeming to overbalance as Spinebreaker thumped against the thick carpet. He even appeared to stumble.

The warrior rushed forward to the side of him, pivoted fast, and came in with a straightforward thrust, but just as he started the turn, so too turned Genoffrey, dropping his foot back as he lifted and re-angled his blade, putting it right in line to pierce the charging warrior.

He thought he had a win, and the necessary quick one so that he could go to the side of his beloved Delaval. But the warrior leaped up high, front somersaulted above the level claymore, and landed in a run past Genoffrey. The soldier tried to turn to keep up and felt the burn in his side, felt the warmth of his blood spilling from a long and deep gash.

To his credit Genoffrey grimaced through the pain, completed the swinging turn, and would have scored a hit on the retreating man had not that man, almost as if he had long anticipated this reaction, dived into another roll, this time along the floor.

This Behrenese warrior was two plays ahead.

W ell, come on then and be done with it," Delaval said to the dark-skinned, slight woman, although he had no way of knowing if she even understood him. She just smiled and circled, her curved and decorated sword down low before her, its tip nearly cutting the threads of the carpet.

"I need not ask who sent you," said Delaval. "Long have we known that the traitorous Ethelbert favored the beasts of Behr."

"You leaders of Honce slaughter your people with impunity," she answered, surprising Delaval with her command of the language. "And yet, we of Behr are the 'beasts'? Tell me, you who would rule the world, how do you measure such a title?"

She came forward suddenly, her sword flashing left, right, and center with three separate thrusts that seemed almost as one to the Laird of Delaval. To his credit, he managed to pick off the first and back out of the reach of the second and third.

She wasn't done, though, quick-stepping forward and turning a complete circuit—something few warriors would ever dare try—bringing her sword in fast at Delaval's side, then doubling the complexity of her form by changing its angle mid-swing.

Somehow, and he knew luck to be a part of it, Delaval managed to block.

"How much is he paying you?" he asked, trying hard to keep the nerves out of his voice. In just those two routines, the man feared he was outmatched. "I will double it!"

"Shallow principles," the woman chided. "We are beasts."

"You intervene where you do not belong!" Delaval growled at her. "You risk a war with all of Honce!"

"Idiot Delaval," she said, and she came again, in a vicious flurry of swings and thrusts that left Delaval dizzy, that left Delaval retreating.

That left Delaval bleeding.

"You do not command all of Honce," the woman finished.

Tademist did not hear Laird Delaval's gasp as Affwin Wi's blade punctured his belly. The young warrior heard nothing but the near constant ring of metal as he and his shaven-headed opponent exchanged vicious and furious flurries. Sword hit sword, dirk hit sword, and so fast was the man from Behr that even as Tademist intercepted his thrust with the dirk and perfectly executed a responding thrust with his sword, he found it fully parried.

If that weren't impressive enough, the man from Behr then immediately launched another thrust routine, left, right, right again, and then right a third time.

Tademist blocked the first three, but his anticipation had him sliding his blade across to block a thrust angled left that never came. He felt the stab in his shoulder, felt his dirk arm go weak, and heard the weapon hit the floor.

Genoffrey did hear Delaval's gasp, a sound he had heard only once before, in a far-off and long-ago battle in the Belt-and-Buckle mountains. He reacted with a sudden and brutal straightforward rush, stabbing his sword then slashing it, then reversing it with a powerful backhand. He didn't get close to hitting his opponent, but he wasn't actually trying for a kill there. He drove the man back, back, and then he turned and charged across the way, behind Tademist and toward Delaval.

He registered that Tademist was in trouble, but there was nothing he could do at that time, for before him the woman was into another wild exchange with Delaval, their blades ringing and screeching with hits and slides, and Genoffrey's fine eye told him that his friend was too slow here, that the woman was outmatching him, strike for strike. He watched her setting Delaval up with every stride he took, and indeed, he felt as if he was running in deep mud, as if everything before him was just out of his reach. She brought Delaval's sword to the right, then a bit farther to the right, and then again, with three short, quick stabs, then she flipped her blade across to the left, actually tossing it to her waiting left hand.

"No!" Genoffrey cried in dismay as Delaval futilely

tried to re-angle his own sword. To the laird's credit, he did manage a central thrust, but the woman stepped away from it, farther to his left, and turned as she went, rotating her hips and shoulders, lengthening her thrust and putting great force behind it.

Genoffrey felt a slug in his lower back—he knew it to be a stab from his pursuing opponent—at the same time he watched the Behrenese woman's sword slide deep into King Delaval's chest.

It occurred to him that it was appropriate that he and his dear friend would die at the same time.

He finished his charge, unable to interrupt his own momentum, slashing Spinebreaker down hard against the woman's blade, but too late, of course, for that only jarred the impaled laird.

Genoffrey stumbled forward, taking Delaval with him hard into the far wall. The king crashed in without any attempt to cushion the blow, slammed face first into the stone, and bounced away, crumbling to the ground. Somehow Genoffrey managed to hold his footing and hold his blade, turning about with his back against the wall. He saw the woman, in obvious distress, looking down at her sword, nearly half its blade snapped off.

Whatever comfort that might have given Genoffrey, though, ended as she thrust her arm at him and launched the remaining piece of her weapon, flying spearlike, spinning sidelong in the air.

Genoffrey heard it hit the stone wall behind him.

It took him a moment to realize that it had gone through his throat.

He slid down to a sitting position. The woman approached him, while the man who had been his opponent, his sword red with Genoffrey's blood, turned toward Tademist.

Genoffrey heard Tademist's cries, one after another, as the two men stabbed at him. Every now and then came the ring of metal as valiant Tademist managed a block, but mostly Genoffrey heard the sickly sound of metal puncturing flesh.

He didn't see any of that desperate last stand, though, for he could not take his eyes off the slight woman walking toward him. She bent low before him, stared into his eyes, and gave that wicked smile once more, then yanked her broken sword out of his throat.

She started for Delaval, but calls from the hall turned her.

She crossed Genoffrey's field of view, running back toward the exit. He wanted to turn to Tademist, wanted to turn away from the sight of his fallen friend, Laird Delaval.

But he couldn't. He hadn't the strength, and even the slightest movement sent fires of agony tearing through his body. He couldn't even manage to close his eyes, and so was forced to watch Delaval's lifeblood pouring from him, pooling around him as he lay so very still.

To Genoffrey, that was the cruelest trick of all.

FIVE

Six Cogs Scattered

The lines of allies couldn't have been clearer to Dame Gwydre as she listened to Bransen relay his tale of capture, escape, and ultimate victory over Ancient Badden. Beside Bransen stood the fallen monk Cormack and the barbarian woman Milkeila, with a pair of powries behind them.

Across the way to the left side of the room sat Father De Guilbe and his entourage, including Brother Jond, who Gwydre knew was the link between these wildly disparate groups. Jond was a good man, an honorable man, who put moral duty first and foremost. Gwydre hoped that to be the case, for De Guilbe had made no secret of his loathing of Cormack.

"We had enough allies to get through the ancient's defenses," Bransen remarked, throwing a sour look Father De Guilbe's way as he spoke.

Gwydre sighed inwardly. Why did things always have to be so complicated?

"It was not our place to go!" Father De Guilbe protested. "I could not know of your predicament, Dame Gwydre!"

"We have already been over this, good Father," Gwydre calmly replied. "No one holds you or your brothers at fault for the choice you made in retreating from the glacier."

"No one?" De Guilbe asked sharply, his glare landing on Bransen.

The man in the black silk clothing grinned, something Dame Gwydre did not miss. "And you slew Badden?" she asked Bransen.

"It would do great injustice to those around me, these four and two other powries, for me to make such a claim, Lady," Bransen replied, managing another sly grin at De Guilbe as he did. "It was my blade that took his head, yes, but only through the sacrifice and efforts of those around me."

"However it was done, it is appreciated," said Dame Gwydre.

"It was done for a price," Bransen reminded, and all in the room widened their eyes at that rather callous announcement, a reminder that stole the joy from the room. "And now, good Lady, with your generosity, I would ask that you extend that reward."

Beside Gwydre, Dawson McKeege and another advisor began to protest, but Gwydre held up her hand to silence them and bade Bransen to continue.

"I would have my Writ of Passage," Bransen demanded. "I will go and collect my wife and her mother and travel Honce as a free man as I was promised."

Gwydre nodded.

"And I insist upon a similar writ for Cormack and Milkeila," Bransen added.

"No!" shouted Father De Guilbe, leaping to his feet. Beside him, Brother Giavno tried to grab his arm, but the large, older man tugged free of his grasp and stormed toward Gwydre. "Cormack does not answer to the laws of the lairds but to that of the Order of Abelle."

"Are you saying that Chapel Abelle will not honor my

wishes?" Gwydre asked. If the cool and calm woman was shaken in the least by the sudden and violent outburst she didn't show it.

"I beg you not to do this, Dame Gwydre!" Father De Guilbe said. "Brother Cormack betrayed us!"

Despite the heightened tension, Gwydre smiled at De Guilbe's clever and selective use of Cormack's title. He only called Cormack "brother" when claiming church jurisdiction, it seemed. She waited for De Guilbe to finally stop his march, just a few feet from her chair, then she turned to Cormack.

"Have you anything to say in your defense?"

"I followed my heart," Cormack replied. "Everything I did, I did because I believed it to be the will and manner of Blessed Abelle, the calling of my order."

"Betraying us to the barbarians?" rasped De Guilbe.

"Ending a needless slaughter," Cormack corrected. "You held the men of Milkeila's clan prisoner. You—we— had no right!"

De Guilbe started to shout back, but Dame Gwydre silenced him and bade Cormack to continue.

"The Alpinadorans of the neighboring islands would all have died at the base of our chapel before surrendering our captives to us," the young man explained. "I could not tolerate that slaughter. There was no need for it."

"So what did you do?" Gwydre prompted.

"I freed the four men and showed them the way out of our dungeon to rejoin their people. The Alpinadorans left our island. The battle ended, and so ended the death— the death of Alpinadorans and of monks."

Dame Gwydre turned to De Guilbe, her expression cold.

"A simplistic review," the monk said.

"Then do elaborate."

"The men we held were not captured, they were rescued. Rescued from certain death and healed of grievous wounds through the power of Blessed Abelle, by the brothers of Blessed Abelle."

"That does not give us the right to hold them as prisoner!" Cormack argued. "You cannot so coerce fealty to faith!"

Gwydre looked from Cormack back to De Guilbe, her expression caught somewhere between disbelief and outrage.

"Our manner is of no concern to Dame Gwydre," Father De Guilbe said to her. "My orders came from Father Artolivan of Chapel Abelle. To him alone do I answer."

"True enough," Dame Gwydre conceded. "But a writ is mine to give, and so I do, to both Cormack and this woman, Milkeila, though I would like to speak at length with you both before it is finalized."

"Yes, Dame Gwydre," Cormack said, and Milkeila graciously bowed.

"I would ask for writs for the other heroes of the fight," Bransen interjected then.

"Bloody caps?" Dawson McKeege gasped behind Gwydre, and, indeed, the Lady of Vanguard, too, seemed more than a bit disconcerted at that suggestion.

To the side Father De Guilbe laughed loudly, as if mocking Gwydre and this path she now walked.

"Go back to your brothers," Gwydre said to him and waved him away.

He complied, but continued his mocking laughter.

"Come forward," Dame Gwydre bade the powries.

"Name's Mcwigik," said one. "And me friend's Bikelbrin. Come from the Julianthes but spent a hunnerd years on that lake, Mithranidoon, with our friends."

"And your friends are still there?"

"Yach, still on the rock."

"You do not wish to rejoin them?"

"Seen too much o' that smokin' lake," Mcwigik replied. "Not for going back, unless going back's for taking them off with us."

"Yach, but more than a few're wanting off that rock," Bikelbrin added.

Dame Gwydre sat back in her chair, and Dawson McKeege immediately began whispering in her ear, his great concern more than obvious.

"You ask much of me, Bransen Garibond," Gwydre said a few moments later.

"I . . . we gave much to you," the Highwayman replied. "At great risk."

Gwydre frowned. "I cannot grant powries the writ to walk freely through the lands of men."

Bransen stood up very straight and crossed his arms over his chest.

Gwydre sighed and looked at the dwarves. "Were I to grant you passage, free of battle, throughout all of Honce, would you agree to lay down your arms?" she asked.

Both Mcwigik and Bilkelbrin began shaking their arms and looking at the limbs curiously. "They're attached to our shoulders," Mcwigik answered. "Ye sayin' we got to cut off our arms to stay with ye?"

Gwydre and the others, even Cormack, chuckled at that. "Your weapons," she explained. "Were I to grant you passage, do I have your word of honor that you will not take up arms against any man or woman? That you will not do battle with any men?"

"Even them that's deservin' it?" asked Bikelbrin.

"Even them. No battle. Not ever. If I am even to consider giving you the writ Bransen desires, then you must promise me that you will not—not ever!—again spill human blood. Can you make such a pledge?"

"Don't hear ye whining that we spilled Badden's blood," Mcwigik retorted. "Last time I looked, he was human. Headless, but human."

"Aye, and we dipped our caps in his blood, and mines shinin' all the better," added Bikelbrin.

"Where we come from, them needing a crack get a crack," said Mcwigik.

"That is not the way among men," said Gwydre.

"Bah, but them men with money and land and power—and them women with such—they get to pick them needing a crack," said Mcwigik. "And when the crack's given, what?"

Behind and all about Gwydre, men bristled at the obvious insult, but Gwydre remained calm, reassuring them all.

"It is by the law, good dwarf," said Gwydre. "The law is bigger than men and women."

"Bigger than most," said Mcwigik. "Not bigger than the lairds and the priests, from what I'm hearing. Even a powrie might walk free, what, if a laird or lady says so."

"I do not know," Gwydre answered honestly. "My writ for you might hold no weight beyond Vanguard."

Mcwigik spat upon the floor.

Dame Gwydre looked at Bransen and shook her head. "This is beyond my power to grant."

Bransen narrowed his eyes.

"But I will offer this. When the weather breaks and the winter is no more, I will send you both back to the lake," she told the powries, "with wagons laden with supplies and with a map to take you and your kin to Brinewind, a port in eastern Vanguard. From there, I will supply you with a boat and star charts so that you can sail for your distant home."

Mcwigik and Bikelbrin looked at each other for a few long moments. Mcwigik stepped forward and fell to the floor, where he sucked up his spit.

More than one person in the room groaned.

Mcwigik stood up straight and smiled at Gwydre.

"I am not sure what that means," she said, caught between revulsion and laughter.

"Means I ain't spitting at yerself anymore," said Mcwigik. "And means me and me friend're liking what ye're saying."

Gwydre watched as Bransen looked at Cormack and Milkeila, both of whom (apparently more familiar and comfortable with the ways of powries) smiled and nodded.

"You would turn them free on the coast to lay waste to innocents," Father De Guilbe said from the side.

"They did not kill me, though they surely had the chance," Cormack argued. "When Father De Guilbe cast me adrift, beaten and dying, the powries took me in."

"More the reason to hate them," muttered the unrelenting De Guilbe, who had only gone as far as the doorway.

"Enough," Dame Gwydre warned him. "Father De Guilbe, you weary me."

"And you overstep your province with Cormack and now with these two little . . . murderers," the monk replied. "I assure you that Chapel Abelle will hear of this, all of this!"

"At the same time they learn of the death of Ancient Badden, no doubt," said Bransen. "And learn that Dame Gwydre has led them greatly in their battle with the Samhaists."

Father De Guilbe looked at him curiously, as if he couldn't believe what he was hearing from this strange man. "Who are you?" he asked.

"The man who helped save the life of one not worth the trouble, it would seem," Bransen replied.

Now Father De Guilbe's eyes went very narrow, a look of absolute loathing and threat.

Bransen grinned at him.

"Perhaps you should not be so secure of Dame Gwydre's writ, Highwayman," De Guilbe said.

Dame Gwydre stood up suddenly, her eyes flashing as she scowled at the obstinate monk. "If you would counsel Father Artolivan to ignore my writ, then you would counsel him badly," she warned in an even and deathly serious tone.

"You war with the Samhaists and you would war with the Brothers of Abelle, too?"

"Chapel Pellinor, all the chapels of Vanguard, exist by my grace alone," Gwydre retorted. "Do not ever forget that."

Behind Gwydre, Dawson McKeege groaned. Behind De Guilbe, Brother Giavno did likewise.

Y ou are satisfied with her decision?" Cormack asked Mcwigik and Bikelbrin when they were alone with Milkeila.

"She didn't attack us, and that's something," Mcwigik replied.

"She assured you safe passage," Milkeila reminded.

"Yach, and we're knowin' it," said Mcwigik. "And we're not thinkin' bad of her."

"She did good by us. We're knowin' that," Bikelbrin added.

"Don't mean we won't kill her one day and dip our caps in her blood, though," Mcwigik said, and when both Cormack and Milkeila's eyes went wide, the two dwarves enjoyed a good laugh at their expense.

"We'll be taking the wagon and the boat, and off we're going back to where we're belonging," Mcwigik proclaimed.

Cormack reached up and grabbed his cap, pulling it from his head. "Will you want this back?" he asked.

"Are ye wanting to give it back?"

Cormack thought for a moment, then shook his head. "I wear it as a reminder of some unusual friends," he explained. "I wear it to remind myself not to be hasty in judging others until I know them."

"Fine words," said Mcwigik.

"To get ye killed to death," added Bikelbrin, and the dwarves laughed at Cormack again.

"We let ye live to put a burr in Prag's fat arse, ye dolt," said Mcwigik. "Weren't for him and ye'd've been gutted on the beach that first day."

Cormack fell back as if slapped.

The powries laughed again.

"How am I to know when you're speaking true and when you're speaking in jest?" the former monk protested.

"Ye're not," Mcwigik answered. "Not now, and not ever."

"Are you friends, Mcwigik and Bikelbrin?" Cormack asked.

"Been friends for a hunnerd years," Mcwigik assured him.

"To me!"

The dwarves looked at each other. "If we're ever in the forest or on a boat and we see Cormack or Milkeila in trouble, then know we'll help ye," Mcwigik said for both, for Bikelbrin nodded his assent through every word of it.

"And we'll be thinking many times o' the one human wearing a powrie cap and glad how he came by it," Bilkelbrin added. "Kicking Prag's ugly face!"

Cormack patted each on the shoulder appreciatively as he left with Milkeila to go to their room across the hall. "I will miss those two," he said to his wife.

Milkeila nodded, hand on the knob. "The world seems less . . . colorful already." As she finished, she led Cormack's gaze down the hall, where several grim-faced guards stood ready with long halberds and armored all in bronze.

"Dame Gwydre did not err in granting them passage," Cormack said.

"You speak to convince yourself, not me."

Cormack looked at his wife carefully and glanced over his shoulder at the closed door of the powries' room. He wondered if he was a fool, for had he been in charge he would have trusted that pair of dwarves, would have given them a Writ of Passage.

"No other laird would have honored that writ," Milkeila said as if reading his mind.

"You know nothing of Honce," Cormack replied.

"I saw the looks on the faces of those here in Pellinor," Milkeila said. "Mcwigik and Bikelbrin would not have much of a life in the lands of your people. What life, I wonder, might Milkeila find there?"

Cormack put his arm about her shoulder and pulled her close as he guided her into their room. "A fine one," he promised, but he glanced back over his shoulder again as he closed the door. He would indeed miss his powrie companions, his powrie friends.

I have little desire to be caught up in the endless drama that so marks your church," Bransen said to Brother Jond.

"You know little—"

"I know much!" Bransen interrupted. "I spent years as a slave in service to the Brothers of Chapel Pryd."

"A slave? Surely you exaggerate!"

"I lived in a hole in the floor and spent my days emptying chamber pots. True, in exchange, they gave me bits of miserable, cold food, and my dungeon wasn't open to the snow and the rain." Bransen gave a little snicker, his eyes looking past Jond and, indeed, into the past, as he remembered those many days he had spent with Father Jerak and Brother Bathelais and Brother Reandu . . . ah, Brother Reandu! Blind Brother Jond couldn't see the confusion on Bransen's face at that moment, of course, but he did tilt his chin in apparent curiosity at the man's pause.

Bransen's mind whirled back to his days as the Stork, living in a tiny, one-room cellar at Chapel Pryd. He almost felt ashamed at the way he had described his time there to Jond. For all the discomfort and for all his outrage at the brothers for what they had done to Garibond, the brothers at Chapel Pryd had not been cruel to the young and wounded Bransen, who, because of his affliction, was known then as Stork. Brother Reandu in particular had often shown him affection and sympathy and, indeed, had aided him in his last desperate fight with Laird Prydae, at the cost of Master Bathelais's life.

"They let me go," he said finally.

"The brothers of Chapel Pryd?"

"Chapel Abelle," Bransen corrected. "They let Dawson McKeege take me here to serve Dame Gwydre, though they knew that Delaval and that pathetic excuse of a man, Yeslnik, would have rewarded them greatly had they turned me over for execution."

"But instead, you were pressed into service you did not desire."

Bransen shrugged. "Aren't we all? I do not think Dame Gwydre wanted this war. Nor did Crait and Olconna and Vaughna. Nor Brother Jond."

The blind monk smiled widely at that, as if he saw something Bransen could not.

"What is it?" the young warrior asked.

"It does my heart good to hear you speak like that, my friend," he explained.

The door swung open to the room, and Father De Guilbe and Brother Giavno entered.

"What are you doing here?" De Guilbe asked Bransen.

"He is here at my invitation," Brother Jond answered. "I have known this fine young warrior for many weeks now. We have shared the road of adventure."

"You speak for him?" De Guilbe asked rather sharply. "I do."

"He befriends Cormack," De Guilbe warned.

"Cormack who saved the folk of Mithranidoon from certain doom, your chapel and clergy among them," Brother Jond reminded.

Bransen noted the big man tense up at that, and so he smiled widely, just to make De Guilbe even more uncomfortable.

"Beware your actions," De Guilbe warned him.

"Cormack helped kill Ancient Badden," said Bransen. "While you ran away, he battled the greatest foe of your order and of Dame Gwydre's holding. Perhaps it is Father De Guilbe and his fleeing monks who should beware their actions."

"Leave this place," De Guilbe commanded.

Bransen looked to Brother Jond, who needed no prompting. "Stay!" the monk from Chapel Pellinor argued.

"Brother!" De Guilbe fumed.

"Good Father, I serve Father Premujon of Chapel Pellinor," Brother Jond answered, remaining very calm. "I name this man as a friend, for he has stood beside me in my trials."

"As you helped me after our capture," Bransen replied.

"I'd no more abandon him than I would abandon my beloved Abelle, Father De Guilbe," said Jond. "He is a man of good heart and great courage, a man we should coax to the ways of Abelle, not a man to be shunned."

Father De Guilbe wore a strange, wicked smile as he replied, "And Cormack? Have you made an assessment of the former Brother Cormack?"

Jond shook his head. "Should he appeal to Father Premujon for reinstatement in the order, I will speak honestly of that which I know regarding the man."

"And you believe that I was wrong in excommunicating him?"

Again Jond shook his head. "I make no judgments of that which I do not know, Father," he said. "I know little of this man, Cormack, but I will speak honestly to that which I have seen . . . heard. His work against Ancient Badden was no small thing, but whether that absolves him of his actions on Mithranidoon is not for me to decide."

"Those actions should absolve him," Bransen insisted. "Particularly since he did nothing wrong on the island on the lake."

"Be gone from this place!" Father De Guilbe insisted, and again Brother Jond started to argue. But this time, Bransen put his hand on Jond's shoulder to quiet him, more than happy to be out of the company of the irascible De Guilbe.

De Guilbe didn't even look at him as he walked past, but Brother Giavno gave him a look that seemed regretful, almost heartbroken, almost apologetic.

Bransen chuckled as he walked from the room, thinking of how much that reaction by the younger brother reminded him of the same sort of conflicts he had seen in Chapel Pryd regarding the young man known as the Stork.

He got into the hall, pulling the door closed behind him, and heard De Guilbe explode at Brother Jond. Bransen just shook his head. He certainly had needed no further confirmation of the many reasons he was no fan or friend of the brothers of Abelle.

E xhausted from the squabbling in her audience chamber, from the incessant complaining of the unlikable De Guilbe, from having to deal diplomatically with powries—with bloody-cap dwarves!—exhausted from her own excitement and anticipation of the possibilities now that Ancient Badden was dead, Dame Gwydre wanted nothing more that night than to fall into the arms of

Alandrais, the brother of Chapel Pellinor who had become more than a friend to her.

The moment she entered her private chambers, where Alandrais was waiting, she knew something was wrong.

The man hadn't dressed down into his nightshirt but was still wearing his heavy brown robes and hadn't untied his uncomfortable sandals. He half stood, half sat on the edge of Gwydre's desk, his strong arms crossed over his chest, his expression stern.

Thinking him distracted by something extraneous (or hoping that to be the case), Dame Gwydre walked over and reached up to stroke his face.

He was looking right at her when he stiffened away from her touch.

"What is it?" she asked, afraid she knew.

"Father De Guilbe is a powerful man in the Order of Abelle," Alandrais replied.

"So is Father Premujon."

"Who supports Father De Guilbe. And Father De Guilbe has the ear of Father Artolivan."

Dame Gwydre stepped back from the man. "I have not spoken to Father Premujon about the new arrivals from Alpinador, nor does it matter much concerning my own words—"

"You should not diminish him or contradict him, particularly on matters relating to the order," Alandrais scolded. "As with the man, Cormack, it is not your concern."

Gwydre nodded her head as she mulled over those words for a few heartbeats. "Cormack, who helped defeat Ancient Badden and thus may have saved my people?" she asked. "That man, Cormack? That hero, Cormack, is not the concern of Dame Gwydre, who rules Vanguard?"

"His disposition in the church is a matter for the Order of Abelle."

"When have I said that it is not? My argument with De Guilbe stemmed from his remarks to my man, the Highwayman."

"Your threat to him, you mean."

"Aland, what is this about?" Gwydre asked, coming forward in a conciliatory manner, again reaching to stroke his bearded face.

This time, he stood straight and turned his back on her.

"Alandrais?"

"Dame Gwydre . . ." he started, and then he took a deep breath and turned around to face her directly. "Gwyd," he restated, using his pet name for her. "I am a brother of Abelle. I will always be such—my first and foremost love is forever my church and my prophet."

"I have never asked you for more than that," Gwydre interrupted.

"Haven't you? When you threaten the very chapels of my order, as you did with Father De Guilbe, you place me in an uncomfortable—"

"And I am the Dame of Vanguard!" Gwydre cut him off. "The people of this land depend upon me for their welfare, as they depended upon my husband before me and my father before him. I will always be as such, and first and foremost in my heart is my responsibility to the people of Vanguard. I have never asked you to betray your order, to place me before Abelle in your heart, and yet you are doing just that to me, right here and right now."

"Your words to Father De Guilbe—"

"Were not an idle threat, I assure you," Dame Gwydre snapped.

Brother Alandrais stared at her hard, but there was no blink coming from the woman, no backing down in the least.

"You should leave," she said after many moments of unsettling silence had passed.

Brother Alandrais started to reply but stopped short, looked to the side for a moment, then nodded and walked past Gwydre, out of the room.

The Dame of Vanguard winced when that door slammed closed. She took a deep breath, wiped away whatever tears were daring to form in her eyes, and walked across the room to her private stock and poured herself a large glass of boggle, a rare and precious wine, rumored to be made by woodland elves or some other such faerie folk.

It had been a long day.

Indeed.

SIX

The Opportune Moment

Laird Ethelbert couldn't hide the smile widening on his face as the scouts offered their reports. So it was true: His assassins had killed Delaval.

Yeslnik had fled to Delaval City, taking much of his entourage with him, including his elite, well-armed, and bronze-armored warriors who had been so devastating to Ethelbert on the battlefield of late. Many of the support groups surrounding Pryd Holding were apparently peeling away as well, falling back to guard Delaval City or falling off simply out of confusion.

Ethelbert had beheaded the beast, and the beast's body was flailing without purpose or direction.

"Yeslnik will become Laird of Delaval Holding," he whispered, nodding. He looked up as he finished to see all his scouts and generals and advisors staring at him, hanging on his every word. "This boy, Yeslnik, who has no understanding of warfare and who has never bloodied his blade on a living opponent."

His emphasis on the word "living" brought a derisive laugh, for it was rumored that the Prince of Delaval had oftentimes wiped his sword on the bodies of fallen enemies to make it look as if he had gallantly struck many mortal blows. The joke among Ethelbert's men and even among the fighting warriors of Delaval's ranks was that Yeslnik must have extraordinarily long arms to reach the battle from his favored position, far in the rear.

"We have accomplished all that we hoped," Kirren Howen remarked, bowing in admiration for his laird's cleverness.

Ethelbert nodded but then addressed another of the scouts who had not yet offered his report. "What news from the north? Has Milwellis pivoted?"

"No, my laird," the man replied, stammering nervously. "I mean, yes, my laird, but not toward us. He went north to Chapel Abelle and the coast. From there, he marched east but then back to the west as if unsure."

"And now?"

"Back east of Chapel Abelle, along the north reaches of Felidan but still west of the Mantis Arm," the scout replied. "He has not sought engagement since his victory at Pollcree."

"Because he thinks his legacy safe," said the smiling Ethelbert. "And thinks the war nears its end. He paused because he expected the battle to commence here, an obvious rout for Delaval. And while I was in retreat to the southeast, Milwellis could move east with ease, against holdings unsure of their allegiance to my, obvious losing, cause."

"Obvious, my Laird Ethelbert," said Kirren Howen, and several others snickered. "But the battle will not commence here, as Milwellis anticipated. And our withdrawal will not be retreat."

Ethelbert was nodding, but his expression did not show agreement. "Delaval's forces slide away. They are confused and demoralized."

Kirren Howen looked at the man slyly.

"Perhaps the battle should commence here, and now," Ethelbert said, grinning at his old general. "We had thought to make the attempt and withdraw posthaste, but since we have been more successful than we ever deemed possible, is it possible that Pryd Holding is within our grasp?"

"They maintain a sizable garrison, but they are in confusion," said Myrick the Bold.

"Do we dare?" asked Kirren Howen.

"Do we dare not to seize the opportunity?" Ethelbert replied. "What might be the gain, I wonder?"

"Pryd Holding," said Myrick the Bold.

"And Prince Yeslnik suing for peace on our terms," added Kirren Howen.

"And Bannagran," said Ethelbert, nodding, his eyes gleaming, for he knew that one well and suddenly understood the potential prize here. "Can we do it?" he asked his most trusted soldier.

Kirren Howen didn't answer. He looked around questioningly at the scouts. "I can know by this very evening," he finally assured Ethelbert.

"Calculate then," Ethelbert bade him. "We must act quickly if we are to act at all. Before Yeslnik's advisors— Laird Delaval's old competent warriors—mitigate their confusion and protect their flanks."

Ethelbert grinned widely at Kirren Howen as he finished. "I believe we can do this. We have struck a mortal blow, but only if we press the wound before it is tended."

Kirren Howen nodded and bowed then went fast to the scouts, and not a man or woman on that field thought for a moment that they would not attack Pryd Holding within the next two days.

Y ou see their eyes?" Lady Olym asked her husband as they were hustled through the streets of Delaval

City, toward the main keep, where Laird Delaval lay in state. "They revere you."

Prince Yeslnik had indeed noticed the many stares—hopeful, pleading, wounded all at once, their intensity nearly stealing his breath and the strength from his legs. Laird Delaval, King Delaval, was dead. Only then did the implications of that reality truly hit Yeslnik, the favored nephew, the Laird of Pryd, the Prince of Delaval's Honce.

Now they all looked at him. No, not at him, but *to* him!

He carried in his every step the hope and desperation of a wounded people. His words now, his every word, would hold great importance and power. His every whim would become edict; dozens, scores, hundreds would clamor to fulfill his every wish.

A smile and squeal of joy would not be appropriate, so the prince managed to hold his somber demeanor as he continued on his way, reminding himself that the weight of Delaval's office, the reality of the war and all the rest, now fell upon his shoulders.

His private giddiness turned to terror when he entered the audience chamber, the hall of state, to see his mentor, Uncle Delaval, laid out upon a stone sarcophagus. The man appeared serene in death, his face chalky but relaxed, arms crossed over his chest.

"I wish for more privacy," Yeslnik said, and immediately the guards began clearing everyone from the room. Yeslnik didn't wait but staggered over to the body and fell to his knees beside it, overwhelmed. He had never thought of Delaval in any terms other than the good the man could do his fortune and ascent to power. He couldn't deny his feelings of guilt now as he knelt by the corpse of the man who had treated him as a son. Never before had the self-absorbed Yeslnik allowed such feelings to invade his consciousness. Never before had he troubled himself with empathy or guilt.

Now it hit him like a shield bash, a great jolt to his

sensibilities, a shocking intrusion into the bubble that was his private domain, and it carried with it a rush of emotion the man had never before felt, a great wave of regret, as if his whole life had been a meaningless thing.

He fell over Laird Delaval, weeping. He grabbed his uncle's hands and squeezed the cold flesh. Delaval's robe opened enough for him to see the wound, still torn open, for in cleaning the man the dried blood had been washed away.

Howling, Yeslnik slapped his hand over the open gash and then pulled it away with a start and a yelp. He stared at his hand in horror, seeing a cut on his palm, his own blood dripping from the wound.

"It is the sword tip, my laird," explained one of the attendants, rushing over with a cloth.

Yeslnik's eyes went wide with shock. "You left it in him?"

The attendant colored. "It is customary to disturb the body as little as possi—"

"You left it in him?" Yeslnik repeated, standing up tall. "The sword that killed him? Take it out! Take it out this moment!"

"My laird," said Pendigrast, the father of Chapel Delaval.

"Take it out!" Yeslnik yelled at him, pointing at the ugly wound.

Pendigrast glanced around nervously. "This is hardly the time, my—"

"Now!" Yeslnik demanded and stamped his foot. "Now! Now! Now! Take it out of him! Now!"

Pendigrast saw the horrified expressions worn by the people still in the room. The father of Chapel Pellinor moved hastily but awkwardly to the body of his fallen laird. He looked around again, his gaze settling on the still-fuming Yeslnik, and then he focused on the wound, working his fingers to widen the gap in the torn skin. He felt like he was pulling against tough leather, but he managed to wriggle his hand inside enough to grasp the back edge of the broken weapon.

He started to pull, but it would not come free. Sweating now, Father Pendigrast glanced anxiously up at Prince Yeslnik again. The man stood resolute and unblinking.

Father Pendigrast took a deep breath and moved his hand in more forcefully to get a stronger grip on the blade. Understanding now the stubbornness of the unyielding flesh and bone, he pulled with all of his considerable strength.

A sickly, crackling sound accompanied the slide of the blade. Pendigrast grimaced, as did everyone in the room, with more than one in attendance giving a horrified gasp. But the monk didn't relent. An edge of the jagged blade cut him, but he continued to pull the item forth.

Finally he freed it and moved quickly to use his voluminous sleeve to try to mitigate the mess on Laird Delaval's chest. He turned at the sound of Yeslnik's approach, showing the obstinate prince the blade as he did.

The slightly curving, etched, and decorated blade.

Prince Yeslnik's eyes went wide and he found himself gasping for breath, his eyes locked on the bloody spectacle. Misreading him, Father Pendigrast moved the blade away, or started to, but Yeslnik reached out and grabbed him by the arm, holding it fast. Ignoring his own wound, an action which in and of itself would have astounded anyone who knew the oft-whimpering man, Yeslnik grabbed the blade, taking it from the surprised father's grasp.

Yeslnik held it up before his astounded eyes. He wiped it fast on Pendigrast's sleeve then held it up again to study it, his expression dumbfounded.

"What is it, my prince?" Pendigrast asked.

"I . . . I know this blade," whispered Yeslnik, twice the victim of the man called the Highwayman.

* * *

Castle Pryd loomed above the tree line behind them. They had been pushed back to the very edges of their town, their backs literally to the walls of their outlying farms.

One after another, the defenders of Pryd glanced back at that keep, their last refuge, and it seemed to offer little hope against the ferocity of the advancing men of Ethelbert dos Entel.

And on the southerners came, roaring in anticipation of victory, charging across the snow-covered field with abandon. A few stray arrows and spears reached at them but proved inconsequential and did nothing to slow them.

A group of defenders took a position at the corral rail up on a bluff. "Hold that spot at all costs!" they had been ordered by the field commander, who had then promptly retreated past the farmhouse and across the back field.

Grim-faced, knuckles white as they gripped their weapons, the proud and battle-seasoned warriors of Pryd Town intended to do just that. This would be their glorious stand to turn the tide against the surprising and ferocious charge of Ethelbert.

The first force came against them, a disorganized mob of Ethelbert's leading line, seemingly oblivious to the defenders crouched behind the bluff. They came on almost casually right to the fence.

Up jumped the defenders, spears stabbing wildly, and behind them came a cheer from the men of Pryd Town. In a day of constant retreat, these warriors had held; the men of Ethelbert scrambled away or fell bleeding to the mud and snow.

Before those retreating few had even crossed the field, however, Ethelbert's main line came out of the trees across the way. Now with the defenders' position clearly defined, the attackers gathered in a tight group in the center and sent out lines to flank, left and right.

Without delay, they came on.

The defenders of Pryd Town kept glancing left and right, kept looking for support, for if the invaders passed their position, where might they flee?

Many broke and ran. Those others who stood their ground held for only a few moments as the full weight of Ethelbert's center came against them, pressing and stabbing and slashing. The attackers dislodged the rails and tossed them aside, then pressed over the bluff, driving the valiant defenders of Pryd under the sheer weight of their numbers. Splashing through mud and blood, they came on.

Across the back field the next line of Pryd defenders looked on in dismay, knowing that they were next.

"Fight them from the trees!" the field commander yelled, though neither he nor the men he led were sure of what that meant. They had few range weapons, few arrows and spears, remaining.

On came Ethelbert's hundreds, seeing the tower of Pryd before them, not so far, seeing victory, not so far.

The men of Pryd Town broke ranks and ran.

The men of Ethelbert shouted all the more eagerly and ran ahead even faster.

"Where is Bannagran?" one fleeing defender cried. "Will the Bear of Honce come to our aid?"

"Where is Laird Yeslnik? He has deserted us with his army and now we are doomed!" cried another. Many of those in full retreat made it to the road and turned fast for Pryd Town with men coming from the trees along either side, scrambling and stumbling, terror clearly stamped upon their faces.

Ahead of them all, the shouting started in the town. Alarm and confusion echoed from the walls, followed by shrieks of surprise.

Among those retreating along the road arose fears that Ethelbert had a second force pressing Pryd from the north. What else could incite such commotion in the town so far ahead of the retreat?

What else, indeed.

Out of the gates of Pryd Town, he came, dressed all in bejeweled bronze armor and driving the chariot of Prydae, a cart of war not seen since the former laird's demise. A rack of spears beside him, his legendary great axe waving high above his head, Bannagran came on in splendor, unafraid, eager for battle. Behind him surged the rest of Pryd's garrison, some on chariot, most just running and waving pitchforks and clubs, rallying to the call of Bannagran.

Those on the road parted as he neared, for he showed no sign of slowing. "Charge ahead!" he cried, his voice strong and resonant. This man, so long the hero of Pryd, the champion of its lairds, shamed those who would flee before Ethelbert.

The road behind him crowded with soldiers, now running back to the south, back toward Ethelbert's approach. All along the sides, among the fields and the trees, cheers went up for the Bear of Honce. "Charge! Charge!" replaced the fearful "Run away!"

Bannagran rushed in front of it all and showed no sign of slowing the fabulous chariot and his mighty team. Ethelbert's leading line loomed before him now, but he didn't make any move to veer or halt. To those before him, he seemed in the grip of suicidal glee, but to those behind him, he appeared as the heart of Pryd, the champion, the warrior.

Ethelbert's men in Bannagran's path set their spears for his charge, digging them in to skewer the team.

But Bannagran dropped his axe to the flooring beside him and took up a spear, veering his team as he neared and letting fly one missile after another. As one man fell

mortally wounded and a second lurched aside, Bannagran turned the chariot back in line and plowed ahead.
For now the integrity of the block was gone, and now the
armored team and the spike-wheeled chariot crashed
through, scattering men. Another spear flew from the
driver, another of Ethelbert's men spiraled down to the
ground in agony.

Bannagran had his axe in hand in a flash and chopped
across to drop another man, then stabbed its pointed tip
back to fell yet another. He turned his chariot, rambling
right off the road, crashing through brush and men alike,
the horses trampling everything in their path.

So great was the spectacle that few of Ethelbert's men
remained focused on that which followed Bannagran, the
weight of Pryd's garrison charging with renewed hope
and eagerness.

The chariot crashed through a thicket and nearly broke
apart as the wheels caught on some roots. Never slowing
in the least, Bannagran merely leaped from the cart, great
axe in one hand, spear in the other. He rushed at a group
of ten men and noted which was giving the orders. That
commander fell, Bannagran's spear deep in his chest.

In leaped the wild warrior, his axe slashing with great
and powerful strokes. No man would stand against him;
his roars stole their strength, his axe sheared their limbs
and crushed their bones and let their blood. He ran back
toward the road, calling for his men to rally behind him,
cutting down enemies with every step, it seemed.

The center of Ethelbert's line collapsed; the men of
Pryd, working in a wedge formation with Bannagran at
their tip, pressed through, widening the breach, splitting
Ethelbert's forces asunder.

Bannagran kept looking for their leaders, kept listening for their commanders. Whenever he spied one, he
rushed that way, cutting his path to the man. Enemies
struck at him from the side but from afar, throwing stones

or knives or small spears, with none daring approach the man, the possessed and crazed warrior.

A dozen wounds marked Bannagran's body, but if he felt any of them he didn't show it. Every hit of stone or knife seemed to spur him on further, more furiously, as if the pain was only granting him greater, almost supernatural strength.

And the spectacle of Bannagran, the great Bear of Honce, commanded too much attention of the men of Ethelbert, allowing the charging forces of Pryd to cut deeper, to gain more strength and momentum.

It was Ethelbert's line that broke that day, the old laird and his forces retreating fast to the south.

Ethelbert knew his folly as he fled. He should have waited for Affwin Wi and the others to return to him before making his move against Pryd Town. He should have had some counter to the strength of this demon warrior from Pryd, a man he had seen in battle a decade before. He had gambled to gain the center and strengthen his hold, and he had lost, but he was not forlorn as he and his forces regrouped that night, several miles south of Pryd Town, with no intention of turning back to the north.

For his greatest foe, Laird Delaval, this man who would be king, was dead.

SEVEN

Abelle's Win

Silent as the shadow he crossed, Jameston Sequin moved along the line of pines, circumventing the drifts of snow with practiced ease. He knew this place, this tended grove, and knew, too, that he was likely being watched. He knew the watcher, though, and had come to see that very man.

Still, he kept his caution and covert manner, unsure of who might be gathered around the one he expected was more than aware of his presence.

A large raven flopped onto the branch of a nearby pine, looked right at him, and cawed loudly.

Jameston straightened and stared at the bird, smiling knowingly.

The bird hopped down and before it ever landed on the ground transformed suddenly and with a bright flash of light into an old man, bald and with a beard braided by clumps of dung, dressed in light green robes, a heavy fur cloak, and open-toed sandals. Only a Samhaist priest could keep his feet from freezing to black with those feeble shoes.

"One day I'll catch you unaware," Jameston said to the man.

"Or I'll grow tired of your trying," the Samhaist replied, but Jameston knew it to be a good-natured threat. Despite all their differences, despite Jameston siding with Gwydre against the troll and goblin hordes of Badden, despite Jameston's obvious disdain for the Samhaist religion, Wisterwhig was not an enemy. Not a friend, perhaps, but not an enemy.

"So, Badden's gone," Jameston said.

"Killed by Dame Gwydre," Wisterwhig replied. "And by his own arrogance."

Jameston raised a bushy gray eyebrow at that startling admission, to which Wisterwhig merely shrugged.

"He did find Mithranidoon, and that is no small thing, of course," the Samhaist said.

"You disagreed with his war?"

Again Wisterwhig, a man Jameston found quite reasonable compared with most of his Samhaist brethren, merely shrugged and then said, "It was not my place to agree or disagree. I do not remember Badden ever asking my opinion."

Jameston snorted. "I love the hierarchy of learned men."

"Spare me your incessant sarcasm, scout," said Wisterwhig. "You come on behalf of Gwydre, I expect."

"Indirectly," Jameston admitted. "As much for my own curiosity as for her needs. There's less activity now. I've seen no sign of goblins or trolls moving south."

"Winter is on in full force in the northland," said Wisterwhig dismissively.

"They fought through the winter last year," Jameston reminded. "Ice trolls favor that season."

The old Samhaist made no move to respond.

"Winter favors them in battle, but your folk aren't sending them to Vanguard," said Jameston.

"If you have all the answers, why do you bother me, scout?"

Jameston leaned back and grinned. "I have all the suspicions. I'm looking for the answers."

"You ask that I would ease Gwydre's mind?"

"Ease the minds of lots of folk," Jameston replied.

"You presume that I have a responsibility to people who have turned their backs on the old gods."

"No," Jameston answered slowly, measuring his words. "I just think you're a decent enough fellow despite those robes you wear."

Wisterwhig laughed. "You're quite wise for an idiot, yes?" he said, imitating Jameston's even tone. Jameston laughed with him. "Or quite the decent murderer, don't you think?"

"I've never hid my feelings for your church or th'other one."

"You have never hidden your feelings on any matter," said Wisterwhig. "Which is why I tolerate you."

"Just tolerate? Should I be insulted?"

"We could banter like this all the day, I fear."

"We have before."

Wisterwhig surrendered with an upraised hand. "I am glad the war is over," he admitted, a startling revelation to be sure.

"Is it?"

"You will not take my word to Dame Gwydre," the Samhaist said.

"I can tell her enough without it," Jameston agreed. "But I'm glad to hear it."

Wisterwhig's nod showed that they had a mutual understanding and agreement here.

"Who'll be the next ancient?" Jameston asked, grinning widely, for he knew that he wouldn't get much of an answer to that one. "Wisterwhig?"

"That is for the old gods to decide."

"And will the one they name then start the war anew?"

"You speak of something a decade removed," answered the Samhaist. "We are not as impatient as the brothers of Abelle. The successor will not be named this year, possibly not even next year, and, after that, he will have many months of work ahead of him in just informing the groves and calling in his disciples."

"You surrender Vanguard to the monks?"

"Not so," said Wisterwhig. "We know that the brothers of Abelle will fail in the end. Their baubles are impressive until the deathbed, and there they have no answers. Just empty promises. Those who follow them pass on unprepared for the judgment of the old gods."

"And those dead ones will come back and discredit the monks?" was Jameston's sarcastic response.

"The ghosts speak to us. To all. In the end, we Samhaists, not the monks, hold the answers most needed. If I did not have faith in that I would not wear these robes."

Jameston conceded the point with a nod.

"Patience," Wisterwhig added. "It is a necessary virtue and one, perhaps, that Badden lost in his last years. Events prompted change in Vanguard, and he wished that errant course corrected before his passing. We do not consider our ancient to be the sole proprietor of godly wisdom, scout. You know that much, at least."

"So, many disagreed with Badden's war?"

"Or thought it an unnecessary provocation. In the end we will win, and we'll need not enlist goblins and trolls and powries and barbarians to achieve the victory. Because we are right, scout—because our gods are true—we will win."

Jameston had been kidding earlier when he had asked if Wisterwhig, not a leading member of his religion by any means, might be named as the next ancient, but truly, Jameston wished that a possibility.

This Samhaist priest, at least, was reasonable and decent enough.

The scout's step as he left Wisterwhig's grove was much lighter than the footfalls that had brought him to this place. Jameston never feared a good fight and was always happy to kill a goblin or a troll, but he knew that the folk of Vanguard had suffered far too much already.

The weather here was trying enough without adding the burdens of a war.

D awson McKeege tried to stay seated, but he couldn't manage it. He kept getting up and pacing around the thick carpet, his eyes scanning the closed door at the side of the room. He knew what was going on in there. Gwydre had asked him to stay with her this evening because she had discerned the tone of Brother Alandrais when he had arrived earlier that day, and Dawson trusted her instincts implicitly.

"Come on, then," he whispered, eyeing the door. He glanced across to a cabinet on the other side of the room where an hourglass drained away; he had upended it almost immediately after his friend had gone to meet privately with Brother Alandrais. She'd been in there nearly a full hour.

Dawson licked his lips. Perhaps things weren't going quite so bad?

The man straightened as the door opened and Dame Gwydre came through. One look at her told McKeege that his hopes for some reconciliation had been in vain.

She stared into his eyes, her face very tight, and she nodded curtly, as if giving any further movement would cause her to dissolve.

Like telling someone when a loved one had passed, Dawson thought. "He's a fool, then," the crusty old sailor said.

Dame Gwydre walked past him and patted him on the shoulder as she moved to sit stiffly on the divan, eyes unseeing. Dawson was quick to her side.

"For the best," he said, putting his arm about her. He was the only man in the world who might tell Gwydre that, he realized.

Gwydre was glad of it at that moment. She slumped at long last and put her head on his shoulder, turning to bury her face in his shirt, her shoulders bobbing with sobs. After just a few brief moments she composed herself and sat back up straight, sniffling away the tears. Then she gave a cleansing sigh and even managed a little laugh at herself as she wiped the moisture from her eyes.

"It's for the best," Dawson repeated without thought. As soon as the words left his mouth he heard them as incredibly inane.

But Gwydre just laughed and nodded. "I would have ended our love affair if he had not," she said. "It was too much trouble now."

"Now that the war's looking to be over, and ain't that the irony?"

Gwydre frowned. "With Ancient Badden looming, I had no time for quibbles with the brothers of Abelle. Now that Badden is gone, I expect that I and the church will face some trying moments of disagreement."

"Alandrais wasn't man enough to keep them separate," Dawson accused. "He'd've kept jumping in at you whenever you took a stand against his masters. As with De Guilbe."

Gwydre nodded. "All true."

"If he loved you—" Dawson started, but Gwydre put her hand up to stop that line of thinking short.

"Once, he did love me," she said. "And I loved him. It was not convenience that brought us together. Indeed, at the time we started this relationship I thought it the least convenient thing in all the world."

"But did he?"

Gwydre eyed Dawson curiously.

"I mean, there's no doubt the brothers of Abelle gained greatly through the relationship," Dawson clarified. "Their fight with the Samhaists added a powerful ally because of Brother Alandrais's loins."

"Dawson!"

The sailor shrugged but didn't retract.

"I would not have sided with the Samhaists in any event, and that much was clear before Alandrais and I fell in love," Gwydre insisted. "As their grip on southern Honce eroded, Ancient Badden grew ever more demanding and desperate and vicious."

"Aye, I know," Dawson admitted. "And Alandrais loved you. I know that, too, though I'm wanting to punch the fool in the nose right now."

"You can't blame him for . . . this," said Gwydre. She reached up and stroked her friends grizzled face. "It's been a long time in coming, and it is for the best."

"Still would feel good to punch him."

Gwydre managed another laugh. She pulled herself to her feet and began to pace in much the same manner as Dawson had earlier. "I am quite the fool," she muttered. "To get involved with a monk at a time such as this—nay, to get involved with a monk at all! Oh, what pain have I brought upon my people? I have betrayed their trust for the sake of my own selfish needs."

"You betrayed nothing!" Dawson shouted and leaped from the couch. " 'Twas Badden who betrayed you, who betrayed us all. He held Vanguard hostage to protect his losses in the south. He demanded of us—of you—that which you could not do! Were you to deny the folk the blessings of the monks' gemstones? Were you to let the sick and injured die because Badden didn't want the monks praying over them with the soul stones?"

"The situation wasn't so bad before my tryst with Alandrais."

"Before the war in the south turned the folk of Honce away from the Samhaists, you mean. Wasn't about you and wasn't about your monk lover. Badden's desperation came from knowing that his priests were being chased from half the holdings of Honce, and even where they stayed in their groves, the lairds weren't listening to them. Delaval and Ethelbert have the whole of Honce in flames, and the folk're suffering. In that suffering they've turned to the brothers of Abelle and their gemstones and away from the Samhaists."

Gwydre considered the reasonable rebuttal for a few long moments, then nodded and smiled her gratitude at this man, her friend Dawson. Dawson took his leave and went back to his own rooms, pleased that he had been able to help his friend through her trying night, for surely Dame Gwydre was as a beloved sister to the old sailor, a woman he would gladly die defending.

Dame Gwydre continued to pace the room long after Dawson had gone. She did feel much better than when she had walked out of her meeting with Alandrais. Dawson was a valuable friend to her, unafraid to speak to her as a friend and not as his liege lady.

Truly he was a shining gem to Gwydre. He kept her grounded, kept her humble, and she knew that his love for her was unconditional, that if she were thrown down the next day from her position of authority and cast penniless into the street, Dawson McKeege would treat her no differently and no less affably.

Some of his honesty that night had stung, though, she had to admit. She didn't think that Dawson had mentioned the gains her tryst had brought to the brothers of Abelle simply to make her feel better. There was a ring of truth in his claim.

Too much, she decided, and so, instead of going into her private chambers to don her bedclothes, Gwydre, Dame of Vanguard, went into the cold winter night.

The brothers of Chapel Pellinor had just finished their evening prayers when she arrived at their door. Father Premujon did not deny her request for an audience. Nor did he say anything when she entered the room and told his attendants, who included Father De Guilbe, to leave them.

"May I help you, Lady?" Premujon said when they were alone. "This is most unusual."

"I was visited by one of your brothers this night," she said.

"I see," Premujon mused. "And who—"

"I'll not speak around it," Gwydre said. "You know well of my relationship with Brother Alandrais, and you know by now that the relationship ended this night."

"Dame Gwydre, I am not—"

"Father," she prompted in an exasperated tone.

The man sighed in surrender. "I know. Of course, I know."

"As you knew of it when it commenced."

The father tilted his head and eyed her curiously.

"Before it commenced, perhaps?" she asked slyly.

"Now how would I have known that?"

"Because you blessed Brother Alandrais's decision, this night and those months ago when first we began our relationship."

Father Premujon sat back very straight, as if he had been slapped. "Good Lady, what do you imply? Do you believe that I sent Brother Alandrais to your bed?"

"Our relationship benefited Chapel Pellinor greatly."

Father Premujon considered that for a moment and conceded the fact with a nod. "Indeed, you were a mighty ally in our struggles with Badden's Samhaists, but I expect that you would have supported us over him in any case."

"A cool war of words and not a fighting battle."

"True enough," said Premujon. "So now you fear that I orchestrated your relationship with Brother Alandrais, that I sent him to you hoping you would fall in love for the sake of Chapel Pellinor?"

Gwydre didn't answer the charge.

"I did not," Premujon stated flatly. "When Brother Alandrais became smitten with Dame Gwydre, he came to me and confessed in full, and he was a man in terrible conflict. He understood the implications of any advances he might make, both for the church and for his continuing role in the order. What would you have had me say to him, Dame? Generally, my order frowns on such relationships, of course, but we often make exceptions, or merely let the situation quietly run its course."

"Quietly?" Gwydre asked sarcastically.

"Such situations do not usually involve a laird or a dame," came the dry reply.

"And in this case?" Gwydre asked. "Which course did Father Premujon prefer?"

"That you and Brother Alandrais would find love, and that such love would bring benefit to Chapel Pellinor and help us rid the land of the vile Samhaists," the man admitted without hesitation.

Dame Gwydre fell back a step, surprised by his forthrightness.

"What would you have me say?" the Father of Chapel Pellinor asked. "What would you have had me do? I saw the gain to my order, to be sure, and did not dissuade such a beneficial outcome." He rose from his seat and walked over to Gwydre, placing a hand on each of her shoulders and looking her straight in the eye. "But milady, good Dame Gwydre, not I nor any of my surrogates sent Brother

Alandrais to court you. In no way. We simply decided not to interfere with nature's course. And now, this evening, no one here bade Brother Alandrais to bring an end to your relationship."

Dame Gwydre didn't doubt him. Somehow, the truth he had just spoken hurt her and comforted her all at once. Her love affair with Alandrais had been real. Of course, that meant that the end of that love was real, as well.

Gwydre reached up with her right hand and pulled Premujon's hand from her shoulder, grasping it tightly. "It is my friendship and trust with you that placed me on the side of your order against Badden's Samhaists, you know. My love for Brother Alandrais did not determine my actions."

"But it spurred many of Badden's," the monk replied. "To the great benefit of Vanguard in the end."

Gwydre nodded. "Thank you," she said softly and took her leave.

She spent a long night thinking of her many days with Alandrais, days in the sun and in the snow. She laughed and she cried that night; she let the light and the darkness have their play in her emotions.

For the next morning, Dame Gwydre had to let it all go, had to be again the leader of her people in a time that was far from settled and far from safe.

EIGHT

Writ and Rebuttal

T he nearest Samhaist's grove is empty, they say," Cadayle said to her mother, Callen Duwornay.

"How would they know, for who would go?" Callen replied.

"They went before the snows," Cadayle insisted, struggling to bite back the desperation she heard in her own voice.

"So before the snows the Samhaist went away."

"And he hasn't returned."

"They're not knowing that," said Callen.

"They're whispering that the war is over."

Callen moved a step away from the blazing hearth. "Every hope to hang on," she said, a common criticism she had thrown her daughter's way these last few weeks. Bransen had been taken from Cadayle to go and fight in Gwydre's war, and each passing day had weighed more heavily on the poor young woman's mind.

She knew that her mother was only looking out for her with her constant words of caution, and she knew, too, that all the people in this new town, Tanadoon, were hanging desperately onto any bit of hopeful information.

They were all refugees here, all displaced from a place they had once called home, and all with family serving in Gwydre's army against the terrifying onslaught of the monstrous minions of Ancient Badden.

A few weeks before, word had gone out that the local Samhaist had deserted his grove, and the people of Tanadoon had taken it as a sign that the war had ended. But new reports of goblin or troll incursions had continued to surface; the war had rolled along. Three of the families in Tanadoon had lost loved ones soon after the initial reports of the deserted grove had begun to raise the hopes.

But over the last three weeks, the reports of battle had slowed to a stop, and no news of further tragic losses had been delivered to Tanadoon. That lull had added life to the excited whispers that maybe, just maybe, the tide had turned.

"There's been no smoke over the grove," Cadayle said. "In the cold, even a Samhaist would need a fire."

"So it might be that he's not there," said Callen. "Might be that he's dead, and you won't ever see Callen Duwornay crying over the death of a Samhaist!"

"They're whispering that the war's over," Cadayle dared again.

"They've been whispering that since we got here," said Callen. "And we're all wanting it so bad that we're listening to every word."

"I miss him," Cadayle said, her voice barely a whisper. She brushed back her long, wheat-colored hair, showing more clearly the redness and moisture rimming her large brown eyes, so much like her mother's. "More and more each day. I know he'll come home to me, but I fear he's lying dead on a snowy field. And then I feel as if I'm betraying my love for doubting him! I don't know—"

"I do," Callen interrupted. "I know that what you're feeling is what I'm feeling. Don't you doubt that I love that husband of yours—he saved my life as his mother and father saved my life. And yours. Keep your faith in him. Bransen has overcome greater trials than most men, and it will take more than a goblin to kill him."

Cadayle managed a smile at that, and a nod, and she turned from her mother to the cabin door, thinking to go out and retrieve more wood for the fire. She pulled her meager shawl about her as she went through the front door into the driving storm, her mother's scolding voice echoing in her ears. For weeks, Callen had been telling Cadayle that she needed to eat more, to put some fat on her body for the coming winter. But Cadayle hadn't found her appetite in a long while and had lost quite a bit of weight since Bransen had departed. She went to the wood pile on the side of her porch and bent to retrieve some, but as soon as she reached for the logs a gust of wind flapped the shawl back over her shoulder. She instinctively went to grab at the flap but froze in fear, feeling another hand at the shawl's edge, pulling it back over her shoulder.

"A woman, poorly dressed and vulnerable," came a whisper behind her in tones suggestive and even lewd.

Cadayle felt her heart pounding, felt her pulse thrumming in her temples. She considered grabbing a log and spinning about to thump the intruder across the head. She considered screaming, or running away.

Callen shouted for her, though, and the cry "Bransen!" almost sent the overwhelmed Cadayle spinning to the ground.

But the hand on her shoulder clasped more tightly and spun her about—spun her to face her husband, standing right behind her, grinning like a happy fool.

The most beautiful fool Cadayle had ever seen. She threw herself upon him, squeezing him to her and kissing him all over his face. She felt the moisture of her tears on her cheeks, felt as if her head would simply explode from excitement and joy.

Callen ran onto the porch and joined in the hug. Bransen

extended an arm to bring her in closer and to loop his cape over her against the freezing wind.

"How? When?" Cadayle stammered, but Bransen hushed her by putting a finger over her lips, and he ushered both of the women back inside. He went out and retrieved a few logs, then came back in and closed the door tightly.

As soon as he placed the kindling down on the hearth, Cadayle wrapped him in another crushing hug. "Tell me that you're home," she whispered in his ear. "That you're really home. That your days in the war—"

"Are over," Bransen confirmed. Cadayle sobbed with joy and hugged him even tighter. Back in her seat at the side of the hearth, Callen put a hand over her mouth, her cheeks streaked with happy tears.

"I killed him," Bransen said simply, pushing Cadayle back to arm's length, and looking at both women as he explained. "Dame Gwydre knew that to win meant to cut off the head of the serpent. I did that. I killed Ancient Badden, who led the Samhaists, who sent the hordes against Vanguard. He is dead by my hand, and there is hope throughout Pellinor that the war is dead with him."

"Hope, but we do not know," Cadayle said with some obvious doubt.

"It is over for me," Bransen said. "By Gwydre's own word." He reached to his belt and pulled forth a rolled parchment. "She told me to kill Badden for the reward of my freedom to go wherever I would go with her Writ of Passage in hand."

Cadayle looked at him, confused, then turned to Callen, who now had two hands over her mouth, as if afraid to make a sound and disturb these wonderful developments.

"We are free, all crimes forgiven," Bransen said calmly when Cadayle turned back to him. "We can go wherever we want."

Cadayle grabbed him again, one hand on either side of

his face as she locked his gaze with her own. "Do not ever leave me again," she said with intensity that widened Bransen's eyes in surprise. "Promise me that you won't ever leave me again."

"I won't—" Bransen started to say, but, surprisingly, Callen cut him off.

"Don't make promises you cannot keep!"

"The war in Vanguard is no longer my affair," he said evenly. "I am done here. I am done with war. I am done with running from guards. We'll find peace now. We'll live in peace, we three. I am at peace and in love," he said directly to Cadayle, now reaching up to similarly place his hands on her soft face. "And happy with you beside me. The fighting is done."

Cadayle could hardly keep her eyes open, so overjoyed was she with that proclamation. She didn't resist when Bransen pulled her closer for another, deeper kiss, and at that moment, both of them felt as if everything in all the world was right.

I have scrubbed it and scrubbed it, and still I cannot re-move all the bloodstains," Yeslnik said with disgust. He held up the broken blade for Bannagran to view. "But enough so that we know this blade."

"It looks like the Highwayman's," Bannagran admitted, slurring his words just a bit, for the side of his face was still swollen from a well-aimed and well-thrown rock during his daring and heroic charge that had sent Ethelbert fleeing.

"It is the Highwayman's!" Yeslnik declared, and he ended with a strange sound that seemed a cross between a growl and a whimper and threw the sword blade to the floor. "I knew that beast would prove nothing but ill to Honce! I implored my uncle to hunt him down and kill him."

Bannagran rubbed his face, fearing where this might be going.

"Oh, would that he had never been allowed to walk out of Pryd Town!" Yeslnik yelled. "With Laird Pryd's blood on his hands!"

"It is not as simple as that," Bannagran dared say.

"Isn't it?"

"No," said the champion of Pryd, the man who, indeed, could have executed the Highwayman quite legally. He chuckled helplessly as he thought back to that terrible time after the fall of his dear friend. The people of Pryd had verged on revolt; if Bannagran had not banished the Highwayman and had executed him instead, the streets of Pryd Town would have run red with blood.

Yeslnik growled again and shook his head forcefully, as if throwing all this turmoil to the side. "You have redeemed yourself in any case."

Bannagran bowed.

"I am the Laird of Delaval now," said Yeslnik, "and the King of Honce. All the holdings will accept that as soon as we are rid of the troublesome Ethelbert. He is on the run to the south—in no small part because of the exploits of Bannagran the hero, the Bear of Honce, I am told. You do smell like a bear, I am sure." He gave a little derisive snort and chuckle.

"Laird Ethelbert backed us into a corner with his bold attack," Bannagran explained, ignoring the insult and reminding himself that if Prince Yeslnik had ever actually been close enough to a bear to smell it, he would have then smelled of his own piss. "Truly, I did not expect that he would move so decisively."

"But you turned him, broke his line and sent him fleeing."

"We had no choice in the matter. Charge and win, or die. We chose to fight."

"No, Bannagran chose to fight, and his choice dragged

along the men of Pryd and those Delaval soldiers I left behind," said Yeslnik. "That is the essence of a leader, and I intend to reward it."

"As you will, my king."

"I will name you Laird of Pryd," said Yeslnik. "No more the steward, but the laird, who will pass the ownership and title down to his own children."

"I have none."

"Then make some, dolt!" Yeslnik retorted. "Or name a nephew as an heir, as did—as wisely did—King Delaval. I will see this done, as soon as we attend to pressing needs."

"To finish off Ethelbert," Bannagran reasoned.

"I will see to that. I have sent emissaries to Laird Panlamaris and his cowardly son Milwellis to dispatch his forces to the east and then south along the inner coast."

Bannagran wisely hid his wince at the adjective Yeslnik had attached to Milwellis. To hear the foppish pretend warrior calling Milwellis a coward strained credulity to be sure!

"I doubt that any will stand against them, but neither shall Ethelbert find his escape in that direction. We will push him right back to his city on the sea this time, and there will be no escape. The lairds of the Mantis Arm will join with me now. Their ships will blockade Ethelbert. There will be no escape, and I will push the imbecile right into the Mirianic!"

"The men of Pryd will march with you, my lai . . ." Bannagran paused, somewhat confused at how to properly address Yeslnik now.

"King," Yeslnik insisted. "The coronation is a mere formality. Honce is mine."

"My king," Bannagran finished.

"And Pryd is yours, Laird Bannagran," he said. Bannagran bowed. "The men of Pryd will march with me indeed. But not all of them. Not Bannagran, the new Laird of Pryd."

The Bear of Honce looked at him curiously.

King Yeslnik bent and retrieved the broken sword, then handed it to Bannagran. "Find him," he ordered. "Find the Highwayman, Bannagran of Pryd. Find him and kill him. You can serve your king no better way than to serve me the Highwayman's head on a banquet tray. Do that, and Pryd Holding is yours and your family's forevermore, with borders we will expand."

Bannagran eyed the sword more closely, remembering when he had done battle against the man who wielded this very blade.

"Find him and kill him," King Yeslnik said again.

The Bear of Honce, champion of Pryd, nodded.

NINE

Stubbornly Entrenched

There is talk that he will be put in line as heir to the lairdship of Vanguard!" Father De Guilbe shouted and waved his arms frantically.

Father Premujon sighed and shook his head. "Cormack is not even of Vanguard. Dame Gwydre would do no such thing as that."

"I heard it!" De Guilbe protested. "Do you deny that he has been named a hero of the holding?"

"All who participated in the battle with Ancient Badden have so been named," remarked Brother Jond, sitting on a bench at the side of the hall. "Except the powries, of course. Dame Gwydre made up some other title for them, one that carries no consequence."

"And you agree with the bestowment?" asked De Guilbe.

"For the powries?"

"For Cormack!" De Guilbe shouted.

Poor Brother Jond appeared uncertain. "Speak freely," Father Premujon coaxed him.

"Why, yes, I do," Jond blurted, with such enthusiasm that those who knew him, Premujon included and perhaps most of all, then realized that his tentativeness had been designed to elicit exactly this explicit permission from his Father Premujon. "Of course I do."

"He betrayed your brethren!" said De Guilbe, and he even took a step toward Jond before Brother Giavno caught him by the arm.

"Dame Gwydre is not of our order and does not answer to us," Jond explained. "Her titles are secular alone. Despite your hatred for the man, you cannot deny that he bravely battled Ancient Badden. Had it not been for him, it is unlikely that Badden would have been overcome—and his fall is to the benefit of us all."

"And if Cormack becomes Laird of Vanguard?" De Guilbe asked. "What then for Chapel Pellinor and the Order of Blessed Abelle in his Vanguard?"

Father Premujon just shook his head at the ridiculousness of the premise.

"I bid you, Father, for your own sake, to search this hatred you hold for this man, Cormack," Brother Jond dared to say, drawing more than a few gasps from around the room. "I have known him but a short time, true, but his character seemed to me in alignment with the precepts of the order."

"Brother!" more than one voice shouted, loudest of all, that of Father Premujon.

But somehow, Brother Jond seemed above them all at that moment, as if he held some insight they could not share, as if the badges of honor he wore—the one from Gwydre's recognition and, more importantly, the garish scar across his face—allowed him to speak truth to power with impunity.

"He betrayed the Blessed Abelle to the barbarians!" De Guilbe roared.

"Did he?" Brother Jond's question, asked so innocently, took the steam from the large man. "Or was it Father De

Guilbe, frustrated after years of wandering the terrible environ of Alpinador, who clung to stubbornness beyond all reason and morality?"

"I will not be spoken to in such a manner by a brother!" Father De Guilbe shouted at Father Premujon.

"Enough, Brother Jond!" Premujon said sharply.

The blind monk settled back on the bench, seeming quite pleased with himself.

"I will not have this," De Guilbe continued. "You will punish this brother severely. And I will have Cormack punished, as well."

"He is in Dame Gwydre's charge," Father Premujon reminded.

"Then demand of the Dame," said De Guilbe. "Cormack parades around in a powrie cap, arm-in-arm with a shaman of Alpinador. He mocks us openly and with impunity. You cannot allow this to stand. His mere presence will erode support for us here in Vanguard and will diminish respect for Blessed Abelle."

"It was Father De Guilbe who demanded of Cormack that he always wear the cap," Brother Jond remarked.

Father Premujon motioned to a pair of younger brothers to take the blind troublemaker out of the chapel.

"And she is a most lovely woman, this Milkeila of Yan Ossum," Brother Jond said as the brothers helped him to his feet and began escorting him from the room. "Calm in temperament, generous in heart, and fierce in battle. I need not see with my eyes to know that she is most beautiful."

"Brother, go in peace," Father Premujon bade him, begged him.

"Our order would be enhanced greatly if we could coax her to us," Jond managed to get in before the younger monks pulled him out of the chamber.

"No more so than if we purchased a mule," Father De

Guilbe muttered. "This Milkeila is rather like a domesti-cated animal, don't you think? And with the appearance of one."

No one but De Guilbe himself chuckled at his joke.

"I would ask you again to exact punishment upon Cor-mack," De Guilbe stated flatly.

"He is not Brother Cormack any longer," Father Pre-mujon reminded. "He is not of our order."

"He was of our order when he betrayed the emissaries of Abelle," De Guilbe replied. "He was meant to die for his treason. Only through unfortunate circumstance does he still draw breath."

"But he did not die, and so he was banished from your island," said Premujon. "Appropriately so!" the father of Chapel Pellinor added with enthusiasm to erase De Guilbe's growing scowl.

"It is different now," De Guilbe said.

"What would you have me do?"

"Take him from Gwydre to be judged by his peers. Take him in chains as a heretic."

Father Premujon looked around the room for support. He knew he was in a corner here: Father De Guilbe was no small player in the Order of Blessed Abelle and had been hand-picked by Father Artolivan, a personal friend, to lead the missionary team to Alpinador. The man's ob-stinacy, so clearly on display, offered little room for com-promise.

And the man's power would demand of Father Premu-jon that he make a stand one way or the other.

H e has suffered his entire life," said Master Reandu. Into his thirties now, Reandu's face showed the strain of the last couple of years. Father Jerak of Chapel Pryd had declined to a point of incoherent babbling, and Reandu had to take up the reins in these most trying times

with all of the responsibilities but none of the imprimatur of the office. No small part of that burden came from
the fact that Reandu's actions had led to the death of Master Bathelais, who would have succeeded Father Jerak.
No action had been taken against Reandu for that confused and tumultuous fight—even Bannagran, who had
been battling the man Reandu had saved, had forgiven
him.

"And he suffers to this day, I am sure. Every step comes
with the grimace of the pained Stork," Reandu finished.

"The Stork who killed Prydae," Bannagran reminded.

Reandu smiled knowingly, sadly. The Stork hadn't directly killed Prydae, after all, but had simply ducked
Bannagran's thrown axe, which had then struck down the
laird. Bannagran's anger as he spoke Bransen's nickname
was rooted in deep guilt, Reandu knew, much as his own
guilt over Master Bathelais gnawed at him, and that was
never a good thing.

"Bransen has moments of . . . surprise, I agree," said
the monk. "But you know his life story as well as any. The
loss of his mother and father, of Garibond Womak . . ."

He stopped there, seeing Bannagran's eyes narrow
dangerously. The fate of Womak was not a good subject
to bring up around Pryd Holding. For the sake of Prydae's manhood, through some ridiculous Samhaist assertion of virility restored, the man had suffered castration.
And for protecting the belongings of his friend, Stork's
father, Garibond had been burned at the stake.

"He carried chamber pots—it was all he could manage," Reandu said, referring to Bransen's stay at Chapel
Pryd as a servant. "He lived in a hole."

"I do not envy him his miserable existence," Bannagran interrupted. He reached to his belt and pulled forth
the broken blade of a fine sword. "Do you recognize this?"

"Is that Bransen's blade?" Reandu asked.

Bannagran shrugged. "It would appear. How many

like this could there be? This blade was pulled from the chest of King Delaval. How many like this one, Reandu?"

"In Behr?"

"In Honce!"

"We know that Ethelbert has many ties to Behr, where such blades—"

"Enough!" Bannagran commanded. "Our own Stork was a party to the group who murdered King Delaval. So says King Yeslnik, and so it is true."

"I know," Reandu admitted. "Yeslnik came to Chapel Pryd this morning." He paused and shook his head. "King Yeslnik?" he said with obvious disdain.

"I would remind you that your tone will hold consequences, Master Reandu," said Bannagran.

"You approve of his ascension?"

"It is not my place to approve or disapprove. It simply is. I am a subject of Pryd Holding, which is indebted to and in alliance with Delaval Holding. We threw our fealty to Laird Delaval, who proclaimed himself king, and his successor was his choice alone."

"You didn't answer my question."

"There is no answer to such a foolish question," said Bannagran. "Yeslnik is King of Honce, by Yeslnik's word. Laird Ethelbert will try to foil him, but Laird Ethelbert will fail."

"And since the King of Honce would see Bransen dead, so Bransen is condemned?" said Reandu.

"Yes."

Master Reandu took a deep breath, saddened by the decision but with no recourse.

"What do you know of his whereabouts?" Bannagran asked.

Reandu shook his head and sighed.

"Brother, I insist," said Bannagran.

"There is word that he traveled through Palmaristown, heading generally east, in the direction of Chapel Abelle.

I do not know if he ever made it there, for there has been nothing more. I do not even know if he truly made it as far as Palmaristown, for that has never been confirmed by the Chapel of Precious Memories."

"When was this?"

"Months?" Reandu said with little certainty, indeed with a shrug of his shoulders. "A couple at least. Not long after his departure from Pryd Town."

Bannagran sighed, and Reandu studied him carefully. "Why do you care?" the monk asked.

"Because the king told me to care."

"You're charged with catching him and killing him," Reandu accused.

"I should have done that long ago, for the death of Laird Prydae."

"No," Reandu replied. "No, you chose wisely. The people of Pryd love you all the more for the mercy you showed . . ."

His voice trailed off as Bannagran held up his hand, begging silence.

"Bransen is not an evil man," Reandu finished.

"That is not my decision. He is complicit in the murder of the king, so he is guilty of treason against the throne. So says Yeslnik, and so it is."

Reandu started to argue, but Bannagran interrupted with finality when he growled, "It simply is."

Cadayle stiffened reflexively, her breath coming in gasps when she heard the horses rambling into town outside her door. The last time she had heard such a ruckus her husband had been taken from her.

Bransen gave her a hug and assured her that all was well. They went to the window together, where Bransen pulled the curtain aside.

They recognized Dawson McKeege immediately,

riding a horse with an escort of several grim-faced soldiers and a single, empty wagon.

"To take us where we wish to go," Bransen insisted when they pulled up outside his door.

"With winter coming on strong?"

"Trust in Dame Gwydre," said Bransen. "I have her word."

Cadayle motioned toward the window then. Bransen turned to see Callen, who had gone across the road to borrow some spices, moving over to speak with Dawson, who smiled widely at the sight of her and tipped his floppy hat.

Cadayle started for the door, but Bransen held her back and bade her to watch the exchange—the undeniably pleasant exchange. Dawson hopped down from his horse and even kissed Callen's hand. Suddenly the men around him didn't seem quite so grim-faced any longer.

The young couple went onto their porch.

"Greetings!" Dawson said upon sighting them, his crooked smile still wide.

"Have you found another battle to which to drag my husband?" Cadayle asked sarcastically.

Dawson paused as if confused, then said, emphatically, "Oh, no, no, good lady. Your husband's heroics in the northland seem to have ended all that!"

"The war is truly over?" Bransen asked.

"What we're hoping, at least," Dawson replied. "No fighting, no goblins, no trolls, and no Samhaists that we can find. I'm thinking that Dame Gwydre's gamble did its work, and wouldn't that be a grand thing for all of Vanguard?"

"It would, indeed," said Bransen. He paused and considered it all for a few moments, then added uncharacteristically, "I hope it's true."

"Then why have you come?" Cadayle asked.

Dawson stepped back as if slapped.

"I mean, you came here for us, didn't you? For Bransen, at least, but it can't be time to sail the gulf."

"Oh, I wouldn't be putting my *Lady Dreamer* out now, so late in the season! Not if all the demon dactyls were chasing me!"

"But here you are, with an empty wagon."

Dawson laughed and bowed. "Guilty, my lady," he said. "We came for you—all three with an invitation from Dame Gwydre for you to winter at Castle Pellinor."

Cadayle looked at Callen, who nodded hopefully. Then Cadayle turned her confused expression to an equally confused Bransen.

"Back to Pellinor?" he asked. "Why?"

"It is more comfortable than here, of course. You've earned that at least," Dawson answered, but Bransen knew better and shook his head in reply.

"There's trouble," Dawson admitted.

"He's done fighting for you!" Cadayle insisted.

"Not that kind of trouble," Dawson said hastily. "I weren't lying to you when I said that all was at peace, good lady. No fighting to be found and none asked of Bransen. Nay, this trouble's with the brothers of Blessed Abelle."

"A group for which I care little," said Bransen. "I put them not so far above the Samhaists, to be honest."

"Brother Jond?" Dawson asked, and Bransen perked up at that. "He calls you his friend."

"I am."

"And Cormack?"

"He's no longer of that order."

"But the order isn't letting him go so easily," Dawson explained. "Father De Guilbe is a fiery one, full of anger, anger aimed at Cormack. Cormack's been arrested."

"Father Premujon put him in chains?" Bransen asked.

"Dame Gwydre took him," said Dawson. Bransen gave a little hiss of disappointment and dismay.

"She had no choice in the matter," Dawson continued. "Father De Guilbe demanded it of Father Premujon—the big idiot De Guilbe apparently has some power in the order and with Father Artolivan, who leads them all. He put Premujon in a tight corner to be sure. Dame Gwydre had no choice but to give in to De Guilbe's demands and arrest Cormack for trial. She's got him, but rest assured he's comfortable and outside the influence of his former brothers."

"To what end?" asked Bransen. "Is he to be sentenced? He risked everything for Vanguard and fought with courage and strength. Without him Ancient Badden would have won the day and your war . . ." He stopped when he noted that Dawson was nodding with his every word.

"There are rumors that he is to be tried before both court and church," Dawson explained. "If it comes to that, it will be fair, I promise. Dame Gwydre will preside and will surely mitigate any demands of the brothers upon Cormack with her knowledge of his heroics in ending the war."

"What of Milkeila?" Bransen asked. He turned to Cadayle and reminded her, "The barbarian woman, wife of Cormack."

"She is well, and within Pellinor with Cormack. They are not ill-treated, I promise you. I came to relay all of this and to extend Dame Gwydre's invitation. I hope you will agree to join us in Pellinor. Your presence would be a great boon to your friend Cormack."

"I have already said everything on his behalf. What influence could I possibly bring to such a trial?"

Dawson glanced back at his men, and they all laughed at that.

"You still do not understand, do you?" Dawson asked. "You, who dropped the head of Ancient Badden at Dame Gwydre's feet, do not understand the power of your mere presence. You're a hero, boy! Your name is being whispered through every vale in Vanguard. To have you there, at Cormack's side, will surely carry great weight. It will bolster Gwydre's hand in this argument and diminish De Guilbe. You shame him, Highwayman, for you went where he would not, and you did what he could not. Cormack's stature rises with the Highwayman beside him. I beg you to join me. You will find Pellinor comfortable for the winter, and you will do a great favor to this man you call a friend."

Bransen turned to Cadayle, who nodded.

"My ma, too?" she asked suddenly of Dawson.

The man turned his smiling face to Callen Duwornay and gave her a playful wink. "Ah, but that I insist upon," he answered.

Callen's blush was not lost on Cadayle.

TEN

A Church on Trial

I can go back, but it's getting cold and I'm getting old," Jameston Sequin said, starting the conversation on that note as Dame Gwydre walked into the room.

"Do you need to go back?" the woman asked.

Jameston shook his head. "It's done and over."

"You have met with Samhaists directly?"

"A couple. One, I trust. The other . . . well, he's a Samhaist, but I don't see why he'd lie to me. The stories were consistent. This was Badden's stand. He wanted to take Vanguard as his own since his order has lost southern Honce to both the warring lairds who just love those monks and their baubles."

Dame Gwydre stiffened at that comment, a curious movement. Jameston looked at her quizzically.

"The brothers of Blessed Abelle have powerful magic, you know," she said, and Jameston nodded. "They can deliver messages over far distances in a hurry, it would seem."

"I'm no expert on Abelle gemstones," Jameston admitted.

"They can," Gwydre replied. "Not an easy task, apparently, and not without danger to the courier. So they reserve this practice for the most urgent messages alone."

"Sounds like you have something important to tell me."

"Laird Delaval is dead, murdered by Laird Ethelbert," said Gwydre.

Jameston shrugged as if he hardly cared. "One of them had to go."

"But while Laird Ethelbert's assassins were killing him, Laird Delaval's men were chasing Ethelbert's army back to the south."

"They'll keep fighting without a laird leading them?"

"They've a new laird and not a promising one from what I could discern. The war rages, escalates even."

"Idiots," Jameston muttered.

"Beyond all reason, Father Premujon told me. This war is to the death."

"Oh, it is," Jameston agreed. "To the death of Honce."

Both paused and sighed at that harsh reality. "Southern Honce," Gwydre added at length. "Vanguard has found peace, it would seem."

"It's true," Jameston assured her. "No goblins or trolls or barbarians to be found. Most of Badden's priests weren't too happy with his decision to employ mercenary monsters. The priests are split now and fighting among themselves, and that's always a good thing. It'll take them a year and more to put a new ancient in place. I expect before that time, you'll be hearing from many Samhaist priests who want to make peace. They'll be asking you to allow them to hold their groves and tend to their followers."

"Do they think they will have any followers in Vanguard after the misery Badden has loosed upon us?"

Jameston shrugged. "Prideful bunch, and I never thought much of the intelligence of the average man or woman."

Gwydre gave a little chuckle at that, a helpless one.

"Vanguard knows peace on the battlefields, perhaps, but not peace of mind."

"I'll go out on a thin trail of old turds here and guess that the Abelle crowd is causing you misery."

Gwydre laughed again and held up her hands helplessly. "They wish to try Cormack for heresy. They demand it."

"Cormack? The tall one who went to the glacier and helped kill Badden?"

"The same."

Now it was Jameston's turn to laugh at the sheer absurdity of it all. He stopped when he noted that Dame Gwydre was staring at him intently.

"How well do you know him?" she asked.

"Cormack? Don't know him at all. Heard about him. Talked to him once."

"How well do you know Bransen?"

"The Highwayman?"

Gwydre nodded. "He arrived in Pellinor this morning at my request."

"I traveled with him for a short time," said Jameston. "Good fighter, that much I know."

"Not unlike Jameston in skill or in temperament."

"I don't think I ever fought like that," the scout replied. "Not that well, but I hope I had better sense than that one even when I was a young man."

"Not unlike Jameston in his disdain for the Samhaist and the brothers of Abelle—oh, and for the lairds of Honce."

"I'm liking him all the more."

"Spend some time with him," Gwydre bade Jameston.

"That an order?"

"A request. I think that you might counsel him well."

"Ah, you mean that you want me to make sure that he likes Dame Gwydre more than he likes the other lairds."

Gwydre smirked at him, and Jameston couldn't suppress a return smile.

"You've earned that much from me, at least," the scout said. He took Gwydre's hand and kissed it. "Since you're th'only one worth a dactyl demon's damn."

"My husband was a good man."

"You do well by his memory."

"You loved my father," Gwydre added.

"Hard man not to love," Jameston admitted. "Were more lairds like him, were more people like him, I might spend less time in the forest."

"Then you'll spend some time with Bransen?"

"For you, pretty lady? Of course."

Dame Gwydre leaned forward and kissed Jameston on the cheek then walked past him and out of the room.

For the first time in several days her smile was genuine.

H e stood alone in the center of the circular room, but he did not bow his head. Nor did he remove his powrie beret, even after Father Premujon, after whispering with Father De Guilbe, ordered him to do so.

Instead, Cormack calmly looked over at Dame Gwydre and asked, "Is it required of me, in this, your chamber, to remove the cap?"

She shook her head. Cormack didn't even bother to glance back at the monks.

From the front of the room, near the door (which was open so that many of Pellinor's citizens could view the proceedings), Bransen watched it all with a grin and a growing respect for Cormack. The man was cool-headed, unconcerned, as if the monks could not truly touch him. They had whipped him near to death and cast him away in a rickety boat to die, and yet he had survived. Perhaps Gwydre was the source of his confidence—maybe she had told him that she would stand with him in these proceedings—but more likely, Bransen thought, Cormack would have acted no differently were this trial in the chapel and governed only by the two fathers.

They couldn't touch him. Not truly. Even if they burned him at the stake, they couldn't touch the soul of Cormack.

Premujon called upon Father De Guilbe to open the trial with an explanation of the man's alleged crime. Bransen listened intently through it all, hearing of the battle at Chapel Isle, where the monks had "rescued" and were "saving" three wayward Alpinadorans when the barbarians came against them viciously. After days of successful defense and another prisoner taken and, De Guilbe declared, with the barbarians ready to break and retreat, Cormack had snuck into the room and ferried the Alpinadorans away, betraying the brotherhood, scorning his superiors, and condemning the four Alpinadorans to eternal damnation.

It was a rousing recanting, Bransen thought, if one were inclined to believe such things. Many in the room, monk and Vanguardsman alike, called for Cormack's head. Of course, to Bransen the courageous actions only made Cormack more the hero.

Dame Gwydre wasted little time in quieting the ruckus and made it clear that she would tolerate no mob mentality here.

"Father De Guilbe," she said, "it would appear that Brother Cormack—former Brother Cormack—did no more than to grant men their freedom. Were they, the Alpinadorans, incarcerated for any particular reason? Had they committed criminal acts against Chapel Isle?"

"They owed their lives to us," said De Guilbe. "To Blessed Abelle. Only through the power of the gemstones did they draw breath, for we found them adrift on the lake, grievously—nay, mortally!—wounded."

"But they wished to leave after you saved them?"

De Guilbe squared his shoulders and did not reply.

"Do you consider their incarceration their cost for your efforts, then?" Gwydre calmly asked.

"I had my charge from Father Artolivan of Chapel Abelle," the man replied staunchly. "My Alpinadoran guests would have come to our way—perhaps they would have then become emissaries of the good word to the rest of their heathen folk. That is a more important healing than the closing of any physical wound."

"The captured Alpinadorans would have come to Blessed Abelle?"

"They were not captured! They were saved! And yes!"

"Never!" a woman cried from the back of the room, directly opposite Cormack, and all eyes went to Milkeila. "Not like that," she added quietly, speaking directly and in apologetic tone to Dame Gwydre.

"It is not your place to speak here," Father De Guilbe said through gritted teeth.

"Unless Dame Gwydre requests it of you," Dame Gwydre added, throwing a disdainful glance at De Guilbe. "And she does, Milkeila of Alpinador, so please, continue." With a steadying deep breath and a nod at her husband, Milkeila stepped tentatively from the gathering.

"What do you know of this incident?" Dame Gwydre asked her directly. "Were you there?"

"I was among those attacking the chapel," Milkeila admitted, and she looked to Cormack again. "Even as the man I love was defending it."

"You admit to a crime punishable by death?" Father De Guilbe demanded.

Bransen put a hand near his sword without even thinking. As he considered his reflexive movement, he realized that if the monks moved against Milkeila here he would indeed draw on them and defend her.

"Continue without fear of retribution," Dame Gwydre

bade the woman. "You are charged with no crime and"—
she paused to glower at De Guilbe—"you will not be."

"Among the prisoners was a very powerful shaman of
my people," Milkeila explained, "one who would not
even willingly accept their gemstone magic, even at the
price of his own life."

"And you, too, are a priest of that barbarian religion,"
De Guilbe accused.

"No longer," said Milkeila. "Like Cormack, I have
come to see that neither side is right."

That brought more than a few whispers around the
room, particularly from the grumbling monks, but Gwydre
again was quick to calm them.

"Father De Guilbe is wrong when he said that we were
nearing the end of our assault," Milkeila insisted.

"We were slaughtering you at our wall!" accused De
Guilbe.

"We would have kept coming, to the last," said Milkeila,
talking directly to Gwydre and ignoring De Guilbe altogether. "Those prisoners were our brethren. We would not
abandon them, whatever the cost. It is not our way. Which
is why, when Bransen came to us with word of Ancient
Badden even though I was out of favor with the leaders of
Yan Ossum, all the tribes came together to defeat the
wicked man." She finally did turn to look at De Guilbe.
"Unlike the brothers of Abelle, who ran away."

The room seemed as if it would erupt.

And yet, again, the power of Dame Gwydre calmed
it. She turned to De Guilbe. "Have you anything else,
Father?"

"The disposition of the Alpinadoran converts is not
your concern," De Guilbe said firmly. "Nor are my orders
regarding our stance against the tribes of Mithranidoon—
we were at war with them for years before this incident. I
saw the men we rescued as perhaps a mediation of that

continuing conflict. But again, I need not explain myself to you in this matter. I was sent to Alpinador, a place outside Dame Gwydre's province, by the Order of Blessed Abelle, acting upon lawful commands issued by Father Artolivan whose sovereignty in these matters Dame Gwydre and all the lairds acknowledge."

De Guilbe leveled his gaze on Gwydre. "This man betrayed my orders, the lawful orders of the Order of Blessed Abelle, and by doing so endangered us all. It is as simple as that," he insisted.

Bransen shifted uncomfortably as he studied Gwydre then, for he saw that the woman had little argument against the simple logic, however she might feel about the larger situation.

"Have you anything to say?" she asked Cormack. It seemed to Bransen as if she was begging the man to give her something, anything, to back down Father De Guilbe.

"Father De Guilbe was wrong and immoral in his actions," Cormack replied without hesitation. "We had no right to hold the Alpinadorans."

De Guilbe started to shout in protest, but Gwydre hushed him immediately.

"Father De Guilbe's decision to hold the men in our dungeon brought actual war to us," Cormack explained. "It is true that we had battled the barbarians on the lake for many months, but not lethally. Our fights were more gamesmanship than serious conflict, until that point. After the prisoners were taken, we were killing them at our wall and they were killing us—not as often, but we had fewer to spare. It wouldn't have ended until one side or the other had been completely destroyed. I could not allow that insanity to continue. If the cost of that is my life, then so be it. I already accepted such a judgment from Father De Guilbe, delivered to me by a brother who was as a mentor to me. I could not allow the killing, senseless and without gain to either side, to continue. I freed the prisoners, as Father de Guilbe charges. In the same situation I would do it again."

Murmurs erupted about the room, some complimentary, some calling for Cormack's death. Truly, Dame Gwydre seemed at a loss.

She was trapped here, Bransen realized. To go against the powerful Order of Abelle so openly as to intervene in their private matters would surely bring disaster to her holding.

"Would anyone else speak?" she asked, a plea if Bransen had ever heard one. He was about to answer that call when blind Brother Jond tapped his cane on the hard floor.

"I will," he said. "I, who know you well, Dame Gwydre, and who went to Alpinador on your behalf to end the carnage of Ancient Badden."

Gwydre's smile showed her appreciation. "Please do."

"I was not at the island, of course," said Jond. "But I watched . . ." he chuckled at his choice of words, and many in the room joined him awkwardly. "With my ears I witnessed the efforts of Cormack against Ancient Badden: He was nothing short of courageous and valiant, fighting for Vanguard and for the good of us all. In the weeks that followed, I had many opportunities to speak with the man—brother to brother—and I find him to be of exemplary character and human decency."

Reading De Guilbe's furrowed brow, Bransen figured that if the father could have gotten away with it, he would have leaped upon Jond at that moment and choked the life from him.

"And with all respect to your office and judgment, Father De Guilbe," Brother Jond added, "my heart grows heavy indeed to think that our beloved order has cast out a man of such fortitude and character."

De Guilbe exploded, shouting at Brother Jond to remember his place, sit down, and shut up. Several monks joined in that chorus, filling the room with the buzz of excited titterings and whispers.

"I will speak for Cormack!" Bransen heard himself yelling above the din. The room quieted instantly, all eyes falling on the Highwayman, on the man who had killed Ancient Badden and delivered them from a horrendous war, on the man who had dropped Badden's severed head in the road, a gift to their beloved Dame Gwydre. "I will echo Brother Jond's words to a one, except to add that it does not surprise me to see the Order of Abelle so confused and wrongheaded regarding the disposition of an honest and decent man. Such a monk is a rare thing, I fear, and one who does not fit their tenets."

Of course, that brought only more shouting and tumult, until finally Dame Gwydre managed to calm it down.

"You have no standing in this, Dame Gwydre," Father De Guilbe pronounced once more. "This matter happened beyond Vanguard and within the domain of the Order of Blessed Abelle. Cormack is ours to discipline."

"Cormack helped Vanguard win a war," Gwydre reminded.

"Nonetheless, you know that I am correct."

The dame rubbed her face, and Bransen held his breath. This was her place to take a stand, a brave one, or to fail, the Highwayman knew, and he sorely hoped that Gwydre would prove herself better than the typical self-serving coward he had come to expect from a laird.

"I will speak for Cormack!" exclaimed another voice, an unexpected source indeed. All eyes in the room, most notably those of Father De Guilbe and Cormack himself, fell to the speaker, Brother Giavno, Father De Guilbe's second.

"This is madness wrought of foolish pride," Giavno said to De Guilbe. "As our stand against the Alpinadorans was madness, and murderously so!"

"Brother!" De Guilbe shouted.

Giavno whirled to address Father Premujon. "Our time in Alpinador was trying," he explained. "We lost men and good brothers to the weather and the beasts and, yes, to Alpinadorans. Worse still, we knew by the time we had arrived on the lake called Mithranidoon that our mission was futile. We were not going to convert any souls in that barbarian land." He looked to De Guilbe and repeated, "We weren't.

"I do not know if Cormack was right or wrong in what he did," Giavno said in more humble and muted tones. "I do not know if Father De Guilbe acted wisely or acted the fool in keeping the Alpinadorans against their will. We punished Cormack for his betrayal. I beat him near to death with a scourge, and we cast him adrift on the lake to die. But he did not die. And how did he repay us for our punishment? By returning with that man, there"—he pointed to Bransen—"to warn us of impending doom. Were it not for them and for Milkeila and her people, Ancient Badden would have succeeded in dropping the edge of a great glacier into our lake, washing us all away to our certain deaths. Enough, please, Father Premujon. Let Cormack go."

He looked to Cormack as he finished, tears in his eyes. "I am proud to say that this man was once my friend and sorry to admit that I failed him miserably."

Again the whispering erupted, more muted and with many heads nodding. Bransen, as surprised as any, watched Dame Gwydre intently. She looked to Father Premujon; the two shared telling nods.

After a long while, Gwydre asked, "Are you satisfied, Father Premujon?"

"I am," he replied.

"Father De Guilbe claims this situation a matter of the Order of Blessed Abelle. Despite my strong feelings here I am forced to agree," Dame Gwydre admitted.

Many around the room gasped, but Bransen grinned and nodded, fully expecting what was forthcoming.

"Then I would argue that Cormack is no brother of the Order of Abelle, that his title was lawfully stripped by a man empowered to do so," said Premujon. "When he was put in that boat and cast adrift he became the charge of Dame Gwydre and not of Father Artolivan or his emissaries."

"But I defer to you, for your guidance, at least," said Gwydre.

With a look to Father De Guilbe that was part apology, part exasperation, Father Premujon said, "We have had our justice on the brother, Cormack. It is up to Dame Gwydre to decide whether his actions merit further punishment or celebration. I have witnessed the cost of this war with the evil Ancient Badden for many months now, my good lady. I would counsel you to leniency at the least."

"Go free, Cormack," Dame Gwydre pronounced immediately. "With my great, great appreciation for your heroic efforts against the most evil Ancient Badden."

The room exploded into cheers, but Bransen watched Father De Guilbe. He even walked among the throng swarming Cormack, veering to be near to De Guilbe so that he could hear the man say to Premujon, "Father Artolivan will hear of this."

"Oh, he will, indeed," the father of Chapel Pellinor replied.

Bransen laughed, and both men regarded him. He almost mentioned that more monks like Premujon, Cormack, and Jond might make him rethink the value of the Order of Blessed Abelle, but he merely tapped his finger to his black bandanna—his head wrap which held the soul stone Cormack had given to him (and the irony of that pleased him all the more)—and turned and walked away.

* * *

The snow fell heavily in spurts this day, but there was little breeze and the temperature was pleasingly moderate, leaving the air dancing with large, lazily drifting flakes. Unlike most winter Vanguard storms, it was not a day where one had to remain huddled beside a fire, though surely many chose that route.

Dame Gwydre, wrapped in a dark blue shawl, was glad to be out, feeling very much like a little girl in a friendly snowstorm. Walking beside her, Bransen was similarly at ease. He had known much snow in Pryd, of course, but there was something very different about the Vanguard winter, something . . . cleaner. In Pryd, the snow came and melted and left a muddy mess repeatedly, but up here, once the snow landed on the ground, it stayed throughout the winter season.

"I trust you are enjoying your stay at Castle Pellinor," Gwydre said. "I have been so busy of late that I have had little time to look in on you and your lovely family."

Bransen continued to look at his companion curiously for a short while, still unsure of why Gwydre had bade him, in no uncertain terms, to come outside and walk with her this afternoon. "We have never been more comfortable, of course," he answered, but with clear hesitancy in his voice, which drew a knowing grin from Gwydre.

"Always expecting *the mule's arse rent*, yes?" the Lady of Vanguard teased.

Bransen stared at her, mouth hanging open as if he had no idea of how to respond.

"You don't know that old saying?" Gwydre asked.

"The mule's arse rent?"

Dame Gwydre laughed at him. "Mules are frustrating creatures, particularly if you have one you don't know well. The mule's arse rent is the extra and unanticipated cost of renting such a beast when it is returned with boot prints on its arse."

Bransen just stood there, gaping.

"An old saying, is all," said Gwydre. "Or is it my use of the crude term that surprises you?"

"You constantly surprise me, Lady Gwydre."

"Good!"

Bransen laughed helplessly.

"To my point, though," Gwydre continued, "you fear that I have some ulterior designs in bringing you here—even above hoping that you would speak for Cormack at Father De Guilbe's spectacle."

Bransen arched a brow. "The possibility has crossed my mind."

"You do not trust me."

"I . . . it's not . . ." Bransen stumbled.

"You have every right to be suspicious," Gwydre conceded. "My man Dawson deceived you initially to trick you to Vanguard, and I demanded of you that you fight on my behalf."

"I understand now that you had little choice," said Bransen. "After meeting Ancient Badden, I better understand your desperation."

"And you forgive me?"

Now it was Bransen's turn to laugh. "Forgive you? You saved my life in tricking me here. I understand that."

"So we are friends?"

"Of cour—" Bransen started to say, but he suddenly felt as if he was walking into another trap here. He stopped abruptly and stared hard at Dame Gwydre, who burst out laughing.

"Oh, but you are insufferable, Bransen Garibond!" she said. "You owe me nothing, of course. I did not demand that you return to Castle Pellinor, did I? Nay, Dawson explained Cormack's time of need. We trusted that you would do the right thing."

"Perhaps I am growing tired of doing the right thing."

"You say that because you suspect that I brought you out here for something other than a friendly conversation."

Bransen shrugged, not denying it.

The dance went out of Dame Gwydre's step, and she said in all seriousness, "I wanted to tell you what is happening in the world, the good news and the bad. You, above many, should know."

"I, above many, hardly care."

"I don't believe that," Gwydre replied. "But even if true you should be told, and I owe it to you to tell you myself."

"I do care about Cormack," Bransen admitted.

"That is part of it," said Gwydre. "Part of the good news, I am happy to say. Brother Giavno's outburst at the trial has caused a great furor in the Order of Abelle. Father De Guilbe is outraged to this day, of course, but he finds few allies. He is a friend of Father Artolivan, so it is said, but still, Father Premujon, at the urging of our friend Brother Jond, has decided that he will travel beside Father De Guilbe to Chapel Abelle in the spring on Cormack's behalf. There is even talk that Father Premujon—who is a good man, I assure you—will ask that Father Artolivan overrule Father De Guilbe and offer Cormack reinstatement in the order. This is a fight that will grow within the ranks of the monks, and it is a fight long overdue, I think."

"Anything to alter their smug faces would be a good thing and, yes, is long overdue," Bransen agreed.

"Worth witnessing, you believe?"

That brought a suspicious, even knowing scowl to Bransen's face, and Gwydre laughed all the more.

"Jameston Sequin assures me that our war here in Vanguard is over," she said. "My plan was borne in desperation, I admit, and yet, because of you and your companions, it appears to have worked. The Samhaists have no stomach for continuing the fight, and without Badden guiding the monsters from the north, they have not been seen in weeks."

"What would you have me say?"

"That this news pleases you," Gwydre replied. "That you care, at least."

Bransen's pause was telling. "I do," he admitted. "Do you think I feel no pain when I see others torn and broken? Do you think me so selfish that I care not at all for the people who are mere victims in the plays of those who seek power above all?"

"You wanted no part of this fight, or of the fight in Honce."

"Because it is a fool's errand," Bransen replied. "Do I kill for Delaval or for Ethelbert? For Prydae, who ruled my home holding and who brutalized his own people? Do I kill for the sake of the Order of Abelle, who would hold a man as flawed and vicious and ultimately wrongheaded as Father De Guilbe in such high standing?"

"So we are all alike, we laird and ladies and fathers and priests?"

"I have seen little to convince me otherwise."

"You wound me to my heart."

Clearly uncomfortable, Bransen shifted and reached toward Dame Gwydre as if to pat her on the shoulder. But even in that, he failed and flailed, so at a loss.

"I understand!" Gwydre said with a good-natured chuckle. "I, my man at least, deceived you and sent you off to a war of which you wanted no part. You do not offend me with your honesty, Highwayman. Far from it. I find you refreshing. Only one other man would speak to me in such a manner, and he, Dawson, I consider my closest friend."

"You humble me and shame me for my harsh words," Bransen said, dipping a slight and awkward bow.

"I appreciate you," Dame Gwydre clarified. "For what you did and for who you are."

"Then accept this as an apology of sorts," said Bransen. "Were you to wind back the days to my arrival in Vanguard and offer me a choice to go after Badden or to leave, a choice and not a bribe conditioned on your writ, I would fight for you. Of my own volition. I would go to Alpinador and again deliver the head of that foul creature."

Dame Gwydre's smile widened, genuine and nearly taking in her ears. "You have no idea how happy I am to hear those words from the rogue known as the Highwayman."

"Don't take it as an invitation to press me back into service of your court," Bransen quipped, and Gwydre laughed again.

"The war is over—do keep your blade in its sheath. I ask nothing more of you, but I wish to make you an offer. Father Premujon and the others, including Cormack and Milkeila, will sail to Chapel Abelle as soon as Dawson deems the gulf safe for passage."

"Cormack should not do that."

"He is safe—his trial is ended and cannot be redone," Gwydre assured him. "And I intend to go with them, so long as the peace holds up here and I am not urgently needed in my court. I would like you to sail with me— you and your family, I mean. I don't know that I will be needed at Father Artolivan's chapel. I expect not, truly, but there are other matters in the southland I wish to discern, not the least of which the disposition of my Writ of Passage for Bransen Garibond, Cadayle, and Callen.

"Laird Delaval is dead, Bransen," she added as the man mulled over her offer. "But Laird Ethelbert cannot claim victory, since he and his army are being pushed back to his holding in the most furious fighting of all. I do not know what will transpire across Honce, but the situation is obviously dangerous."

"Dangerous and none of my business," said Bransen.

"You say that now, as you said it when first you came to Vanguard," Gwydre reminded.

"Would you have me save the world?" Bransen answered with obvious sarcasm. "Is there another Badden to slay?"

"I know not what needs to be done, nor do you. I go to learn and to see if there is any way in which I might use my standing to help the people who suffer because of the prideful fighting between two powerful lairds. Do you not wish to learn the same? Do you not wish to learn if you are truly free to walk the lands of Honce? You owe that much to your wife, I would expect."

Bransen sighed as if cornered.

"And to Cormack, as your friend, if there is anything you can contribute to his argument against Father De Guilbe."

"I will go," Bransen said suddenly, silencing her further comments. "I know not how long I will stay, and I intend to hold you to your promise that I will be delivered to a location of my choosing."

"Our agreement holds," Gwydre assured him.

Bransen looked at her with a sly smile. "You believe that I will wish to entwine myself in this fight," he accused.

With a light laugh Dame Gwydre turned away. Bransen watched her dance off through the continuing snowfall. Was she asking too much of him?

Or, he wondered, was he demanding too little of himself?

The world, his world, was on fire. How far could the Highwayman run?

PART TWO

The Wider World

The woman has shaken me to my core, has taken my ex-
pectations and twisted them into unrecognizable knots.

I am not unused to such unsettling realizations of the
true nature of the powers of Honce. From Father Jerak
and the brothers of Chapel Pryd to that horrid Prydae
who so disfigured Garibond, my father, I came to under-
stand that many of the qualities that put a man in power
in the first place seemed also to disqualify him from prop-
erly tending the flock in practice. So much had this axiom
become a mantra for me that I was hardly surprised by
the idiocy of Prince Yeslnik, who is truly an exaggerated
collection of every flaw I had ever seen in those who had
attained power. Yeslnik, so much a caricature, did not
surprise me in the least and did not shake me (other than
to make me shake my head in resignation).

I had known minor exceptions, of course—Brother
Reandu comes to mind, and even Brother Bathelais had
moments of great decency. But truly, Yeslnik the liar, the
fool, the pretend hero, the hapless lover (judging from
his wife's desperation), and, ultimately, the coward, em-
bodied the extremes of my expectations of a laird. How
appropriate, it seemed, that he who would stand above
the lairds would be even more the fool than they.

But now I have come to know Dame Gwydre. I hardly
know how to speak to her, to view her; I have to admit
that she frightens me. I don't believe her to be secretly

*sinister and conniving. Quite the opposite! The idea that
there is no underlying deception and selfish intent about
the woman is a notion foreign, one that mocks me in my
certitude and endless petulance.*

*Nay, she doesn't frighten me, except that she makes
me afraid that she will shame me. For if this perception
of goodness I believe of Gwydre is indeed the truth of
Gwydre, then who am I? No hero, certainly.*

*When the snow fell deep this cold winter in Vanguard,
the people of Pellinor struggled to retrieve enough wood
to keep warm. With the drifts piled high, the forest was
not safe for individuals or small groups to venture. So
Gwydre, as she has apparently done many times before,
held a grand ball in Castle Pellinor, with all invited. All!
Every person about the town of Pellinor. And with the
great celebration came a feast that lasted for days. And
during that time, at Gwydre's behest, Dawson and her
soldiers ventured often into the forest and retrieved piles
of wood for the folk of Pellinor to take with them as they
at last departed the castle.*

*And Gwydre ate with them and danced with them and
led them in song. I looked upon her and wished that she
were not so atypical a laird, that all the people of Honce,
of all the world indeed, could be so blessed to live under
the care of such a ruler.*

*She shames the callous heart of the Highwayman. She
frightens me because she did something to me. Dame
Gwydre made me, at long last and against all expecta-
tion, hope.*

*Hope. She made me hope. She made me believe that
the world could change. But hope is not as easy an emotion as is surrender. For that is what I have done, Dame
Gwydre has shown me to my great discomfort. When the
Stork became the Highwayman, the Stork surrendered.*

I care not for the war in the south, so I declare. I cared

*not for Gwydre's war, so I declared. I fought only be-
cause of Gwydre's deception and blackmail. Beyond
Cadayle and Callen and my own needs, I declared myself
removed, uncaring, not responsible.*

*She shames me, and the hope I feel when I look upon
her scares me.*

*Who would I be had I been raised in Pellinor instead of
Pryd? I doubt that the Highwayman would exist, and that
is a notion that bothers me profoundly. But how might
that persona of the Highwayman have grown in such a
climate as Pellinor? Would Father Premujon have treated
me as the brothers in Chapel Pryd treated the Stork?
Would Gwydre have allowed it?*

*No. Not up here. Up here, even the relationship be-
tween Castle Pellinor and Chapel Pellinor is a very different one than that I experienced in Pryd Town. Back
home, the brothers were terrified of the laird and would
not go against him even when they knew he was wrong.
But here Premujon and Gwydre are friends, and she
supports him in his work most of all when his work is
benefiting the people, the common folk. Both Gwydre
and Premujon act as if they serve the folk and not as if
the people were put here as pawns for their pleasure.*

*Perhaps it is the harsh climate of Vanguard and the
simple pragmatism the difficult environment demands. Up
here, the folk stand as one, or die alone. Would the common folk suffer the selfishness so typical in the southern
lairds and nobles? Would they sit idly by, freezing and dying, while their leaders of castle and chapel hoarded the
winter supplies?*

*I doubt they would . . . but as I reflect on this matter, I
realize that I am applying a pragmatism to my observations of character that is unfair to Dame Gwydre. I so
clearly see her heart in the way she dances in a snowstorm or sings to the people of Pellinor.*

She would be a good leader of good heart wherever her holding. And had he grown among the pines of Pellinor, the Highwayman would not exist.

And Garibond Womak would still be alive. Alive and friend to Bran Dynard and Sen Wi.

So it is not Gwydre I fear in the end but the hope she lights in my heart and soul, in the way she forces me to feel responsibility beyond the boundaries of my own needs.

Had I known the light that is Gwydre before, I wonder what I might have answered when she came to me with no threat or deception and asked me, for no reason other than the good of the folk of Vanguard, to go north and do battle with Ancient Badden.

She has shaken my beliefs to the core.

—BRANSEN GARIBOND

ELEVEN

Just As the King Had Planned

W e're driving them hard," shouted Erolis, a nobleman from Pryd who had so distinguished himself in the fighting that Bannagran had given him one of
the ten chariots in his elite team.

Bannagran could only nod as others chimed in above
the din of pounding hooves and rolling wheels. They had
started to the north on the hunt for the Highwayman, as
Yeslnik had demanded. That alone had bothered Bannagran more than a bit, given the Highwayman's reputation
among the commoners. Indeed, Bannagran had let Bransen go after the death of Prydae for just that reason, a
potential revolt among the people of Pryd Holding.

Word had caught up to them after their departure,
though, that King Yeslnik was soon to be engaging the
forces of Laird Ethelbert far to the east of Pryd, along
the western banks of Felidan Bay, the long inlet that
separated Honce proper from the large peninsula of the
easternmost regions known as the Mantis Arm. Yeslnik
had recalled Bannagran with all speed.

And so the good general had followed his orders,
wheeling his group of ten back to the south and then east,

rumbling to the limit of the horses' strength along the cobblestone roads. They were getting close, Bannagran knew, and that was a good thing, for more than a few of the twenty horses drawing the war chariots would need to be replaced.

"Smoke in the northeast," Erolis called as they neared an intersection in the road.

"Stay east," Bannagran replied. He knew this land—he and Prydae had battled powries throughout this region, driving them to the sea, years before.

"Some town is burning," one of the others said.

"Good enough for them," another added.

Within a half hour, they came upon the stragglers of Yeslnik's rearguard and, they learned, southern flank.

"Ah, but never have me eyes looked upon a more blessed sight!" cried one man—a man from Pryd, Bannagran knew.

Bannagran pulled his chariot up beside the beleaguered footman. "You are Farmer Grees?"

"Ah, Laird Bannagran," the man replied with a low bow.

Bannagran scowled at him from the chariot for using that title, one not yet officially proclaimed. "Where is King Yeslnik?"

Grees halfheartedly waved generally north.

"The town and smoke?"

"Nay," Grees answered. "That'd be Milwellis, we're hearing. The king's due north of us—might even be back to the west a bit."

Bannagran didn't have to probe further to get the hidden meaning there, that Yeslnik, as usual, was safely to the rear of the fighting.

"Can ye go to him?" the man asked suddenly. Bannagran looked at him with surprise.

"Might I be speaking without getting yer spear in me chest?" Grees asked, his voice low.

"What are you about?"

"About to die, I'm guessing," Grees answered.

Bannagran scowled; behind Grees several other footmen shifted nervously.

"Go and tell King Yeslnik, I beg ye," Grees pressed.

"Tell him what?"

"He's got us spearheading straight east," Grees explained. "And the front groups're making great gains. The enemy're falling back before them." He sighed and lowered his voice as he added, "None to the south of us. None of us, I mean, guarding our flank. But there's a road there."

Bannagran looked to the east, then the south, trying to get a feel for the situation. Farmer Grees was a veteran of many battles, as were most of the men of Pryd. His tone spoke volumes more than his actual words.

"Mighty spearmen are the folk o' the Mantis Arm," Grees added. "Who spend their days harpooning the fishes."

"They've crossed the bay?"

"Aye, Prince Milwellis hit them hard in the north and cut them off from the mainland—he's built a fortress at the north tip o' Felidan to keep the men o' the peninsula *on* the peninsula. But aye, they've got boats a'plenty."

"You're being flanked to the south," Bannagran reasoned. "While the Felidan Bay villagers retreat, their allies from across the bay are sliding in beside and behind you."

Grees didn't have to answer.

"How many? How far west have they pushed? And how far east are the front runners of your surge?"

"I can't be knowing, but they're there. They're falling too fast afore us, letting us push east and stretch thin. These folk are no strangers to the way of battle—they've been fighting powries all their lives."

"Why are you men back here?" Erolis interjected, accusation heavy in his tone. "If your line advances with all speed, then why are you so far behind?"

Farmer Grees pointed down at his foot, which was heavily bandaged, but showing blood through the wrap. "All of us here been taking hits and can't keep up."

"And when you heard of the southern flank, you hesitated more," Bannagran remarked, and Grees and many others shifted uncomfortably.

"Good fortune that you did," Bannagran said even as Erolis started to launch another accusation. "And good fortune that you are rested." He turned to his charioteers. "We go south, and these men will run behind us. We'll cut the enemy off along the road." Turning back to Farmer Grees, he instructed, "Your men come in behind us and turn fast to the east. Our enemies will be in rout and retreating, so run among them and kill them."

"What of them that's already crossed the road?"

"The chariots will hold the road," Bannagran declared, loud enough for all to hear. He snapped the reins and his team leaped off, rambling across an open field to the road running south beyond.

"For the Bear of Honce!" he heard more than one man cry enthusiastically behind him. He hated that nickname, hated being compared to some animal, but he couldn't deny its power to rally men, and he surely needed that energy and hope at this time.

Flames hungrily ate the thatched roofs, billowing thick black smoke into the air. Men, women, and children screamed and rushed about in stark terror as horsemen weaved through the village, launching torches onto the roofs, launching spears at the pursued, or just running down the smaller ones and trampling them under hoof.

Prince Milwellis of Palmaristown kept his horse running and couldn't stop laughing at the frenzy before him.

This village, of no name worth remembering, had sent some men to the north to . . . to what, Milwellis still wondered. To parlay? To defend? In either case, they had utterly failed, since Milwellis, eager to be the first to Yansinchester, the target city of King Yeslnik's diversion to the coast, just sent his large force swarming over them and into their village.

Out of the corner of his eye, Milwellis noted a man darting behind the corner of a building. He kicked his mount into a short gallop, spinning around the corner, spear ready, to find the man huddled with his back against the stone, his hands open and defensively against his chest and belly.

"Oh please, good sir, please don't kill me!" he cried. "I'm with no one, not Ethelbert. Just a fisherman, I am."

"Be at ease, good man," Milwellis said and lowered his spear across his lap.

The man straightened, his arms going down by his sides. "We're just simple folk," he started to say.

"Then no real loss," Milwellis interjected. He thrust his spear into the man's gut. The fisherman shrieked and doubled over as Milwellis tore his barbed weapon back out, taking along the man's entrails.

"I would carve the crest of Palmaristown in your forehead for your treachery against King Yeslnik, fool!" the merciless prince shouted as the man crumbled to his knees. "But I haven't the time!"

The fisherman fell flat on the ground, and Milwellis whirled his horse about, stomping over him as he went back to the fun at the village center.

A large group moving east-to-west," Erolis confirmed from his perch up in a tree. "Slipping in behind Yeslnik's line as they spearhead east."

"Heartbeats?" Bannagran asked from his chariot below.

"Hundreds, five hundred, perhaps."

Bannagran nodded and motioned his man down from the tree (and since the wind carried great bite this day, Erolis was more than happy to follow that order).

"You follow as swiftly as you can," Bannagran commanded Grees and the fifty other footmen he had rounded up. "We will turn them and send them running, and the quicker you are among them, the more confusion they will find. So, for your own lives, warriors, run!"

As soon as Erolis stepped up into his chariot, Bannagran set his own off along the road, the other nine quickly sweeping up in his wake. Bannagran kept the pace measured for a short while, trying to gauge his timing for maximum effect at the enemy crossing point.

As usual, his instincts proved perfect, and when he set his team into a full charge along the last span to the enemy crossing, more than three dozen warriors from various villages of the Mantis Arm were within striking distance of the road.

Bannagran's armored team and chariot roared down at the Ethelbert soldiers. The warrior led with a series of spear throws, plucking them from the stand before him, launching them with precision and great power, all the while aiming his team at the largest concentration. A couple threw spears back his way, but they were more concerned with trying to get out of Bannagran's path, and their missiles proved ineffective.

Men rushed about wildly, and some broke. Some who thought they had dodged the brunt of the charging horse team found their legs literally cut from under them by the great jagged blades protruding from Bannagran's wheels.

Screams echoed east and west of the road, including cries of alarm that the Bear of Honce had come. And

from the north, where the other nine charioteers similarly pounded into Ethelbert's forces, the fifty footmen
howled and hollered and ran on at full speed.

The road was cleared in moments. Bannagran pulled his
team up to the side, took up shield and spear, and leaped
away. None could stand before him. Indeed, his enemies
knew him and shouted his name in terror as they broke
and fled before him.

All that Bannagran had hoped came to fruition in short
order. The concentration of enemies moving to flank the
southern end of Yeslnik's line fell apart almost at once,
and those who managed to escape the catastrophe ran
back the way they had come, to the east.

Bannagran and his nine fellows gave short chase, launching spears, inciting further terror. Grees and the others
swept by, cheering their leader, the great Bannagran, who
had arrived to turn certain disaster into victory yet again.

"To your chariots," Bannagran ordered the nine. "Those
who have already crossed the road will try to strike at us
from the west. They are caught alone!"

As predicted, the peninsula warriors did come on from
the west, trying to break through to secure their reinforcements. But this was Bannagran, the Bear of Honce, the
hero of Pryd, the hero of Yeslnik's Honce. Their spears
were met by brutal and unforgiving charges of chariots.
At one point Bannagran even grabbed a handful of jave-
lins, leaped from his chariot, and chased after a group of
five who ran back to the west.

Not fast enough for one, who caught a spear in the
back, and then another, who took one in the back of the
thigh, and then a third, whom Bannagran hit with a flying tackle, burying him in the dirt.

Just before Bannagran cut that one's throat open with
the serrated edge of his short sword, the man cried, "I
surrender! Oh, but it's not my war! I've children!"

Bannagran held his slash, stood up straight, and hoisted the man to his feet beside him. He looked back to the man he had hit in the leg, thrashing on the ground, and to Erolis, closing in for the kill.

"All quarter!" Bannagran called, and Erolis nodded. "These, too, are men of Honce!"

"Hail King Yeslnik!" Erolis called back.

Bannagran scowled at his prisoner.

"Hail King Yeslnik!" the terrified man answered, and Bannagran nodded grimly and pulled him back toward the road.

Soon after, Grees and the others returned, full of cheer and bluster. "We ran them off for good!" the farmer asserted. "And many're down."

"Well done," Bannagran congratulated him. "Now we turn west and quickly. Those out there are cut off from their allies and families, and they know it."

"How many?" Grees asked, concern in his tone.

"It matters not," Bannagran assured him. "They'll have no heart for the fight."

Proud of his men and glad that he had again ably led them, Bannagran left the western fields of victory, driving for Yeslnik's position in the center of his extended line. As it seemed that the fighting had ebbed— all warriors he passed on his way told him that the enemy had retreated to the fortified coastal towns—Bannagran eased his pace, so that his charioteers and footmen and their hundred prisoners, taken in those western fields with hardly a fight, as he had predicted, could somewhat pace him.

He wanted them to arrive in view of King Yeslnik soon after he and the unpredictable young nobleman had begun their conversation. In dealing with Yeslnik, Bannagran knew, it was always wise to somehow gain an advantage.

He found the young king basking in luxury in a grand tent, surrounded by so many layers of sentries that Ethelbert's entire army, had it come at them, would not likely have gotten to Yeslnik. Inside, around a table set with lavish foods, Yeslnik and his field commanders dined and drank.

Bannagran wasn't surprised.

"Ah, but the great Bear has come," said Yeslnik.

Bannagran winced at the mocking tone.

"I expected your arrival this morning," Yeslnik went on. "You were seen not far to the west many hours ago. I told you not to tarry."

"I happened upon a situation that needed to be addressed, for the good of my king," Bannagran explained. "I had not the time to ride to you and to correct the breach in your defenses."

"Breach?" Yeslnik replied, his tone going higher and betraying his sudden anxiety.

Always the brave one, Bannagran thought.

"The success of your maneuver at your southern flank was obviously unanticipated," Bannagran carefully explained. "Huzzah for the men of Delaval, so obviously eager to please their new king!"

Yeslnik smirked at him, and Bannagran knew that the king understood the criticism behind the compliment. A buffoon in many ways, too prideful for his or his subjects' good, and possessed of ridiculous vanity and deceit, Yeslnik was nevertheless not a simpleton, particularly not in matters politic. Bannagran silently reminded himself never to forget that.

"The peninsula warriors made a fatal mistake," Bannagran went on. "They tried to flank your spearheading advance by secretly advancing to the south of the southern end of your line. But they stretched themselves too thin. They are more used to fighting on the sea, methinks, or at the seacoast."

They heard a commotion outside the tent, and Bannagran knew that his men had arrived with the prisoners—and not a moment too soon, he thought.

"They were desperate against your bold gambit in the south, and so they erred," the Bear of Honce finished. He led Yeslnik and the other commanders present to the tent flap, coming in view of Bannagran's forces leading the long line of captives.

"What is the meaning of this?" Yeslnik asked Bannagran, surprising the champion.

"It means that our enemy's gambit has failed," he started to answer, but before he could finish, before his group even fully entered the encampment, horns blew from the other direction and a great cheer went up among King Yeslnik's forces.

Yeslnik led Bannagran and the others from the tent to come in view of the new arrivals, Milwellis and his forces.

"They have razed a line from the neck of the Mantis Arm to here," King Yeslnik explained to Bannagran. "They have struck fear into the hearts of the fools who would oppose my reign. Never again will the men, what few remain, of the Felidan Bay villages take up weapons in support of Ethelbert. The region is nearly secured."

He turned to Bannagran. "Do you notice anything absent among Milwellis's ranks?"

Bannagran looked hard, but found no answers to the curious and curiously leading question.

"Laird Bannagran did not hear of your edict, my liege," one of Yeslnik's other commanders remarked. Yeslnik nodded.

Bannagran looked at them with puzzlement.

"The days, the months, nay, the years, of merciful war are ended," Yeslnik explained.

"Merciful war?" Bannagran echoed with confusion.

"Merciful?" Yeslnik spat. "The reason this uprising of Ethelbert continues is because of false mercy!"

Bannagran let the description of the war as the "uprising of Ethelbert" go without the obvious challenge. This war was more a matter of Laird Delaval's expansion of his substantive holding than anything else. As soon as the roads had been completed, Laird Delaval, with his large resources, had moved to unify Honce under his banner. Ethelbert, the second strongest laird, with the support of many other lesser lairds and with ties to Behr in the south, had opposed him.

"Only when the cost of their choice is clear to those who would oppose me will they cease in their folly," Yeslnik explained.

"What would you have me do, my king?" Bannagran asked, a bit tentatively, for he was truly afraid of where this curious conversation might be leading.

"Tell me what is missing from Prince Milwellis's grand entrance," Yeslnik replied, and loudly, so that the approaching Milwellis clearly heard.

Bannagran scratched his head, not wanting to answer.

"Prisoners," Yeslnik said with a hiss. "The day of false mercy is ended. We do not offer quarter."

Bannagran swallowed hard, his mind whirling through the myriad of troublesome implications of such a ruthless edict. Why would any of those loyal to Ethelbert ever surrender with such a fate before them? He wanted to speak out, to explain to King Yeslnik that his own victory that very day would have been hard to achieve and would have cost him dearly had not the disoriented and fearful warriors of the Mantis Arm surrendered in those western fields—surrendered, despite outnumbering Bannagran's forces two-to-one, because they knew there was no long-term solution to their dilemma.

"Execute them," Yeslnik instructed Bannagran, the

king's words snapping at the champion like a jolt of lightning.

"I took them fairly, upon my word," Bannagran dared to argue.

"My word overcomes your word."

"Yes, my king," Bannagran stammered, "but you cannot take from me my honor if you wish me to remain valuable to your cause." His justification sounded inane to his own ears as he improvised the words, but he had to say something, anything, to dissuade Yeslnik from this course. Bannagran could kill any man or woman in battle without the slightest regret; he was a warrior and had been since his youth. But to kill unarmed, defenseless prisoners on such a scale, many of them simply folk caught up in the folly of lairds?

"Are you refusing me?" Yeslnik asked, the threat clear.

"No, my king, I am asking your deference in this matter."

Yeslnik stared at him hard.

"Oh, just kill them quickly and be done with it," said Prince Milwellis. "My liege, allow me," he added, staring at Bannagran as he spoke, as if this request was surely elevating him against the champion of Pryd, who many believed to be Milwellis's primary competitor for the favor of King Yeslnik. "As a reward for my efforts in the north."

Yeslnik looked from Milwellis to Bannagran and gave a little laugh, then motioned for Milwellis to proceed. The fearsome prince of Palmaristown eagerly climbed back upon his horse and motioned for a few of his most deserving and trusted comrades to follow.

"It would seem the situation here is well in hand," Yeslnik said to Bannagran in dismissive tones. "I expect that you are not needed after all. Take your charioteers and return to the hunt of the Highwayman."

Bannagran gave a curt bow and spun away, rushing to his chariot and motioning his nine to follow quickly.

"And do not fail me again," King Yeslnik said to him.

Bannagran snapped his reins and sent his team charging away, hoping to be far from this place before the screams of terror and agony filled the air.

No such luck.

TWELVE

Moral Outrage

Bransen and Cadayle stood arm in arm by the prow of *Lady Dreamer* as she bounced and splashed her way through the springtime swells. The sky above loomed dark and foreboding, and some drizzle had filled the morning air, but Dawson McKeege had assured them and all the other nervous "stiffleggers" (as he called those who hadn't spent much time on a boat) that it wasn't much of a storm.

"Just a pall," he had called it. "Worse on the spirits than on *Lady Dreamer*." The couple knew his words to be sincere. After all, Dame Gwydre herself was aboard; Dawson would never take a chance with the life of his beloved Lady of Vanguard.

"Chapel Abelle," Cadayle mumbled after a long while of silence. "What will you say to them when we arrive?"

"Nothing," Bransen answered. "Unless they ask. Then I will ask them why they found the need to so torment my family. What threat was Brother Dynard, truly? Or are they afraid to learn, as Father De Guilbe was so fearful of the barbarians that he would kill them all before speaking with them honestly?"

"They will welcome you with open arms, then," Cadayle replied sarcastically.

"They should hear the truth, if they ask."

"You would not have waited for that invitation a few months ago."

Bransen looked at his wife curiously before nodding in concession. "Father Premujon understands—and accepted Cormack despite great risk." As he spoke, he glanced back across the deck, to the sails of the vessels trailing them. De Guilbe and his people were on one, with the notable exception of Brother Giavno. Giavno sailed on *Lady Dreamer* with Father Premujon and his closest advisors, including Brother Jond, and with Cormack and Milkeila, as well.

"Not so great a risk for the father," Cadayle corrected. "Not with Dame Gwydre by his side."

"This meeting at Chapel Abelle will be interesting, even for me, though I hardly care for the affairs of the Order of Abelle," said Bransen.

"The Order of Blessed Abelle," Cadayle corrected with a wry grin.

Bransen rolled his eyes.

"But you will still offer your opinion if asked," Cadayle said with her unending playful sarcasm.

"Your own mother was thrown in a sack with venomous snakes, then hanged by her wrists and left to die," Bransen reminded, stealing her giggle.

"Samhaist justice, not Abellican," she said somberly.

"The brothers of Chapel Pryd sat silent at her trial, at her sentencing, and at her intended execution," Bransen reminded. "And those brothers were more than passive in the death of Garibond Womak!"

Cadayle hugged him close. "I did not mean to upset you," she said.

"It is the way of a difficult world," Bransen replied, returning the hug.

"Where will we live?" Cadayle asked.

"If Dame Gwydre's writ is accepted, anywhere we choose."

"And where will that be?"

Bransen looked at her carefully, trying to weigh the wistfulness in her beautiful eyes—those same eyes that had steadied him and warmed him when the other children had tormented him in his youth. In looking into Cadayle's eyes, Bransen could truly see her soul, her gentle and kind and loving soul. The wonderful view brought peace to him then, on *Lady Dreamer*'s damp deck, and reminded him how much he loved this woman and how fortunate he had been to find her.

"Pryd Town," he said. Cadayle started in surprise, and then a telling grin spread across her beautiful face. "Home."

"I would like that."

"So would Callen, I think."

"And Bransen, who offers it out of his boundless generosity?"

"It was my home on the lake. Although I am pained by the ending Garibond found, I think he would like it if we built our home there, in his memory. Also, if Yeslnik is laird, I will like it all the more simply because I know that Dame Gwydre's writ will bring frustration to the dimwit every day."

"And how many times will you rob him?"

Bransen laughed and hugged her tightly again. "No more," he said, shaking his head. "Dame Gwydre says that all is forgiven: that is our freedom. Our time in flight from pursuing soldiers is ended."

"Have you thought of becoming a father?" Cadayle asked. Something in her tone gave Bransen pause for a few heartbeats. His eyes popped open wide.

She looked up at him and smiled, then slowly nodded. The next hug was the tightest yet, and the warmest.

* * *

He uses Laird Delaval's own seal overlaid with a *Y*," Father Artolivan observed as he held the rolled parchment to arm's length so that his failing eyes could make out the insignia.

"He names himself Yeslnik Delaval, King of Honce," Master Reandu, the courier, explained.

"He would, wouldn't he?" Artolivan asked with a snort. "And before I read this, good Brother, would you desire to forewarn me of anything?"

Reandu looked at him curiously. "King Yeslnik is in a foul mood," he admitted. "His beloved uncle was murdered, after all. Is there something you fear, Father?"

Artolivan chuckled and looked around at his attendant, Brother Pinower, who seemed equally as sadly amused.

"We had a bit of a disagreement with Prince Milwellis of Palmaristown regarding our role in the disposition of prisoners," he explained. "I expect that the young man of hot humor complained to Yesl . . . to King Yeslnik, who no doubt wishes to chastise us for our impertinence."

"If he could think past the gains of the next day, he would understand Milwellis's posture to be one of disaster," Brother Pinower added. "I have little affection for the coldhearted prince of Palmaristown, I must admit."

"More than I," Artolivan mumbled.

"The events in the south move quickly," Reandu said. "Since the murder of Laird Delaval, Laird Ethelbert tried to assault Pryd Town. He was turned back by the brave men of Pryd and a great champion whom I name as a personal friend. The battle has turned vicious and furious. King Yeslnik will see this through, whatever the cost."

Father Artolivan held up a hand for him to pause, then broke the seal, unrolled the parchment, and began reading.

Almost immediately his jaw went slack, his eyes went wide, and he began to shake his head.

He passed it off to Pinower, who truly seemed as if he had been slapped in the face as he read it and gave a yelp of protest.

"King Yeslnik demands the release of all the Delaval prisoners held at Chapel Abelle and at any other chapels," Father Artolivan explained to the concerned Reandu, taking the scroll back from Pinower. "And he wishes us to serve as executioners for those captives of Laird Ethelbert's army."

"Impossible," Reandu started to argue, but Artolivan thrust the scroll into his hand, and he couldn't deny the meaning of the words on the parchment.

"What are we to tell our brethren at Chapel Entel in Ethelbert? Or at any other of our chapels in holdings under the domain of Laird Ethelbert?" Master Reandu asked.

"To barricade their doors and pray," Father Artolivan asked as much as stated, so ridiculous was the answer.

"This is insanity," Brother Pinower dared declare.

"It is the unbridled vengeance of a man answerable to no one but himself," Artolivan said. "The old graves of Honce are filled with the results of such folly." He cast a sympathetic glance at the obviously uncomfortable Reandu. "Speak freely, brother from Pryd," he bade. "What do you think of King Yeslnik's designs?"

Reandu swallowed hard and shook his head. "I do not . . . I don't," he stammered, shaking his head again more forcefully. "I must reflect on it, Father."

"Truly?" asked Artolivan with evident surprise.

"I . . ."

"Be at ease, Brother," Artolivan mercifully said. "We are all caught by surprise. We must all reflect. I will write and seal my response for you to take on your return to Father Jerak and Chapel Pryd."

"Thank you, Father Artolivan," Master Reandu said with a bow.

After a long and uncomfortable silence, Father Artolivan, who thought their audience at an end, looked at the younger man curiously.

"There is one more matter," Reandu explained, "though I hesitate to even mention it in light of the gravity of the previous issue."

"Come out with it," Artolivan bade him. "I am old, but my heart is strong enough for your surprises."

Reandu smiled and nodded, obviously appreciating the levity. "There is a man traveling the roads of Honce. His name is Bransen Garibond, a man of my home holding."

Behind Artolivan, Pinower shuffled nervously.

"He is known as the Highwayman, a great warrior, but he also travels in the guise of an awkward and damaged man often called the Stork," Reandu explained.

"Yes," Artolivan prompted.

"He is charged with the murder of Laird Delaval," Reandu explained. "It was his sword that slew the great man."

That news, of course, confused the two monks of Chapel Abelle. As far as they knew, the Stork was still in Vanguard, a long way from Delaval City. They both did well to hide that fact, however.

"If you find him and capture him, King Yeslnik will be pleased, no doubt," said Reandu, who couldn't hide his grimace as he spoke.

"You are pained by the prospect," Artolivan observed. "You know this man?"

"For many years."

"And you believe that he killed Laird Delaval?"

"He is capable of great anger. It is not unexpected, given the tragedy of his life," Reandu explained. "The evidence seems strong, though I am surprised that Bransen would go to the lengths of murder. I . . . I simply do not know."

"He was seen west of here, along the road to Palmaristown," Father Artolivan said. "Though that was before the onset of winter. I have heard reports that he went to Vanguard."

"Those reports must have been in error," Master Reandu said.

"Or it wasn't his sword."

Reandu paused at that. It seemed to the others as if a dark cloud left his face, however briefly. "I will report that back to King Yeslnik as well," he assured them.

Father Artolivan let that sit for a few moments before nodding. "Is there anything more?"

"No."

"Good," said Artolivan. "You have given me more than enough, I am sure. Allow me now to reflect on King Yeslnik's demands so that I might properly fashion a response. But do tell me, how fares Father Jerak?"

"No better, no worse," Reandu replied.

"Your service in his stead is not unnoticed, Brother," Artolivan assured him.

Reandu swallowed hard.

"With the accidental death of Master Bathelais the chapel will likely fall to you in full."

Reandu shifted from foot to foot, too overwhelmed to reply.

"Father Jerak is an old and dear friend of mine. I am glad that he trained such competent successors," said Artolivan. "I am sure that your work would please him, as it pleases us. Go with grace, good young Master Reandu."

Reandu breathed a sigh of relief, bowed, and quickly took his leave.

"You need to reflect?" Brother Pinower asked Artolivan, his tone full of doubt.

"On whether or not it would be politic of me to publicly spank this young twit who thinks himself King of Honce," Artolivan replied.

"What are we to do?" Pinower asked.

"We are not to free the prisoners sent to us in good faith by Laird Ethelbert and his commanders," Father Artolivan insisted. He took a few deep breaths, but far from steadying him, he seemed to grow more agitated as he continued, his voice reflecting a deep-seated outrage. "To do so would be to betray our word to the people we serve. And of course the brothers are not going to act as executioners for a young king drunk with power! The Order of Abelle was founded as a gentle alternative to the vicious Samhaists. We have won over Honce's people with the utility of our blessed gemstones, true, but also with our determination to reduce the suffering of men, not to play as the Samhaists in inflicting misery. This is who we are. We are not murderers and executioners!

"This is madness!" he roared, though he quickly calmed and lowered his tone, suddenly fearful that Re-andu was not far enough away and might hear. "Tell no one of this edict."

"Of course, Father," Pinower replied.

"Oh, what a week of ecstasy and agony," Father Arto-livan lamented. "To hear the grand news of Dame Gw-ydre's victory and now to see the truth of King Yeslnik laid bare."

"Perhaps Dame Gwydre will aid us in our conflict with King Yeslnik," Brother Pinower offered. "Surely she will not agree with his brutal tactics."

"How far out is *Lady Dreamer*?" Father Artolivan asked, for only a day earlier, the advance ship from Van-guard had slid into Chapel Abelle's long wharf with news that Gwydre was on her way.

"Three days. Perhaps two. The weather has held across the gulf, we believe. She departed only four days behind the advance ship. No one is faster across the dark waters than Dawson McKeege."

Father Artolivan reflexively turned to glance out the

window of his room, overlooking the dark waters of the Gulf of Corona. "Write our response immediately," he instructed. "Advise King Yeslnik—all proper respect in the use of his formal title!—that we will take his edict under advisement."

"Delay," Brother Pinower reasoned.

"Better that than to invite immediate war," said Artolivan. "We will indeed enlist Dame Gwydre in this trouble, should she be willing."

"Then the longer we take in replying the better."

"No, write it immediately—not with our decision, but with a promise that our decision will be forthcoming in short order. I want Master Reandu as far from here as quickly as possible, before he is even made aware of the impending visit of the victorious Lady of Vanguard. Reandu is spoken of in the highest terms, and he seems a man of mature and moderate temperament despite the unfortunate incident that led to the loss of Master Bathelais. But I'll not have our true feelings revealed beyond this room."

"Yes, Father."

"Let us hope that Dame Gwydre offers a solution," Artolivan said.

"Perhaps the solution will come from within," Pinower replied. "From the heart of Father Artolivan, who is closest to the spirit of Blessed Abelle."

He and Father Artolivan exchanged a long reflective look as the gravity of that statement weighed upon them.

Master Reandu left Chapel Abelle the next day, bound for his home of Pryd and bearing Father Artolivan's rolled and sealed response, which, of course, wasn't really a reply at all. Brother Pinower spent most of that day and the next two on Chapel Abelle's high wall, staring out at the gulf. When at last the sails of Vanguard ships appeared in the distance, he rushed to Father Artolivan and then down through the winding tunnels and stairways descending through the hundreds of feet of rocky cliff upon which sat their home. Much of Chapel Abelle lay within that mountain now, as the monks continually fashioned the deep limestone caves into chambers grand and humble. From the lowest chambers the two entered a long tunnel, its sides sculpted like the ridges of a clamshell, its air thick with brine and torch smoke. The fortified back door of Chapel Abelle, hundreds of feet below the main structures, opened onto a small beach in a deep, secluded bay.

With *Lady Dreamer* clearly in sight, Pinower rushed along the wharf past the brothers gathering up lines. He spotted Dawson, who often docked here. Beside him, to his sincere relief, stood Gwydre herself.

The young monk felt a sense of great elation at that, relief that she, this woman who might be the only hope against the insanity of Yeslnik, had indeed made the journey south from Vanguard.

"Praise Abelle, for he must have guided her heart," Pinower said with a hopeful smile. He looked back to the approaching ship and his smile became a look of concern, for moving up beside Gwydre came another distinctive figure dressed in black silk.

"Aye, but there's that Highwayman fellow," one of the wharf hands remarked.

"We should put him on a boat right back to Vanguard for his own sake," another added. "Afore Yeslnik hangs him, I mean."

"We know now that he could not have participated in the murder of Laird Delaval," said Pinower. "Unless he found some blessed spirits to fly him to Delaval City in the south and back again."

"Blessed?"

"Cursed spirits, then."

"I am not so certain that our new young King Yeslnik will accept any evidence contrary to the notions that fill his mind, given Master Reandu's description of him," said Pinower.

The ship moored alongside the long wharf then, monks and sailors fast tying her off, and soon the impressive procession moved down the plank to join Pinower and the other monks working the docks. Pinower was glad to see his old friend Father Premujon disembark beside Gwydre.

"All news from the north is good," Premujon said after the formal greetings, where Dawson did all the introductions.

"And so we have brought an eclectic entourage," Dame Gwydre remarked. "Brothers of the order and a priestess of Alpinador. A man of legend," she said, looking at Jameston Sequin, whose name was known along the southern coast of the Gulf of Corona, "and one in the making," she added, looking to Bransen.

"And of course, the hero of Vanguard and all of Honce, the lady who has renewed hope in our order with her victory over Ancient Badden," Brother Pinower said as they all began walking toward the doorway and the many staircases that would bring them back to the top of the great cliff. "It is a grand day in Chapel Abelle, indeed!"

"A day of hope," Gwydre agreed.

Pinower's expression flashed with both concern and tempered hope at that, but he said no more.

THIRTEEN

Cornering a Snake

E very village along the Felidan Bay is ablaze," General Kirren Howen reported to Laird Ethelbert. "We will find no allies from that direction. And the villages of the Mantis Arm have been cut off from the mainland."

"They have many boats," the laird replied.

Kirren Howen shook his head, his expression grim. "They have been battered, laird. I doubt they'll come forth and leave their families to the mercy of merciless Milwellis of Palmaristown."

"But Yeslnik has broken off and moved back inland," Ethelbert remarked.

"Leaving Prince Milwellis of Palmaristown and his vile forces free run of the inner coast," the general reported. "Now the both of them, Yeslnik from the northwest and Milwellis from the north, would seem to have entered into a race to see who might arrive at our gates first."

Laird Ethelbert poured two glasses of shinaba, a potent liquor distilled from tart roots from the steppes of To-gai, a brutal land of horsemen and vile beasts to the west of the deserts of Behr, south of the Belt-and-Buckle.

"To a good try, then," he said, handing one to Kirren Howen.

"I am not yet ready to surrender Ethelbert dos Entel to that putrid Yeslnik," the general said as he took the drink, then quaffed it in a single gulp. With Ethelbert's nod of approval, the man moved across the room to pour another.

"Surrender?" Ethelbert echoed incredulously. "Not Yeslnik or Milwellis will see the streets of my Entel, unless it is through the eyes of a disembodied head."

"A good try, you said. You speak as if we have lost."

"And we have, though we have stung our enemies profoundly," Ethelbert replied. "I fear that we haven't the resources to again march north and challenge for Honce, nor would I deign to put the people of the holdings through a continuation of this . . ."

He stopped when he noticed his general staring at him hard and disapprovingly.

"Your men fight because they love you," Kirren Howen declared. "You fought, not out of self-gain, but because you were the only one who could slow the thievery of Laird Delaval. Most men of Honce understand this."

"You are too kind, my old friend," Ethelbert replied. "And I do not doubt your loyalty or love, or that of many others like Myrick and the warriors of my holding. But for many of the others, the men and women of other holdings whose lairds decided that my gold was better than Delaval's, there is only misery and blood and agony and death. They hold my name no higher than the name of Delaval, or Yeslnik now (though I dare to believe that he will be less loved than either I or Delaval could ever have been). They fight because they are told to fight. They die because they cannot escape. They hate us all, no doubt, and hate their own miserable lives almost enough to make death a welcome alternative."

Kirren Howen didn't disagree, but the look on his face was one of utter dejection.

"We are not surrendering," Laird Ethelbert assured him. "And not Yeslnik or Milwellis will march into Ethelbert dos Entel. That much I promise. We are now the great biting turtles of the Belt-and-Buckle's end stones." He brought his hands together, fingers interlocked, and drew them tighter. "We close ranks and fight from positions where ten men might fend off a hundred. And whenever our enemies carelessly venture near our point, we bite at them and teach them pain.

"And we are more than a huddled turtle," he continued, a sinister smile coming over him. "We have vipers to send forth, a most venomous group."

Kirren Howen considered the words for a few heartbeats, then grimly nodded. "And when the vipers poison the attackers and send them reeling?" he asked. "Do we march forth and drive our enemies before us?"

"Eager for another try at the Bear of Honce?" Ethelbert asked slyly.

"A worthy opponent!" Kirren Howen replied. "So, yes."

"I do not like battling that one," Ethelbert admitted. "I fought beside him and Laird Prydae those years ago."

"I remember it well. Would that Bannagran—Laird Bannagran, I am told—had decided to ally with Laird Ethelbert!"

"Would that Laird Prydae had kept his loins, and then his life," said Ethelbert with a great sigh as he considered the tragic events that had ultimately driven Prydae and Pryd Holding from his side. He noticed Kirren Howen looking at him curiously.

"I thought to name Prydae to my line," Ethelbert said, surprising the general.

"He was a good man," Ethelbert explained. "But he lost his ability to continue his line, his balls taken by a powrie. Still, I blame myself for not acting forcefully enough to enlist him and his important holding, a holding become all the more important by the rise of the Bear of Honce." He ended with a profound sigh, one that had Kirren Howen nodding his head in agreement.

"To the vipers, then," Kirren Howen said and handed a second glass of shinaba to Ethelbert, who drained his first, then brought the other up to tap the general's, a toast they were both glad to acknowledge.

Are you ready, my prince?" asked Dimitri Raetu, holding back his obviously eager horse. The scouts ahead had reported confusion and terror in the ranks of their enemies, with most fleeing south. This next charge, back to the east and the Mirianic, would take the rocky hill anchoring the southern bank of a large bay just north of the city of Ethelbert dos Entel. That strong position would ensure that no ships could put in and off-load soldiers right behind their lines and would also serve as a fine vantage point for the short run to Ethelbert's city.

Milwellis, victorious all through the morning and all the day before, beamed with glee. Was he ready to win yet again? How could he not be? "King Yeslnik is still two days from Ethelbert City, and we'll be at her gates by evening."

"Is this a bad thing, my prince?" asked Harcourt, another of the commanders. He was the oldest of the generals who had set out from Palmaristown with Milwellis those weeks before. He also had fought with Panlamaris, Milwellis's father, in the powrie wars and in many sea battles when Panlamaris had seized control of the western reaches of the Gulf of Corona, thus ensuring Palmaristown's place among the most highly prized and important ports in all of Honce.

Milwellis looked at him curiously, not understanding

how the prospects before them could possibly be considered as such. Still, his father had made it clear to him to heed well the advice of the veteran Harcourt. "You fear that I will outshine the king? Do you think me impolitic?"

"No, of course not, and we . . . you have earned all honors," the old general answered. "Your march south will be remembered throughout Honce for generations to come—already the bards are writing their songs of Milwellis's great victories—and never will a Palmaristown ship be out of reach of a friendly port, since you control them all now, from the river through the southern coast of the gulf and down the length of the Mantis Arm. All glory to Milwellis. Young prince, you've done your father proud, and no easy task that!"

Milwellis's stare took on a harder edge. "But . . . ?" he prompted.

"King Yeslnik is new to the throne, and the throne itself is new," Harcourt replied. "As such, he is no doubt unsure."

Several of the other Palmaristown knights, splendid in their shining suits of bronze, shuffled uncomfortably on their horses and looked to Milwellis, seeking to gauge his response to the possible affront.

"Unsure and insecure," Milwellis added, nodding his approval at the blunt-speaking Harcourt, which reassured the others. "So we are faced with a dilemma. I desire credit to Palmaristown's brave warriors for the taking of Ethelbert dos Entel, but I fear to walk too tall above Honce's new king, to whom my father has pledged fealty. What am I to do?"

The way he had asked, grinning from ear to ear, told them that he had already sorted out the solution, and so the knights just glanced at each other with confident nods and waited for Milwellis to explain.

"I will take my leave of you now," he told them, "riding west to King Yeslnik's line and camp. You proceed as we had planned. You will have no trouble smashing to the city's gate. And when I arrive, King Yeslnik will find his path clear to victory, Ethelbert dos Entel, the greatest prize of all, presented to him by my minions. All glory to Yeslnik for leading the march into the city, but all the men of the king's many holdings will know that it was Palmaristown and Milwellis who truly won the day."

He looked to Harcourt, who was nodding with approval. "Aye, but your father has raised a son who will well lead Palmaristown and more," the general said.

With a stern look Milwellis dismissed the others. As they walked their mounts away, he brought his horse up very close beside Harcourt.

"You find me too forward in front of the others?" the general asked.

"I have never heard such compliments flowing from the lips of Harcourt," Milwellis answered. "I find them unsettling."

"Perhaps you have never deserved them before."

Milwellis sat up straight as if the man had slapped him.

"I promised your father that I would counsel you and protect you," Harcourt pressed. "And protect you particularly from yourself. This is not easy business—oh, killing our enemies is simple enough, and a task you've learned well."

"But the politics of it," Milwellis reasoned.

"Trickier by far," said Harcourt, and he lowered his voice as he added, "And more so given that our new king is a man of exceeding vanity and unworldliness. Would that Laird Delaval had known an heir as worthy as Milwellis."

"You say so only because you fear you have angered me."

"I speak only because I do not fear to anger you," Harcourt answered without hesitation. "My loyalty is to Laird Panlamaris first, and I was fighting beside him before you were born. He charged me with fulfilling his own role beside you, to criticize when needed and to counsel always."

"And to praise?"

"Only when deserved. As now. There are two men in particular making names in this war, yourself and Bannagran, the champion of Pryd."

"He is a peasant."

"The warriors love him, and Yeslnik has named him Laird of Pryd."

"That does not change his peasant blood," Milwellis said with a scowl.

"And the warriors love you," Harcourt was quick to add. "And you have the advantage, young prince, for they fear you, as well. All who watched the burning of the Felidan villages understand well the severity of Prince Milwellis, and fear is a tool that will serve you well in the days after Ethelbert's certain defeat. As King Yeslnik sorts out his new and vast domain he will wisely and warily defer to you."

"All Honce's coast for Palmaristown, eh?"

"That is your father's greatest wish, one that you have made possible, even likely."

"My choice in going now to Yeslnik?" Milwellis asked. "Wise?"

"Brilliant beyond your years," Harcourt answered.

"Ride with me?"

"With honor, Prince of Palmaristown."

Aye, General Dimitri," one of the Palmaristown's knights replied with striking emphasis on the man's newfound title. The others, peers all until this point, laughed at their new commander's expense.

Dimitri Reatu laughed with them. This was his first command, handed to him by Prince Milwellis himself when Milwellis and Harcourt had departed. The mission seemed straightforward enough. The armored horsemen had a clear run to the hill and a clear trail up it. The fact that their enemies held the higher ground seemed inconsequential and had been to this point. For the Ethelbert defenders hadn't bows strong enough or spears heavy enough to inflict any real damage against the bronze plating and hadn't the heart to continue the fight anyway, having been in retreat for days now. A few stubbornly (or under orders) kept their positions along the hillside, a few light spears had reached Dimitri's band, and an enemy occasionally climbed on rocks, sword or long spear in hand to block the way.

But the Palmaristown knights had ridden right through the diversions, ignoring the flimsy missiles and cutting low the peasants, who wore no armor, who carried shields of ill-sewn leather, and who wielded weapons that bronze armor easily turned. In a gallop more often than a trot, Dimitri Reatu led his men up the side, with the top, the goal, clearly in sight.

Through the slit in his full helm, Dimitri hardly noted the Behr features on the shaved-headed man who appeared among the branches of a tree to his right or his strange black clothing.

Just another peasant to ignore or, if he ventured too near, to slay, so the new general thought.

Only one of Dimitri's band of ten even noted the stranger's sudden movements, his leaping from branch to branch with the grace of a squirrel, bounding to the top of a small pine just ahead and to the side of the lead rider. The knight called a warning, but his voice was filled more with curiosity than alarm.

The stranger disappeared into the thick boughs of the pine.

The knights charged forward.

The pine tree leaned over suddenly, as if to grasp at

them. It was the black-clothed stranger, holding its top branches and leaping to the side, his weight and momentum taking the tree down with him in his descent. He came across Dimitri's horse, both men disappearing in a swirl of green.

And the knights gasped in unison as the tree swung back up, a flailing Dimitri affixed to it, the stranger sitting in Dimitri's saddle, hoisting the general hard to help the recovering tree gain momentum.

The nearest knight leaped his horse ahead and readied his sword to slash at the attacker, but as if he had anticipated that very movement, as if Dimitri's horse was no more than an extension of his thoughts, the stranger slapped the mount and it reared on cue, bucking and double-kicking back, slamming the charging horse in the chest. The jolt sent the knight tumbling from his seat to crash hard at the side of the trail.

The stranger whirled Dimitri's mount around and produced a strange weapon: two black poles as long as a forearm fastened end to end by an equally long length of dark leather. He held one of the poles and sent the other spinning as he brought his horse in line to pass by the next charging knight.

That man yelled, veering in and leveling his sword.

But the spinning pole went about that sword and wrapped it. A quick twist by the black-clothed warrior snapped the blade in half and freed the strange weapon in the same instant.

The knight tried to turn in closer, to stab with his suddenly shortened half sword, but the stranger veered his horse opposite, keeping just out of reach. As they passed, that curious twin-poled weapon snapped in against the back of the knight's bronze helm with such force that the back plate buckled in hard against his skull. The knight howled and reached up with both hands to clutch at his aching head, caring not that he had let go his reins, thinking only to get his cracking skull out of the bronze prison. Half mad with explosions of agony, the man never let go of the sides of his helm even as he toppled from his mount, even as he hit the hard ground headfirst, all of his weight crushing down upon his neck, pulverizing his spine. He flopped on the ground and rolled, coming to an awkward rest, having no control, no strength to straighten himself out.

The warrior from Behr turned to bring himself straight between the next two knights in line, and they adjusted their swords accordingly, thinking him mad and foolish despite his impressive display.

Just before the three horses passed, the stranger leaped to stand upon his saddle and sent his leather-tied sticks into a whirling display, moving them from hand to hand, over one shoulder then behind him and back under the other shoulder and all about his head with amazing precision.

The two knights tried to ignore the diversionary movements, tried to focus on taking the warrior's legs out.

The horses passed, the knights stabbed repeatedly, and the stranger from the southland danced and leaped and worked his sticks into a spin, into a forward rolling action before him. He caught the flying pole tight under his right armpit suddenly, leaped the stabbing blades and landed sidelong, pulling hard all the while on the other pole with his right hand, building tension against his own lock. He back-kicked his left foot just as he released the trapped pole from under his arm. It snapped forward like a To-gai viper with such force that it drove right through the knight's bronze helm and through the side of his skull.

The knight across the way fared little better, the back-kick hitting him with a force he could not have anticipated and at just the right angle to lift him from his seat. He went over the far side of the horse, his left foot still caught in the stirrup, and that tether twisted him underneath the galloping beast. Hooves pounded against him, which only frightened the horse more. It ran off across the hillside, the knight bouncing along the stones behind it.

The other horse continued to run as well, its rider quite dead, slumped over its neck.

The trailing knights, wanting no part of this southern creature, tried to turn aside, but other southerners appeared from the brush, leaping at them, kicking at them, stabbing them with long and thin poles. Only one managed to turn about completely, thinking to ride away to warn Prince Milwellis. He broke free and fought hard to balance his mount, refusing to relinquish the gallop even though he was in a steep descent. As the sounds of fighting receded behind him, he gradually relaxed and tried to ease his horse, but he realized his folly when he noted movement within the brush to the side of the path.

Another black-clothed warrior, a woman.

She closed in a confusing blur, springing to her hands, then over to her feet, then up into the air in a dizzying spin, landing again on her hands and springing away once more. With stunning speed she moved toward the trail, and the knight knew that he could not get past this somersaulting demoness.

Hands down, feet down, full airborne somersault, she came on, and he aimed his sword to the side at her as he crossed before her on the path.

But she just sprang higher in her next leap, climbing far above the sword, and the knight could only gawk.

She came out of her curl as she descended, her muscles and momentum driving her extending legs out to crack against the knight's shoulder and neck. He jolted down, then bounced back up and didn't even realize that he was clear of his saddle and mount and flying free to the ground, didn't even realize that the horse this black-clothed demoness from Behr was now astride was his own. He hit the ground, and all consciousness flew away.

The woman now riding paid him no heed, charging

instead up the hill. Almost all the knights were down by the time she arrived, rolling and fighting, but one man remained in the saddle, and one of her warriors lay bloody on the ground beneath him.

Outraged, the former Jhesta Tu charged right for the man, who turned to meet the charge.

Except that suddenly she wasn't there! The horse remained but was riderless. By the time the knight understood that the woman had tucked her legs and leaped away and was now descending across his own mount, it was too late. The graceful woman barely touched the horse's back as she crossed over and flew away. The knight started to cry out a warning to his companions.

But he could not yell, could not make a sound, other than the gurgle of bubbling blood. He reached up to grasp his throat, flung aside his heavy gauntlet to get his fingers under his helm. To feel the warm blood, his throat slashed from side to side. He glanced back at the woman and saw a small, decorated sword barely more than a long dagger in her hand and stained with his own blood.

As he fell, he realized that it was not a dagger but a broken sword. In the last moments of his life he recalled that a sword had been broken in half in the chest of King Delaval.

The same sword, he knew with dying certainty. No comfort as the darkness closed.

U nworthy enemies," Merwal Yahna complained when the battle had ended.

Affwin Wi, her broken sword dripping with blood, glanced around, her gaze focusing on the one of her warriors who was writhing on the ground.

"Not so unworthy," she argued.

"It was not their worthiness, but Ti'ragu's own error,"

Merwal Yahna assured her. "His leap fell short of his target."

Affwin Wi nodded, then indicated Merwal Yahna's bloody nun'chu'ku, the two poles tied with leather.

With a grim nod in reply, the fierce half-To-gai-ru, half-Behrenese warrior walked over to his badly wounded companion and again sent his weapon into a spin, catching the flying pole under his arm. His muscles bulged and strained as he pulled against the hold, taking sure and merciful aim at the base of Ti'ragu's skull.

All of the other Hou-lei gang began to hum in a low and somber key.

Merwal Yahna released the trapped nun'chu'ku pole, and it snapped forward to devastating effect.

Ti'ragu lay very still.

Caught in the top branches of the swaying pine, Dimitri Reatu rolled around just in time to see the execution of the wounded Behrenese warrior. Somehow that cold-blooded act, killing one of their own with such impunity, brought the first-time general to a new plane of terror. His fingers turned bloody as he desperately forced them under the rim of his helm and under the fine silk rope tied about his neck and hanging him from the trunk.

All of his knights had been slain within moments, the black-clothed southerners moving about them with deadly precision. He dared hope that maybe they had forgotten him or believed him already dead. He closed his eyes, tightened his neck muscles as much as possible to fight the choke, and tried to go very still.

He knew their laughter was directed at him before he even opened his eyes again.

The one who had caught him, the tall one with the

shaved head and the strange weapon, moved to the low
boughs right below him and pulled forth from them a silk
rope—the other end of the one binding him, Dimitri understood, just a moment before the southerner tugged it and the
clever knot unwound and the young general crashed and
bounced to the ground in the midst of his laughing, victorious enemies.

Prince Milwellis and Harcourt did not receive the
greeting they had anticipated when they at last came
to King Yeslnik's encampment. Traveling through the
tree-lined dells of the region, they had not seen the developments in the east along the shore until they crested the
tall hill to stand beside Yeslnik and his commanders.

Milwellis noted immediately that the king's eye was
not turned to the southeast and the city of Ethelbert dos
Entel as he had expected, but to the northeast.

"You are here?" Yeslnik blurted with surprise when
the Prince of Palmaristown rode up beside him.

"What is this about?" Milwellis demanded, sliding down
from his mount and running to the edge of the hillock.

"Your army is being routed," one of Yeslnik's commanders remarked.

"And you are here!" Yeslnik added.

"Routed? They should be at the gates of Ethelbert by
now!" Milwellis declared, and he began stomping about
like a caged beast.

"They've lost a league of ground," Yeslnik grumbled.

"Did Ethelbert come at them with all his force? Even
then, we should have routed—" Milwellis stopped when
he noted Yeslnik's generals shaking their head.

"Our scouts saw no sizable force moving from the city
gates," one said. "Are you certain that your men simply
did not retreat?"

The scowl Milwellis gave him was all the answer he needed and more than enough to silence that notion.

More scouts went out from Yeslnik's camp soon after, and more came in, with reports of dead Palmaristown soldiers and the main force in fast retreat. Milwellis wanted to ride to them, but Yeslnik would hear none of that.

"He's more interested in making sure that he's surrounded by strength," Harcourt dared to mention to Milwellis as they wandered about the encampment.

Milwellis looked at him incredulously but finally nodded, glad again that his father had thought to put this candid and seasoned warrior beside him.

Long after the sun had set, the riddle of the retreat was finally solved, for some of Yeslnik's scouts returned with a pair of Milwellis's men, both wounded.

"Demons!" one insisted. "They walked invisible through the trees!"

"Demons?" Yeslnik and two of his commanders said in unison.

"Not demons," the other said. "Men, sure enough—and women! Southerners. Beasts of Behr. Ah, but they're demons when they're fighting, none should doubt!"

"A sizable force?" Yeslnik asked.

"A handful."

"Backed by?" Milwellis asked.

"Just a handful," answered the soldier. "And our knights're all gone."

"Gone?" asked Yeslnik.

"Dimitri Reatu?" asked Milwellis.

"All gone," the soldier answered grimly. "They went up the hill—"

"And the demons came down," the other soldier added.

King Yeslnik lifted a hand to silence the plethora of questions the others started to ask. "You saw them? Up close?"

The soldiers nodded.

"What weapons did they wield?"

"Strange ones for some, swords for a couple," one answered.

"And one used a half sword," said the other.

Yeslnik looked at him curiously.

"Broken, maybe," the man explained. "But half a sword and with a jagged tip."

King Yeslnik looked as if he might topple over. He turned to regard his commanders and Milwellis.

"What is it, my king?" the Prince of Palmaristown asked when it appeared as if Yeslnik couldn't find his voice.

"The assassins who killed King Delaval," one of the commanders explained.

"Where are these enemies now?" Yeslnik demanded of the soldiers. Even in the dim light it was obvious that the blood had drained from the young king's face.

The two looked to each other and shrugged, then turned back sheepishly to the king. "The fighting has stopped, my king," one of Yeslnik's scouts said for them. "The enemy disappeared into the hills, likely exhausted."

King Yeslnik began glancing around, eyes darting nervously from shadow to distant shadow.

"And so the war continues," he said, his voice cracking and uneven. "Ethelbert has averted disaster—we cannot push him into the sea."

"A full attack, north and west, my king," one of the commanders offered. "A few assassins will not stop the prepared lines of our army!" He looked to Milwellis accusingly as he spoke.

"No, no, no," Yeslnik replied, shaking his head and walking about in circles. "No, we should not remain here. Not now. Ethelbert has turned the tide against us. He is wounded and battered and will not come forth. And so we can go, quickly."

"Go?" the commander asked.

"To lands more familiar and more to our liking," Yeslnik explained. "Yes, that is the course. We will retreat to Pryd Town, or to Delaval."

"Delaval was no defense against the assassins before," the commander dared to remind him.

"But we will be more vigilant!" Yeslnik screamed. "We will back away—and parlay. Yes, parlay. Perhaps Ethelbert will stay in his city and we can go. We can take the rest of Honce. Yes, yes, I must consider our course. But not here. Not now. Break the camp, and be ready to depart."

He walked off as he spoke, and it did not escape Milwellis and Harcourt that more than one of King Yeslnik's commanders rolled his eyes.

"He is a man of great courage," Harcourt whispered to Milwellis as they rode from the camp soon after, heading back to where the army of Palmaristown had regrouped.

Milwellis didn't bother to reply to the sarcasm. There was no answer.

FOURTEEN

Aimlessly Wandering

A dejected Master Reandu walked into the small village of Eskald three days' north of Pryd Town. An inconsequential place, Eskald had no chapel and only a tiny keep, barely more than a stone house atop a cleared hill, to serve as the castle for its laird.

The day was young, and Reandu thought to travel right through Eskald and continue on his way home. There was another community, Chud, a cluster of huntsmen's houses several hours farther to the south. As he passed along the main road through the bulk of the houses, though, the monk saw that the people were all astir, and he knew that their agitation was not on account of his arrival.

He turned a questioning gaze on one young woman whose response was a chin nod toward the laird's house on the hill. Following that look, Reandu noted a familiar sight: the chariot of Bannagran.

With a sigh of relief—perhaps he could ride south with the man—Reandu moved up the hill. He didn't even have to tell the lone guard to announce him to the laird, for Bannagran was coming out the door even as he approached.

Reandu thought that a good thing, for the Laird of Eskald, a man of great mouth and little repute by the name of Mackwok Boln, was one of the most insufferable and self-absorbed men Reandu had ever met. A visit with him would involve hours of time, listening to the man recount the exploits of his long-lost youth, how he rode with Prydae in the powrie war (which wasn't true, though the pompous laird had probably claimed as much to Bannagran, who had led Prydae's forces in that very conflict), and how Laird Ethelbert had not come to attack Eskald out of respect, nay fear, of the heroic Mackwok Boln. Reandu had heard it all before and on several occasions, including the first steps of his journey north to Chapel Abelle.

The look on Bannagran's face, like it was locked in a permanent sigh, told Reandu that his friend had not been spared the recounting.

"Has he saved the world this day?" he greeted.

Bannagran laughed at that. "Twice, methinks."

"I did not expect to see you here," said Reandu. "I've been told that the fighting has moved south."

"All the way to Ethelbert dos Entel."

"And you are north of Pryd. On the hunt for the Highwayman?"

"I've been tasked with that," Bannagran reminded. "King Yeslnik has determined that his finest general should don the mantle of bounty hunter, and this at a time when his greatest enemy might soon be pushed into the sea." His voice trailed off as he noted that Reandu was smirking at him. "What do you know?"

"His finest general?" Reandu echoed with a wide grin.

Bannagran snorted at him, waved his hand and walked past, heading for the chariot.

"I am just unused to such aggrandizement from you, about you," Reandu explained, hounding him every step.

"Be at ease, monk," said the warrior. "Else I will show you the truth of the claim."

Reandu laughed at the empty threat.

"What news of our masked friend?" Bannagran asked.

"He was seen on the road to Chapel Abelle," said Reandu. "He passed through Palmaristown but did not arrive at Chapel Abelle."

"One of the villages to the west of that place, then? Or did he pass to the east by the chapel and move along Felidan Bay? If that is the case, then he is likely dead. Milwellis offered little quarter to the people of the holdings who joined with Laird Ethelbert's cause."

Reandu blew a deep sigh, certain that Bannagran would not be pleased with his information. "The whispers claim that our friend Bransen went to Vanguard before the winter."

"The whispers are wrong, then," Bannagran said, and he nodded his chin to the spear bucket set on the chariot, in which stood the broken half of the sword blade that had been taken from the chest of King Delaval.

"Or that is not Bransen's sword," Reandu replied. "He went to Vanguard before the winter, they claim, and claim with some confidence. It is rumored that Bransen joined with Dame Gwydre in her struggles against the Samhaists. We both know that Bransen had no love for that cult."

Bannagran suddenly appeared more tired, and he rubbed his face.

"You believe that King Yeslnik will send you there in pursuit?"

"If the Highwayman is there, then he will," Bannagran replied. "Without doubt. He wants our friend dead. More than anything in the world, he wants the Highwayman slaughtered."

"If Bransen is in Vanguard, then he couldn't have killed King Delaval," Reandu said plainly. "The distance is too great, and the seas and land impassible through the winter months. Surely King Yeslnik will understand this and will rethink the best course for his finest general."

Bannagran shook his head through every word. "It

would hardly matter. Yeslnik's hatred of this one was strong before the evidence of the Highwayman's complicity in King Delaval's death, before King Delaval had even been killed. Twice now has our little friend robbed him, and both times shaming him in front of his insuffera . . . his wife. To a man like Yeslnik, that is a more egregious crime than murder."

"A vain man like Yeslnik, you mean, and with an insufferable wife."

"Your words, not mine, and words to get you slain."

Reandu just shrugged. "King Yeslnik has invited great strife within the Order of Abelle. Father Artolivan cannot do what he has demanded of us."

Bannagran looked at him curiously.

"To free all prisoners loyal to Delaval who were sent to the keeping of the brothers," Reandu explained. Bannagran nodded as if he did not think that so egregious. Reandu let that notion sink in just a bit more before adding, "And to kill all loyal to Ethelbert."

Bannagran's face screwed up for a moment, but then he just shook his head and snorted, as if hardly surprised, as if nothing Yeslnik did would ever surprise him.

"He will send you to Vanguard?" Reandu asked, and Bannagran nodded.

"To the edge of the world and over it," he replied. "Our young king is not in good humor. He is wounded by the death of Delaval."

"And he is afraid," Reandu dared to say, and again Bannagran nodded.

"And he is frustrated by Ethelbert's stubbornness and fight," the warrior added. "Yeslnik is focusing all of those emotions on the Highwayman now, as if he is the source of all the prince's ills. He will not rest until he has the head of Bransen Garibond."

"So you are certain and will head straightaway to Vanguard?"

"No, and I hope that I am wrong!"

"You are returning to Pryd, then?"

Bannagran nodded. "Though I fear my rest will be short."

"And you will offer a brother a ride in your fine chariot?"

"No, but I am sure that Reandu is so forward that he will take one anyway." He moved up to his driver post. Grinning, Reandu stepped up behind him.

They made Pryd Town the next day, just as the first advance scouts of King Yeslnik's army were arriving with news of the stinging reversal at the gates of the southern city. The news that the war was still on in full, that Ethelbert had stayed the seemingly inevitable conclusion, was not as unwelcome to Bannagran as it was to Reandu. At least for Bannagran, it offered some hope that he wouldn't be sent to the cold north of Vanguard.

FIFTEEN

That Which Is Right

"They'll not be any quicker because of your pacing," Cadayle said to Bransen later the very same day that *Lady Dreamer* brought them to Chapel Abelle. Sitting beside her on the long bench in the antechamber, Callen gave a laugh.

"He's blazing a fine trail across Father Artolivan's rug," she said.

Bransen did stop his pacing momentarily to regard the women. They had been waiting in the antechamber to Father Artolivan's audience hall for more than an hour, expecting to be called in to speak on behalf of Cormack, who was in front of the Court of Chapel Abelle facing the impassioned appeals of Father De Guilbe.

"He's got Father Premujon speaking for him, and Brother Giavno, even," Cadayle reminded. "And Dame Gwydre herself. She had to preside neutrally over the court in Vanguard, but here she makes no secret of her support for Cormack and Milkeila."

"I've seen too much of the likes of men akin to Father De Guil—" Bransen started to say, but he stopped fast as the door swung open and Father De Guilbe stormed from the audience chamber. Brother Giavno came close behind the large and angry man and tried to speak.

De Guilbe turned suddenly and snapped, "Do not follow me, Brother, else I will be spending my next days inside Chapel Abelle's dungeon!"

At first, Giavno looked as if he had been slapped, but as De Guilbe stormed from the antechamber and across the open courtyard the monk just sighed and shrugged at the three witnesses.

"I'm guessing it went well for Cormack and Milkeila," Cadayle said with a grin.

"Beyond anything I could have hoped," said Cormack from the door. Arm in arm, he and Milkeila moved from the audience hall.

"Father Artolivan would like to sanction our marriage formally," Cormack explained.

"Then you are forgiven," said Bransen.

"And offered a return to the order," Milkeila said.

Bransen's face twisted uncomfortably at that. "You'll not go back," he said.

"I've made no decision," said Cormack. "But it was good to be asked."

From inside the audience hall Dame Gwydre called out, "Hurry along, then!"

"They would see you now," said Milkeila.

Bransen and the two women exchanged surprised looks, for they thought they had been brought here solely to speak on Cormack's behalf, which was apparently no longer required. With a shake of Cormack's hand and a hug for Milkeila, Bransen entered the audience hall, his wife and Callen close behind.

"I had thought to be speaking for Cormack," he said as he walked to the center of the carpet. He faced a long table, behind which sat Father Artolivan and Father Premujon, Dame Gwydre, several other monks Bransen did not know, and, surprisingly, Jameston Sequin and Dawson McKeege. He couldn't help but feel as if he were standing before some kind of inquisition, though he took faith in the friends seated at that table.

"It was not necessary," Father Artolivan replied. "Cormack's character was well presented and represented."

"We have heard news of you, young man," Artolivan continued before Bransen could ask why he had been summoned if not for Cormack. "Information regarding the Highwayman."

"It is good to be famous." Bransen's sarcasm didn't brighten the grim faces staring back at him, which didn't bother him so much concerning Artolivan, but Dame Gwydre seemed equally uneasy.

"You are hunted, friend," Artolivan said, "accused of a crime against the throne of Honce."

"I did not know that Honce had a throne," Bransen replied, all glibness gone from his voice. "Just a bunch of petty lords with petty concerns and not a care at all of who they destroy to see their desires fulfilled."

Father Artolivan smiled and glanced at Dame Gwydre.

"A notable exception to the rule," Bransen quickly added, bowing deferentially to the Lady of Vanguard.

Dame Gwydre waved it off and seemed hardly to care, but Father Artolivan cleared his throat, bringing the conversation back on topic. "You are accused of a serious crime, Highwayman."

"That I robbed that idiot Yeslnik in Delaval City?" Bransen replied. "Of that I admit my guilt. I robbed him as well in Pryd right after I rescued him from certain death at the hands of marauding powries. I have already admitted my past deeds, though in my heart I fear that my biggest error was in saving Yeslnik from the dwarves." He bowed as he finished, and when he came up, he saw the principles at the table all exchanging somber and concerned looks. Bransen looked back to Cadayle and Callen, and then all three of them shared confused shrugs.

"Dame Gwydre's Writ of Passage was offered with knowledge of those thefts," Bransen said somewhat more defensively than he had intended.

"Laird Delaval—King Delaval—was murdered in the same tower where you robbed his nephew," Father Artolivan said.

"At the same time?"

"No. Recently," said Artolivan.

"While you were in Vanguard," Dame Gwydre added.

Bransen held up his hands, not quite understanding. "I am sorry?" he asked as much as stated.

"King Yeslnik—" Father Artolivan started, but Bransen interrupted with a cry.

"King?" he blurted.

"He proclaims himself King of Honce as the rightful heir of Delaval, who similarly demanded the title," Artolivan explained.

Bransen snorted with obvious derision.

"He believes you complicit in the death of his uncle, King Delaval," Artolivan explained.

"My arms are not that long," Bransen quipped, but he saw Gwydre, grim-faced, shaking her head at him. "I did not know the man. Why would I want to kill him? And if I haven't killed the loathsome Yeslnik, then why would I go out of my way to kill his uncle?"

"Your contempt for the new King of Honce is noted," Artolivan said dryly. "As is your proclamation of innocence."

"I have been in Vanguard throughout the winter," Bransen replied, growing more animated with every word. "With him." He pointed to Dawson. "And with Brother Jond, and Cormack after him. How could I have been involved in a murder in Delaval City?"

Father Artolivan held up his hands to calm the man. "We are not your judge and jury. We know that you could not have been involved in this tragedy. But King Yeslnik will not be so easily swayed, I fear, given all that I have heard of him."

"What does that mean?"

"It means that my Writ of Passage to you may not be enough," Dame Gwydre answered. "It means that you and Cadayle and Callen should remain here or perhaps even sail back to Vanguard with me when I go."

Bransen stared at her hard, angrily, suspiciously.

"I honor the Writ of Passage," Father Artolivan was quick to say, "and will not detain you in any manner. You and your family are welcome at Chapel Abelle."

Bransen never blinked and never stopped staring at Gwydre.

"Yeslnik claims that Bransen, the Highwayman, killed Delaval," Gwydre said.

"We know otherwise," said Bransen.

"We do," Gwydre agreed. "But he does not. Nor do the lairds who do his bidding. It was Master Reandu of Chapel Pryd who delivered the news, only right before we arrived here."

Bransen's face brightened at the name.

"You know him?" Gwydre asked.

"Quite well, I am told," said Artolivan. "And if it means anything to you, young man, I think that Master Reandu doubted in his heart the claims against you."

At that moment the words meant nothing, for suddenly the weight of it all came clear to Bransen. He felt as if the walls were pressing in on him. He could hardly remember to draw breath. He had no response to this surprising news or to the involvement of Reandu, his old . . . what? Friend? Mentor?

"We will work to clear your reputation," Dame Gwydre assured him.

"If Yeslnik is King of Honce, then your work will be in vain. Know that he will always hate the Highwayman," Bransen finally replied. "As much because of his own failings as a husband and a man as because of the robberies."

Behind him, Cadayle gave a little yelp of surprise.

"His wife was rather taken by a man who would fight against enemies instead of sniveling inside the coach," Bransen explained to her and turned back to the table. "If Yeslnik is your king, then, as much as I would have thought it impossible, my estimation of the nobility and leadership of the Honce Holdings has sunk even lower. He is a fool and a fop, a vain and preposterous coward, and—"

"Enough, Bransen," said Artolivan. "We will work to clear your name as Dame Gwydre insisted. We are interested in justice."

"That is not my experience with laird or brother."

"Enough," Artolivan bade him. "We ask that you remain here for your own sake and the sake of your family until we can clear away all this confusion."

"Or we will be sailed to Behr," Bransen said, staring again directly at Gwydre, then sliding his gaze to take in Dawson McKeege, who was nodding his agreement.

"Give us time," Gwydre said. After a stone-faced moment, Bransen nodded.

"And now you will excuse us," Father Artolivan said. "For we have other matters to discuss."

Before Bransen and the two women turned to go Dame Gwydre interjected, "No, I wish Bransen to sit with me as we discuss the situation."

Father Artolivan looked at her with surprise and something less than enthusiasm.

"He has earned it," Gwydre insisted. She turned to Bransen and motioned to an empty chair at the end of the table. "He may be quite important as this goes forward. The Highwayman is not unknown in Honce and not unloved by many of the people we seek to serve."

After a moment Artolivan sighed. "Would the two of you please excuse us then?" he said, indicated Cadayle and Callen. Cadayle moved up and kissed Bransen on the cheek and squeezed his hand, then took her leave with her mother.

For all his bravado, Bransen felt quite unsure of himself as he moved to take the seat between Jameston and Gwydre. He sat quietly as the group began discussing Yeslnik's new edict regarding disposition of prisoners. He wasn't surprised by the foppish, self-proclaimed king's lack of simple morality, of course.

"And you will react how?" Dame Gwydre asked after Artolivan had explained every detail regarding Yeslnik's demands for the prisoners entrusted to the Order of Abelle and his further demand that the church declare allegiance to him in his struggles with Ethelbert.

"We must refuse this man who calls himself King of Honce," Father Artolivan declared. All the monks around him nodded and whispered their agreement.

Bransen arched his eyebrows in pleasant surprise.

"And I will support you, of course," said Dame Gwydre. "Let us hope that King Yeslnik will listen to reason on this matter."

"He won't," Bransen interrupted, surprised at himself for saying that aloud. Everyone turned to him, so he continued, "He is stubborn and vain beyond description."

"In that case we will be faced with more difficult decisions still," said Father Artolivan. He sighed and seemed very old and tired at that moment. "But we will forge our way through the obstacles as they are presented to us. For now King Yeslnik awaits our further word on his edict regarding the prisoners. He will not be pleased, but we must follow that which is right and just and in concert with the teachings of Blessed Abelle."

For some reason the decision and declaration of the father of the Order of Abelle unsettled Bransen even more than the unsurprising news of Yeslnik's continuing and escalating stupidity. He left the meeting much later on, his thoughts spinning, both for himself and his family and their place in the world and for the larger issues of Honce and this new king who could be nothing more than a catastrophe.

The couriers went from Chapel Abelle soon after the meeting had adjourned. While watching them depart, still surprised by the continuing actions of the church, Bransen heard a familiar voice call to him.

"How do you fare with the new order of the world?" asked Cormack.

Bransen turned and greeted him as he approached. "I am not surprised by the actions of Yeslnik, to be sure. I have encountered the man a couple of times in the last months. Neither meeting has left me impressed with his wit or his wisdom."

"I mean regarding Bransen," Cormack clarified. Bransen stared at him curiously.

"You expected to walk Honce a free man," said Cormack.

"And so I shall."

"By your stubbornness and your sword? Is there not the matter of your wife and her mother to consider?"

"Dame Gwydre—"

"Is powerless against Yeslnik at this time. Her Writ of Passage will not be honored for a man believed to be the killer of King Delaval. And, honestly, it would be foolhardy to not rescind the order. If you go and present that document, then she, too, will be complicit in the killing of King Delaval."

"I had nothing to do with that. I was beside you, was I not?"

"And you believe that matters?"

Bransen gave a helpless laugh. "No," he admitted.

"So what will you do?"

"I don't know. Dawson McKeege has pledged to sail me wherever I wish to go. Perhaps to Behr."

"Jacintha?"

Bransen furrowed his brow in puzzlement.

"The principle city of the desert kingdom," Cormack explained. "Just south of the city of Ethelbert dos Entel around the Belt-and-Buckle mountains, whose rocky spurs jut into the Mirianic as if god himself did not want the men of Honce and of Behr to mingle."

"Jacintha, then."

"It is a strange place with strange ways," Cormack warned.

"A fine choice you offer," Bransen replied.

"Father Artolivan will not expel you or your family, nor will he turn you over to Yeslnik's soldiers if they come."

"So you offer me imprisonment in a chapel of a faith I do not hold true or a journey to a strange and dangerous place," Bransen reasoned. "Shall I thank you for creating great contentment within my tumultuous soul?"

Cormack couldn't suppress a laugh at the deserved sarcasm. "Vanguard," he said a moment later, and again he drew a puzzled look from Bransen.

"It is a wondrous place," said Cormack. "Full of freedom and personal responsibility. It is the perfect location for one who wants no part of the politics and intrigue of Honce, or of Behr, I am told."

"Will Cormack be there?"

"And Milkeila. Dame Gwydre speaks of dividing up her vast holding into smaller duchies and has hinted that she will offer one to me."

"And you would like the Highwayman as a subject," Bransen said dryly.

"Or as a neighboring duke."

Bransen laughed all the more, and all the more helplessly. "I thought you just said . . ."

"I did, and I hold to it," Cormack replied. "I only mean that if you wished more for yourself and Cadayle, then you will find an ally in Dame Gwydre, do not doubt. She expressed deep gratitude to me when we spoke quietly about a possible appointment, though she counseled me to consider Father Artolivan's offer to return to the Order of Blessed Abelle."

"And will you?"

Cormack shrugged, and Bransen knew that the man was truly uncertain here, truly torn. "I would be a liar if I said that I was not intrigued. Great healing might be accomplished between the Order of Abelle and Milkeila's shaman brethren and between Vanguard and the Alpinadoran tribes. Father De Guilbe did great damage on Chapel Isle. Our battle with the many tribes of Mithranidoon Lake—"

"And De Guilbe's refusal to join in the common cause against Ancient Badden," Bransen interrupted, and Cormack nodded solemnly.

"Perhaps I can do some good," Cormack finished.

"As a monk or as a duke?"

"That is the question, is it not?"

"Why not as both?"

It was Cormack's turn to wear an expression of surprise, which shifted to one of intrigue. He paused for a few moments, then took a deep and steadying breath and looked back to Bransen. "But what for you?"

Again, the young warrior shrugged. "I wish at some point to travel to Behr—I must. But Honce is my home, and I do not count that lightly. And there is another matter . . ." He stopped just short of telling Cormack of Cadayle's pregnancy, deciding instead to remark, "Honce is Callen and Cadayle's home, as well, and they should be free to remain here and wait for my return—particularly Callen, who long ago grew weary of the road."

"You would trust Yeslnik to honor the Writ of Passage for them and not imprison them to use against you?"

"Of course I would not."

"And so we are back where we began."

"I will go to Pryd Town to test Dame Gwydre's Writ of Passage," Bransen decided then and there. "And if it is not to be honored, I will do what I need to clear my name and to demand the commute of any claims made against me. I served honorably under a bargain from a Honce Lair . ... Lady. I expect, when the truth is known that I could not have participated in the murder of King Delaval, that my covenant with Dame Gwydre will be respected."

"You will march south and demand all that?"

"I will journey south more quietly, and learn and adapt," said Bransen. "I am the Highwayman, have you not heard? And the Highwayman has many friends in Pryd Town."

"And many enemies?"

"That is what I intend to learn."

S he knew.

That truth permeated Bransen's thoughts as he navigated the corridors and courtyards of the sprawling complex of Chapel Abelle. He had tried to hide his decision from Cadayle for the time being—out of cowardice, he admitted to himself—but she had seen through him, and his tenuous and halting answers, stuttered even though he had the soul stone firmly tied against his forehead, had led Cadayle to more incisive and determined questioning.

By the time Bransen had managed an appropriate dodge

to the larger question of his intentions, Cadayle had already confirmed her suspicions.

She knew, Bransen believed, that he was planning to leave her once again despite his promises to her in Vanguard.

The look on her face as he had walked out of their room that morning, a combination of resoluteness and sadness, had nearly made him change his mind, had nearly turned him toward a different course—perhaps back to Vanguard with Cormack.

But now, as he walked the ways of the great chapel complex, as he heard the familiar dialect of the many men hard at work, Bransen understood that he must go at once to Pryd Town, to confront Reandu with the hard evidence, the letters of proof from many reliable affiants. He had to believe that somewhere, somehow, even in the holdings of Yeslnik, the truth would ultimately win out and he would be exonerated and that Gwydre's Writ of Passage for him and for his family would be honored.

If there was any justice in the world, this course would be the correct one to walk.

But Cadayle knew.

His inner tumult slowed his steps as he neared Father Artolivan's chambers, and he slowed further as he came to hear loud arguing from behind the solid oaken door. Growing up as the Stork, where so many people had thought him an idiot and had spoken about him and about important matters right before him, it didn't even occur to Bransen that he shouldn't eavesdrop.

Right before the door, the words became clear, as did the voices of fathers Artolivan, Premujon, and De Guilbe.

"You would have me kill them," Artolivan shouted, "these men who were given to Chapel Abelle and put under our care on condition that for them the war had ended?"

"We must choose between Yeslnik, who will win, and

Ethelbert, who hides in the south," De Guilbe argued. "The greater movement of the kingdom is beyond our control. Delaval won and gave his winnings to Yeslnik, and thus Yeslnik is the King of Honce."

"That simply?" asked Premujon.

"Yes! Unless you know of some great army stirring to oppose him."

"His victory over Laird Ethelbert seems assured, by last reports," Father Artolivan unhappily agreed, speaking lower so that Bransen had to move right up and put his ear to the door to understand.

"Then we are to recognize Yeslnik as King of Honce," said De Guilbe. "What other choice is before us?"

"Recognition with precondition," said Artolivan. "Perhaps. We can force King Yeslnik's hand on this and other matters, promise our fealty, but only to a goodly king."

De Guilbe snickered loudly. "You think yourself the king," he accused.

"Father De Guilbe!" Premujon scolded.

"If Yeslnik is the King of Honce, then the decisions are his to make," De Guilbe continued, undaunted. "We cannot say that we agree here and disagree, and therefore will not abide, there. Is he the King of Honce or is he not? And if he is, then we are bound to honor—"

"I will not murder unarmed prisoners!" Father Artolivan cried.

"Then you should not have involved our order in this secular business of war!" Father De Guilbe scolded.

"Father!" Premujon shouted again.

"It is true!" De Guilbe shouted right back at him. "We heal the wounded for both sides. That is a good thing, and all the chapels agreed. But then you agreed to turn our most holy and important monastery into a prison?"

"A prison that sent men to the aid of Vanguard!" Premujon reminded.

"That matters not at all! Father Artolivan took it upon himself to involve the order in matters where it did not belong. You cannot make such a stand and then decide at a later date that you don't like the outcome."

"We retained our neutrality," Father Artolivan argued, and De Guilbe snorted as if the notion was absurd.

"Until one side or the other gained the advantage," De Guilbe said. "For surely, had Ethelbert won the field, his demands upon you would be equally harsh and distasteful."

"I do not believe that, nor do I believe that Laird Delaval would be possessed of such . . . cruelty."

"Then you are a fool," said De Guilbe. "And you have softened to the point where your leadership is a danger to the Order of Abelle."

"Father!" Premujon shouted again, but De Guilbe shouted back at him to shut up.

"I demand a Council of Fathers," De Guilbe said.

"Denied," said Father Artolivan.

"You cannot deny it alone!"

"Denied," echoed Premujon. "Two to one, then. Find more fathers of similar humor to yours and make your request at a later date."

"And until then, know that I will not execute the men of Laird Ethelbert, taken under honor and sent here under promise of my protection," Father Artolivan assured him.

"And the men of Laird Delaval?"

"Are here as agreed. King Yeslnik will not have them turned free to serve his cause until the war with Laird Ethelbert is settled."

Father De Guilbe began to laugh, a chuckle that rang of little mirth in the ears of Bransen.

"Our order has gone soft," he said. "As with Cormack, who betrayed us."

"This was about Cormack all along," Premujon accused.

"It is about a church that forgets the harsh lessons of the wider world," De Guilbe replied, but calmly now—

and that seemed far more imposing to Bransen than his fiery rant of a few seconds before. "A church so steeped in false hope and idealism and tolerance that it ensures its own inevitable collapse."

"If I gave you a sword and the order from King Yeslnik, would you kill the prisoners with your own hand, Father De Guilbe?" Father Artolivan asked.

"Yes," the man replied without the slightest hesitation.

Bransen did well to hide his own gasp as both Artolivan and Premujon issued theirs.

"Because I look beyond the lives of a few and the immediacy of our current situation," De Guilbe clarified. "War is cruel, and need be, to end it swiftly and to make the mere thought of it cause men to piss in their breeches."

"You sound like a Samhaist," said Premujon, his voice subdued now as if De Guilbe's stark admission had simply broken his will to argue.

"You are dangerously wrong in your decisions, Father Artolivan," said De Guilbe.

"If you believe that, then find enough support among the brethren to force your council," Father Artolivan wearily replied. "Truly you tire me. I sent a man of spirit and hopefulness to Alpinador those years ago, a mission that I thought De Guilbe might accomplish in bridging the differences between our ways and those of our northern brothers. This man who returns to me these years later hardly resembles the one I knew."

"Because I am wiser."

"Because you are hardened, and stubborn."

De Guilbe snorted, and Bransen heard heavy footfalls coming his way. He managed to jump back a couple of steps and tried to appear as if he was just arriving when the door was flung open and the large monk rushed out. With only a cursory glance at Bransen and a dismissive shake of his head, De Guilbe stormed away.

"Greetings, Bransen Garibond," Father Artolivan said—to Bransen's back, since the Highwayman had turned to watch the angry De Guilbe's departure. "To what do I owe the pleasure of your visit so early in the day?"

Bransen turned about. "Your pardon, Father," he said with a bow. "I have made a decision and wished to inform you first of all."

"A decision? I did not know that you were faced with a question."

"Concerning my destination and my place in the world."

The monk nodded and waved for Bransen to enter the room.

"I will take my leave of Chapel Abelle this day," Bransen explained. "With Dame Gwydre's Writ of Passage in hand, I will go to clear the name of the Highwayman."

"King Yeslnik will kill you," Father Premujon remarked, but Bransen merely shrugged.

"Yeslnik seems not to be a reasonable man," Father Artolivan added.

"I know him well," Bransen assured them both. "And I do not disagree regarding his temperament. But there are others I know to be reasonable and just."

"You will build support for your cause?"

"That is my hope," said Bransen. "And I hope that Father Artolivan will lend that support." To the side, Father Premujon shifted uncomfortably, as did Brother Pinower, who had walked into the room behind Bransen.

"I will speak truthfully to that which I know, of course," Artolivan said. "What more would you have from me?"

"A second Writ of Passage."

Artolivan looked at him incredulously, while Premujon and Pinower said no in unison.

"You cannot ask this of Chapel Abelle," Premujon elaborated against Bransen's obvious disappointment. "We are in difficult straits with King Yeslnik as it is."

"And with some in your own ranks?" Bransen asked, and Premujon didn't disagree.

"You appreciate the difficulty I have in openly defying King Yeslnik at this time, on this issue?" Father Artolivan asked.

"I do."

"I cannot offer you any imprimatur that would serve you against the king's men," Father Artolivan said. "But perhaps I can fashion some writ to add my voice to Dame Gwydre's, some imprimatur to ensure those favorable to your cause that I witnessed Dame Gwydre's testimony on your behalf and found it credible." He looked around as he finished and both Pinower, who had moved up to stand beside him, and Premujon nodded their agreement, albeit with some obvious reservations.

"That would be most helpful," said Bransen.

"Your wife and her mother are welcome to remain here at Chapel Abelle," Artolivan added. "I trust you will not be bringing them along on your undoubtedly perilous journey."

Bransen sighed deeply; the thought of being away from Cadayle again after only a few short months together gnawed at him. Thoughts of traveling to Behr flickered through his mind once more, along with a nagging feeling that he should sail north again with Gwydre and Dawson and make his home in Vanguard. It had been a fine winter, the most peaceful and enjoyable Bransen had ever known. Beside Gwydre and Dawson and Cormack and Jond and even Premujon, Bransen and his family had felt as if they were truly among friends.

"Bransen?" he heard Artolivan remark, and realized that he had fallen deep within himself and had missed a question or two. He shook the doubts away and looked at the leader of the Order of Abelle.

"Your wife?" Artolivan asked.

"I have to go," Bransen said, as much to himself as to the others. "If Yeslnik is to be King of Honce, then I have to clear my name and regain the freedom I earned from Dame Gwydre."

"King Yeslnik is a stubborn one," Father Artolivan warned. "He will not be easily swayed."

Bransen, knowing Yeslnik better than any in the room, nodded, but he smiled as he did, and in a flash drew out his magnificent sword. "For the third time, I will put him at the tip of my sword," he promised, and he didn't fight that mischievous, almost reckless, smile from widening on his face as he went into a sudden slash and thrust move, ending up in a powerful pose, sword forward. "I suspect that while his eyes are seeing the sharpened edge, his heart will see the truth of Bransen."

Brother Pinower looked horrified, and Father Premujon cleared his throat uncomfortably, but Father Artolivan let forth a great squeal of laughter and clapped his hands. "Brilliant!" he congratulated. "I only hope that Honce will forgive you for stopping short your deadly blade."

"Father!" Pinower and Premujon said together, but Artolivan waved them away and walked up to Bransen, patting the young man on the shoulder.

"I would like for you to stay, Highwayman," he said. "Though I know you cannot. Return to me, if you find the time."

"To retrieve my family, of course."

"And to sit with me! I have only heard small stretches of the history of Bransen Garibond and this hero known as the Highwayman." He paused and looked at Bransen as if seeking permission, before finishing, "And of the Stork. I would like to hear the whole story."

"Ask Cadayle," Bransen replied. "She can tell it as well as I, since she was there for most of my steps, even the awkward ones of the Stork, that as often as not left me face down in the mud."

"Sometimes in the mud of Chapel Pryd, with buckets in hand," said Artolivan, and Bransen looked at him, surprised that he knew so much.

"Small stretches of your history," Artolivan assured him. "And there is one more thing." He reached up and touched the front of Bransen's black bandanna, tapping right atop the soul stone hidden beneath it and secured to his forehead.

Artolivan turned to Pinower and pointed to the desk, and then pointed more emphatically when the younger monk hesitated.

"I have had a long discussion with Brother Cormack," Artolivan said, and it took a moment before Bransen realized that Artolivan had added the church title to his friend's name.

Pinower walked over with a small, decorated box. With obvious reverence, he handed it to Artolivan, who held it before Bransen as he slowly opened its hinged lid.

Bransen's eyes widened as he stared at the contents: a small star-shaped brooch, no more than a fingertip across at its widest point, centered with a soul stone and containing in its five tips other stones of various colors. He recognized the ruby at its top point, flanked left and right by malachite and a particular type of agate known as cat's eye. The striated stone set in the bottom left point he thought to be serpentine, and the other he knew as quartz, but a cloudy variety whose properties Bransen did not know.

"This was made for Laird Delaval's grandfather, ironically," Artolivan explained, "in the early days of the Order of Abelle. To Father Abelle's surprise, the laird refused it, despite its obvious powers, since we were not as accepted back in those days, when the Samhaists dominated Honce." He lifted the brooch and slowly turned it so that Bransen could better see its wondrous craftsmanship, including small hooks and pins on the backing. "It is fashioned of silverel, the same metal as your unusual sword, and edged in graphite, the stone of lightning."

"What does it do?"

"Separately, the gems are each possessed of their own blessing."

Bransen, who knew of the gemstones, of course, nodded. "They are all enchanted?"

"It is a fine item," Artolivan confirmed. "It was crafted to be sewn to the chest, above the heart, but perhaps on your forehead . . ."

Bransen reached up and touched his bandanna. "To the cloth?"

"To the skin itself," said Artolivan, and Bransen's eyes widened in surprise and a bit of trepidation. He calmed quickly as he remembered the fight on the road with Dame Gwydre's raiders, when his bandanna and stone had been knocked away and he had been helpless against the troll enemies.

"I have spoken about you at length with Brother Jond, as well," Father Artolivan explained.

"Women in Behr wear gemstones in such a manner," added Brother Pinower. "They call it tikka, and it is considered quite beautiful."

"And those are simple and mundane jewels," said Artolivan. "Magically speaking, I mean. You will find these stones useful in other ways."

He handed the brooch to Bransen, who slowly lifted it to his forehead with one hand, slipping free the other soul stone as he slid the new one in place. He closed his eyes and fell within the flux of energy offered by the gems.

His *ki-chi-kree,* his line of life energy, remained straight and strong, as with the other soul stone. And other possibilities flitted through his thoughts, a jumble at first, but gradually sorting themselves out.

Possibilities.

"You would give this to me?" he asked, opening his eyes to stare hard at Father Artolivan.

"An extraordinary gift for an extraordinary man," Artolivan replied. "It does my old heart good to see that brooch, so long in the coffer, upon your forehead."

"And it looks quite good," Father Premujon added with a smile.

Bransen left Artolivan's quarters with his bandanna in his hand, and he walked with the sure gait of the Highwayman, not the awkward stumble of the Stork.

You hate me," Bransen said solemnly after a long and uncomfortable pause.

Cadayle looked up at him; across the room, Callen laughed.

"For a hero, you're sure for saying some stupid things," the older woman remarked. "She's no more for hating you than you are for her, and you should be able to see that clear enough in her eyes by now."

"Of course I don't," Cadayle added, and she hugged Bransen close. "But I am afraid, and I'll miss you dearly, as I did in Vanguard those weeks you were gone from me."

Bransen hugged her back even more tightly. "I know. But I have to do this. My name is clear, as Dame Gwydre agreed."

"We'd be free enough in Vanguard," said Cadayle.

"I've spent most of my life trying to figure out how and where I belong," Bransen replied. "Honce is our home— Pryd is our home. Even if we choose not to live there, we should be able to return at our leisure."

"When we left, you left a dead laird behind," Cadayle reminded him.

"But even that is forgiven by Gwydre."

"By Bannagran?"

"I don't know, but I will find out." He paused, his next admission coming hard. "I want Brother Reandu—Master Reandu, I mean—to know the truth of it, to know that I am no criminal and that his order, at the very highest level, has deigned to honor and accept me."

"Because of your life at Chapel Pryd. Because of the way Reandu and the others treated you."

Bransen couldn't deny the obvious truth of Cadayle's observations, so he just slid back from her a bit and shrugged helplessly.

"If Bannagran or Yeslnik catches and kills you, I'll never forgive you," Cadayle said, ending with a spreading grin.

"Then you don't hate me?"

Callen let out a great burst of laughter.

"I know you have to do this. I only wish I could go with you," said Cadayle.

"Not now."

"I know."

"Here, you hero," said Callen and she took a couple of steps toward Bransen and tossed him his bandanna, which she had been sewing. He caught it and examined it, then slipped the now thin eye-mask on.

"The dashing Highwayman," said Callen.

"They know who I am," Bransen replied. "And now I need not hold a gemstone in place. There is no point to the disguise."

"Yes there is," said Callen.

"The common folk of Pryd know the Highwayman more than they know Bransen Garibond," Cadayle agreed. "Your reputation is your advantage against Bannagran."

Bransen's step was sure-footed but much less animated as he walked out of Chapel Abelle that afternoon. He was confident that his course was correct, and that he had justice on his side, but the thought of leaving

Cadayle for an extended period yet again—even though
he expected to be gone from Chapel Abelle for no more
than a couple of weeks—wounded him. He glanced back
to see Dame Gwydre and Dawson McKeege watching
him from the wall, Gwydre nodding her approval.

Cadayle was not there, though, and Bransen was glad
of it, for had his beautiful wife been watching, he would
have turned and rushed back to her.

He sighed and laughed at himself for his own weakness,
then adjusted his hat, brim low to cover the gem-studded
star set in his forehead, and hoisted his pack higher on his
shoulder and moved on his way. He stayed mostly to the
side of the road, moving along the brush and trees, enjoying the solitude and the sounds of a world awakening in
the full bloom of spring.

He let his guard down—who wouldn't in so idyllic and
peaceful a setting?—and so he was caught by surprise
when a voice called out, "You've got a longer road before
you if every step forward is taken with half a step back-
wards!"

Startled, Bransen jumped back, his hand going reflexively to the hilt of the sword set on his hip. He relaxed
when the speaker, Jameston Sequin, walked out of the
shadows.

Bransen glanced all around and back the way he had
come, back toward Chapel Abelle, which was long out of
sight by then.

"What are you doing out here?" he asked.

"Been a long time since I've walked the ways of Honce."

"Vanguard is part of Honce," Bransen said, but Jameston, like most Vanguardsmen, dismissed that notion with
a snort and a wave of his hand.

"Haven't been here in more years than you've been
alive," he continued. "Thought this'd be as good a time as
any to reacquaint myself."

"Heading where?" Bransen said suspiciously.

"You'd know that better than myself."

"I am going to Pryd Town."

"I am going to Pryd Town," Jameston echoed.

Bransen put his hands on his hips and stared at the man. "Dame Gwydre believes I need a bodyguard?"

"Doubt that, since she sent you against Badden."

"But she asked you to come with me on my journey."

Jameston shook his head. "Was my idea."

"One she thought wise."

"I'll give you that much. But I do want to walk the ways of Honce again, and I know more than a bit about staying out of sight and out of notice. I think you'll find that helpful."

"I am no novice."

"Could've fooled me with the way you were dancing down the path. And if I was one of Yeslnik's men, one with a bow, you'd be lying dead in the brush."

Bransen just stared at him hard.

"Oh, but quit pretending," said Jameston. "You know I'll be helpful, you know I won't slow you down, and you know you don't want to walk alone. You also know, but you're too proud to admit it, that you might learn from my long experiences. Sure, you know how to fight—you're as good as any I've ever seen, and I've seen many!—but you could learn a few things about when to fight and where to fight from, I'm thinking."

Bransen didn't reply, but his visage did soften.

"You know you don't want to go alone," Jameston said with a grin under that outrageously thick mustache of his.

Bransen couldn't resist that smile, and returned it.

"Good thing we've got a long road ahead of us," Jameston said, moving beside Bransen as he walked by. "Because you've got a lot to learn and I've got a lot to teach you."

Bransen didn't reply, other than to widen his smirk. He

had spent his life in learning, from the Book of Jhest his father had penned, from the brothers of Chapel Pryd, and, more recently, from Dame Gwydre. He wasn't about to let foolish pride get in the way now, not with the likes of Jameston Sequin offering him the lessons!

SIXTEEN

Moments of Private Clarity

Young Brother Pontitious huffed and puffed as he ran along the road to the west, his precious cargo, the edict from Father Artolivan, set in a scroll case and slung over one shoulder. Until that morning, he had been jogging along with three other brothers, but they, with their scroll cases, had turned down the southern road for other destinations.

Pontitious's pace was much greater that day, for he hoped to reach Palmaristown, his goal, before sunset. Suddenly he felt very vulnerable there alone on the road with so important a letter, and those feelings only increased when he heard the clip-clop of a horse and the rattle of coach wheels behind him. Pontitious veered off the side of the road, moving down into a gully behind some brush, where he crouched and looked back the way he had come.

He relaxed when he saw the horse, adorned in a bridle that showed the evergreen symbol of Chapel Abelle and his beloved order. He knew this horse, and recognized the small wagon it pulled. He scrambled back up to the road, waving for his brethren.

"Ho, Pontitious, Brother," hailed the driver, a man named Josaul, and he slowed the horse to a stop. "I'd hoped to find you on the road. You've made a fine pace!"

"Would that Father Artolivan had decided to afford me a coach all the way from Chapel Abelle," Pontitious said, moving to climb up beside Josaul. "My feet are sorely bruised."

He reached up, but froze in place when the coach's door flew open and Father De Guilbe leaned out, lifting his head over it and scowling fiercely at the young courier.

"Father," Pontitious stammered and fell back.

"I do not recall hearing an invitation for you to ride with us," De Guilbe said.

Josaul started to say something, but Pontitious spoke over him. "No, Father. I assumed that a coach from Chapel Abelle would afford a brother a seat."

"You deliver Father Artolivan's message to Laird Panlamaris?"

"That is my duty, yes, Father."

De Guilbe offered an unsettling grin in reply. "Do you know Laird Panlamaris, boy?"

"No, Father. But I met his son when Prince Milwellis passed through Chapel Abelle."

"And your impressions of the young man?"

Pontitious realized that his expression and body language were giving away his feelings for the brutish man, none of them positive. "I . . . I . . . I didn't know him well."

Father De Guilbe laughed at him, and he knew that he needn't say any more. The large and imposing father then motioned toward the bench seat beside Josaul. "Do join us," he said in a tone as unsettling as that wicked smile. "I wish to see the look on Laird Panlamaris's face when you deliver to him the notification of Father Artolivan's treason."

Brother Pontitious swallowed hard and never stopped

staring at Father De Guilbe as he made his way onto the
seat beside Josaul. Behind them, the door closed, and
Josaul urged his horse back into motion.

Pontitious looked at him with concern, but he just
shrugged and shook his head helplessly.

They made the great port city by mid-afternoon, and,
with Father De Guilbe guiding Josaul, for the father was
obviously quite familiar with Palmaristown, the Chapel
Abelle coach soon rambled right up to the coach house of
Panlamaris Keep.

Ordering Josaul to stay with the coach, De Guilbe es-
corted Pontitious into the castle, and, again, this time as a
diplomat and not a navigator, had them at their destination in short order, standing before the throne of old
Laird Panlamaris.

"De Guilbe, young fool, is that really you?" greeted
Panlamaris, a grizzled old man, still thick and strong and
carrying the scars of a thousand fights.

"Not so young anymore, laird," De Guilbe replied.

"Aren't you supposed to be in Alpinador, converting
barbarians to the light and the stones?"

De Guilbe waved the notion away. "Too stubborn and
stupid a lot for that," he replied jovially, for these two
were obviously old friends (which of course made Pontitious even more nervous). "I could not convince them, so
I killed a bunch instead."

Laird Panlamaris laughed heartily, as did the many
attendants in the room, as did Father De Guilbe. Only
Pontitious, so obviously and painfully nervous, did not
join in.

"Your order is better for it," Laird Panlamaris said.
"I've met a few Alpinadorans in my sailing days. Not one
worthy of civility. Fierce warriors, though, huh? So I
count those among my finest kills!"

Another round of laughter made Pontitious want to
crawl into a crack in the floor. Never in his young life, not

even on his first day at Chapel Abelle, had he felt so out of place.

"So what brings young De Guilbe to my humble city?"

"Not so young, though I wish I were, and there is little humble about the grandeur that is Palmaristown. I do believe that your fine city has grown as powerful as I have grown old."

"A flagon of mead for that man!" Laird Panlamaris called to an attendant, who scurried from the room. "And, aye, we have prospered under the fine friendship of King Delaval, may the old ones see fit to seat him at their table."

"Aye!" Father De Guilbe agreed, while Brother Pontitious winced at the reference to Samhaist, and not Abellican, tradition.

"And you must know, De Guilbe, that everyone in the world seems young to me," Laird Panlamaris added with a laugh.

"Father Artolivan?" De Guilbe said slyly.

Laird Panlamaris snorted and waved his hand dismissively. "No, perhaps not that one. The gods don't want him so they make us keep him."

Brother Pontitious's eyes widened at that, and he looked to Father De Guilbe for some guidance but found instead the man smugly smiling at him. Brother Pontitious knew at that moment, beyond all doubt, that Father De Guilbe had injected Father Artolivan's name into the conversation to elicit exactly that response.

"Your pardon, brothers," Laird Panlamaris said with obvious insincerity. "I do not suffer that one well."

"Your son would agree," said De Guilbe, and Panlamaris nodded.

"The rebuff of Milwellis will be remembered the next time Father Artolivan calls upon Palmaristown's fleet for transport or supply or defense," Laird Panlamaris promised.

Smiling all the wider, Father De Guilbe reached around Brother Pontitious and removed the slung scroll case. "I expect none of those to happen anytime soon," he explained, handing it to Panlamaris.

An attendant rushed up and took the case, popping off one end and rolling wide the scroll. He read it quickly, bending low and reciting its contents into the ear of Laird Panlamaris.

The man sat stone-faced. Another attendant came in with Father De Guilbe's flagon of mead, and the monk took his first swallow just as the reader finished, stood straight, and stepped back.

"You would drink with me after delivering this?" Panlamaris said, his voice calm but in a manner that promised violence. Brother Pontitious took a step away from the throne.

"I?" De Guilbe replied. "Not I. Brother Pontitious here delivered the note. Would that it had never been penned, but Father Artolivan would not heed my advice."

"You know what it says?" asked Panlamaris, his tone growing stronger and darker.

De Guilbe nodded.

Panlamaris fixed a withering gaze on poor Pontitious. Not a large man to begin with, the young brother seemed to melt into the floor.

"He is a courier and nothing more," De Guilbe explained.

"Then get out of my chambers!" Laird Panlamaris yelled. Pontitious began stammering and stuttering and looked to De Guilbe for guidance.

"Get out," De Guilbe quietly advised.

Bowing with every backward step, mouthing words though no sound came forth, Brother Pontitious executed a graceless departure.

"Has Artolivan gone mad, then?" Panlamaris asked when the young brother was gone at last.

De Guilbe shrugged and sighed.

"Yeslnik wins—has won!" Panlamaris insisted. "Ethelbert is pushed to the sea and will not break out. More of Honce's holdings pledge fealty to Yeslnik daily."

De Guilbe nodded.

"This . . ." Panlamaris fumed and reached over and tore the scroll from his attendant's grasp. "This is treason."

It occurred to De Guilbe that he could diffuse the situation at that point by mentioning the extraordinary nature of Yeslnik's request regarding the disposition of the prisoners and the awkward situation it presented for the church. But the wounds regarding Cormack were too raw for the man who for the first time in his life had miserably failed his mission—a failure he still believed was due to Brother Cormack's treachery.

"It is far worse than you think," he heard himself saying. "They harbor not only the prisoners from Ethelbert's army, they hold in chains not only the men loyal to King Yeslnik, but there is another in their chapel who is much sought after."

Panlamaris, fist clenched up beside his strong, bearded jaw, leaned forward in his seat, eyes locked on De Guilbe.

"They harbor the Highwayman," De Guilbe announced.

Panlamaris's eyes popped open wide, and he mouthed, "He murdered King Delaval."

"Dame Gwydre has provided him with a Writ of Passage, forgiving all crimes."

"She forgives the murder of the king?" Panlamaris roared, and De Guilbe saw no reason to clear up that little matter and merely shrugged.

"How many brothers are at Chapel Abelle?" the Laird of Palmaristown demanded.

"Less than three hundred."

"How many prisoners of each side?"

"I know not the exact count. A couple of hundred of Yeslnik's men, perhaps twice that of Ethelbert's."

"Would that my son were returned from the Mirianic coast," Panlamaris muttered. "He has many of my finest commanders and warriors with him."

De Guilbe looked at the man curiously, for only then did it occur to him that his words might be escalating this incident above the level of parlay and disagreement. "What do you mean?" he asked as Panlamaris rose quickly and forcefully from his throne.

"Ah well, then," the man said. "It wouldn't do for Milwellis to have all the fun, would it?"

"What will you do?" De Guilbe asked, but Panlamaris wasn't listening to him.

"Since Yeslnik's decree I've got more men free of duties, what with fewer prisoners to watch," Panlamaris said, nodding his head as he worked through the details. "Couple hundred monks, a few hundred others . . ."

"Dame Gwydre is there with four ships of men."

"Skinners and drunkards, no doubt. She won't follow the course of Artolivan. She's nobody's fool, from all I've heard. She'll get on her boat and go home. This isn't her fight."

That last word resonated in De Guilbe's thoughts, at first uncomfortably. As he considered the wheels that seemed to be turning here, however, the fiery monk grew more and more at ease, coming not to regret at all his decision to tell Panlamaris of the Highwayman.

Good enough for Father Artolivan, he thought but did not say.

You've got to know what they see," Jameston explained. "If you were up on that rock, where would you be looking? What movements would catch your eye?"

Bransen squinted in concentration as he followed Jameston's pointing hand.

"Or over there by the stream in that stand of oaks?" the scout asked.

"There are a million places to hide, and surely there is no path invisible to all of them," Bransen replied.

"Am I telling you anything different than those who taught you to fight?" Jameston retorted, his expression finally showing that he was growing weary of Bransen's constant arguing. "Is there any perfect defense? Or a swing that can't be parried?"

"Measure your enemy," Bransen admitted. He laughed at himself then and waved his arm wide. "So where would enemies most likely hide in wait? What vantage points are most likely and how to avoid them?"

"You couldn't have admitted that an hour ago and saved me my talking?"

Bransen started to reply but stopped short and laughed instead.

"Pretty wife you left behind," said Jameston.

"It's been a long road," Bransen admitted.

"We just left!"

"Not from Chapel Abelle," Bransen started to explain, but he realized that Jameston had been playing with him with that last comment. "For so many years my life moved in a slow and straight line," he explained, as much to himself as to his companion. "Everything around me was solid as stone even when I wasn't."

"When you were this Stork fellow, you mean?"

Bransen nodded. "Even as I began to find those moments of escape from the Stork, there were so many constants. It was as if the world was there, one place known to me, and I could play with it as it amused me. But now there is so much tumult, so many things changing."

Jameston shook his head. "Now you've got others depending on you," he said with a knowing grin. "That's the only real difference."

Bransen stepped back as if he had been slapped and let the scout's words sink in.

"I've seen it happen a thousand times," Jameston said. "You've got your wife, now with child, and her mother all needing you."

Bransen sighed as he considered the truth of the statement.

"So you're more careful with every step and smiling less because you've got something to lose. For the first time in your life, you've got a lot to lose."

"Thank you for pointing that out," Bransen sarcastically replied.

"And you're making the biggest mistake of all," said Jameston, slipping past the sarcasm. Bransen went silent. "You've got more to lose because all the world—all your world—is better, but you're smiling less. You're letting those bad maybes bury the good that is."

"What?"

"Lighten your step!" Jameston scolded. "I spent many hours with Callen on the boat. She told me of a masked man who challenged the Laird of Pryd and defeated him. She told me of a masked man who leaped from a Samhaist bonfire to slay a powerful priest. Of a masked man who saved Yeslnik, then robbed him and stole his powdered wife's heart at the same time. Oh, and then robbed him again in his own castle for no better reason than to witness the foolish expression on his face."

"It does seem as if everyone is prying into my past."

"Everyone but yourself," said Jameston.

"What does that mean?"

"It means you're forgetting to remember where you came from and how far you've walked," the scout replied. "It means you're losing your joy in your worry. You see powries raiding a coach and take them on, then take on the men in the coach when you're done with the dwarves. You see a high castle wall and decide to climb it

for treasures you don't even want. Now there's a man I
want to walk beside."

"I'm right here."

"No. Wish that you were." Jameston finished and
walked down the path, leaving Bransen to ponder his
words.

They were apart for nearly half an hour, Jameston continuing along the road south, when finally a voice came
out of the trees to Jameston's right not so far away.

"If I was one of Yeslnik's bowmen, you'd be lying dead
in the brush."

Jameston froze at the sound of his own words coming
back at him. He slowly turned to regard Bransen, sitting
easily on a branch, his legs dangling, his mask down over
his eyes low enough so that the star-shaped brooch
showed clearly on his forehead.

"And how did you know to be there instead of up on
that rock?" Jameston asked.

"Because I know that you know what your enemies are
likely to see and from where they're likely to be watching." He pointed across the way to a thicket up on a bluff
on the other side of the stream. "They can't see you from
there. You were careful to make sure of that."

"Good to know that you listen to me, boy," said
Jameston.

More than you realize, Bransen, who was smiling
widely inside and out, thought but did not say.

Father Malskinner and Brother Honig of the Chapel of
Precious Memories entered the keep of Laird Panlamaris somewhat tentatively, expecting an angry berating
from the volatile man. Brother Pontitious had stopped by
the chapel of Palmaristown before his return to Chapel
Abelle to inform the monks of the stern and defiant message he had just delivered on behalf of Father Artolivan.

"Ah, good," Laird Panlamaris greeted warmly. "I always count on Father Malskinner to be on time."

His apparent good humor had the three monks visibly relaxing.

"I trust that your son is well?" Father Malskinner said.

"Since your church has taken its stand he had better stay away from Ethelbert's swords," came the rather sharp reply.

"The brothers would not refuse to care for any man's wounds," Father Malskinner replied.

"Yes, any man of either side. Under Father Artolivan, your order has perfected the art of—"

"Neutrality," Father Malskinner finished.

"Cowardice," corrected Laird Panlamaris. His arm sliced to his side. Immediately a dozen men dropped their halberds level with the monks and closed in on them in a nearly complete and inescapable circle. The two monks were herded together as sharp bronze spear tips prodded at them.

"Laird Panlamaris, I protest!" Father Malskinner said.

"I expect you would!"

"What is the meaning of this?" Malskinner demanded.

"Your Father Artolivan has declared opposition to King Yeslnik," Panlamaris calmly explained. "So it follows that he has declared his opposition to me, loyal to Yeslnik as I am. If your leader is going to declare war you would be wise to be better prepared than to walk into your enemy's castle."

Malskinner bristled impotently. "I demand that you release us!"

Panlamaris laughed at him and motioned to the guards. The prodding of halberds quickly had the two monks moving toward the room's side door.

"Take their gemstones," Panlamaris instructed.

"I demand you release us to the Chapel of Precious Memories!" Father Malskinner cried again.

"Where my guards are even now collecting the rest of your treasonous band," Panlamaris declared. "Your chapel is my chapel now, monk. I will have your inventory of gemstones and all the gold you have taken from the people of Palmaristown these last decades. Your welcome in my domain is at its end."

Father Malskinner started to protest but stopped walking as he did and got stuck hard in the arm by one of the long weapons. He yelped and clutched at the wound then reached reflexively for the small pouch of stones he had hanging on a sash at his left side.

The tip of a halberd pressing against his throat stopped that movement. A second guard produced a knife, stepped in to cut the pouch free.

"You and your flock will remain as my guests," Panlamaris said. "For as long as I decide. Perhaps you will know freedom again. Perhaps not, but I assure you that any actions you take against me, my people, or my king will be returned with . . . vigor."

Brother Fatuus had spent many of his days down at the dock section of Palmaristown and so knew the group of men who walked into the Chapel of Precious Memories. These were the dock masters, even the harbor master himself, tough and disciplined and loyal to Laird Panlamaris.

They were armed, though they came in with their weapons sheathed, but Fatuus felt the hairs on the back of his neck tingling. He alone among the brothers of the Chapel of Precious Memories had been to Chapel Abelle in recent months to warn them of the approach of the Highwayman, and so he appreciated the gravity of Father Artolivan's declaration perhaps most of all. He had seen the prisoners of both Ethelbert and Delaval and understood the insanity of King Yeslnik's demand that one group be freed and the other executed. These men and women worked side by side at Chapel Abelle; the lines of loyalty had been blurred to nothingness. And not one of them by Fatuus's estimation would prefer to be sent from Chapel Abelle if that meant going back to the front lines of the awful war. Even offering complete freedom and land, Dawson McKeege had been unable to convince more than a handful to sail with him to Vanguard!

Thus King Yeslnik's declaration had been a fool's writ. But for Father Artolivan to make such a bold response, as relayed by Brother Pontitious, was no small thing.

Brother Fatuus knew Laird Panlamaris well, too. He had watched the man swell with pride over the last few months as his son scored great victories across the land in the name of King Delaval and now King Yeslnik. Panlamaris remained unwavering in his support for King Yeslnik.

These armed loyalists were not in the Chapel of Precious Memories by accident or coincidence, nor was the sudden and unexplained absence of Father Malskinner and Brother Honig a coincidence.

"Tell the brothers to quietly slip into the streets," Fatuus whispered to a nearby pair of monks. "Move to the eastern gate with all haste and with as many gemstones as can be carried."

"Brother?" one of the monks asked incredulously.

"With all haste," said Fatuus. "And beware the men in the nave."

"Laird Panlamaris's men," one of them said, as if that fact should be reassuring.

"Shed your robes and go dressed as common folk," Fatuus added. "Go now."

When the pair hesitated, Fatuus shoved them hard, launching them on their way. Then he took a deep breath, recognizing his duty here. Accepting his lot as the highest-ranking brother within the chapel, Fatuus went to the nave to greet the visitors.

Less than half an hour later, Fatuus was dropped in chains before Laird Panlamaris's throne. Throughout the rest of the day, he watched as brother after brother, often severely beaten, was brought in and dropped unceremoniously on the floor.

The next day, Laird Panlamaris's dungeons swelled with monk prisoners, for only a handful of the fourscore brothers of the Chapel of Precious Memories had managed to escape the city.

SEVENTEEN

Saving Future Allies

Jameston Sequin was not a sound sleeper. Living most of his life alone in the wilds of Vanguard and southern Alpinador, the man had trained himself to react to the slightest of sounds or movements.

His eyes opened wide this dark night, and he was surprised indeed when he looked to the side to see that Bransen's bedroll was empty. Jameston silently congratulated the young man; escaping Jameston unnoticed was no small feat!

The scout lay very still for a few moments, allowing his sensibilities to fully adjust to the darkness. He rolled silently to his side, tucked and set his foot under him, then just as silently rose up tall and gathered his bow and quiver. He heard another sound then, a slight shuffle, and followed it to a small clearing.

Bransen stood in the middle of the lea, working his fine sword furiously through a series of practice cuts and blocks, a brilliant dance of perfect balance, which again reminded Jameston of just how good a fighter this young man truly was. Jameston rested the tip of his bow on the ground beside him and leaned on it, enjoying the show.

Bransen turned in one mock attack to the side and then spun all the way around, looking right at Jameston.

Jameston knew that he had been seen, and that confused him and unnerved him more than a little. For the night was not bright—only a few stars twinkled above—and he was fully engulfed in the darker shadows of a stand of thick spruce. Bransen couldn't have seen him from that distance, not viewing from the lighter open lea to the darker shadows.

But Bransen had seen him. Of that Jameston was certain.

The scout shook his head and continued to watch as Bransen finished with a flurry, moving from a series of defensive poses and blocks to a sudden and violent forward movement, sword thrusting. The young man ended by lifting that magnificent blade high to his right. To Jameston's astonishment the blade erupted in a sudden burst of flames!

"How the . . . ?" Jameston stuttered, compelled to walk forward. His surprise only heightened as Bransen, seeming as surprised as Jameston by the flaming sword, reached over with his free hand and felt the burning blade.

"They're not hot flames, then," Jameston reasoned as he walked up beside Bransen. He reached toward the fiery sword, snatching his hand back immediately. An all-too-real fire danced on the shining metal of that beautifully etched sword blade.

Bransen looked at him with puzzlement and shrugged.

"I never saw your sword do that before," said Jameston. "I never heard of any sword doing that before!"

"It's not the sword," Bransen replied. He pointed to the star set on his forehead, three of the gems—ruby, serpentine, and the agate—twinkling. "The ruby gave me the fire. The serpentine shielded me from its heat."

"Nice brooch."

"I grew up among gemstone users in Chapel Pryd," Bransen explained. "My connection to the stones and their powers is considerable." He paused and smiled widely. "The cat's eye let me see you as clearly as if you were standing in the midday sunlight." He looked at his sword as he spoke, and with a thought, winked out the fires, leaving the silverel blade unscarred.

"Full of surprises," Jameston remarked.

"Even to myself."

"And what else can you do with that toy you've got stuck on your head?"

Again Bransen shrugged. "I don't know—yet. But I will find out."

Jameston stared at him for a few moments then headed to the campsite. "Long walk tomorrow," he said without looking back. "And not many hours left before we start it."

Bransen nodded, though Jameston wasn't watching him. The young man didn't immediately follow. Instead he stood under the stars, staring at his sword, trying to sort out the unexpected benefits the brooch had shown him, and wondering what more might yet come.

They were off early in the morning, Jameston setting a swift pace. Signs along the road indicated a village not too far in the distance, and Jameston wanted to get there before they set their next camp. "Maybe we can try out that writ of yours," he said. "Or you can just wear the deerskin coat and pants and keep a hat on your head."

"No," said Bransen. "My clothing suits me. I am Bransen the Highwayman. I will not hide who I am. Dame Gwydre says I need not."

"The man who calls himself King of Honce says you do."

Bransen couldn't help but snort at the reference to Yeslnik. "I expect that I will have to visit with the man who calls himself King of Honce, then."

"To convince him?"

"To take his money. To make his wife swoon for no better reason than to see the anger on his face."

"Then he'll want you dead even more."

"Then I'll have to kill him and hope his successor is more reasonable."

Jameston stopped abruptly and stared at his companion, who was grinning and obviously enjoying the banter. "Took my advice, did you?"

In response, Bransen hopped and skipped lightly, landing in an exaggerated heroic pose. Jameston enjoyed the best laugh he had known in many years.

"I should thank you," Bransen said.

"Oh?"

"You don't have to do this."

"Dame Gwydre's a friend, and she's better served if you learn to keep your head on your shoulders."

Bransen, smiling all the more widely, shook his head through every word. "This isn't about Dame Gwydre. Not entirely, at least. So I thank you for teaching and most of all for reminding me."

"You do have a way of talking in riddles, boy."

"Reminding me to smile," Bransen said. "And to enjoy this, as trying as it may be."

"Well, what's the point otherwise?"

"There is none!" Bransen gave a little laugh and dropped a hand comfortably (surprising to both) on Jameston's shoulder. "And so I thank you, Jameston Sequin. Because of you I have remembered my past and what I have overcome to get to this point."

Jameston gave an exaggerated deep bow.

"I've been in love with Cadayle since I was a boy, you know," Bransen said.

"Good taste."

"But I never, ever dared believe she could love me in return."

"Because you were the broken boy, the Stork?"

Bransen stared at him and couldn't respond past the lump in his throat.

"You figured she loved you after you found a way around that infirmity?" Jameston asked. Bransen's tight expression turned into a perplexed look. "So now you doubt that she—"

"Never!" Bransen retorted. "I doubt nothing about Cadayle."

Jameston's smile relaxed him a bit. "And you shouldn't," the scout said. "Easy enough to see in her eyes. Cadayle loves Bransen, not the Highwayman. Cadayle's always loved Bransen, but she probably wasn't sure that he could ever love her. Could you?"

"What do you mean?"

"When you were the Stork, could you have loved Cadayle?"

"I did!"

"And you would have married her, even if you hadn't found the answer to your problem in that gemstone you wear on your head?"

"Jameston, of course! I have loved her . . ." Bransen paused then and assumed a pensive pose, truly asking himself that question for the very first time. If he was still an infirm and unsteady creature and Cadayle professed her love for him, would he have accepted her proposal?

"No," he answered at last. He looked at the scout, dumbfounded, and shook his head. "I would not have let her marry me."

"I know. And I know that she wouldn't have let your condition stop her from wanting to marry you. Don't ever let yourself think that you weren't good enough for her, boy. You're still the Stork, and he's still you, and Cadayle loves you."

The two men stared at each other for a bit longer before Jameston complained about needing sleep. He patted Bransen on the shoulder and walked back to their camp, leaving Bransen with the realization that the High-wayman wasn't the only one full of surprises this night.

Bransen was still considering the conversation of the previous night when they broke camp the next morning. His gratitude to Jameston Sequin had only grown as he had pondered the great gift the man had given him. Jameston had seen into his soul, it seemed, and had offered a salve to a wound that lay there, one that Bransen had never even openly acknowledged to himself.

There was a new spring in Bransen's step. He was feeling quite good about himself, about the possibilities of the gemstone brooch, and about the woman he had left behind in Chapel Pryd. That step did slow as the sun lowered in the west, however, as he and Jameston moved down the cobblestones into the heart of Eskald.

They heard the whispers coming at them from every direction as they entered the town.

"The Highwayman!"

"That's him!"

"The Highwayman has come!"

"You've made quite a name for yourself, boy," Jameston said.

"We're not far from Pryd Town," Bransen whispered back. "And, yes, something important happened there of which I was more than a small part."

"They appreciate it," Jameston observed.

Bransen didn't reply, but his smile showed that he was not so far above basking in the compliments. Jameston liked seeing that from the young and exotic man. Though he had been a loner, nearly a recluse in recent years, Jameston Sequin was no neophyte in recognizing and understanding the foibles of men and women. Bransen's acceptance of the complimentary remarks with such inner satisfaction reinforced the depth of Bransen's humanity in Jameston's mind. No man or woman, not laird nor dame nor general nor cobbler nor blacksmith, could work for the betterment of others without some measure of personal pride. Many people viewed that as a failing, as hubris, but Jameston knew it to be a simple and acceptable truth of human nature. Charity came from the heart, and accepting the compliments only reinforced the notion that such charity was correctly given.

If Bransen had not been smiling, if Bransen had not quietly acknowledged the whispers of the villagers around him, Jameston would have worried that Bransen's actions—the very actions which had inspired the awe-filled whispers—had not been taken for their benefit.

The pair made their way to the village's common room, where all eyes turned upon them as they took seats at a small, round table. The serving girl began to move their way, but the tavern keeper, an older and severe-looking woman with short hair curling tightly to her rather square forehead and a small but tight frame, held the serving girl back and went to see to the guests herself.

"Ye got some belly for walking in here open," she remarked.

"A fine day to you, too, good lady," said Jameston.

"It could be," she replied curtly.

"Would you prefer that we leave?" Bransen asked.

"Makes no nevermind to me. Go where ye want, but go looking over yer shoulder if ye got any sense between yer ears."

"I have a Writ of Passage from a Honce laird . . . err, lady," Bransen said, holding it up.

"One loyal to Ethelbert or Yeslnik?"

"I do not really know."

"Best be hoping it's Yeslnik and that he's listening," the tavern keeper said. "So are ye eating or drinking or both?"

"You would still serve us?" Jameston asked.

"Am I looking like a soldier to ye?"

"A little bit, yes."

That brought a chuckle from the woman. She told Jameston of a fine stew and a finer brew, and that seemed like just the thing for the road-weary duo.

When she went to get their meal, Jameston kept up the small talk, chattering to Bransen about the weather and other nonsense. So out of character was the man of few words that Bransen looked at him strangely.

"I thought that squirrel was going to jump down and bite your neck," Jameston said.

Bransen's jaw hung open at the gibberish.

"What with them two by the door staring at us like that," said Jameston. "More than a furry-tailed rat can take."

Bransen's mouth started to form the question "What?" when Jameston's words began to register. He began laughing, a bit too much, and used the hopeful distraction to get a look at the men by the door.

That quick glance confirmed Jameston's concern as valid: grim faces staring intently—too intently—at Bransen.

He turned back to Jameston and began talking about a squirrel chasing a skunk, the pair by the door enough in view out of the corner of his eye for Bransen to see them depart.

"Trouble," Jameston said seriously.

"Do we eat or do we leave?"

"If you leave, I'll just eat yours, too."

Their meal went off quietly. One of the too-curious men who had left returned to his previous seat by the door and did a poor job pretending that he wasn't staring at them.

"Try not to look too intimidating, and we'll have a bit of fun," Jameston remarked as they rose to leave.

The pair passed right near the spy as they exited the tavern. Jameston dipped the tip of his tricornered hat to the tavern keeper. Bransen tossed a mischievous wink at the seated man. Outside they found the street strangely empty, the long shadows stretching into a wider darkness as the sun fell below the western horizon.

"We should not remain here through the night," said Bransen.

"Thought you wanted to test that writ Gwydre gave you."

Bransen considered that for a moment but shook his head. "Not here in some village whose name I hardly know. Pryd Town is only a few days march south of here."

"Got more friends there?"

"And probably more enemies," Bransen admitted. He let his thoughts slip back to his last days in his hometown as he and Jameston set out, moving off the road as soon as they were out of sight of Eskald. He thought of Bannagran and Laird Prydae and the look on the warrior's face when his thrown axe had spun right over the ducking Bransen to dive deep into the chest of Prydae, mortally wounding the nobleman. How Bannagran had wanted to kill Bransen for that!

But the people wouldn't let him. They marched on the castle, demanding the release of the Highwayman.

Bransen nodded as he replayed it all, remembering that the final brokers in the standoff had been the monks of Chapel Pryd, mostly Reandu. Where would they stand now, and was Bransen acting the fool to begin to believe that they would do the right thing? Was he deluded, drunk with optimism, because of his unexpectedly positive experiences with Dame Gwydre and Chapel Pellinor and with the brothers at Chapel Abelle?

This was the church that had burned his beloved Garibond at the stake, he reminded himself.

"Best get your thoughts back to what's around you," Jameston whispered, drawing him from the inevitable memories inspired by being so near to Pryd. Bransen perked up immediately but gave no indication that he and Jameston were on to whomever might be watching them.

Bransen began using the techniques Jameston had shown him. If there were men in the area watching him, where would they be? And if they were watching the road and not the two men walking in the brush to the side of it, then where?

Bransen felt his blood pumping, felt the rush of adrenaline coursing his veins. The brooch on his head called to him then, a confusing jumble of possibilities.

And a pathway, he saw suddenly, an invitation. He grabbed Jameston's shoulder and motioned for him to stop, then closed his eyes and let his spirit fly free of his corporeal form, sliding through the brooch into the open air. Invisible, propelled by will without constraint, the disembodied spirit of Bransen Garibond darted all about the area impossibly fast.

He passed near one would-be ambusher, crouched in a tree, and marked the spot, thinking to move along. He sensed the man's thoughts completely and honestly; as expected, he was here hoping to catch or kill the Highwayman. The man was thinking of the bounty, of the glory, of how King Yeslnik and Bannagran would reward him when he brought in the Highwayman's head.

Not surprised, Bransen again started to move along to will his spirit back.

But he couldn't. Suddenly Bransen felt a compulsion he had not known before. Unable to mount a defense or argument against it, he found himself sliding into the ambusher's body.

A wall of outrage and denial came up against him, the man instinctively battling against this awful intrusion, this invasion into his very being. He flailed mentally and physically, and the movement cost him his balance and he tumbled from the branch, crashing through the tree to land in a shocking jolt against the hard ground.

The jarring landing expelled Bransen's spirit instantly. A wave of disorientation overwhelmed him and left him lost in the ether. He saw one spot of light, warm and inviting, and instinctively made for it, not realizing until he had passed through it that the brooch was showing him the way home.

Back in his own body, Bransen nearly swooned and fell over. He started to talk, but a hand slapped over his mouth and held him fast then pulled him to the ground. He realized where he was when he was finally able to open his eyes and see Jameston staring at him incredulously. Bransen could only shrug in response, since he wasn't even really sure what had just happened.

Commotion began to grow around them. The fallen man howled in pain; Bransen had felt more than one of the poor fellow's limbs breaking. Others nearby shifted in the branches and the brush, wondering if battle was upon them.

"They're here to kill us," Bransen silently mouthed.

"Well, yes," Jameston replied, rolling his eyes.

Jameston held up four fingers and pointed toward the noise. Bransen somehow understood and nodded, slipped his mask down over his eyes, and started that way. The scout pulled and strung his bow in one fluid motion, then moved off the other way, disappearing into the brush.

Circling wide of the fallen man, keeping him between them and the road, Bransen noted more movement. After his spiritual flight he knew exactly where to look. He made out one man creeping toward the writhing victim, another in the tree, as well as a third.

Another man appeared along the road the way Bransen had come. The man started to call out, "He just fell—"

The whizzing sound of an arrow slicing through the tall grass cut him short and stole his breath as he suddenly lurched over.

"I'm shot!" he managed to cry, tumbling from Bransen's view.

"Where?" called a man from across the road.

"What direction?" shouted another from the tree above the first to fall.

A second arrow cracked into the wood at that location, a perfect shot that pinned the speaker's hand to the branch.

"Down! Down!" the man in the next tree yelled. "To the northwest!" He leaped to the ground beside his fallen friend.

"And here!" Bransen added, springing into their midst. Swords rose against him, but he was already past their range, rushing between the men and turning as he went, cutting a downward stroke across the back of one man's legs. The second man cried out and thrust at him, but Bransen's powerful blade picked off that thrust with enough force to send the sword flying from the man's hands.

He wouldn't have been able to do anything with his weapon anyway, for Bransen, far too fast for him, sent his fine sword slashing across, but purposely high of the mark. The man yelped and instinctively ducked, and Bransen continued his sword's movement, turning around and stepping forward. He threw his left arm up high as he spun, still coming forward. His elbow hit the man hard in the nose, shattering it and snapping his head back. Bransen planted as the man recoiled and hit him with a vicious right cross, pommel in hand.

This time the man's head snapped to the side. He staggered only a step before falling face down with a groan.

Bransen paid him no heed, knowing the man to be out of the fight. He turned instead on the man he had slashed, still standing exactly as Bransen had left him, reaching back to grasp his torn leg. Two steps brought Bransen directly behind him. He stepped again to gain momentum, then leaped and laid flat out, his legs tucked tight.

His double kick sent the man flying to the ground. Bransen, too, fell flat, and a pair of arrows soared past above him. He landed lightly and sprang back up just as the man Jameston had shot in the hand dropped to the ground before him. His right hand bloody and tucked in tight, he brandished a dagger, waving it frantically at Bransen, grimacing in pain with every movement.

"You would make me kill you?" Bransen asked, punctuating his question with a sudden thrust that left the tip of his sword resting under the man's chin.

The man gave a little squeal, and his dagger fell to the ground.

Bransen dove away, another arrow coming at his position. The knife man cried out and stumbled away. Bransen let him go, focusing instead on the two archers who had a bead on his position.

One archer, he corrected silently, as Jameston's next arrow took one through the upper arm. He fell onto the branch and managed to hold tight. To Bransen's relief, the second man turned and let fly to the northwest. He sent off another arrow, ducking as one cracked into the tree by his face.

Bransen let it go, leaving the man to Jameston, as three more men appeared directly across the road and coming hard for Bransen, two brandishing shields and swords, the third a shield and bronze-tipped spear.

"I arrest you, Highwayman!" one cried.

Bransen met their charge with one of his own and hit them with a barrage of thrusts and slashes, his Jhesta Tu sword slamming against bronze shields, slapping against one sword then the other, severing the spear tip when his opponent stubbornly brought it back to bear. He leaped and rushed left and right, sword working every step as he moved to defeat the integrity of their line, to push them apart enough so that he could get between them.

But these were not simple peasants seeking a bounty. They had obviously known battle and carried the scars of many fights. Still the Highwayman of fame kept all three on their heels with his speed and side-to-side movements, his sword finding any opening they presented or just slashing hard against a shield, digging deep grooves.

He slid to the right in fast steps, stabbing hard to make the man on that flank fall back, then went to the left, flipping the blade to his left hand and stabbing with equal precision and speed.

Bransen cut the second course short with a sudden stop and complete turn, tossing the sword to his right hand. The three men skidded to their own short stops. Bransen used the moment to heed the call of his brooch, though he knew not what it was saying. Driven by some subconscious thought, he thrust his arm and the blade high to his right and felt the ruby tip of the brooch tingle.

His opponents widened their eyes in obvious shock and fell back in unison.

Bransen heard the crackling and managed to glance up at his blade.

At the flames dancing about the carved silverel blade.

Grinning, he slashed the sword down and across. The defenders exaggerated their dodges, trying to stay far from the fiery weapon. Using those wild and erratic movements against them, Bransen slashed left at one man, then back at the man standing to his left. Both yelped and faded far from danger, opening the path the Highwayman sought.

Bransen jumped between them, and his brooch screamed new possibilities. He grabbed the half spear of the man to his left, neutralizing any immediate attacks, and sent his sword in a down and around parry at the sword coming at him to his left. He caught the blade with his own and continued his movement, sending both weapons up high, then turned and snapped off a succession of quick elbow smashes above the off-balance man's shield, cracking him one, two, three in the face.

The spearman bull-rushed from the right, or started to, but Bransen quickly let go of his spear, planted his hand against the leading shield, and let the power of the brooch flow through him. Before he even realized what he had done, he noted the spearman flying backward, as if he had been thrown from a catapult. The man landed hard on his feet but staggered back a couple of quick steps and fell to his bum, where he sat, scorched shield before him, hair dancing wildly at its ends, a confused and dazed look in his unfocused eyes.

Bransen spun fast to see the swordsman he had elbowed rolling on the ground, the one remaining foe coming in hard.

Again the Highwayman invoked the power of his new brooch, and the attacker stopped suddenly and turned, slashing with abandon. He kept on, fighting as if against some unseen demon.

Jameston walked up to Bransen and looked at the swordsman with puzzlement, then back to Bransen. The Highwayman merely shrugged, took a step forward to the side of the fighter, tapped him on the shoulder, and when the man finally glanced his way, smashed him hard in the nose with the pommel of his sword.

"What was that about?" Jameston asked.

Bransen pointed to the tip of the brooch holding the smoky quartz, the gemstone of illusion. "I guess his eyes were crossed," he said somewhat sheepishly.

Jameston shook his head and sighed. "Gather them that aren't dead and disarm them," he instructed.

Bransen started to round up the rogues, slapping them up to the road with his sword, when he noticed the first man Jameston had shot in the gut curled on the ground, groaning softly.

"That one's near dead," Jameston explained, leading two more from across the way, one with an arrow halfway through his bicep, the other leaning on him and limping badly with two arrows stuck deep into the back of one leg.

"Watch them," Bransen said, rushing past Jameston to

the mortally wounded man. He eased the man onto his back, wincing at the gruesome sight, the arrow deep into the man's belly, his guts all torn up.

"Shh," Bransen soothed him, putting one hand up to his brooch and setting the other firmly on the man's stomach, the arrow shaft tight against the crook between his thumb and forefinger.

"Shh," he said again, sending waves of healing energy into the man, almost anesthetizing him with a blast of concentrated warmth.

Bransen yanked the arrow out, the man howling in agony. The others cried out in surprise. Bransen held the wounded man down and put his hand immediately back to the ghastly wound. Gradually, the injured rogue eased to lie flat and his breathing improved. Many heartbeats passed, Bransen holding the pose, continuing the flow of healing magic. He found the man's line of *ki-chi-kree* fluctuating wildly; he used the connection of the soul stone to coax it back to straight. Drawing some of the man's agony into himself, Bransen winced and clenched his jaw.

After many minutes, the man's *ki-chi-kree* finally settled. Bransen leaned over him and whispered into his ear, "The Highwayman is not your enemy." Repeating it a couple of times, Bransen straightened on his knees and turned to regard Jameston and the prisoners.

"The Highwayman is not your enemy!" he proclaimed. "Now be quick and get your friend to a warm bed. Care for him, and he will live." Bransen leaped to his feet and walked back toward the group.

"Go on, then," Jameston said above them. "And go fast, before I slip with this bowstring and put one of you down to the dirt!"

They scrambled at that, past Bransen, who seemed not to notice.

"Good choice," Jameston said to him as he approached.

"I couldn't let him die."

"He tried to kill you."

"He didn't know any better. But now . . ."

"Now what? Now you don't know, and the whole group might come back at us in a day or two."

"You said it was a good choice," Bransen protested.

Jameston grinned slyly. "Yep. And I think I figured out why that pretty Cadayle fell in love with you."

Bransen just shook his head and, with a glance back at the group, followed Jameston into the brush.

"If you're thinking this to be a clean war of minor wounds, then you're the fool," Jameston warned. "I hope you've got the stomach to kill a man when you need to."

"I know a couple of former Samhaist priests, a young thug, and a former laird who would vouch for me on that point."

Jameston nodded and held his knowing grin. "Glad you can do it," he said. "And gladder still that you don't prefer it that way."

Bransen nodded.

So was he.

EIGHTEEN

In the Arms of My Loving Mother

"Alas, Brother Fatuus," Brother Pinower said as his fellow monk from the Chapel of Precious Memories was shoved before the imposing line of Laird Panlamaris's considerable force. Pinower leaned on the crenellated wall of Chapel Abelle's gate tower roof, along with all the principals of the mother chapel and the visiting dignitaries from Vanguard, including Cadayle and Callen.

Hands bound behind his back, poor Fatuus couldn't hold his balance and fell hard to the ground.

A few feet behind the battered monk, sitting astride a large gray mare and dressed in splendid bronze armor, Laird Panlamaris didn't blink, and none of his attendants moved to help poor Fatuus back to his feet.

Panlamaris said something to the man standing beside his horse, who sprinted across the field to the man who was positioned not far below Chapel Abelle's imposing wall.

"Your answer to King Yeslnik's edict is unaccceptable," that courier relayed.

The brothers of Chapel Abelle weren't surprised by the appearance of the Palmaristown soldiers that morning, for a handful—just a handful!—of Palmaristown's monks had managed to get to Chapel Abelle with word of the takeover of the Chapel of Precious Memories by the angry Laird Panlamaris.

"You will release the prisoners loyal to King Yeslnik!" Panlamaris's courier shouted. "The others, and the Highwayman, will be turned over to Laird Panlamaris!"

"The Highwayman?" Brother Pinower remarked. "How could he know . . . ?"

"De Guilbe," Brother Giavno reasoned, shaking his head.

"Good, they think he's here," Cadayle couldn't help but whisper, and her mother pulled her close.

"It saddens me to see how far my old friend De Guilbe has fallen," said Father Artolivan, who seemed very weary and old indeed that day. "And all because of foolish pride."

"What say you, Father Artolivan?" the courier demanded. "My laird grows impatient."

Artolivan started to reply, but Dame Gwydre begged his indulgence and stepped up beside him. "I, too, rule a Holding of Honce," she called down. "A large one and no enemy of, or stranger to, the sailors of Palmaristown. Make your Laird Panlamaris aware that an attack on Chapel Abelle at this time is also an attack on Dame Gwydre of Vanguard."

The relay man looked to the courier, who nodded. He ran back across the field and the dame's words were told to Laird Panlamaris.

His answer came back immediately, for he obviously had known that Dame Gwydre and her contingent were present in Chapel Abelle.

"My Laird Panlamaris offers you sanctuary, good Lady of Vanguard," the courier explained. "You and those loyal to you may leave Chapel Abelle now by ship or through the front gate. This is not your disagreement."

"My fight, you mean, for you come with swords."

The courier had no response. Gwydre looked around at the monks, who were all staring at her with breath held, and smiled her assurance.

"There your laird errs, my friend," she called down. "This is my . . . disagreement. I and my Vanguardsmen will not leave Chapel Abelle at this time. Tell Laird Panlamaris that Dame Gwydre and Vanguard stand with Father Artolivan as guests in his good house. Explain that your laird, too, is welcome here, where we may speak of these pressing issues before rash decisions are made that cannot be undone."

Laird Panlamaris's response came back in mere heartbeats. "Father Artolivan's decree of disobedience to the throne, if it stands, thus does end all discussion."

"It stands, and I stand with Father Artolivan," said Gwydre. "Pray tell your laird that he should consider very wisely his next actions."

The proclamation, so final and clear, lifted the hearts of all the brothers.

Word went back and came forward, and the courier's pause as Panlamaris's response was whispered into his ear foretold ill.

"We have prisoners, Father Artolivan," he said with a backward motion. On Panlamaris's responding wave, a dozen or so captured brothers from the Chapel of Precious Memories were shoved forward to stand beside the kneeling Fatuus.

"Surrender the prisoners loyal to King Yeslnik," the courier demanded. "Or these men who would not denounce you, your brethren, are declared guilty of treason against the throne of King Yeslnik and shall be punished accordingly."

"Treason?" Father Premujon shouted before Artolivan could reply. "They have done nothing!"

"They refused the leniency of Laird Panlamaris and the choice of the new father of the Chapel of Precious Memories, Father De Guilbe," the courier said. Gasps sounded all along the wall.

"This is my Laird Panlamaris's last word," the courier finished. "Release the prisoners loyal to King Yeslnik at once or witness the consequences." He bowed and ran across the field to join his companions.

"I cannot do this," Father Artolivan lamented. "But am I to witness the executions of innocent men?"

"Perhaps we should let them go," said Gwydre.

"And then he will demand that we turn over the men of Ethelbert for execution as King Yeslnik has decreed," said Artolivan. Gwydre had no answer.

But across the field, Brother Fatuus did.

"Abelle!" he cried, his voice clear, unafraid, slicing loudly through the windy day. "My prophet, my saint, oma tula mere!"

"Saint?" said one monk down the wall. "That is heresy. The beatification has only just—" Others hushed him.

Brother Fatuus rolled over and managed to slip his bound hands around his tucked feet to bring them in front of him. He flipped up from his knees to his feet and began walking toward Chapel Abelle, repeating that cadence every step, his voice strong and without a quiver. "My prophet, my saint, oma tula mere!"

"Oma tula mere?" Brother Pinower and others asked.

"He's got Vanguard blood, he does!" Dawson McKeege explained. "Oma tula mere—in the arms of my loving mother."

"What is he doing?" asked Brother Pinower.

"He is giving his soul," Father Artolivan replied, his eyes growing moist.

Cries of "Halt!" resounded from Panlamaris's line, to which Fatuus merely lifted his arms and eyes to the sky and continued his march and his chant.

Panlamaris motioned a spearman to his side and pointed emphatically at Fatuus.

"My prophet, my saint, oma tu—" Fatuus gasped as a missile hit him square in the back. Everyone watching from the chapel walls and tall buildings—monks, Vanguardsmen, and even the men who had been sent to Chapel Abelle as prisoners—gasped when the point of that spear drove through the monk's back and out his belly.

Fatuus dropped to his knees, arms still high, gasping for breath. Somewhere, somehow, he found a moment of great strength and wrenched his hands apart, loosing the bindings. Fatuus found his voice again. "Oma tula mere!" The wounded monk miraculously regained his footing, impaled though he was, and resumed his march, his arms high and wide.

A furious Laird Panlamaris summoned other spearmen; a barrage of missiles soared at Fatuus. Again and again the spears violated his flesh, plunging into his shoulder, his back, his calves.

Fatuus kept walking, kept chanting, now more like singing to a beloved. "My prophet, my saint, oma tula mere!"

"Stop him!" Laird Panlamaris howled, but those soldiers around him seemed frozen, awestruck, as were the witnesses within Chapel Abelle.

"My prophet, my saint, oma tula mere!" Brother Fatuus sang, joined by a dozen other prisoners of Laird Panlamaris, who began to walk toward Chapel Abelle.

Spears reached for them. Riders broke from Panlamaris's ranks, running down the brothers, cutting them down with heavy bronze swords. But not one stopped chanting until the moment of his death. Not one cried for mercy or in pain.

Ahead of them Brother Fatuus, impaled by seven heavy spears, kept walking and singing. A rider bore down on the monk.

"Shoot him dead!" Father Artolivan shouted.

"Stop him!" Cadayle screamed.

"We can't reach!" Brother Jurgyen cried in reply. All winced at the expected moment of Fatuus's death.

Suddenly the rider's mount stopped and bucked, then spun about, hurling him to the ground. The horse began pawing the ground wildly, kicking and neighing as if it had gone mad. The swordsman crawled away, dragging a broken leg.

"My prophet, my saint, oma tula mere!" Brother Fatuus cried in glory and passion.

"Open the gate! The gate!" men shouted while others ran for the huge beam that sealed Chapel Abelle's massive doors.

When at last it opened, there knelt Brother Fatuus, a look of complete serenity on his pale face. "Oma tula mere," he rasped.

And then he died.

Across the field Laird Panlamaris began his charge, hundreds of Palmaristown soldiers churning the ground beneath their running feet and the hooves of their mounts and chariot teams.

The monks dragged Fatuus inside and scrambled to close and secure the gate. All eyes turned to Father Artolivan.

"Turn them," he grimly instructed. "With all the power of beloved Abelle—nay, of Saint Abelle, for we have seen now his miracle, turn them!"

Grim-faced, the brothers began sorting their gemstones, holding back until Brother Pinower gave the call.

A barrage of lightning reached out from Chapel Abelle the likes of which had never before been seen in Honce. When at last the flashes ceased and the ground stopped shaking and the spots no longer danced before their eyes, many men were down, crawling, writhing, burning. The charge had turned to retreat.

"You are besieged!" Laird Panlamaris cried in outrage. "You shall never leave!"

Old Father Artolivan, feeling strangely alive at that terrible moment, did not reply, silencing any responses from monk or Vanguardsman. He watched Panlamaris for only a moment before his reverent gaze shifted below to where brethren and prisoners from Ethelbert and Delaval alike knelt around Brother Fatuus in shared prayer.

Y our allegiance in the face of Laird Panlamaris has renewed my hope, Lady of Vanguard," Father Artolivan said to Gwydre as the group of leaders made their way across the courtyard toward the main chapel. Across the field Panlamaris's army was at work setting tents, though many, including the laird himself, had moved down to the small town of Weatherguard.

"The inspiration for this day belongs to a monk I do not know," Gwydre replied. She nodded her chin toward the courtyard, where Brother Fatuus lay wrapped in a decorative shroud of the type used for a church father.

A large group had gathered on the far side of the courtyard. It seemed as if all the prisoners were there. Before them a pair of their ranks stood speaking with Brother Pinower.

"I would ask one more thing of you, Dame Gwydre," said Artolivan. "Laird Panlamaris will not be foolish enough to assail your ships, so your way home is all but assured. I ask you to take these men, Laird Ethelbert's at least, so that they may be spared the fate King Yeslnik has decreed. They deserve better."

Dame Gwydre turned to stare directly at the old father. Everyone else stopped as well, hanging on her every word, confused by the wry smile she wore.

"Good Father Artolivan, I would ask a favor of you,"

she said. He looked at her curiously, which seemed to please her greatly, as if she wanted this to be a surprise.

"Privately," she added.

"Of course."

The group moved toward the gathered prisoners and Brother Pinower.

"What trouble, Brother?" Father Artolivan asked.

"None, Father. This is Malcombe of Delaval City and Elefreth Pavu of Ethelbert dos Entel," he said, indicating a sturdy man with piercing blue eyes and curly black hair, the classic Delaval specimen. The other was a swarthy man, no less striking or imposing, obviously of the south and perhaps with a bit of Behrenese blood in him.

"Of course. Greetings to both of you this troubling day," said Artolivan. "The events have unsettled you, no doubt."

"We know of King Yeslnik's demands," Malcombe said.

"Yes."

Malcombe straightened his shoulders. "I was a knight in Laird Delaval's army," he said. "Among the elite warriors who rode with Delaval himself."

"This, too, is known to me," said Artolivan. "I am not so old as to have forgotten your pomposity on the day you arrived here at Chapel Abelle, all broken and outraged."

That seemed to shrink the proud warrior a bit, but he managed a smile. "Broken and near death, and, save the work of your brothers, I would surely have gone to my grave."

"Praise Abelle that you did not."

"I do," said Malcombe with a simple sincerity that added great weight to the statement. He nodded at Artolivan, then turned to his fellow Delaval prisoners watching from afar. To a one they signaled their agreement with him, with whatever pact had brought him to stand before Artolivan at this time.

"I—we—ask that you do not turn over my friend Elefreth and the other good men of Laird Ethelbert," Malcombe said.

More than a few of those with Artolivan gasped.

"Most of us have been here for more than a year, some for nearly two," Malcombe explained. "We have been treated well by the brothers, and we have come to know one another as friends and companions, not as enemies."

"We will fight one another no longer," said Elefreth with a heavy Entel accent.

"I expected as much and am glad for you that you have found your way from the darkness," Father Artolivan told them. "I was just now arranging with Dame Gwydre passage for all of you, or at least for those condemned by King Yeslnik's wrongful order, to Vanguard and freedom."

Malcombe and Elefreth looked at each other, a flash of hope fast giving way to looks of grim determination.

"I would let my men make that decision," said Malcombe.

"And I mine," Elefreth agreed.

"But this is my home, and I will not leave it now," said Malcombe. "Particularly not now."

"What then?" asked Father Artolivan. "To return to your respective lairds that you may be once more pressed into battle?"

"Nay, never that," said Malcombe, Elefreth nodding with every word. "For too long we've been fighting and bleeding and dying for the wants of the lairds."

"And you are weary of the battle, understandably so," said Artolivan. "But what, then? Do you ask to live out your lives here in Chapel Abelle?"

Malcombe straightened again, as did Elefreth, and behind them, all the prisoners, hundreds of warriors, stood as one and at rigid attention.

"Not weary of the battle," Malcombe corrected. "Weary of the cause."

"There is no cause in their battle," Elefreth agreed.

"But we're ready to fight if that's what is needed," said Malcombe.

"To fight? For whom?"

"For ourselves!" a man shouted from the ranks, and others cheered and agreed.

"To fight for you!" said another. "And for those monks, and for that one, Fatuus, who just showed us a good way to die!"

The cheering erupted at that, so sudden and heartfelt that Artolivan's eyes, and those of all around him, grew wet with tears.

"We are here at your call, trusting in your judgment," said Malcombe. "If you arm us and send us forth, we will crack open Laird Panlamaris's siege. Perhaps we could go out as if freed and chase them from the field as they naively welcome us into their ranks."

Father Artolivan was emphatically waving his hands to stop the line of thinking, for it was all too sudden for him and too overwhelming. He looked to Dame Gwydre for support.

"You are men I would be proud to have in Vanguard," she said. She and Artolivan retreated fast for his private quarters, with Dawson and Brother Jond in tow.

I t is all so unsettling," Callen said as she sat with Cadayle, Cormack, and Milkeila. "This day, I mean."

"We have witnessed the depths of treachery, the horror of inhumanity, the miracle of faith, and the hope of men's souls in the span of a single hour," said Cormack.

"I have seen it before, on a warm lake in the north," Milkeila added, tossing a wink at her husband, who nodded his agreement. "I am no longer surprised by the potential and the depths of the hearts of men."

"What will it all mean?" asked Cadayle. "How will it end?"

Brother Pinower walked over as she spoke. He regarded the four before nodding his chin toward a small window in the tower of the large chapel. "They are seeking the answers to that question even as you speak," he said.

"You know Father Artolivan well," said Cormack. "What will he do?"

"You know Dame Gwydre. What of her?"

Cormack smiled and pondered the question for a few moments, then smiled with confidence. "She will not abandon Father Artolivan to the whims of King Yeslnik. Of that I am sure."

"Perhaps the whole of our church will flock to Vanguard, and southern Honce be damned," said Brother Giavno.

"And what would you do, Brother, if it were up to you?" Cormack asked him pointedly. For a brief moment, all felt the tension in the air. This man, a disciple of Father De Guilbe, had whipped Cormack to within an inch of his life on De Guilbe's command.

"I would not have left Mithranidoon, save to follow Cormack and Bransen to the glacier and Ancient Badden," Giavno replied. "Or at least I pray that had the decision fallen to me I would have had the courage of Cormack and Milkeila." Embarrassed by the reminder of his previous failures, he bowed then and started away.

But Cormack called him back. "Sit with us," he bade the man who had once been his mentor, who had once been his friend, who had nearly been his executioner. "Let us solve the problems of the world and muse on the miracle of Brother Fatuus."

A look reflecting both gratitude and great sadness flashed on Giavno's face, and he did indeed join them for a discussion that nearly mirrored that taking place behind the window in the tower.

* * *

I ask that you allow me to remain here at Chapel Abelle and that my ships can sail north and return, laden with soldiers," Dame Gwydre said flatly, her tone indicating no sway in her position.

"Soldiers? To what end?" asked Father Artolivan.

"To the defense of Chapel Abelle," Dame Gwydre replied. "To the support of your courage. I had not thought this war of southern Honce to be the affair of Vanguard, but I see now that I was wrong. This is no petty fight between warring lairds. It is a battle for the soul of Honce. And a fight whose victory or loss will determine the future of Vanguard, I do not doubt. For if he wins here, Yeslnik—a man who claims a throne that does not even exist—will turn his eyes and his armies north."

"Because you were here when Laird Panlamaris was humiliated, both by Brother Fatuus and by the complete rejection of his assault," Father Artolivan reasoned.

"It would not have mattered," Gwydre said. "Unless I promised fealty to Yeslnik."

"There remains that option."

"At the cost of my soul. For how could I give credence and fealty to a man who would murder the men of Ethelbert you hold here? How could I keep my own soul if I were to ally with a man like Panlamaris after what he just did to the innocent brothers of the Chapel of Precious Memories? I will not abandon principle and what is right for political expediency, Father Artolivan. I did not do so when Ancient Badden demanded freedom to continue his reign of terror against the folk of Vanguard. A sorry and false woman I would be to turn my back on my fellows to the south."

"This is truly an unexpected day," said Artolivan. Weary, he moved to his chair. "A day that will echo in the songs of the bards for lifetimes hence, perhaps. Or one that will quickly spell our utter doom. I do not know."

"Aye, and that's where a measure of courage is needed," said Dawson McKeege. "And without that measure—" he gave a snort to reflect complete disgust "—then what's worth singing about, anyway?"

Father Artolivan looked at the man incredulously, but then gave a much needed chuckle of agreement.

"Do you understand now why I keep him around?" asked Gwydre.

"Do you understand the magnitude of what you are proposing?"

"I will annex Chapel Abelle for Vanguard, but fear not, for you will continue with all freedom to do as your heart instructs," said Gwydre. "My action will be only to reinforce Vanguard's commitment to you and your brothers."

"You will be declaring war with Delaval City and Palmaristown, both of which can muster a garrison much larger than Vanguard's."

"Then we will fight better," said Gwydre.

"Or die better," Dawson added. "Like Brother Fatuus. I'm not knowing how long they will be singing of our choices this day, but the grandsons of the grandsons of the grandsons will be singing of Brother Fatuus. Of that I am sure."

"For Brother Fatuus, then," Gwydre proclaimed. "It is a good way to die!"

After many nods and hopeful smiles, Father Artolivan said grimly, "There is one more thing that must be done this day. De Guilbe will no doubt begin a rival order in Palmaristown—it has already happened, I am certain, since many brothers were not among those executed on the field. Laird Panlamaris will seek to justify his stand here, in any case."

"Your reasoning is sound, I fear," said Gwydre.

"We have seen the miracle," said Father Artolivan. "All of us. The strength of Brother Fatuus, the turning and bucking of the horse when Fatuus was surely doomed before he reached the gates of Chapel—" He paused there to smile.

"You will finalize the beatification of Abelle!" Father Premujon cried in joy.

"Blessed Abelle," said Artolivan. He paused again, his mind still sharp, still weighing every possibility, working fast behind his sparkling eyes. "From this day forth let it be known that we are the Order of *Blessed* Abelle, the Abellican Church, and that this place will be named St. Abelle—no!" He paused again for effect, grinning so widely that it seemed as if he would explode into joyous laughter. "St. Mere Abelle!" he finished.

Dame Gwydre and Dawson McKeege cheered, and Father Jond wept with overwhelming good spirit.

NINETEEN

The Impetulant

H ere, then," Master Reandu said to Bannagran. He
handed the man a long knife. "Do it yourself."
Beside him a pair of younger brothers stiffened.

From the sill of a high window in Chapel Pryd, Bransen listened carefully to every word. A short while earlier, the monks had spoken of King Yeslnik's edict that all prisoners of Delaval be released and all those taken from Ethelbert's ranks be executed. Bransen was glad of their reaction, particularly the angry foot stomping of Reandu. For some reason he did not quite understand, Bransen needed to believe the best of this man. He remembered a day when Reandu had helped him finish his chore of lugging chamber pots to the dumping area, when Reandu had subsequently washed the filth from him. There had been tenderness there, once, though it had been suppressed under the orders of severe Bathelais and the even more severe Father Jerak.

Bransen shrank back when Bannagran had stormed into the chapel, full of unfocused anger and agitation.

"Do not try my patience," Bannagran warned. "My

road has been long and wearying. I've no tolerance for your stubbornness this day."

"I have released the Delaval prisoners," Reandu calmly replied. "Against my better judgment but for your own sake."

"That was half the edict."

"You would have me murder helpless captives?"

"King Yeslnik did not demand that of you."

"Of course. I am simply to turn them over to you so that you might employ some valorless and immoral cad to stab and beat them," Reandu said, his voice thick with sarcasm that surely spelled defiance. "How easy it is for King Yeslnik to make such a demand, his own hands clean of the blood. How easy it is for Bannagran to follow such a command . . ."

Up above, the Highwayman could hardly believe that Reandu was showing such independence, such . . . humanity. This was the man who had declared Garibond's heresy, which had doomed the innocent man to the fire.

"Silence!" Bannagran yelled.

"Then bloody your own hands, warrior!" Reandu spat back in his face.

"Do you think these hands clean?" the Bear of Honce roared, holding his large, strong paws up before him. "In this war and a dozen before! Do you think I have not killed many men?"

"These are helpless prisoners!"

"Many men undeserving? Men whose only crime was to serve the losing laird? So stained are these hands that your own Abelle could not wash the blood from them! There is no place in your heaven for Bannagran!"

"Then take this dagger and murder the five men of Ethelbert held within Chapel Pryd," said Reandu. "Cut their throats or stab their hearts." He held the dagger again, and Bannagran narrowed his eyes and stared at him angrily.

"Because you cannot!" Reandu lectured and pulled the dagger away. "You are a warrior, not a murderer!"

"This is an execution of the convicted, no murder," Bannagran said.

"Murder!" Reandu reiterated. "These men have committed no crimes."

Bannagran seemed to gasp for breath for a few moments before replying, "They are to be turned over. All loyal to Ethelbert are to be executed by order of King Yeslnik."

But Master Reandu was smiling by then, the Highwayman noted from far above. "You'll not kill them," he said with confidence.

"Their loyalty to Laird Ethelbert dooms them," Bannagran answered.

"You cannot ask a man to exchange his loyalty to an opposing laird," said Reandu. "You know as much." Reandu paused, and it occurred to Bransen that both he and Bannagran had known all along where this conversation would lead, almost as if they had choreographed it beforehand.

"But if they expressed loyalty to a third party, one neutral in the war, perhaps," Reandu posited.

"None who don the robes of the Order of Abelle fall under the edict of King Yeslnik, certainly," Bannagran replied. His guards looked at him curiously, as did all the monks in the room, except Reandu standing before him.

"Of course, because then they will serve the order and not Laird Ethelbert," Reandu said. "It is curious that you mention that, new Laird of Pryd, for this very morning, all five of the remaining prisoners expressed just such an interest. I happen to have several extra robes that will fit them well."

"I will see them dressed as such, and this very day," Bannagran warned. "Else they will face the wrath of King Yeslnik."

Master Reandu, who looked quite pleased with his cleverness, bowed. Bannagran and his soldiers left the chapel.

D o not hesitate," Yeslnik said to his brutish guard. "It is imperative that you react as soon as I indicate, true and fast."

"Me pleasure, me king," said Brawnwin, a three-hundred-pound behemoth of a man. He carried his great axe casually on one shoulder and could wield it with one hand as easily as most men could wave a short sword. Brawnwin's head was shaven and looked as if it had been melted on atop his massive shoulders, large rolls of skin falling down the back of that neck and great jowls that seemed to grow out of his collarbones in the front.

"They may come to his defense," Yeslnik warned. "Their magic is potent."

"One cut, me king," Brawnwin assured him.

Drawing power from the imposing brute so readily at his command, Yeslnik stepped a little more lightly as they ascended the long stairs of Chapel Delaval. Until recently, this church of the Order of Abelle had been known as the Chapel of Weeping Brothers, a name dating to the slaughter of the first monks in the city, who took their own lives rather than denounce Abelle in the great tragedy of Cordon Roe. Many of the brothers currently in Chapel Delaval still referred to the place by its older name, a more fitting title this dark day.

Yeslnik and his entourage of a dozen armed and armored guards shoved past the brothers who answered their knock on the heavy wooden doors.

"Father Pendigrast, immediately," Yeslnik commanded. "And bring forth all the prisoners delivered to you who have not yet been ushered north to Chapel Abelle."

"The prisoners, King Yeslnik?" a young monk asked.

"At once! All of them, and in chains!" He waved the young monk away emphatically, giving him a shove with his foot when the monk didn't move quickly enough. The hapless monk flew several feet before he stumbled and crashed into the side wall.

In moments, Father Pendigrast appeared with three of the higher-ranking brothers. He was one of the younger fathers in the order, not yet forty, promoted because of the untimely death of the father before him and the man's two expected successors, all taken by the same bout of the grippe that had swept through Delaval City. There was no missing the trepidation on Pendigrast's face as he moved into the nave and walked along the worn fabric of the carpet that led between the chapel's center pews. Pendigrast had obviously expected this visit. How could he not, given that Father Artolivan's edict of disobedience had reached Delaval City that very morning?

"I sent one of your young brothers to fetch Ethelbert's men," Yeslnik said as the man approached. "To save you the trouble, of course."

Pendigrast glanced to his monk companions, closed his eyes briefly, and breathed deeply to steady his obviously frayed nerves. "You have seen the edict of Father Artolivan of Chapel Abelle, who rules my order," he said quietly.

"Of course," said Yeslnik. "A meritless writ I will ignore, as will you. Where are the prisoners?"

Pendigrast swallowed hard. "King Yeslnik, Chapel Delaval serves at your pleasure, as it served at the pleasure of Laird Delaval before you."

"King Delaval," Yeslnik sharply corrected.

"Yes, of course. King Delaval. But we serve Father Artolivan above all."

"Get the prisoners," Yeslnik interrupted.

"My king, I cannot," said Father Pendigrast.

Yeslnik gave a bored glance at the giant Brawnwin, who

came forward suddenly and with a single chop of his axe cut Father Pendigrast apart from shoulder to hip. The man's legs crumbled beneath him, blood spewing for just a few heartbeats before Pendigrast fell sideways, quite dead. Monks cried out, but Yeslnik's guards were among the most fierce and violent in all the city. Brandishing their weapons they formed a defensive ring about the king, spear tips thrusting to keep Pendigrast's entourage back.

Yeslnik looked up. "Who is the new Father of Chapel Delaval?" he calmly asked. The monks all stammered and stuttered until finally one pointed to a man about the same age of Pendigrast.

"Congratulations, Father," Yeslnik said to him. "Now send your minions to retrieve the prisoners." Never taking his withering gaze from poor, frightened, newly appointed Father Dennigan, Yeslnik watched as a dozen ragged men were led into the nave in chains.

Yeslnik smiled widely, a most wicked and pleasing idea coming to him. He reached to Brawnwin's belt and pulled the man's bronze short sword from its sheath, then tossed it on the ground before Dennigan.

"You kill the first one," he instructed. "Then hand the blade to the next most superior brother and on down the line."

"I am no warrior, King Yeslnik," Dennigan stammered.

"Kill him. Now," said Yeslnik. "Or explain your failing to Father Pendigrast."

Hands trembling, Dennigan picked up the sword and moved on shaky legs to the nearest of the prisoners, a young man barely out of his teens. The boy pleaded with his superior to be spared.

"Do it!" King Yeslnik cried.

Dennigan leveled the blade at the prisoner's throat and whispered that he would try to make it clean. The boy began to cry. Dennigan dropped the blade to the floor and vomited.

"Pathetic," Yeslnik said. "All of you!" With a flick of his white hand he motioned to two guards, who rushed to the chapel doors and flung them wide. More soldiers charged into the chapel.

"Arrest the brothers and drag those miserable wretches from Ethelbert into the streets," Yeslnik commanded. He turned to Brawnwin. "I trust that you will find ways to execute them that will amuse me."

He led Brawnwin's gaze over to Dennigan, on his knees now, shoulders bobbing violently with great sobs. Yeslnik gave a derisive snort. "Wound him," he whispered to the brute. "But leave him with enough to make the journey to Chapel Abelle bearing my response to Father Artolivan."

"And yer answer will be?" Brawnwin asked eagerly.

"The brother who delivered Artolivan's treasonous writ," said Yeslnik. "Put his head in a sack."

Brawnwin's grin nearly took in his ears.

The next morning, Brother Dennigan felt a heavy boot kick against his back, shoving him from Delaval City's north gate on the eastern side of the great river. In his hand he held a sack that bore the severed head of Brother Piastafan, the courier from Father Artolivan, his mouth locked wide open in a final, horrified scream. As Dennigan pulled himself from the mud to a kneeling position, a wagon rolled out of the gate and splashed beside him. Brawnwin came forth and grabbed him by the collar. With tremendous strength the brute lifted Dennigan over the side of the wagon and unceremoniously dumped him in.

"With all haste to Chapel Abelle," instructed King Yeslnik, sitting astride his mare just inside the gate. "And you, monk, tell your Father Artolivan that when I am soon finished with Ethelbert, the Order of Abelle will be held accountable for his treason. This is our time of great need, the moment of triumph for the line of Delaval, and

I will never forget that Artolivan and your church did not stand with me."

Dennigan managed to shift to a sitting position and looked back vacantly at the young tyrant.

"Oh, about that boy you were too weak to kill," Yeslnik said to him. "We stripped him naked, bound his hands, and put him in a sack with some poisonous snakes this morning. Perhaps you heard his screams. They lasted a pleasingly long time."

Dennigan closed his eyes and shook with silent sobs.

I knew that Yeslnik was an impulsive child, but this surprises me," Bransen said to Jameston when they regrouped in the woods behind Chapel Pryd after both had witnessed the conversation between Reandu and Bannagran from opposite windows high on the side of the nave.

"You knew he had done as much," said Jameston. "We heard this at the other chapel, and you said then that Yeslnik's murderous mind didn't surprise you."

"Not Yeslnik," Bransen corrected. "Nothing bad that comes from him would surprise me. The reactions of Brother Reandu and Bannagran, however . . . I never thought them so possessed of moral boundaries," Bransen explained and Jameston nodded. "Especially not Bannagran."

"Is that the reason?" asked the scout. "Or are the both of them weary already of King Yeslnik?"

It was Bransen's turn to nod. "Could it be that King Yeslnik is so far beyond the moral boundaries that even the always callous lairds will be put off by his demands?"

"Or it might be that these callous lairds you speak of have a bit of sense and know that they can only ask so much of those they dominate before they find the tines of a pitchfork aimed their way. It didn't take much convincing by Gwydre to get the people of Vanguard to turn and fight against Ancient Badden."

"Yeslnik is an idiot."

"An impetulant one, for sure," said Jameston.

Bransen nodded, for the word sounded right. After a moment's reflection, though, Bransen screwed up his face curiously and echoed, "Impetulant?"

"Aye."

"I don't know that word," said Bransen.

"But you know what it means."

"Impatient? Impetuous? Petulant?"

"Yes."

Bransen gave a helpless laugh.

"It's from an old hunter's song," Jameston explained. "'The Herstory of History.'"

"Herstory?"

"You can figure that part out."

"True, but why?"

"When you live alone in the forest you learn to speak little and listen a lot," Jameston explained. "Putting words together to make a quicker point saves you breath."

"Crazy V would have had a herstory," said Bransen.

Jameston laughed. "And a good one! And more than a few who knew her would be embarredassed by the tales told of V."

"Embarred . . ." Bransen started to echo, then he could only chuckle. "Red-assed? What did you call him?"

"Who? Yeslnik?"

"Impetulant?" asked Bransen.

"Fits him, don't it?"

"Better than any. King Yeslnik the Impetulant. We should put it on his headstone. Soon."

"Then let us start the carving of king and stone."

Jameston paused and let the moment slip aside, watching Bransen as the young man glanced back toward Pryd, the town that had been his home for so many years.

"You are proud of the laird and the monks," Jameston remarked. "Their actions in dodging Yeslnik's verdict give you hope."

Bransen considered that for a few heartbeats. "I cannot deny that. My relationship with Brother Reandu is . . . complicated."

"He's the closest thing you've got to family after your wife and mother," said Jameston. Bransen didn't argue with that assessment. "Is it time for us to go see him?"

Bransen nodded but did not move. Jameston stepped aside and motioned him to lead the way, but Bransen still made no move.

"You think it harder to test that Writ of Passage now," Jameston reasoned. "Now you're hoping they might honor it, and now, with such hopes, you're more afraid of how you'll feel if they don't."

Bransen took a deep breath.

"Put your mask down over your eyes and walk openly through the town," Jameston advised. "The people here will remember you. They saved you once. Maybe once again?"

Bransen took off his farmer's hat and his mask and shook his hair out, which parted it in the middle and showed the star-shaped brooch set on his forehead. His deerskin coat fell to the ground with the hat, and he tied the mask on securely. He looked different from the Highwayman who had left Pryd Town months before. His dark hair was longer, and, of course, he now wore the brooch. His bandanna, once a mask and hood, was now rolled so that it was just a thin strip across his eyes. But the black silk outfit was unmistakable, with one sleeve long, the other torn off at the shoulder, and with a black strip tied about his otherwise bare upper bicep.

The gasps of recognition and whispers of "The Highwayman!" began as soon as Jameston led him from the forest and onto the main road far across the way from Chapel Pryd. The pair moved toward Chapel Pryd, with many people following in their wake.

They knew the Highwayman here in Pryd Town. And they loved him.

Chapel Pryd was close to Castle Pryd, and as the monks obviously heard the approach of the Highwayman and his considerable entourage, for their courtyard gates opened before Bransen even approached, so too, he figured, had some in the castle heard.

He didn't think about that as he walked through the chapel's outer wall, a flood of memories greeting him the moment he stepped again onto Chapel Pryd's courtyard. Up the white stone path, the doors to the chapel proper were also opened, brothers peering with obvious apprehension.

Bransen moved into the large foyer, Jameston beside him, and before he could even ask the astonished young brothers standing there to see the leaders, Master Reandu appeared flanked by several others.

"Bransen!" Master Reandu blurted. "What are you doing here? Are you mad? You left under condition of a strict penalty."

"Good to meet you, too," Jameston muttered so that only Bransen and a couple of nearby monks could hear.

"And I return to insist that the condition be revoked," Bransen said.

"Are you a madman?" Reandu repeated, apprehension growing on his face.

Bransen reached over his shoulder and produced Dame Gwydre's Writ of Passage from the scroll tube he had tied diagonally across his back. "On the contrary, Brother Reandu," he said, handing it over.

"Master Reandu," one of the monks behind corrected sharply.

"I find this to be a most glorious day," Bransen announced. He offered a smile before finishing, "Master Reandu."

Before the monk could respond, a shout came from the courtyard. "You!" came the resonating voice of Laird Bannagran.

"The Bear of Honce!" the monk behind Reandu breathed with obvious terror.

"It would have to be, would it not?" Bransen asked as he turned. But any intention he had of parlaying here, of letting Dame Gwydre's writ carry any weight for him, disappeared as he swung about.

Great axe in hand, a look of sheer outrage on his face, Bannagran didn't seem to be in any mood for talking. The laird charged with a roar, his axe upright before him, not tipping his hand about the intended angle of his initial cut.

Jameston moved for his bow, but Bransen, drawing his sword with his right hand, pushed Jameston to the side with his left. His sword came out in the blink of an eye, which seemed to surprise Bannagran. He kept coming, though, his axe head slipped over his left shoulder. He turned his foot in with his closing step at the Highwayman, also to the left.

A lesser fighter would have cringed and braced, and thus been cut in half, but the Highwayman anticipated every movement. When Bannagran went into his sudden spin, axe flying to arm's length, Bransen was already moving. He shifted to his left, dancing past the retreating Jameston. When Bannagran came around, axe slashing powerfully, he hit nothing but air. Too fine a warrior to leave himself open despite the daring move, Bannagran recovered almost immediately, stopping short his swing as soon as he realized the Highwayman's dodge. Reorienting himself, he squared up with his opponent.

"Are we to do this dance again?" the Highwayman

asked. "And who will die this time when you throw your weapon at me in frustration?"

That last question made Bannagran narrow his eyes with anger. He stepped forward fast, chopping down left to right, right to left, and back to the first strike. The Highwayman swayed to his left, to his right, and to his left again, causing three near but complete misses. He countered with a sudden stab of his sword, but Bannagran threw his hips behind him, less gracefully than the Highwayman had dodged the axe swings but effective nonetheless.

The Highwayman thrust again. Bannagran, his hands wide on the handle of his great axe, drove his weapon down to deflect the blade low, then stepped ahead and threw forward his right hand, the lower on his axe, punching the handle at the Highwayman's face.

Bransen dropped under it and came on lower this time. Bannagran had to throw his feet out behind him wildly to save his shins. He staggered and scrambled as the Highwayman pressed the attack, stabbing at one leg, then the other.

"Read it!" the Highwayman shouted to Master Reandu, the Writ of Passage still rolled in his hand.

The Highwayman duckwalked in a crouch, his sword prodding faster and faster to keep the retreating Bannagran off balance, to keep him working furiously with his feet and his weapon so that the great warrior of Pryd Town could not begin a counterattack.

"I did not return to Pryd to fight you," the Highwayman said to him.

"I told you to stay away," Bannagran growled in response. "Forevermore!"

"Things have changed," the Highwayman insisted.

"The worse for you!" Bannagran shouted as he leaped up and forward, clearing the Highwayman. The warrior landed in a forward roll and came up and around with a great sidelong slash designed to keep the Highwayman far away.

But Bransen was right beside him as he turned. The sword blade hit the axe handle before Bannagran could build any momentum. The Highwayman slid it right up to slam hard at the crook between axe handle and head.

The Highwayman grabbed Bannagran's chest with his free hand. "I don't want to fight you!" he yelled in Bannagran's face.

"Hold, Laird Bannagran!" cried Reandu, who had finally recovered his wits enough to read the scroll.

Bannagran pulled his left hand free of his trapped axe, retracted immediately, and moved to slug the Highwayman, a heavy and powerful punch that would have surely crushed the young warrior's face. But Bannagran flew backward before he had barely begun the swing, jolted by a blast of lightning-like energy. He landed on his heels but stumbled down to a seated position on the floor some ten feet away, his long black hair flying wildly.

"You cheat with the gemstones!" Bannagran growled through chattering teeth.

"He has a Writ of Passage from Dame Gwydre of Vanguard!" Master Reandu shouted, "Forgiving him his crimes of theft and praising him for the great victory in the north!"

"What?" Bannagran scrambled to his feet, giving no indication he intended to abandon his battle.

"I fought for her," the Highwayman explained. "I killed Ancient Badden of the Samhaists and freed her people from the grip of horrible war."

"That means nothing to me." Bannagran hoisted his axe as if he meant to charge again.

"In return, Dame Gwydre has pardoned me for my past . . . difficulties," the Highwayman said.

"A Writ of Passage," Master Reandu said again.

"Does that include your murder of King Delaval?"

"My what?"

"I thought not!" Bannagran said and charged again. He came in furiously, his axe working brilliantly in short strokes and stabs with its pointed iron top. Almost any other warrior in Honce would have been cut repeatedly by that barrage, and all in the room gasped and winced, expecting the Highwayman to fall to the floor in pieces.

But to the Highwayman, it seemed as if Bannagran was moving in slow motion. Bransen easily worked his sword, tip up, tip down, left and right, to slap against the axe every time and always before the powerful Bannagran could gain momentum behind his swing.

Silverel rang against iron and tapped against the wooden handle. The Highwayman's hand moved in a blur before him, perfect aim, perfect angle. The exchange went on for what seemed like an eternity, though it was not more than a score of heartbeats. More gasps echoed in the nave of Chapel Pryd.

Bannagran came in hard, swinging left to right. The Highwayman chopped a shortened downstroke, sliding his sword again along the blade to hook the axe under the head. He continued his rotation through the backhand, high over their heads, then down to the left and low to the right, where an extra shove of that sword nearly swung Bannagran around.

The Laird of Pryd fought to hold his balance but didn't even recognize that the Highwayman had disengaged and turned his sword with such precision and speed that the tip was in at Bannagran's throat before he had begun to move his axe again.

All in the room gasped to see the great Bannagran, the Bear of Honce, defeated. But Bannagran wasn't quite finished yet. With a suddenness that startled everyone except the always cool Highwayman, Bannagran threw himself over backward. At the same time he used his tremendous strength to bring his great axe sweeping up from the side so that as he pursued, the Highwayman had to suddenly retract his blade or have it raked aside by the axe.

Bannagran hit the ground in a roll, throwing himself over and stumbling fast back to his feet, slashing his axe the rest of the way to his right, then back again to the left.

Fast and balanced, the Highwayman rushed in as the axe went to Bannagran's left, stepping quickly past the man's right. He flipped his sword to his left hand and stabbed behind his back to the right. Bannagran turned and lurched in a desperate dodge as Bransen ran by him. Though the fine sword did whip past, it seemed to all that he had avoided the blow.

He turned and the Highwayman continued back a couple of steps, then spun to face him directly once more, tossing his sword back to his main hand.

A curious expression crossed Bannagran's face, and he slyly slipped one hand behind his hip to feel his torn tunic and shirt under the back of his breastplate. He looked questioningly at the Highwayman.

Bransen half shrugged, half nodded to confirm Bannagran's suspicions: He had lost this fight not once but twice, for in both the movement that had removed the sword from under his chin and in his dodge from the Highwayman's charge, the only thing that had saved him was Bransen's mercy. Twice in the span of a few heartbeats, the Highwayman had beaten him.

"Are we to continue this folly all the day?" Bransen asked. "Read the Writ of Passage."

"You murdered King Delaval!" Bannagran snarled.

"His sword is whole!" Master Reandu cried in sudden realization.

The Highwayman glanced back at him curiously, then looked to his magnificent blade.

"He repaired it!" Bannagran insisted.

Bransen snapped his sword down beside him and retreated three fast steps. "What are you talking about?" he demanded. "My sword, my mother Sen Wi's sword, has never been broken."

"The sword that slew King Delaval was broken in half," Reandu explained.

"In the man's chest," another monk added.

"Surely not a blade like this," said Bransen, presenting his sword before him.

"Exactly so!" Reandu replied pointing to Bannagran. When he looked to the laird, Bransen saw Bannagran draw the top half of a delicately curving blade from a sheath on his hip, a scabbard that Bransen had thought for a long dagger and empty since no hilt had shown there.

"The blade that killed King Delaval," Bannagran said, holding it up for Bransen and all the others to clearly view. "So much like your own. Too much like your own!"

Bransen turned his blade over up before his eyes, noting the unmistakable similarities. "Where did you get that?" he asked, finding it hard suddenly to even draw breath as the implications of that blade—unmistakably a Jhesta Tu blade—began washing over him.

"From King Delaval's chest," Bannagran answered. "And for it, King Yeslnik has declared you guilty of murder."

"But it is not my blade," Bransen protested, turning his own over again to accentuate his point.

"It is too similar, possessed by one of like mind and training as you," Bannagran said.

Bransen had no answer other than to shake his head. Eventually, he managed to say, "I was in Vanguard when Delaval was murdered. Dame Gwydre will confirm my claim. Last time I was in Delaval City was before the winter, and Laird Delaval—"

"King Delaval!" Bannagran corrected.

"King Delaval," said Bransen, not wishing to argue

such points. "He was very much alive when I left, and I have never returned. That is not my sword, and I have never seen another sword of this type in my life until just this moment!"

Bannagran stared at him hard. If he was softening at all to Bransen's reasoning, he wasn't showing it.

"Does the truth not matter?" Bransen asked.

"Not to King Yeslnik," said Bannagran.

"What is this insanity that has gripped all of Honce?" Bransen asked as he spun around, sheathing his sword in a single fluid movement to address all in the chapel. "Is there no limit to the misery these lairds will inflict for the sake of their own gain?"

"Enough of your speeches!" Bannagran yelled at him. He turned his gaze wider. "All of you be gone!" he demanded. "Now!" Brother, soldier, and peasant alike scrambled to escape the volatile man's wrath, leaving only Bransen and Jameston, Reandu, and a pair of Bannagran's guards in the wide nave.

"You have seen Dame Gwydre's Writ of Passage," Bransen said when the commotion died away. "She offered to me and my family a full pardon in exchange for my actions on her behalf against Ancient Badden. Will you honor her decree?"

Bannagran paused and continued to stare at him. "Your family? Callen Duwornay and her daughter, you mean."

"Yes."

"For them, yes," said Bannagran. "For you, no. Not until you clear your name with King Yeslnik, and I think that unlikely."

"And if I do? Am I to be welcomed back in Pryd with Callen and Cadayle beside me?"

Bannagran looked to Reandu, gave a deep and profound sigh, and then stated, to Reandu's obvious surprise and to Bransen's, "Yes."

"Bannagran?" Reandu asked.

"Yes," the Bear of Honce said again more forcefully and confidently. "I'm sick of it all."

"I did not mean for you to kill Prydae," said Bransen. "But I went to his tower to protect my love and would do so again!"

"Silence," Bannagran warned. "I have given you what you desire and all that I can. Ask no more of me. Understand, Highwayman, that I'll not tolerate any of your indiscretions should you ever return."

"I will return."

"King Yeslnik will never agree."

"But, my family? You said—"

"They can return to Pryd Town at their leisure," Bannagran assured him. "That poor woman, Callen, never deserved the sack, though her sniveling lover surely did. The Samhaists are long gone from Pryd Town, so I care not if the Duwornays walk here openly. But you remain another matter."

"I will clear my name," Bransen said.

"I am tasked with killing you," Bannagran admitted.

Bransen laughed. "Care to try again?"

"Bransen!" Reandu and Jameston scolded in unison.

Bannagran held up his hand to silence them and assure them that all was calm here. "Be gone from my town and my holding."

"I ask two things of you before I leave."

The Bear of Honce put his hands on his hips and stared at Bransen hard, thinking to question the young man's nerve in making requests. However, remembering their fight and noting that the young warrior did not flinch or back down, Bannagran merely waited.

"First, I would speak with Master Reandu."

"You have until the noontime hour."

"And, second, allow me that broken sword."

"It is not mine to give."

"Let me study it at least," said Bransen, desperation

creeping into his voice. Bannagran, Reandu, and particularly Jameston looked at him with surprise.

"Please," said Bransen. "I believe that to be a Jhesta Tu blade."

"Like your own."

"Perhaps."

Bannagran tossed the blade to the floor at Bransen's feet. With trembling hands the young man picked it up and turned it over and over, pointing it away from his eyes so that he could study the break.

Wrapped metal. Just like his own sword. Only the Jhesta Tu were known to create such blades. Bransen could hardly draw breath. He closed his eyes and considered the possibilities here, if the Jhesta Tu mystics had truly come to Honce. That long road, that long-avoided road, now loomed before him, within his grasp, as never before.

"Then Laird Ethelbert has hired Jhesta Tu mercenaries from Behr," Bannagran remarked.

Bransen blinked out of his contemplations. "No," he said as he tried to sort through Bannagran's claim. "No."

"It is such a blade," said Bannagran.

"Jhesta Tu are not mercenaries. They cannot—"

"That blade slew King Delaval. The wielder of that blade, part of a small band by all reports—and dressed as you are, by all accounts—scaled the castle walls and defeated King Delaval and his elite warriors in short order."

Bransen couldn't doubt the claim, but he did not understand the concept of Jhesta Tu mercenaries. If they were fighting for Laird Ethelbert, which seemed likely, then it was for philosophy and preference and not for coin. The notion shook the young man profoundly. "May I keep this?" he asked.

Bannagran held out his big hand. Bransen reluctantly set the sword blade in it.

Bransen turned to Master Reandu. "In private?" The monk nodded and started for a side room.

"Noontime," Bannagran reiterated as Bransen walked past. "Then be far from Pryd, and return not other than on pain of death unless King Yeslnik has declared your innocence and freedom."

Bransen didn't bother to respond.

Master Reandu's visage and posture changed noticeably when he and Bransen were away from Bannagran and alone in a side room of Chapel Pryd. His face brightened and his step lightened, and his smile seemed truly genuine.

"My heart warms at seeing you walking so tall and straight," he said.

"You saw it before I left, when you took me to kill Laird Prydae," Bransen replied curtly. Reandu stiffened and took a step back at the grim reminder of that fateful day.

"But that was because of the soul stone."

"As is this," said Bransen. He brushed his long hair aside and indicated the brooch set in his forehead.

Despite his reservations at the initial sharp retort, Reandu moved closer, eyeing the marvelous piece of jewelry. "Yes, but even so," he said, reaching up to touch the brooch. "You seem more comfortable and stable."

"I am."

"All the gems . . . are they magical? Where did you get such a marvelous piece?"

"They are, and this was put upon my forehead by Father Artolivan of Chapel Abelle," Bransen answered.

Reandu fell back another step and looked at him incredulously. "Father Artolivan gave that to you?"

"I just said as much."

"It is . . . unexpected."

"That he would offer it, or that I would take it?" Bransen asked.

"Both!"

Bransen chuckled. "I served Dame Gwydre in exchange for her Writ of Passage. I dealt a great blow to the Samhaists when I took Ancient Badden's head from his shoulders. Father Artolivan knows that I am no enemy to him or his church. Does Brother Reandu?"

"Of course!"

Bransen eyed him doubtfully, then smiled as he produced a second parchment, the writ from Father Artolivan. He handed it to Reandu, who read it with eyes so wide that they seemed as if they might roll from their sockets.

"I understand your actions here, Bransen. Perhaps better than anyone. I saw the punishments you endured at the hands of the people of Pryd, at the demands of Laird Prydae, at—"

"The punishments my innocent father endured?" Bransen interrupted. "At the hands of the Samhaists and Laird Prydae?"

"And at the hands of Chapel Pryd," Master Reandu admitted without further prompting. "What am I to say, my old friend? I did not approve of the treatment of Garibond, nor do I think the treatment offered to your mother and father fair or wise, though I was not involved in those decisions. I was not a voice of power within Chapel Pryd. . . ."

Reandu's voice trailed off when Bransen put up a hand. It occurred to Bransen then just how much of the upper hand he had gained in the last few months. Here was Reandu, Master Reandu, the acting leader of Chapel Pryd, stuttering and stammering excuses to him. Bransen did well to hide his amusement for Reandu's sake. He reminded himself of Reandu's commitment to him, such as it was, in the dark days.

"I am glad that you were not punished for your actions at Castle Pryd," Bransen said, referring to Reandu's intervention against Master Bathelais when Bathelais had sought to stop Bransen with a blast of lightning.

"Master Bathelais did not recover from his fall," Reandu said, his voice low, his guilt all too clear. "I am not proud of how I attained my current position, but I am grateful to Father Artolivan and the masters at Chapel Abelle for their understanding and faith in me."

"I have not forgotten the sins of your chapel," Bransen said. "But neither have I forgotten the day you helped me with the chamber pots or when you washed the filth from me. I am not your enemy, Master Reandu."

That proclamation brought a profound sigh of relief from the brother. "It does my heart good to see you standing so straight and tall," he said once again after a few heartbeats of slow and steady breathing. "I do not lament the passing of the Stork."

"Even if in his stead comes the Highwayman, whom King Yeslnik hates above all?"

"King Yeslnik is wrong," said Reandu.

The startling words had Bransen lifting his eyebrows.

"And more the fool for the edict he issued to Father Artolivan," Reandu said, trying to keep his voice low. "He would have our order act as executioners and go back on our promises. Does he believe that the holdings of Honce will rally to his flag when he would so callously murder the many men whose only crime was to serve the lairds they had known all their lives?"

"I watched your conversation with Bannagran earlier this morning," Bransen admitted, and Reandu looked at him curiously. "Regarding the disposition of the prisoners, who are now brothers, it would seem. I was in a high window overlooking the nave."

Though they were not in the high-roofed nave, Reandu reflexively glanced up before shaking his head and reminding himself to doubt nothing about this surprising young man.

"I would not have allowed the prisoners to be killed," Reandu said after he sorted through the startling information.

"You handed Bannagran the knife."

"Because he would never have killed them," said Reandu. "Bannagran is no murderer."

"Garibond," Bransen said.

Reandu shook his head. "His fire has dimmed with the wisdom of age. He has served the people of Pryd well as steward and now as laird. They have come to trust him and love him, and they follow him into battle."

Bransen shrugged as if he hardly cared. "I hope you are right, for the sake of the people of Pryd."

After a long and uncomfortable pause, with Master Reandu clearly caught between his hopes for Bransen and his growing loyalty to Bannagran, the monk asked, "Will you return to Pryd Town when you have cleared your name?"

Bransen replied with a grin that revealed . . . nothing. For only when he had heard that question had he realized that it hardly mattered. The entire reason for his journey to Pryd, to secure a home for his growing family, hardly mattered to him at that time.

The Jhesta Tu had come to Honce.

While Bransen was meeting with Master Reandu, Jameston Sequin walked out of Chapel Pryd and over to the next impressive structure. He was stopped at the gates of Castle Pryd by grim-faced guards, crossing halberds before him and looking very much like they would enjoy eviscerating him.

Jameston just laughed at them. "Go and tell your laird that a friend of Dame Gwydre of Vanguard would like a word with him," he instructed.

Neither guard budged.

"Would you deny the Dame of Vanguard access to your Laird Bannagran?" Jameston asked. "Without even asking Laird Bannagran? I've known more than a few presumptuous guards. They're all dead now, of course, but I admire their spirit."

The guards looked at each other for a moment, then one backed away and started into the castle. He picked up his pace almost at once, which amused Jameston greatly.

Soon after, Jameston found himself standing before Laird Bannagran.

"Jameston Sequin at your service, good Laird of Pryd Town," he said with a bow. "Come from Vanguard to your door."

"If you wish to ingratiate your Lady Gwydre to me you would have been wiser to come in to Pryd Town separate from the Highwayman."

Jameston laughed. "Wouldn't even have found my way to your town."

"You find this amusing?" Bannagran asked grimly.

"All of it, in a sad manner," Jameston replied. "Guess that's why I spend most of my time walking the forests of Vanguard and Alpinador."

"What do you want?"

Jameston nodded at Bannagran's short response. "I'm a good friend of Dame Gwydre and empowered to speak for her. I'd be a sorry emissary if I didn't pay a visit to the laird."

"A visit? Should I set a banquet table?"

"I'm not your enemy, nor is Dame Gwydre," said Jameston.

"The politics of the world are not my own to decide."

"Just yours to laugh at, helplessly," Jameston quipped. "Oh, I see that in your eyes, Laird Bannagran of Pryd. Tired of war, tired of stupid lairds and stupider kings and stupider reasons for men killing men."

"You pretend to know more than you do," Bannagran replied. "I have no time for your pointless banter. You came seeking audience, and, as you claim to be a spokesman for Dame Gwydre, I granted your request. Do you have anything of value to say, or are you just here to annoy me?"

Jameston laughed at that.

"Do not try my patience," Bannagran warned. "Other men who have done so have lost their heads."

"That wouldn't be a wise choice for you," Jameston replied. "Gwydre's got no fight with you, nor do I, and I doubt King Yeslnik would appreciate you starting a war with Vanguard."

"What do you want?"

"I want to tell you of Bransen, the Highwayman," Jameston replied. "He had nothing to do with the murder of King Delaval. He was in Vanguard, maybe even in Alpinador, at the time, and I've been with him every moment since he sailed south across the gulf with Dame Gwydre."

"Gwydre is in Honce proper?"

"Left her at Chapel Abelle," Jameston explained. "I'm not thinking she's pleased with what she's seeing here in the south."

"That is not my concern."

"But the Highwayman is."

"And?"

"He had nothing to do with the murder of Delaval."

"So you believe that matters a whit?"

"Not in your world," Jameston replied with a snort. "But I think it does to you."

Bannagran stared at him hard.

"He's a fine fighter, that one," Jameston said. Bannagran didn't blink. "He could have killed you."

"Your insults do not serve Dame Gwydre here."

"No insult, just observation," said Jameston. "You might have saved yourself when he had his blade at your chin, I suppose, but he had you when he went past you, and you know it."

Bannagran continued his unflinching stare.

"But he didn't stick you, did he? And he could have, in a fight you started."

"Do you have a point here, other than to insult?"

"No insult intended," Jameston said and bowed low. "I'm only saying so because I'm thinking you should take a closer look at this young man you call the Highwayman. There's more to him than you think."

"Thank you for your advice. I will inform Dame Gwydre that her observant emissary is a wise man."

Jameston grinned at the unrelenting sarcasm, seeing it for what it was. "Bransen had nothing to do with Delaval's death," he repeated. "That doesn't matter to King Yeslnik, but I believe it matters to you."

"Take care your words."

"Bransen's not the reason you're so mad right now," Jameston dared to press on. "I see the twist in your face, Laird Bannagran of Pryd. You know what is right and what simply is. When what simply is doesn't match with what is right, it sticks you harder than Bransen's sword ever could."

"You presume a lot, emissary."

"I've seen a lot, good laird," Jameston replied, bowing low again.

"Is there anything more?"

"I'll pass along your well wishes to Dame Gwydre when I see her again."

Bannagran just sighed as Jameston took his leave.

TWENTY

Focusing Purpose

Dame Gwydre sat on the balcony of her lavish room at St. Mere Abelle, looking across the expansive courtyard to the front wall and beyond, where the first flickers of evening campfires began to sprout among the ranks of Laird Panlamaris's besieging force.

"Second thoughts?" Dawson McKeege asked her from the middle of her room. She turned to regard the man, managing a slight smile.

Dawson understood her dismay. News had come in a short while before of Prince Milwellis's rampage along the populous region known as the inner coast, the western banks of Felidan Bay, with many villages burned to the ground and many, many people killed. Devastation was reported all along the coast, with too many bodies to bury, including many warriors who had come from the wilder reaches of the Mantis Arm.

Yeslnik's victory seemed assured in short order. His apparently overwhelming win did not bode well for St. Mere Abelle and Father Artolivan, nor for Dame Gwydre and her decision to throw in with the monks.

"He says that he is the King of Honce, and so he may well soon be," Gwydre replied.

"We do not know how far south the prince managed to go," Dawson reminded her. "And some of the monks here who've been to Ethelbert dos Entel say that it's a formidable city."

"Let us hope. If Laird Ethelbert can hold back the tides of Yeslnik, then our chances here are greater indeed, but—"

"But if he comes against us with all he's got, then you're wondering if you chose right in standing by the monks, because we're sure to lose. But ye knew that, and didn't we talk about the songs they'll be singing when we're long gone from the world?"

"I know," Gwydre admitted, turning her wistful gaze to distant fields where campfire after campfire flared to life now.

"But now that it seems real, you're wondering about what your choice will mean for them that follow you," Dawson reasoned.

"Perhaps we should sail for Vanguard. All of us, with the monks and the prisoners, too."

"That'd take a lot o' boats."

"Or fast ships turning back."

"To what purpose?" Dawson asked. "He'll come for ye. For all of us."

"We know the ways of Vanguard. Yeslnik does not."

"I'm thinking his armies will cut new ways."

"It may be the wiser course. Perhaps the people of Honce will have no will to pursue. . . ."

"We'll not abandon St. Mere Abelle," said Father Premujon, entering through Gwydre's partially opened door with brothers Giavno and Jond beside him.

"Not for Chapel Pellinor?" Dame Gwydre asked.

Premujon shook his head. "Father Artolivan has made

a bold stand, and we stand with him above all. Brother Fatuus has shown us the way."

"The way to die," Dawson deadpanned, but no one laughed.

"St. Mere Abelle is the most defensible structure in the world," said Premujon. "Both in natural blessings and constructs. The brothers have built and fortified this place over the decades. The only approach by land is up a steep hill, and a slow-moving army . . . we all witnessed the fate of Laird Panlamaris's charge. The small, narrow harbor is nearly unreachable by any who do not know the rocky reefs about it, and it, too, would be easily defended by merely a handful of brothers with the proper gemstones. A single sinking could prevent other sizable ships from even attempting the approach. And even if Yeslnik's sailors somehow gained the wharf area, the tunnels are easily defended or, if need be, easily shut down."

"You inspire confidence, Father," Dame Gwydre remarked.

"Look again to that wall, milady," Premujon went on. He, too, seemed to be gaining strength from his own words. "The wall of St. Mere Abelle is thicker and taller than any in Honce, and forget not that behind the wall wait scores of brothers well trained in the use of potent magic."

"I saw as much when Panlamaris dared approach," Gwydre admitted.

"Then we're decided," said Dawson. "St. Mere Abelle is part of Vanguard, if Father Artolivan agrees."

"He is on his way here this very moment," said Premujon. "To do just that, as he indicated when first you proposed it."

"And this chapel will hold strong against King Yeslnik, a safe harbor for any who want no part of his Honce," Dawson proclaimed, smiling widely at his beloved lady, knowing well that she needed his confidence in this dangerous hour.

"Would that it were that simple," Gwydre replied, though she did flash her own smile to show her appreciation to her trusted friend. "When Yeslnik is through with Ethelbert he will likely reinforce Panlamaris's siege."

"St. Mere Abelle can hold forever and longer," Premujon assured her. "They have access to all the water and food they would ever need."

He continued on, but Gwydre, not disagreeing, finally managed to stop him with an upraised hand. "I do not doubt the might of this sacred place," she assured the three monks. "When first I sighted Chapel . . . St. Mere Abelle from Dawson's boat, my heart leaped in awe. I do not doubt the strength of this place or the resilience of those who reside here. Of all my holdings, this one on the front line of the expected war and under siege even now is the one for which I least fear."

"Lady?" an obviously confused Premujon asked.

"While we are trapped here, what mischief will Yeslnik wreak behind us in Vanguard?" The others suddenly wore concerned expressions, as if that little matter had escaped them. "With a few of the great warships of Delaval or Palmaristown to blockade us, what might those still in Vanguard do against the approach of Yeslnik's thousands should he choose that route? To whom will they look to lead them with Dame Gwydre, Father Premujon, and so many of our finest warriors here south of the gulf?"

Beside Premujon, Brother Giavno gasped audibly, accurately reflecting the sudden trepidation of all in the room.

"Never said it'd be easy," Dawson muttered under his breath.

Almost as if to accentuate Dawson's point, Father Artolivan knocked on the partially opened door then and shuffled in, and old indeed did he appear. The great weight of the monumental events had taken a toll on him. It seemed that, as with Dame Gwydre, doubts had begun to surface.

"We are part of Vanguard," he announced without prompting. "St. Mere Abelle is within the domain of Dame Gwydre. That is my decision, though I do not come to it easily. Your generous offer is accepted, good lady, may Abelle watch over us all." He bowed slightly as he turned to leave again. "You will forgive me, but I must retire early."

Father Premujon nodded to Brother Giavno, who rushed to catch up to Father Artolivan and help him back to his private quarters.

"I worry for him," Premujon said. "These are difficult times, all the more so because of the decline of Samhaists, making this a time that should be the golden age of our church."

"It will be," Dame Gwydre assured him. "If good people stand strong."

"Stand strong and sail swift," Dawson added.

"That is indeed our plan and our need," said Gwydre. "We can hold St. Mere Abelle—of that, I have no doubt. But you must lead my ships with cunning and skill. We cannot allow Palmaristown to seal off the sea routes and control the coast. You have been beside me for so long, my friend Dawson, and now what I ask of you is no less than that I asked of Bransen, Jond, and the others in sending them after Ancient Badden. We must be mobile, quick, and strong. The fewer options we offer to King Yeslnik, the more likely he will be to accept any terms or compromise."

"Fair winds and following seas," Dawson replied with a wide grin and a look of sincere love for his dearest friend.

* * *

Callen Duwornay moved tentatively toward her bedroom door, surprised by the knock. She expected it to be Cadayle, of course, and feared that something might be troubling her daughter at this late hour, for indeed, the night was past its midpoint.

She flinched, her rich brown eyes going wide to see Dawson McKeege, his floppy cap in hand.

"What trouble?" she started to ask, but Dawson hushed her gently.

"No trouble, pretty lass," he said. "Or might be for me, but nothing to get yourself upset about."

"It is very late," Callen said, and she reflexively grasped the front of her loose nightshirt and slipped a bit farther behind the cracked door.

"Begging your pardon."

"Given, but what is the matter?"

"It's about you and yours going to Pryd to live," Dawson explained, his voice shakier than Callen had ever heard it. "That's what I'm hearing."

"That is the plan if Bransen can manage it."

"No water near Pryd."

"No water?"

"No sailing water—river or ocean, I mean."

Callen looked at him as if she did not understand.

Dawson, clearly uncomfortable, rubbed his stubbly, weathered face. "I'm sailing in the morning. Not knowing when I'll be back."

"Going home?" Callen asked.

Dawson shook his head and rubbed his face again. "I'll be on *Lady Dreamer* for all the season, until winter puts me in dock, either here or back in Port Vanguard. It's not what I'm wanting, but Gwydre needs me, and that's a call I've never let pass."

Callen smiled and nodded, though her expression drooped just a bit as she asked, "So you have come to me to say farewell?"

Dawson seemed to Callen as if he might cry. He shook his head. "I'm not wanting to, pretty lady. Not since the first time I saw you."

"Dawson!" Callen said.

"I know I'm not proper here, and I'm not knowing how to tell you otherwise, but I had to tell—"

He stopped then. He had to, for Callen Duwornay came through her doorway and wrapped him in a great hug and a passionate kiss.

She hadn't even realized how much she had longed to hear words like that from this man, hadn't realized the depth of her feelings for Dawson, so busy had she been in the teasing and lighthearted banter with him.

So she kissed him with passion she hadn't shown since the long-ago night when a wicked Samhaist and the people of Pryd Town had mutilated the one man she had ever dared to love and had thrown her in a sack with a snake for her crime of loving him.

Clearly nervous, and clearly not knowing what he was supposed to do next when Callen broke off the kiss, Dawson stammered and glanced around.

Callen tugged him into her room.

M a?" Cadayle asked, gently knocking on Callen's door. It was long past breakfast, and it was typically Callen who awakened Cadayle for their morning meal. Cadayle knew Callen to be a prompt and responsible woman, and her unusual tardiness this morning brought real fears to her daughter.

"Ma?" she asked again and pushed open the door.

To come face-to-face with Dawson McKeege.

"What?" she started to ask, when she noticed Callen,

standing off to the side of the shade-darkened room, wrapped in a blanket and apparently nothing else.

"Ma?" Cadayle stammered, and then, "Oh, oh, oh!"

Callen started to call to her, but Cadayle didn't wait and reflexively slapped Dawson across the face. Then, in horror, Cadayle sucked in her breath and threw her hand over her mouth, her eyes darting from Callen to Dawson to Callen to Dawson.

"Why'd you do that?" a surprised Dawson asked.

"I don't know!" Cadayle cried, and with a final look at her mother, she gave a sharp yelp and ran off down the hall.

But by then she was laughing, giggling like a young girl.

"Ye've got yerself a strange girl there, Callen," Dawson muttered.

"Have you met her husband, then?"

"Can't wait to see their kids," Dawson said with a helpless chuckle. "Ye think the girl's sensibilities scarred?"

"I think her surprised," Callen admitted, walking over and reaching with her blanket-gown to wrap Dawson next to her naked form. "And I think her happy, because she's always happy when I'm happy."

"And ye are?" Dawson asked.

"Fool," Callen teased, kissing him, sealing his lateness for his meeting with Dame Gwydre.

Bransen stood with Jameston in the forest to the east of Pryd Town. Jameston leaned on his bow, watching the young man, who seemed confused about his next steps.

"You'll not find an easy path to clearing your name," Jameston remarked. "Back to the north and Chapel Abelle, then? Be good to see your family. Let Dame Gwydre take the lead in arguing your case with the idiotic Yeslnik. That's my advice."

"You go and do that, with my gratitude," said Bransen.

"What's that supposed to mean?"

"My road is southeast. To find the other half of a broken sword."

"You're thinking to kill the murderer and bring his head in to toss at Yeslnik's feet? Much like you did with Badden?"

Bransen shook his head through every word.

"Bring him in alive, then, so he can speak the truth that you weren't involved."

Still Bransen shook his head.

"Say it, boy," Jameston prompted.

"I'm not going to fight with the one who killed Delaval."

"Then how're you to clear your name?"

Bransen turned and looked at the scout directly. "I'm not sure I care any longer," he admitted. "So please tell Cadayle and Callen that they may have to remain at Chapel Abelle a bit longer."

"Bannagran said—"

"I would not trust their safety outside of Chapel Abelle, particularly if Yeslnik or his lackeys come to understand that I go to find he who killed Delaval not out of anger or for vengeance or for their perceived justice."

"Then why?" Jameston smiled as Bransen took a deep breath. "Because they're like you—like your ma, at least."

"Jhesta Tu," Bransen confirmed. "Long have I wanted to embrace the mystics of that which has guided me from Stork to Highwayman."

Jameston considered the words for a few heartbeats, then nodded and shrugged. "Your road to choose."

"And you will go north?"

"Only following your own steps. This is your journey."

"Because that is what Dame Gwydre asked of you, but now I travel for myself and not for Dame Gwydre."

Again Jameston shrugged. "Doesn't matter to me. I

travel for myself and have been enjoying the road beside you. And that's the whole point of it, isn't it?"

"Enjoyment?"

"Aye."

"There is more than that," said Bransen.

"Never!" Jameston said with a grin.

Bransen knew better than to argue with the stubborn scout. Besides, though he wouldn't admit it aloud, he was glad for the company—particularly the company of this man, this friend. He took a deep breath and took a bold step to the southeast, toward Ethelbert dos Entel, toward this unknown Jhesta Tu who had slain Delaval the king, toward the realization of his greatest hopes or his greatest fears.

But he didn't slow.

Not this time.

PART THREE

THE MEANING OF HIS GIFT

I met Jameston Sequin on a road east of Pryd Town. I had first been introduced to him on a winding trail in Alpinador, far, far away, when he had intervened to help me and my companions in a fight with trolls. His reputation preceded him by only a few sentences, mostly revealed in the wide-eyed admiration from that most unlikely source of such animation, Crazy Vaughna.

I had known Jameston Sequin for months and had spent many hours with him and many alone with him before I ever truly met him. There was always something about him and his unusual appearance and demeanor that had drawn me to him and had made me glad indeed (though I wouldn't openly admit it) when he had unexpectedly joined me on my perilous road out of Chapel Abelle. So many extraordinary visual clues had revealed to me long before that this was no ordinary scout, with his huge mustache and amazingly long-legged strides and that distinctive hat he wore, named after him because its triangular design served him as a sight for his deadly bow. Truly Jameston seemed larger than life, a man, perhaps the first I had ever met, whose reputation was not diminished, indeed was enhanced, by familiarity.

So I had known him, had traveled with him, had battled beside him, but it wasn't until one morning a week out of Pryd Town, the smell of recent battles heavy in the air, when I actually met Jameston Sequin, and all because the enigma that was this formidable scout finally forced me to ask him a simple question.

"Why?"

He looked at me, and I knew at once that he understood the context and the depth of my inquiry. Maybe it was my stance, or the tone I had used in asking, or the simple lack of context for such a question, uttered suddenly on a faraway road. Whatever the reason, Jameston knew. I could see it in his eyes and in that grin he often wore, a look that made anyone around him know for certain that he, Jameston, knew more than they knew or at least understood better.

"Where?" he flippantly replied. "When? Who?"

I wasn't letting him get away. Not then. I needed to know. He had surprised me by deciding to stay with me even after I had learned of the presence of Jhesta Tu and had proclaimed that my journey was my own and not for Dame Gwydre. To understand his decision, I needed to know the truth of Jameston Sequin. "Why?" I responded.

"Any answer I gave would work, I suppose, since your word works for any question." He grinned wider because he knew that I knew that he knew, if that makes any sense, and he was determined to play it out fully.

"Why are you who you are?" I clarified, though it certainly wasn't necessary. "Why a scout? Why do you spend your days in solitude?"

"I'm here with you."

My sigh made him grin all the wider.

"You are becoming predictable," I told him.

"When people think that, it makes me more dangerous."

"Or are you afraid to tell me? To tell anyone?"

Finally, I could see that I had hit his sensibilities, and hard. His expression changed, as if a cloud had passed overhead to darken the day. He moved off the road to a small grouping of rocks large enough to serve as seats, bidding me to follow. I saw weariness in his step that I had never before detected.

"You want to know why I went into the emptiness of Alpinador?" he asked me as he took a seat, still looking older than before.

"I want to know why you're here with me."

"That's what I said," he replied. Was he always one layer ahead of me in my thinking?

"Pride and money," he said then, and his smile became self-deprecating. "I went to Vanguard as a young man, younger than yourself. I was a confident one, almost as much as you are, and I was good enough to back it up. Things that seemed so simple to me, like how to hide and how to find someone else who's trying to hide, befuddled others. I understood animals—I don't know why or how, but everything about them and the way they were likely to behave just seemed obvious to me."

"And goblins and trolls and powries," I remarked, and Jameston nodded.

"With all that behind me, with all the folk of Vanguard looking north for furs and timber and exotic items, the road seemed obvious. I wanted to make a name for myself, boy, and make a fair amount of coin at the same time."

It all made sense to me, of course, but I knew, too, that the young man who had first gone out from civilization for those reasons was not the same person now sitting before me. As Jameston continued his tale of exploration and building his reputation and fame as a guide and hunter, one question became apparent: What had changed his mind?

"I had the coin. It came from the caribou moss, from leading teams to it, from protecting caravans, and from this hat!" He tipped his "sequin," that triangular cap favored by archers across Vanguard and even in northern

Honce proper. "All the coin in the world, and nothing I wanted to spend it on," he answered, plainly and again with that self-deprecating chuckle, as if it had all been a bad joke he had inadvertently played upon himself. "The fame led to a line of the same questions being asked over and over again. To some I was a hero, but I wasn't any such thing. To most I was a curiosity, something to gawk at.

"Aye, that's what I was," he said, sadness in his tone. "And there was no point to any of it, so I went on without any sense of purpose."

"Even mocking those who claimed such purpose driving their own lives," I dared remark. Jameston's corresponding nod was more enthusiastic then, as if I had grasped exactly his point in telling me all this.

"My purpose was all for me when I was a young adventurer, looking to conquer the world," he said. "Then I had no purpose at all, and for a long time."

"And now?"

"Now? Dame Gwydre's father cut a new trail in front of my wandering feet. I didn't walk it, not far anyway, until I had to, many years later." As he finished, he looked up at me, locked gazes with me, and I knew then, in that moment, that I had truly come to know Jameston Sequin.

"When you met my group in a fight on the trail," I reasoned.

"That was part of it."

"You walk with me to find purpose in the life of Jameston Sequin."

My proclamation was met with a somewhat accepting and somewhat incredulous look. Finally, he shook his head. "You're just on the trail Gwydre's da cut for me."

Part of the bigger whole, he meant. Part of the purpose that was not self-centered, as was the one that had driven Jameston Sequin to the wilds of northern Vanguard and Alpinador, the one that had brought him fame and false *fortune. It wasn't until he realized that his journey through this life wasn't about him alone, but about a greater sense of brotherhood and community, that Jameston Sequin had found a trail worth walking.*

As I pondered that unexpected conversation throughout that day, I knew, too, why Jameston had shared it with me.

Dame Gwydre, like her father before her, had cut a trail, but it was one I was reluctant to walk.

And so it was that even as I directed our journey, to the east and the Jhesta Tu and my greatest question and challenge, even as I led, so I was being led.

It was . . . comforting.

—BRANSEN GARIBOND

TWENTY-ONE

Let the Word Go Forth

A calm spread over St. Mere Abelle. Panlamaris's army remained entrenched across the field, but they would not come on. No monks were out to guide the many prisoners, who, suddenly, did not seem to be prisoners any longer. Their work was not diligent this day as they milled about, whispering about the grand changes that had come to the world and to their corner of it. Ethelbert man and woman and Delaval man and woman mingled effortlessly and without thought, their old boundaries and battles now, finally, fully left behind.

In every prayer room of the great chapel, the brothers did their work, those lesser monks assisting the more powerful as they used a soul stone to soar out from their bodies, to travel spiritually to every corner of Honce, to their brethren with the word of Father Artolivan.

Come gather in Chapel Abelle, the blessed St. Mere Abelle, their spirits implored their brethren. Or to Ethelbert dos Entel if you must, and pray for the mercy of Laird Ethelbert. Hide, brethren, from the fires and follies of King Yeslnik.

The finality of the decision, a frank admission that the

Abellican Church had severed ties, had declared a complete and likely irrevocable break with King Yeslnik and thus the bulk of Honce itself, had weighed heavily on Father Artolivan and the others, but when Father Dennigan of Chapel Delaval had arrived, carrying the head of Brother Piastafan, what choice had been left?

"Let the word go forth," Father Artolivan had told his brethren, his voice thick with regret and sad resignation. And so the brothers went to their work this calm morning, their spirits soaring from their corporeal bodies and from St. Mere Abelle, flying to the distant chapels to the limits of their power, then entreating the brothers of the outward chapels to spread the word to the wider corners of Honce.

"This ability of the monks to spread the word wide and far is an advantage for us," Dame Gwydre said to Dawson, Cormack, and Milkeila at the windswept docks of St. Mere Abelle. "Should it come to war, our armies can remain in coordination. Our enemies might wait a week to hear word from a distant battlefield, but we can know . . ."

"You overestimate the power of spirit-walking," Cormack dared to intervene. "This is a highly unusual event—we did not dare try it even in those hours when our situation in Alpinador grew desperate. This is most extraordinary for Father Artolivan to command it, or even allow it."

"He did as much to relate to us the happenings in the southland when we were in Vanguard," Dame Gwydre protested.

"And paid a dear price. One of the brothers who came spiritually to Vanguard—"

"One of? There was only the one."

"Only the one who made it," Cormack corrected. "Out of a dozen who made the attempt. Most fell short, weary before they ever managed to float their spirits across the

Gulf of Corona. Another never even made the gulf, having fallen to possess a poor girl he saw along the road. He has recovered from the shock of that ill-fated meeting, but she remains a stuttering fool. And another brother did cross the gulf, only to be drawn into the corporeal form of a dockman on the wharves of Port Vanguard. He did not manage a possession and was driven mad in the attempt."

"Why would they attempt such a thing as possession?" Milkeila had to ask, her eyes wide with shock.

"Aye, it seems an evil thing!" added Dawson.

Cormack nodded. "It is a compulsion that breaks the greatest of brothers, a temptation borne out of no rational thought and rarely controlled by rational thought. Spirit-walking is outlawed within the order, other than by specific exception. A brother trapped in the forest, freezing to death, would be violating church edict if he so used a soul stone to seek out aid."

Dame Gwydre started to argue against that reasoning, but stopped and swallowed hard and glanced back at the long tunnels that would take her back to the cliff-top structures, only then truly appreciating the enormous weight that had bowed the shoulders of Father Artolivan.

"They use it now, as previously to inform you of the great events in Honce, because of the magnitude," Cormack explained. "Even should a few brothers fail, even should a few bystanders be driven mad by an unintended possession, the cost is worth the gain, for Father Artolivan knows well that many of his brethren and the prisoners they shelter are in dire peril now, and he would not have them go to unwitting slaughter."

"His brethren, or your own?" Dawson asked, drawing a sidelong glance from Cormack. "You sound like one who's thinking the church a good place to be."

Cormack glanced at Milkeila, who grinned knowingly, not disagreeing with Dawson's assessment.

To that, Cormack merely shrugged.

"Sail swift and sail safe," Gwydre said to them. "To Vanguard, one ship, to Ethelbert dos Entel the other."

Dawson nodded, then stepped up and gave the woman a hug. "I'll be for Entel," he whispered. "So my journey's the long one."

"What will I do without Dawson beside me?" Gwydre whispered back.

"The right thing," he replied and squeezed her tighter. "I lost me heart last night," he whispered even more quietly. "And now I'm leaving her here under your own protection."

"Callen?" said Gwydre, loudly enough so that Cormack and Milkeila caught it and looked at the hugging couple curiously. She pushed Dawson back to arm's length. He didn't answer, other than to smile.

And Gwydre's own smile more than matched his own. How strange the fates could be! A deception to bring Bransen to Vanguard to serve in a war had brought Dawson together with a woman who stole his heart, an event that neither he nor Gwydre had ever expected would happen again.

"Sail swift and sail safe," she said, her voice breaking. "And come back to your lady, who will be by my side."

The good news carried Dame Gwydre back through the tunnels and stairs to the high ground of St. Mere Abelle. When she arrived, though late for a meeting, she did not go straight to Father Artolivan's audience hall. Instead she climbed the ladder of the back wall, overlooking the narrow bay that sheltered St. Mere Abelle's docks.

Lady Dreamer was just putting out, all lines away. A second ship was already out from the docks, awaiting Dawson's craft. The two would travel together throughout the first couple of days, moving to the middle of the gulf, before Dawson turned east to run the coast all the way to Ethelbert dos Entel at the end of the Belt-and-Buckle and the other went north.

The tide brought *Lady Dreamer* out a short ways, and one sail dropped open, Dawson tacking hard and expertly to turn his bow out to open waters.

Gwydre took comfort in the great confidence she held in Dawson McKeege. If anyone could get to Laird Ethelbert and properly deliver her message, it was he. The comfort helped her to get past the great sadness that enveloped her as *Lady Dreamer* started away, for she missed her longtime companion already. He had become a true brother to her, a confidant and the one man who kept her focused on and honest to what was in her heart. How would she get through these trying days without him?

She made a mental note to look in on Callen and Cadayle. She was quite fond of the mother and daughter, and if Dawson saw so much in Callen, then Gwydre figured her positive impressions of the woman must be valid.

When she finally arrived at Father Artolivan's gathering, she found the elderly church leader with Father Premujon, brothers Pinower, Jond, and Giavno, and several other monks she did not know by name engaged in a heated debate about their next moves.

They stopped chattering as one when Dame Gwydre entered, Father Artolivan motioning for her to take a seat beside him on the raised dais that centered the gathering.

"My ships are out for Vanguard and for Ethelbert dos Entel," she explained. "Our break with King Yeslnik is complete." Several deep breaths, signaling fear and determination, came back at her. "We cannot turn back from our stance now, Father Artolivan," she pressed. "Yeslnik will not forgive."

"Let us hope your good man Dawson gets to Laird Ethelbert's side before Yeslnik pushes him into the sea,"

Brother Pinower remarked, and Gwydre winced at the proposition.

"King Yeslnik and Laird Panlamaris will not forgive, Lady of Vanguard," said Father Artolivan. "We must hold them off long enough to diminish their appetite for war. Perhaps then we might find some common ground upon which a peace can be enacted."

"Or we must win," said Brother Pinower, and all eyes turned his way.

Their expressions told Gwydre that this was exactly the argument into which she had walked.

"Yeslnik proclaims himself King of Honce and there seems to be no one who can stop him," Pinower explained. "But his actions have already wrought great disdain. Almost to a man and woman, the prisoners we hold here have pledged their loyalty to our cause. They will fight, though the option of sitting to the side of the battle is open before them without ill consequence. How many men in Yeslnik's army would be so willing and eager for more battle, I wonder?"

"How many of Laird Panlamaris's men did not look on in horror when our brethren were evilly murdered on the field outside St. Mere Abelle?" Brother Giavno agreed. "And if Brother Fatuus so touched and inspired us, what might be the effect of his determined march on those among Panlamaris's ranks who witnessed it?"

"Our hopes may prove correct and will aid us," Father Artolivan warned. "But they alone will not turn the tide against the power of Delaval City and Palmaristown and Pryd and all the rest."

"We sit and wait, and we fight if we must?" Dame Gwydre asked. She made it clear with her tone that she was not enamored of that passive course. "And we seek Ethelbert for alliance, though we know not what he has left to even continue in this war. Dawson might well arrive at Ethelbert dos Entel's docks to find Yeslnik's soldiers manning them. Or to find Laird Ethelbert helplessly trapped within his city, as we seem to be here."

Her grim assessment was met by blank stares, until Father Artolivan offered, "We are seeking other routes of resistance and alliance."

"Other routes? Surely any allies we could find would be welcomed."

"There are two names being spoken across the breadth of Honce behind those of the warring lairds," Artolivan explained. "Two men have distinguished themselves and have led Yeslnik to near-certain victory. Every prisoner in St. Mere Abelle, Ethelbert and Yeslnik man alike, knows of these generals: Bannagran of Pryd and Milwellis of Palmaristown."

"You wish to find alliance with Yeslnik's generals?" Dame Gwydre tried to keep the incredulity out of her tone. How desperate were they, truly?

"Not Milwellis, certainly," said Artolivan. "He is a man of ill temperament and great hubris. He holds no love for St. Mere Abelle."

"Particularly since we just sent his father scurrying away with lightning prodding his arse every step," Gwydre added.

Artolivan conceded that point with a nod and just a hint of a much-needed grin.

"Master Reandu of Chapel Pryd is a good and temperate man, and he has the ear of Bannagran, whom he considers a friend. Perhaps . . . ?"

"If Master Reandu still holds court in Chapel Pryd," Dame Gwydre warned.

"He does," said Giavno. "I went to him in spirit this morning, though I had not the strength to impart the message of Father Artolivan. Still, I sensed calm about that town."

"I doubt that King Yeslnik would force Bannagran to move against his friend Reandu, but should Yeslnik do such a thing it is possible that Bannagran would take great exception."

"It seems a desperate plan, but I see few other options," Gwydre admitted. "If we could turn this General Bannagran to our cause, then it would bolster our hopes, of course. But to what do we ask him to pledge his fealty? To Vanguard? That seems unlikely, at best."

The monks all glanced around at each other and Gwydre realized that she had touched upon the very heart of the debate into which she had intruded, the backdrop that had inspired the notion that they might "win."

"Yeslnik and Ethelbert have torn Honce apart with their war of greed," Father Artolivan began, his tone measured. "We have rejected Yeslnik and have little connection to Laird Ethelbert, though we seek him, not to serve him, but as an ally against our common foe. We will not serve King Ethelbert, Dame Gwydre. The Abellican Church will fight beside him, perhaps and if he is willing, but we will not serve him."

"He is very tied to the ways of Behr," Brother Pinower explained. "And to the religions of Behr. He is not hostile to our order, but neither is he a believer."

"So if we gain ground, if we can hold against Laird Panlamaris and even begin to move against King Yeslnik, then to what end?" Gwydre asked. "Am I to declare autonomy of Vanguard from Honce? Will the Abellican Church then become the Church of Vanguard?"

"Suppose we show the people of Honce a third way, beyond Yeslnik and Ethelbert?" Father Artolivan asked.

"And that would be?" Gwydre asked. "Compromise?"

"A queen."

"You are mad!"

"Perhaps," Father Artolivan conceded. "It is a difficult proposition."

"A desperate one, you mean," said Gwydre.

"And are we not desperate?"

Gwydre sighed.

"You saved Vanguard, Dame Gwydre," Father Artolivan said. "Can you save Honce as well? Two lairds hungry for power have driven the land to near ruin. Every family has been devastated now by a war that will not end."

"Will it not?" asked Gwydre. "It seems that Laird Yeslnik has a strong upper hand, by all the reports and your own admission."

"That result might prove the most disastrous one of all," said Artolivan. "Yeslnik is a merciless, privileged beast of the highest order. He would have me murder all the prisoners he has sent while freeing all the men sent by Laird Ethelbert, and both by treaty for honorable recusal from the war!

"Nay, Dame Gwydre, that outcome cannot be allowed. The Samhaists have been driven from most of their groves, Blessed Abelle be thanked, and now King Yeslnik has declared war with the Abellican Church. Indeed, I expect him to declare Father De Guilbe as Father of the Order of Blessed Abelle and to enlist his phony interpretation of the teachings of our Blessed Abelle as his official religion. You wish to sue for peace and to declare autonomy, but you know that this man, Yeslnik, will not agree and will not relent."

"Have you come to regret your words and actions against King Yeslnik and Laird Panlamaris, Father Artolivan?"

The old monk smiled more widely than ever before, and, for the first time in the meeting, serenity washed over his wrinkled face and his eyes twinkled with hope. "Not for a moment," he replied. "Though I have come to realize the difficulty of the road such principles demand."

"Cordon Roe," said Brother Giavno, surprising them all with the reference to a most terrible incident that had

occurred in Delaval City in the early days of the Order
of Blessed Abelle. "Brother Fatuus," he added, grinning,
against the confused expressions. "We all will die, after
all, be it now or in a decade or in several decades. Better
to die contented. Better a life guided by principle, even a
short one, than a century of misery wrought by the knowledge of personal cowardice."

"Queen Gwydre of Honce," remarked Father Premujon. "It rings of hope."

"It rings of presumption and arrogance," said Dame
Gwydre.

"Perhaps it is the time for both, good lady," said Father
Artolivan. "Perhaps it is time for both."

D awson stood near *Lady Dreamer*'s prow, his favor-
ite place when his ship found a good wind and
threw her spray up high. She opened her sails now, leaving the docks of St. Mere Abelle far, far behind. The
slight splash of salty water felt good to Dawson, made
him feel alive and gave him a burst of that brine smell
that seemed to define his life. He came up here to be
alone with his thoughts, to reflect on his life and the point
of it all.

And today, Dawson needed that contemplative energy
more than ever. The night with Callen Duwornay had
thrown his emotional balance into a delicious swirl, a
jumble of possibility. Terrifying possibilities, since Dawson had stepped away from his typical course. But that
was the way of the world right now, was it not? Honce was
at war with itself in a struggle that would dramatically
redefine the old feudal holdings, however this insanity
ended. And the roads! Dawson had long been among the
most worldly of people in parochial Honce and even more
parochial Vanguard. *Lady Dreamer* was his freedom, his

transport to exotic lands. Until these last few years, only the sailors and the marching armies typically saw any of the world beyond their own home villages. The average person in Honce would spend the entirety of his or her life knowing only a few square miles of land and a few score, perhaps a hundred, other people.

While that no doubt remained the truth of the land, the roads connecting all the major holdings of Honce proper were taming the land and making possible many more journeys to Delaval City or Pryd Town or St. Mere Abelle. The world was changing, and the tumult of those monumental shifts was a big part of the reason for the war.

Now Dawson's world, too, was changing, had changed. He couldn't believe that he had found the courage to be so forward with Callen, couldn't believe his good fortune to find his feelings reciprocated. He could only hope now that he would be able to get to the city of Ethelbert dos Entel and back in time to realize the sweetness of his courage. Suddenly, he couldn't imagine his life without Callen.

Dawson took a deep breath. If Callen went home to Pryd Town, then was he to abandon his life at sea? How could he give up *Lady Dreamer*? How could he give up Callen?

"I say, Captain!" said an insistent voice from behind, in such a tone that Dawson realized he must have been hailed several times already.

"What? What, then?" Dawson stammered. He focused on the situation at hand, noting that they were fast closing on *Shelligan's Run,* the ship he had selected to deliver Dame Gwydre's message back to Vanguard. At first all seemed as it should, but Dawson's face crinkled a moment later when he noted the commotion on the deck of the other ship, with sailors running to the port rail and to the rigging.

"West, Captain," Dawson's crewman said.

Dawson looked that way and felt his heart sink.

Palmaristown warships, three of them, each twice as large as *Lady Dreamer,* sailed in tight formation. Their decks were full of crewmen, archers with their deadly longbows. Even from this distance Dawson could make out the distinctively high poop deck of a Palmaristown warship, for those craft had each been equipped with a large ballista, a gigantic crossbow set on a rotating platform.

Giant sails full of wind, the ships came on fast.

Dawson's thoughts whirled. Could *Lady Dreamer* tack fast enough and fill her sails with the westerlies quickly enough to outrun them?

He shook his head doubtfully. *Lady Dreamer* could get up to speed and outmaneuver anything on the water, true, but she wasn't even at full sail, and she couldn't straight-line outrun Palmaristown warships, the greatest vessels in all of Honce.

Dawson glanced back the way they had come, thinking that maybe they could turn about and get into the protection of St. Mere Abelle's harbor before the warships got in range and laid waste to his two ships.

And there, Dawson McKeege saw his doom, for he sighted two more Palmaristown warships running the coast.

He had sailed into a trap.

Five ships, fully manned and armed for battle, any one of which could probably defeat both *Lady Dreamer* and *Shelligan's Run.*

Two of the ships in the west continued their straight charge, while the third had veered to the north to cut off any attempt to flee into the open waters of the gulf.

There was nowhere to run.

He thought of Dame Gwydre then and how he had failed his friend. He thought about Callen. Once the notion of the beautiful woman entered his mind a great despair washed over him. He knew that the beautiful possibilities had just flown away.

Would he take comfort in the memories of his last night when the Palmaristown fleet put him into the dark water? he wondered.

TWENTY-TWO

The Wake of War

W ell, you know an army or two marched through here," Jameston Sequin said somberly—the only tone appropriate for the images around them. They were nearing the Mirianic coast now, far to the southeast of Pryd. Torn roads, burned forests, and carrion birds, so many carrion birds, greeted them at every turn.

A ground fog covered the region this day, thick with the smell of death.

Bransen had fought in several battles, most notably in the large and wild fight outside Ancient Badden's castle, so he was not unused to the aftermath of war. But this was different, darker and more sinister. For he knew that this time the smell of rotting bodies was not fully from, not even mostly from, the corpses of combatants, the soldiers of Ethelbert and Yeslnik who had fallen in their struggles. No, the air was thick with the smell of rotting, dead children and other innocents caught between the bloodlust of the warring lairds.

"You got no belly for it," Jameston said, obviously seeing the sour expression on Bransen's face.

Bransen looked at him hard. "You do?"

Jameston gave a helpless chuckle. "You're starting to understand why I live in the woods."

"And yet, here we are."

"I already told you . . ."

"I know, a purpose bigger than your own life," said Bransen. "Are you, am I, possessed of magic enough so that we can just lift a gemstone and utter a phrase and repair all of this?" As he finished, he swept his arm toward the south, where a trio of burned-out cottages stood. Even the animals on the small farms had been killed, and several cows lay on the field, covered with pecking birds.

"Not thinking that, and you're not either," said Jameston. "We'll find ways to help. That's something."

Bransen nodded, his expression grim. They set off again, heading east, and Jameston's words seemed prophetic soon after, when cries for help and of fear rent the heavy air.

The pair rushed through a stand of thick trees and around a rocky bluff, Jameston stringing his bow as they ran. With the sounds coming from over an old and crumbling stone wall—crumbling, but still taller than a tall man—Bransen reflexively called upon his brooch and his Jhesta Tu training, reaching into his concentration and the malachite stone simultaneously, instantly, instinctively. He leaped high. Too high. He felt weightless, the malachite working its magical levitation and amplified by his Jhesta Tu understanding. He had meant to grab a hold on the top of the wall and pull himself over, but he climbed into the air to the wall top and above, floating right over, almost as if he was swimming in the air.

He remained in control of his body and kept his wits about him as he crossed over the stone wall. From that bird's-eye view, the Highwayman witnessed the chaos. Before and below him poor peasants scrambled among several small cottages, while armed men chased them and beat them down. Out of one house rushed a young warrior, his hands full of bread, a peasant woman charging after him, screaming for him to stop. One of his companions stepped up from the side and cracked her across the back of the neck with a heavy club, throwing her face down to the ground, where she lay still.

The Highwayman noticed a bow aimed his way. He reached into the gem again, to the smoky quartz stone. The archer let fly, and the arrow missed cleanly but the bowman cheered, thinking his shot dead center, for it had surely hit the decoy image the Highwayman had created of himself.

Below, the man who had clubbed the woman lifted his weapon to strike her again as she lay in the dirt.

The Highwayman dropped to the ground before him.

"Wha—" the man managed to gasp before he was hit with a series of short punches and flying elbows that sent him spinning away. The Highwayman turned as the stealer of bread spun back and dropped the loaf, sword in hand.

The Highwayman's fabulous blade came forth, slashing across to cleanly intercept the warrior's thrust, parrying the enemy blade, a second then a third time. Any unwitting onlooker might have thought the warrior deftly picking off the attacks of this strange, black-clothed warrior. But Bransen and the warrior knew the truth of it: The poor warrior had no idea of the fast-changing angle of the longer and stronger sword coming at him and the only reason his smaller iron weapon was parrying was because this far superior swordsman was aiming for that iron weapon!

"Affwin Wi!" the warrior cried desperately. "Ethelbert! Ethelbert!"

The Highwayman knew the first words as a name, so much like his mother's own, but the stunning realization didn't slow his assault. He hit the iron sword again and again, sending numbing jolts up the warrior's arms, and finally he maneuvered the man where he wanted, at the same time using the noise of the fight to bring another pair of marauders charging at him.

His blade came across left to right, driving the iron sword out before it. The Highwayman stepped forward in a spin, elbow flying high to snap at the warrior's throat as he came around, sending the man gasping to the ground but leaving the Highwayman perfectly balanced and squared up against the newest two attackers.

One attacker, Bransen mentally corrected, as one of the charging enemies lurched suddenly and went staggering aside, an arrow deep in his hip.

The other man charged in, screaming, lifting an axe above his head for a powerful chop.

But in the blink of an eye the Highwayman was up against him and inside the angle of any strike. The sword slashed above the attacker, lopping the head off the high-raised axe even as Bransen's free hand grasped the handle. With the weighted head suddenly gone the attacker lost all balance. Bransen twisted his arm that held the axe handle, repeatedly slamming it down against the man's forehead.

The man stumbled, dazed. The Highwayman let go of the handle, grabbed the man by the front of his leather tunic, and again reached into the power of the Jhesta Tu and of the brooch, two properties together.

He used the malachite's levitation powers to lessen the weight of the man and the jolting power of the graphite backing to add lightning into his throw.

The warrior went flying away up high, over the side of the small cottage, to land on the thatched roof. He lay twitching in violent spasms that made him bite the tip off his own tongue.

The Highwayman looked to the fallen woman, blood running from her ear. Rage gripped him. He charged the center courtyard of the house cluster where several warriors had gathered, some setting a defense against him, others lifting bows and firing off to the north—at Jameston, Bransen assumed.

They were ready for him and too many, but he didn't care. The image of the peasant woman, her skull broken, haunted and drove him on. He lifted his sword, and the blade burst into flames.

An arrow shot out and struck him in his left shoulder.

Nearly blinded by rage and pain, the Highwayman yelled and charged all the faster. He grabbed at the power of serpentine, the fire shield, and then demanded more of the ruby firestone. Now flames covered not only his sword but his entire body!

Like a living bonfire, half-blinded by flames, and with agony biting him from the arrow deep in his shoulder, the Highwayman surged into their midst.

They ran, terrified, overwhelmed, and confused. The Highwayman caught one and cut him down. He heard the whizzing of arrows cutting the air nearby as Jameston Sequin took down a second and then a third.

Weariness and pain overwhelmed him. The Highwayman dropped the magic enacting the fiery cloak, then dismissed the serpentine shield and fell fully into the central gem of the brooch, the soul stone, seeking the warmth of its healing magic.

Bransen knelt in the dirt while all around him townsfolk cheered and screamed and cried. Glad he was to see the familiar boots of Jameston before him, to feel his companion's hand grasp him under his good shoulder and help him back to his feet.

"Pull it out," Bransen said through gritted teeth, meaning the arrow.

"I'll get whiskey and something for you to bite."

Bransen grabbed him hard as he started to turn away. "Now!" he demanded.

"Boy, you can't—"

"Now!" Bransen insisted, tugging Jameston's hand toward the arrow shaft. Jameston still resisted, so Bransen reached for the bolt himself and grimaced all the more as he tugged on the arrow.

"Push it through!" Jameston enjoined. He grasped Bransen's hand with his own, reversing the pressure.

Waves of agony assaulted Bransen, but he fell into his meditation and into the soul stone. A moment later he felt a sudden looseness in the wound as Jameston pulled the arrow from the back of his shoulder.

"You won't be using that arm anytime soon," the scout lamented. Bransen didn't even hear him, his thoughts fully immersed in his discipline and the gemstone magic even as his free hand grasped the wound.

The townsfolk gathered about them, clapping and nodding their appreciation, but Bransen's focus remained absolute. Jameston began talking to the people, but Bransen didn't hear. He stood straight and let go of his shoulder: No blood came forth. Jameston and the others looked on in amazement as Bransen reached down and retrieved his sword—with his left hand. He spun the weapon over and slid it expertly into the sheath on his left hip, showing only a trace of a grimace.

"I'll be using the arm sooner than you believe," Bransen said softly to his friend.

"How'd you jump that wall like that? How'd you throw a man onto a roof? How'd you do that with the fire?" Jameston came back at him, one, two, three.

Bransen smiled coyly, though in truth he really had no idea. Something momentous was happening here, some joining of his Jhesta Tu sensibilities and the powerful brooch upon his forehead. He had walked through flames before, stepping from the log pile of a Samhaist bonfire to strike down the evil Bernivvigar. His Jhesta Tu training alone had assisted him in keeping the flames from his body, but it had been a very temporary effect. This time was different. He had magically summoned the flames about his whole body and had hardly felt their warmth. Not a wisp of smoke now arose from his clothing. Skilled monks could use their serpentine to enact such shields against fire, of course, but the speed and completeness of Bransen's work with the gems at his disposal had surprised even him. Made him ponder what other wonders lay before him.

"Oh, but ye saved us!" one old woman cried, taking Bransen from his private thoughts. He looked around at the gathering of townsfolk then, noting the absence of men. This village was old and very young, but there was little in between, like so many of the other villages of war-ravaged Honce.

"Who were these marauders?" Jameston asked. "What laird do they serve?"

"Ethelbert's own," an old man answered. "And ain't yerself?"

Jameston's head shook most emphatically. "We serve at the pleasure of Dame Gwydre."

The old man looked skeptical. "But he's looking like one o' Ethelbert's," he said, pointing to Bransen.

The clothes, Bransen knew. He sucked in his breath at the reminder that there were Jhesta Tu about, that he was close to his goal, his last best hope.

"Not with Ethelbert—never met the man," Jameston assured them. "But these soldiers were from Laird Ethelbert's ranks?"

"This time," the old man replied. The resignation in his voice was not hard to hear. "Next time it'll be Delaval's men."

"Yeslnik's," a girl corrected, and the old man snorted as if that mattered not at all. It didn't, from the perspective of the poor villagers caught in the middle of violent chaos.

"They be all about the land, roaming like animals," another elderly man explained. "Prince Milwellis is fighting at the coast again, but in here there's just pieces of the armies, scattered and finding food where they can."

"And who do you serve, Ethelbert or Yeslnik?" Bransen asked to many a blank stare.

"Don't think they care," Jameston suggested in a whisper.

N o camps, no food wagons, no one giving orders," Jameston elaborated as he and Bransen made their way out of the small village. "Just a bunch of broken soldiers, hungry and scared and with nothing to believe in. I've seen it before."

Bransen shook his head, not able to grasp it.

"They fell off the side of the armies—both armies," Jameston explained. "Or they ran off the side. There's a point where it's too much fighting. Drives a man blood-crazy, takes the point of it all from him."

"Was there ever a point to it?" Bransen asked. "More than the greed of a couple of selfish lairds, I mean?"

Jameston shrugged. "Pride of home, fear of not defending what's yours. Starts that way, might still be that way for many in the ranks of both armies, but for some there comes a time when they can't remember their home, at least not well enough to connect it to what they're doing way out here. Maybe some just have nothing left to fight for."

"So they slaughter defenseless villagers?"

Jameston shrugged again. "I'm not excusing it, boy. I'm telling you what is, not what should be."

"And it will only continue to get worse," said Bransen.

"Or so many will just be dead that there won't be enough left to make it worse," said Jameston.

"Your optimism inspires me."

"You don't care about it anyway, boy. Remember?"

Bransen shot him a cold look. "We should go straight

to Ethelbert dos Entel," Jameson said, his laugh a pitiful sound.

"We?" Bransen asked. "I should go. Where Jameston goes is for Jameston to decide."

"Already told you I was following you."

"Have I told you that you needn't?"

"Every step."

"Have I told you that I don't want you to?"

"You'll get to that eventually," Jameston replied with a disarming grin. "But I'm here now, so I can tell you that you'd be quite the fool to walk into Ethelbert's city."

"How so? How am I to find the Jhesta Tu I seek? Should I just walk from village to village?"

"Going to Ethelbert's city might get you to meet them, indeed, but not in the way you're wanting."

"What are you implying?"

"I'm not implying, boy, I'm saying. There's a laird in Ethelbert dos Entel who might be thinking that it's past time to negotiate a truce. We're not far from his home, with nothing but the sea behind him. Wouldn't he have a treasure to offer King Yeslnik if the Highwayman walked into his midst?"

"But he above all must know that I was not involved!" Bransen protested.

"You're still believing that matters? After all this and all you've seen?"

Bransen considered it for a moment, then gave a helpless shake of his head. "No."

"What do you want?" Jameston asked him. "You want to meet these assassins Ethelbert's brought from Behr—"

"They are Jhesta Tu, not assassins."

"King Delaval would disagree. If he were alive, I mean."

"If they killed King Delaval . . ."

"You saw the sword."

"It was because they believed in the cause against him," Bransen stubbornly finished. "The code of Jhest is not mercenary, it is principle. If the Jhesta Tu have allied with Laird Ethelbert, then that speaks well of Laird Ethelbert."

"And if I give you that, will you answer my question? What do you want, boy?"

"First, I want you to stop calling me boy."

Jameston nodded. "What would be your perfect life? To live with Cadayle and your child, your children, and with Callen nearby? All in peace? To farm the land or hunt for food? To go to church and pray to whatever gods you find?"

"Yes, and no."

"What *do* you want?"

"I want . . ." Bransen took a deep breath and truly considered the question. "I want a home for my family, and peace, yes. I'm sick of smelling corpses."

"Are you sick of battle? Even when it means battling someone like Badden or that priest Bernivvigar before him?"

Bransen looked at Jameston as if the man had just slapped him across the face.

"You spend your hours working that sword and working your body through practice—practice for fighting," Jameston remarked. "You just found strength back there in that village that I've never seen before. Did you hate it, b . . . Bransen? Do you hate the fighting even when you're thinking the fight to be just?"

"Just? For which laird? They are two sides of the same ugly stone!"

"Forget that!" Jameston scolded. "Forget the greed and the pride behind it all and make it personal, just for now. Just so you can answer—to yourself and not to me. What drove you to rescue Callen and Cadayle? What did you feel when Badden's head flew from his shoulders? What do you want, Bransen Garibond? What do *you* want, Highwayman? Who is the Highwayman? Why is he the Highwayman?"

Every word stabbed at Bransen's sensibilities profoundly. He wanted to shout at Jameston that Dame Gwydre had obviously put him up to that line of questioning, so much had it echoed her more gentle nudging over the winter in Pellinor.

He knew what he wanted regarding Cadayle and his coming child—and more children, he hoped. For them, with them, he wanted peace and security and enough comfort to give them the room to love and enjoy one another.

But Jameston was right, he knew, though he wouldn't openly admit it at that strange moment. There was more to him than Bransen Garibond.

There was the Highwayman.

TWENTY-THREE

From the Depths

We might be able to get to smoother and deeper water," the helmsman reported to Dawson as he ran back amidships. "I'm betting *Lady Dreamer* can run from them warships when the swells ain't so tall."

"Aye, and what o' *Shelligan's*, then? She's not so fleet," another crewman reminded.

"What of her, then?" the first replied angrily. "If we're to fight beside her, then we're to drown beside her!"

"Enough o' that," Dawson implored. He turned to Cormack and particularly to Milkeila. "You've got some magic, I'm hoping."

Milkeila glanced at the vast and powerful ocean waters, then back at Dawson doubtfully.

"A few tricks?" asked Dawson.

Both the young fighters nodded reluctantly.

"And so we aren't leaving *Shelligan's Run*," Dawson declared loudly. He focused his gaze on the helmsman. "A sorry group o' friends we'd be and a sorrier commander by far for meself if we'd leave our friends to certain doom."

"But it's certain doom for them if we stay and fight, too," the helmsman stubbornly reminded.

"Aye, might well be, but we'll sting the Palmaristown dogs, don't you doubt. And we won't be sailing the seas the rest of our days remembering them we let die!"

That last statement had the crewmen gathered about pumping their fists with determination.

"Signal *Shelligan's*," Dawson ordered. "Fill the sails and start east and just a bit north. We'll split them wider as they try to box us, then turn back to fight two on two to start it up."

"Two on four, ye mean, since they're twice our size," the helmsman grumbled, but the man beside him slapped the back of his head and bid him shut his mouth.

Lady Dreamer signaled her sister ship and waited patiently as she readied her sails. All the while the five Palmaristown ships continued weaving their net, two to the south, one to the north, and two more coming straight in at the prey from the west.

"Go then!" Dawson called when *Shelligan's Run* signaled she was ready and began to tack, turning her prow east. "And don't outrun *Shelligan's*!"

The chase was on, seven ships crashing through the swells at full sails, oak beams creaking and groaning in protest, crewmen pulling hard on the ropes to try to keep the sails angled perfectly to make the most of the strong spring breeze. As the ships leaped away, it seemed like they were holding their own against the two in pursuit. Dawson briefly wondered if they might just try to keep running.

But the Palmaristown caravel in the north was too fast and would soon enough be able to turn south to cut them off and slow them enough for the two behind to catch and rake their decks with volleys of arrows and giant ballista bolts.

Dawson moved to the taffrail, Cormack and Milkeila

beside him, watching the run, gauging the progress of the chasing warships and the one in the north. He had to make his dramatic turn before that one started south, or it would catch them before they could get in a straight run again.

He'd wait until the last moment, for that northern ship was outdistancing the two chasers, and the two by the coast were making no move to close, instead ensuring no escape to the coast and freedom.

"Did you see that?" Milkeila asked suddenly, pointing. Both Cormack and Dawson turned to her, following her finger to the north, to the Palmaristown ship. Angled strangely, her prow suddenly too much pointed northward, her sails slack, her momentum stolen.

"She hit a rock!" Cormack exclaimed, for indeed it appeared as if the ship had struck something, and hard.

"No rocks, no reefs this far out," Dawson muttered with certainty. He knew every bit of the gulf waters better than any man alive.

But the other ship was stopped. She shuddered again as they watched, her masts trembling violently, her sails whipping back and forth. They were too far away to make out any distinct movements on her deck, but they saw commotion there, sailors running about.

"What is it?" Cormack asked.

"I'm not knowing," said Dawson. "Break north!" he shouted to his crew. "And signal *Shelligan's* to the same!"

Heartbeats later *Lady Dreamer* leaned low to port, *Shelligan's Run* in her wake.

Yach, but they got her!" Shiknickel cried to his crew, a score of bandy-legged powries pedaling hard to turn the screw on their deadly, ram-headed barrel boat. "Cracked her wood and told the sea to come aboard!" The powries gave a cheer.

"Well, turn us to her, then, so's I can wet me cap in human blood!" one cried to the agreement of all.

"What ho now?" Shiknickel asked, glancing to the side out the one conning tower on the cylindrical, mostly submerged boat. "Two more coming to play."

"Two o' her friends, or the two they were chasing?" asked one of the crew.

"The runners. They're thinking the way clear, they are. Yach, but we'll show them the bottom!"

Others cheered, but two dwarves near the back of the barrel boat glanced at each other and stopped their leg pumping. One hopped up and made his way forward.

"What're ye about?" Shiknickel demanded as he came to the side of the sturdy captain.

"About seeing the flag on them new-coming boats," answered the dwarf, a recent addition to Shiknickel's crew.

"Well what're ye knowin', Mcwigik?" Shiknickel asked, showing great deference for this one, who had been hailed as the savior of a lost powrie band that had been missing for one hundred years.

Shiknickel stepped aside as Mcwigik moved to the small top port to climb the three-step ladder and poke his head out, staring to the south.

"Dame Gwydre's flag?" called Bikelbrin from the back.

Mcwigik strained to make out the pennant. "Aye!" he said at length. "Flying the flag we seen over Castle Pellinor."

"The Vanguard queen who sent ye back to fetch our lost kin?" Shiknickel asked.

"That don't matter!" one of the bloodthirsty crew protested.

"Shut yer mouth, or I'll be fillin' it with me fist!" Shiknickel barked at him, for indeed, three of the dwarves who had been retrieved from Mithranidoon, including gray-beard Kriminig, were of Shiknickel's own clan.

Kriminig, whose beret glowed as brightly as any dwarf's in all the Julianthes, had long been regarded as a (missing) hero of the dwarf captain's clan.

"Aye, it's Gwydre's boat," Mcwigik replied when the captain looked his way.

"And ye don't want us to hit it?"

"Not with bigger boats chasing it," Mcwigik reasoned, assured that he had hit a good note when Shiknickel's face brightened. The captain pulled out a small, reflective device to signal the other barrel boats in the water, moving past Mcwigik to the top. Shiknickel stopped Mcwigik when he started back for his seat.

"Stay beside me a bit," he ordered. "We'll be going close by them littler ones, and if they're not what ye're thinking they'll be the first to drown."

More than one set of eyes focused on Dawson when the screaming started from the Palmaristown ship to the north. Something terrible was happening there, and *Lady Dreamer* was sailing right toward it.

The warship shuddered again and her mainmast lurched over to port, and, even from this distance, the crew of *Lady Dreamer* could discern that it had cracked down by its base. The ship was taking on water, evidenced by a pronounced list.

"What's hitting her?" more than one crewman asked, voices tinged with fear.

Dawson, too, was more than a little afraid of this course that would bring them so close to whatever was destroying a great warship so efficiently, but when he glanced behind, he saw the two Palmaristown ships in full pursuit. To stop or even turn was to fight them; to fight them was surely to die.

"Powries." The almost breathless call came from a crewman working hard at the rigging at the bow.

"Powries?" Cormack echoed beside Dawson. Cormack and Milkeila chased him to the rail.

In the distance they saw the rounded wood and the small conning tower of a strange craft, her barrellike shape and terrible ram smashing through a swell before settling into the dark water.

Blood drained from Dawson's face, and a million thoughts swirled in his mind as he finally came upon a desperate plan: Join with the Palmaristown ships against the even more ruthless powrie enemy.

Yach, but we're takin' her down, Gwydre's boat or no!" Captain Shiknickel cried. "'E's wearing a powrie cap, he is! Double-time left!"

As calls for the righthand turn echoed the length, Mcwigik's eyes opened wide. "A powrie cap?" he mouthed. Gulping hard, he shoved his way back to the short tower to stand beside Shiknickel.

Below, the dwarves shouted and sang of getting to ramming speed, of dipping their berets in the blood of men.

Shiknickel's call of "Hold yer feet!" stopped them cold.

Shoot it dead!" one man cried, but Dawson held his hand to belay that order and to keep everyone calm as they stared at the powrie barrel boat, nearly stopped and splashing in the rough waters barely thirty yards off *Lady Dreamer*'s starboard bow. A red-bearded dwarf crawled from the conning tower, holding it fast as he settled his feet on the concave deck, waves rolling over the wood.

"Mcwigik," Cormack and Milkeila said in unison before Dawson could mutter the same.

"Yach, ye dogs, and know yer good deed's not been forgotten," the dwarf hailed them as *Lady Dreamer* fast closed on the barrel boat. "Ye keep on running with yer partner there, and we'll be giving a good poke to them two that're chasing ye, not to worry."

Dawson swallowed hard and looked to his companions.

"Good Mcwigik, and the best to yer kin!" Cormack yelled, taking the cue and moving up beside Dawson.

"Aye, and Bikelbrin's below!" the dwarf replied.

"How many boats have you?" Cormack called.

"More than a few, and good ones. Ye wanting them's wearing that flag as them's chasing ye put to the bottom? Hope ye do, because that's where they're going, don't ye doubt!"

"You will let the ships under the flag of Dame Gwydre pass?" Milkeila dared to ask.

"Aye, a debt repaid, and fun repaying!"

Mcwigik gave a great laugh then as *Lady Dreamer* glided past, a chuckle filled with such wickedness that Dawson, Cormack, and Milkeila were glad to have him on their side.

"We should tell them to be gone from the gulf," Cormack said quietly to Dawson.

"Aye, but that's giving the waters to Panlamaris, now ain't it?" the older Vanguard sailor replied.

Ahead, the Palmaristown ship keeled over, dropping sailors into the cold waters. Like sharks, a trio of powrie boats rushed the scene, dwarves scrambling on the decks, serrated knives in hand. Dawson and the others on *Lady Dreamer* watched in revulsion as one poor woman was hauled up by the hair onto the side of the powrie boat, her throat quickly slashed open. Powries swarmed over her, slapping with their berets.

The three on *Lady Dreamer* glanced back to the boat carrying Mcwigik, already pedaling fast to the south to intercept the Palmaristown ships.

"Weren't a thing we could do to stop them, anyway," Dawson mumbled. Given the carnage just ahead, his justification rang hollow even to him.

"Every choice we make, every battle we fight, takes a piece of my soul," Cormack said and leaned heavily on the rail.

Lady Dreamer and *Shelligan's Run* continued to the northeast under full sail for a long time, long after the two ships giving chase broke apart under powrie rams, long after the screams of more Palmaristown men and women rent the early spring air, long after the remaining Palmaristown ships, hugging the coast, turned and fled west.

Finally, the two Vanguard ships dared to separate, *Shelligan's Run* turning north to deliver Gwydre's message to Vanguard, *Lady Dreamer* turning straight east on their critical mission to ally with Laird Ethelbert.

There was no cheering on either boat for their improbable escape. Nearly every sailor on both of the ships more than once uttered the justification that "the Palmaristown crews would've shown us no mercy."

They had to say that, and had to believe it, given the sight of powries with knives slaughtering helpless crewmen as they splashed about in the dark and cold waters. They had to say that, because they had left fellow men of Honce to the merciless, brutal dwarves.

They had to say that, and so they did, and like Cormack, every one of them lost a little bit of his soul.

TWENTY-FOUR

The Center, the Flank

Prince Milwellis grabbed the man by the front of his threadbare tunic with one hand and hoisted him up to tiptoes. "And where did you find this food?" he demanded.

The man's eyes darted all about as if he was searching for an escape route. But the whimpering sounds that came from him showed that he realized there was no way and nowhere to run. A former soldier in Milwellis's ranks, he and a pair of his companions had been caught in the forest, settled around a substantial stash of food they had procured from area villages. Caught so completely by surprise, the poor fellow's companions were still sitting, soldiers towering over them.

"We didn't . . . we didn't know what we was to do," he finally blurted.

"You are a soldier of Palmaristown. I am your prince. What more do you need to know?"

"Please, lord," the man gasped as Milwellis pulled the tunic up a bit more, tight against the bottom of his chin. "When the demons came north—"

"The demons?"

"Ethelbert's demon warriors!" one of the other two blurted. The soldier standing over him kicked him hard in the ribs for daring to interrupt.

"Aye, them demons," the man in Milwellis's grasp quickly added. "We saw them come down from the hill. They killed the knights, and we were next. And we tried to fight—" His response was cut off into indecipherable garbles as Milwellis, outraged by the reminder of the loss of his elite warriors, tugged him up even harder, and growled as he did.

"Please, lord!" he gasped.

"You battled them?"

"Tried, lord."

"Tried?"

The man whimpered and Milwellis threw him to the ground, turning on the other two, particularly the one who had interrupted earlier.

"We couldn't fight them," the man stammered. "We couldn't see them. Just men dying. Screaming and then dying. And they were above us in the trees! All about us—as if there were ten thousand of them!"

"Ten thousand? How many were there?"

"Just a few," the man he had thrown to the ground squeaked in response. Milwellis turned back on him, hands out in confusion.

"Demon warriors," the other one added.

Prince Milwellis took a deep breath. "Pull the lines in tight and strengthen the flanks," he instructed his commanders.

"Back to the north?" Harcourt asked quietly, moving by his leader's side.

Milwellis shook his head. "Back to Ethelbert dos Entel," he said. "Back to Ethelbert's lair."

"We've no support from King Yeslnik," Harcourt reminded. "He has left the field."

"More the glory for us, then."

"You don't fear Ethelbert's demon warriors?"

Prince Milwellis looked at him hard, and Harcourt chuckled.

"Do you disagree?" Milwellis asked honestly.

"Keep the lines tight," Harcourt recommended. "Laird Ethelbert has a few tricks, but in the end, the weight of the army will win out. It'd be a great thing for your father to put our enemy back in his box."

"And better for Palmaristown since Yeslnik fled the field," said Milwellis.

"King Yeslnik, my prince," Harcourt teased, and both men laughed.

Strong Prince Milwellis stroked the growing beard on his face and looked to the south where lay, five days' march away, Ethelbert dos Entel.

Nothing," Bannagran assured Reandu one warm morning in Pryd Town. "Not an Ethelbert soldier to be found."

"And not a Yeslnik one, either," Master Reandu replied.

Bannagran gave him a look of mock anger.

"And that is a good thing," Reandu pressed on anyway. "The folk of Pryd have time to get their gardens and fields in, perhaps. It would do my heart good to see an easier summer this year than last."

"You're glad to have your young brothers home at Chapel Pryd," Bannagran said.

"And our laird, who is needed at this troubling time," Reandu replied.

Bannagran nodded, knowing well that Reandu's compliment was heartfelt.

"King Yeslnik was truly unsettled by the Behr assassins and their efforts against Milwellis's force?" Reandu asked.

"Terrified. And I'm not certain that I blame him."

"You said the field was won."

Bannagran shrugged. "It seemed as if the sides were closing in on Ethelbert. The outlaw laird had no escape, save the sea at his back. I believe that if we had come to his walls, both forces, Yeslnik and Milwellis, Ethelbert would have boarded his private ship and fled his city, leaving it an easy victory and an end to the war."

"And how much better that would have been for everyone," Reandu remarked, watching Bannagran closely as he did, suspecting a rather curious undertone here.

"Yes," the Bear of Honce replied more than a little unconvincingly.

"Would you measure King Yeslnik against your old friend, Laird Prydae?" Reandu asked. "Or against Prydae's father, Laird Pryd before him?"

Bannagran's expression became an open scowl then, and Reandu was quick to back off the explosive question. He knew that Bannagran was not enamored of young King Yeslnik, of course, particularly since Bannagran had offered Chapel Pryd a dodge to avoid Yeslnik's awful order that all Ethelbert men and women held prisoner were to be put to death.

"Compared with King Delaval, then?" Reandu pressed.

Bannagran's face remained very tight.

"What will Honce be like when King Yeslnik takes full control?" Reandu asked. "What will life in Pryd be like?"

Again Bannagran shrugged. "I cannot predict what will someday be, other than to tell you that I believe the war nears its end and that the forces of Delaval will prevail. You, too, have heard the news from Chapel Abelle . . ."

"The edict said St. Mere Abelle," Reandu corrected.

Bannagran nodded. "They have thrown in with Dame Gwydre, who, I am told, opposes Laird Panlamaris of Palmaristown and King Yeslnik."

"Will Bannagran lead the folk of Pryd on a campaign through the wilds of Vanguard, then?"

The question made the big man visibly shrink. The Laird of Pryd did not say that he would do as his king asked, as would be appropriate. "Let us hope for a peaceful summer, that the folk of Pryd Town can heal their wounds," was all he said.

Too many," Harcourt said to Milwellis as the reports came in one after another regarding the strength of their opponents. "We will sweep the field of them, perhaps, but will not have enough might left to tear down Ethelbert dos Entel's tall walls. The city is well fortified, with many engines of war lying in wait behind her stone barriers."

Prince Milwellis rubbed his face. He knew that Harcourt was responding not only to the reports regarding Ethelbert but also to those concerning his own force. His men were growing tired and increasingly glancing back to the northwest. Attrition was already beginning to work against him, with men simply disappearing from his ranks, and the whispers said that it was from more than confrontations with Ethelbert's soldiers.

"Have the runners returned from King Yeslnik?"

"King Yeslnik is long gone from the field, my prince," Harcourt replied. "He is almost directly south of Delaval City by some reports. Others say that he and his private guards have gone back to Castle Pryd."

"We have Ethelbert in a trap from which there is no escape," Milwellis protested. "We have turned his desperate attempt to break out. It was a showy and dramatic response by Ethelbert, to be sure, but without the numbers to back up any change in the course of the battle!"

"All true," said Harcourt. "But King Yeslnik is not to

be found, and I doubt we'll get him and his warriors back to the field in time to finish this grim business."

Milwellis blew a frustrated sigh.

"And Yeslnik's tactics work against him, and us, regarding such an event," Harcourt went on. Milwellis looked at him curiously.

"His retreat was marked by the scorching of the world," Harcourt explained. "Every village, every field of crops, every garden, and most every animal was trampled under boot. So fearful was he that Ethelbert and his assassins would pursue, he destroyed the ability of Ethelbert's army—of any army—to follow his route back to the west."

"He intended to put Ethelbert in a box of barren ground?"

Harcourt shrugged. "Likely he means to send the fleets of Delaval and Palmaristown to assault Ethelbert from the sea. Or perhaps he hopes to keep Ethelbert in his city while he solidifies his grasp on the rest of Honce, and by sheer weight of support force Ethelbert into a truce."

"A truce that would include no assassins from Behr, no doubt," Milwellis remarked with a knowing chuckle.

"Let us hope that he is wiser than he is brave," Harcourt dared to say, knowing that some levity was needed here, since Milwellis's dream of finishing off Ethelbert seemed suddenly an unlikely thing.

"Sweep the field," Milwellis ordered.

"My prince?"

"Chase Ethelbert's ragged band back into the city," Milwellis explained. "Let us see if the walls of Ethelbert dos Entel are as solid as you fear."

"And if they are?"

"Then we will turn back to the north."

"How far?"

"Let us follow Yeslnik's lead." He grinned as he added, "Around Felidan Bay to the Mantis Arm? A few fortresses under the flag of Palmaristown scattered about the Mantis Arm would serve my father's seaborne designs well."

Harcourt smiled and nodded his approval. "A wise leader has more than one road before him and keeps both trails open for as long as he can."

"And has wise advisors to help guide his course," said Milwellis.

The regrouping and advance was on in full that very day, Milwellis's army, promised a swift victory or a swift return to Palmaristown, marching with eagerness once more. They crashed through two of the villages they had already flattened on their first pass, and all the people of those hamlets fled before them.

They found only meager resistance from a couple of small Ethelbert encampments that were not fast enough in flight before them.

They arrived in Yansinchester yet again, the last sizable town before Ethelbert dos Entel itself, the high-water mark of Milwellis's advance. This time they found the town itself deserted; they knew the survivors to be in the one structure in Yansinchester that had escaped the first march intact, Chapel Yansin.

"Bring the wounded to be tended by the brothers," Milwellis ordered his commanders. "And harm no one in the chapel. Allow these peasants some manner of peace. Perhaps they will think Laird Panlamaris beneficent when our pennants snap in the strong coastal breezes above this land."

He and Harcourt got a laugh out of that order.

They were not laughing a short while later, however, when the first couriers from Laird Panlamaris's force arrived with news that Milwellis's father had marched and been met with a magical barrage outside Chapel Abelle and was besieging the monks of the mother chapel.

Milwellis's face twisted in anger at yet another dire turn in this unfolding drama.

"Trust in your father," Harcourt said to calm him. "He is as fine a general as has ever ridden the ways of Honce."

Milwellis chewed his lip, his dark eyes flashing dangerously, his hands clenching into fists at his sides.

"My prince?" Harcourt asked.

"Are we to battle for useless land in the name of a king who had not the courage to stand and fight on his own behalf while our brethren and my father and laird battle treachery near to our own home?" Milwellis blurted, his breath coming in ragged gasps.

Harcourt put a hand to his shoulder to calm him.

"Advise me," Milwellis demanded, pleaded.

"Do as our king," Harcourt said. "Turn and burn the land behind your march."

Milwellis began to nod. "To Chapel Abelle," he whispered, as if he couldn't put anything more behind his voice.

"Most of Ethelbert's minions are back in his city now," Harcourt offered hopefully. "We can run to the gates of Ethelbert dos Entel within a matter of hours."

"Tomorrow," Milwellis decided, his voice suddenly strong once more. "A fresh march. Let us get close enough to shoot our arrows at them and turn quickly enough to persuade them that we leave of our own choice. Perhaps we can even send a message to Laird Ethelbert, a warning that if he comes forth we will destroy him."

Harcourt nodded, glad to see that his prince was continuing to think on his feet, adapting, and wisely, to every new twist.

"Tomorrow," he echoed. "And today we camp here in Yansinchester?"

"We have unfinished business here," said Milwellis, turning his angry stare right at Chapel Yansin. "For here we discover enemies of Palmaristown."

They came within sight of Ethelbert dos Entel's northern reaches the following afternoon, staring down from the same hills where Milwellis had lost his knights. The carnage of the battle remained all too clear. Milwellis trembled with rage.

Harcourt did not miss that reaction. "My prince," he said comfortingly, drawing the volatile young man out of his fuming contemplations.

"Would that I had Ethelbert's head on the ground before me," Milwellis growled.

"But you do not, though take heart in that you have surely wounded him more profoundly than he you."

Milwellis looked up from the body of a Palmaristown knight—Erolis, he recalled, though the carrion birds had done too much to disfigure it for him to be sure—and offered a thankful nod to his honest companion.

"What can we do to sting Ethelbert one last time before we turn?" he asked. "What can we do to make him know that we are here, right before his wall, and that he daren't come forth?"

Harcourt grinned and nodded.

Under the cover of darkness, on that cloudy and moonless night, every archer in Milwellis's force crept down from the hill to the field before Ethelbert dos Entel's north wall.

They couldn't see their target any better than any defenders might see them, of course, but then, their target was the size of a city.

A hundred bows lifted to the sky and let fly. Then again and again and many more times after that until at last cries came from the city as Ethelbert's people realized they were under attack. The last volley was flaming arrows, five score streaking through the night sky to cross over the wall and seek further fuel within.

A response finally came, but by then the Palmaristown archers had turned and fled.

Several fires erupted within the city wall, Milwellis and Harcourt saw from the hilltop. Perhaps a few people had been injured or even killed, perhaps those fires, though surely quickly attended, would cause some damage. But none of that was the point, after all. Milwellis had just told Ethelbert that he was here in the dark within striking distance of the desperate laird's last refuge.

The next morning Milwellis's army moved back to the north, driving livestock and villagers before them, destroying the gardens and the fields.

And dragging with them the twenty-three brothers of Chapel Yansin bound for Chapel Abelle.

TWENTY-FIVE

Worthy

They're running," Jameston remarked to Bransen. "Like deer before the wolves."

The pair stood looking to the east from opposite branches of a tree. Something was happening there, some fighting or other commotion, but they couldn't make out what, exactly, for a line of hills blocked their view even from the high perch. That was the nature of this ground along the southernmost Honce coastline, as if the towering mountains just south of their position, the great Belt-and-Buckle, had collided with the sea in days long lost to the world and had strewn great broken mounds all about the region.

Suddenly soldiers were scrambling past the trees as if the demon dactyl itself was close on their heels. Not far before them, one spearman stumbled as he headed down a slope, nearly thrown from his feet as the back quarter of his spear shaft collided with a tree. Finally orienting himself, he just threw the spear to the ground and continued his desperate run.

Bransen got Jameston's attention and pointed up above.

"Too thin," the scout replied, meaning the branches.

Bransen shook his head and started up anyway, falling into the malachite in his brooch. He lessened his weight greatly, his hands easily propelling him skyward. Within only a few moments he had climbed nearly twenty feet to the tree's tiny top (which wasn't bending under his weight in the least). He looked back to see Jameston gawking at him and shaking his head in disbelief.

Bransen suppressed his smile and looked to the east again. Though he still couldn't see as widely as he had hoped, the view proved enough to make out the pennants flying over a large force.

"Palmaristown," he muttered, turning his gaze south. The structures of Ethelbert dos Entel, built on steps up the mountainsides, were in clear view only a couple of leagues away. Was the war nearing its end? And what might this mean for his quest to find the Jhesta Tu? Bransen danced his way back down to Jameston and relayed the information.

"So these are Ethelbert's men," Jameston remarked, glancing down at the fleeing force. "They'll run all the way to the city, I'm guessing."

"Not all of them," Bransen determinedly replied. To Jameston's gasp of surprise, he leaped from the tree and floated—floated, not fell!—to the ground. He was running as he landed, scrambling through the thick copse to intercept nearby soldiers.

"I've got to get me some of them damned stones," he heard Jameston mutter as the man carefully and painstakingly worked his way back down to the ground.

The Highwayman slipped into a grove of pines, sliding silently through the dense branches. He followed a movement out of the corner of his eye to his left, and he glided as a shadow to intercept.

The man ran before him; the Highwayman's foot thrust out to strike the trailing foot of the fleeing soldier, kicking it behind his other ankle. The man tripped and tumbled forward, landing awkwardly in a skid on his knees and hands. Apparently still oblivious to the source of his fall, he started to scramble back to his feet.

A fine sword blade atop his shoulder, its sharp edge barely an inch from his neck, froze him in place.

"Please, sir, I've a family," he begged.

The Highwayman retracted the sword, grabbed him by the collar and hoisted him to his feet, turning him as he stood to look him in the face. The soldier gasped, eyes widening as he considered the black clothing and the unusual gemstone brooch.

"Affwin Wi?" he asked.

The Highwayman paused at hearing that name yet again. "You know Affwin Wi?" he asked.

"Of her all do," the terrified soldier replied.

"Let him go!" came a cry from the side where a pair of soldiers appeared, swords in hand. They advanced slowly toward the Highwayman, their blades raised threateningly.

"Oh, I'm not thinking that you're in a place to be telling him what to do," came an answer to the side of the newcomers, who both looked and blanched at the sight of Jameston Sequin, his bow drawn, arrow leveled.

"Easy," the soldier with Bransen instructed his companions. "He's one o' Affwin Wi's boys."

The other two certainly did relax at that.

"Praise the ancient ones," one muttered while the other gave the sign of the evergreen.

Bransen and Jameston exchanged glances, both of them noting yet again that curious combination and juxtaposition of the major Honce religions. The ancient ones were Samhaist gods, the evergreen the sign of the Order of Blessed Abelle.

"If ye're to sting him, then now's the time or never's the time," one of the newcomers remarked.

"Him?" asked Bransen.

"Prince Milwellis," the other newcomer clarified.

"Aye, that one came back mad because you and your friends stung him so hard the first time," said the first. "So stick him again, we beg, and this time stick his own body, if ye're getting me point."

"He's a dog what's killed a thousand mothers and more than that o' children," said the man standing beside Bransen.

"To see his blood staining the waters o' the Mirianic would do our hearts good when we come from Entel, and don't ye doubt that we'll be back," said one of the others.

"Where is Affwin Wi?" Bransen asked. "Has she returned to the city?"

The three soldiers exchanged shrugs.

"She's still out, I'm thinking," said the one near Bransen. "Not far from here, last I heard."

"Be gone," Bransen told his prisoner and the others, and they were happy to oblige.

Bransen fixed his gaze on Jameston, who nodded solemnly and slipped back into the thick grove of pines, with Bransen close behind.

Two other sets of eyes watched the exchange between the strangers and the soldiers, all the more carefully when they took note of Bransen's sword.

Merwal Yahna motioned to Pactset Va, and the two men slid away from the scene, no less silent than the black-clothed stranger carrying a sword he should not possess.

"Jhesta Tu," Merwal reported to Affwin Wi soon after. "There is no doubt."

"He wore our clothing," said Pactset Va, a young and strong specimen with small dark eyes and his hair bound in a topknot. "And carried a sword as your own traced with vines."

Affwin Wi drew her broken blade and rolled it over in

surprisingly delicate hands that had many times driven right through the throat of an opponent. She looked to Merwal Yahna with an expression that was not hopeful. The Jhesta Tu had hunted them in Behr, but they had thought their mercenary stint with Laird Ethelbert would allow them reprieve from their continual trials against Affwin Wi's former masters. Had they found her again?

Affwin Wi took some solace in the likelihood that this new mystic would be acting mostly alone; the Jhesta Tu considered the adjudication of the matter of a rogue like Affwin Wi to be a personal challenge for their disciples, whereas the Hou-lei traditions Affwin Wi had come to follow, much more forceful and warlike, called for as many warriors as needed, and then some more, for any given task. In simple terms, Hou-lei didn't fight fairly. Three times before the great warrior had helped her fend off Jhesta Tu.

Since the Jhesta Tu's companion in the woods earlier was surely not of Behr or Jhesta Tu, Affwin Wi had no reason to believe this time would be different.

"Well, you do look like a southerner," Jameston quipped as he and Bransen made their way to the southwest, tracing a wide perimeter of Ethelbert dos Entel. "You've got the skin for it."

Bransen could only shrug. Though Jameston was teasing, his words were true enough. With his brown skin and jet black hair, the black clothing and his exotic sword, the Ethelbert warriors had thought him from Behr. And they understood the significance of his dress. "Affwin Wi," he mumbled, and he found it hard to breathe. They were close; the Jhesta Tu were close.

"And what are you planning to do when we find these folk?" Jameston asked as if reading his mind, which was probably not a difficult thing to do at that moment.

"Learn from them," he replied. "You cannot understand, but I am trapped in an infirm body."

"Are you, then?" the scout asked, his eyebrows rising along with the sides of his mouth as he put on an incredulous grin.

"Without this," Bransen explained, pointing to his brooch, "I am a helpless, babbling fool, the one you saw being dragged toward the glacier after the troll fight."

"Wasn't it a knock in the head?"

"A knock in the head that dislodged the gemstone," Bransen explained.

Jameston nodded and smiled. "I wondered on that. I saw you walking—being dragged, actually—and thought you knocked silly beyond any chance of regaining your senses."

Bransen lifted an eyebrow. "Thank you for the assistance."

"Told you not to fight the damned trolls."

Bransen let it go with a laugh, not willing to recount all those earlier questions at this pressing time.

"You think these strangers we're hunting will free you of that stone?" Jameston asked.

Bransen saw that the scout didn't understand. He was simply too edgy at that moment to go into great detail. "They will," he replied.

He turned to glance at Jameston and ensure that the explanation would suffice just as the scout froze in his tracks, his eyes locked.

"Looks like we're going to find out," Jameston whispered out of the side of his mouth. Following his gaze to a pair of thick pines across a small open patch of ground, Bransen saw a warrior, lithe and strong with tightly wound muscles. His brow, furrowed and pronounced with the dark, thin lines of his eyebrows, made his black eyes seem even angrier, fiercer, an imposing appearance that grew only more so for his shaven head. He was dressed in black silk clothing akin to Bransen's own and casually swung a strange weapon at the end of one arm, a pair of forearm-length solid wooden poles secured at their ends by a short length of leather.

"Nun'chu'ku," Bransen mouthed as he considered the very deadly weapon he recognized from his lessons reading the Book of Jhest.

The warrior said something in a strange tongue, and Bransen tried to unwind the words. He knew the language from the book his father had penned, but he had never heard it spoken before. The warrior repeated his phrase, a demand from the insistent tone.

"You know what he's saying, boy?" Jameston whispered.

"Something about Jhesta Tu," Bransen answered, shaking his head. "Asking if I am Jhesta Tu, I think, but I cannot be certain."

"Act certain, then," Jameston replied.

"Jhesta Tu," Bransen said loudly.

The warrior's dark eyes narrowed immediately, and he began to walk slowly to their left, putting himself more in line with Bransen.

"Wrong answer," Jameston said.

"Jhesta Tu?" Bransen asked this time, and he pointed at the warrior. That stopped the man in his pacing, and his expression turned more to curiosity.

"Who be you?" the warrior asked in the common tongue of Honce, though heavily accented in the dialect of Behr, a rolling and bouncing singsong effect of consonants bitten off and vowels exaggerated.

"I am Bransen Gari—" Bransen started, but he changed direction and said with confidence, "I am the son of Sen Wi of the Jhesta Tu and of Bran Dynard, trained at the Walk of Clouds."

"But you have de sword," the warrior said, his accent thick.

"I wield the sword of Sen Wi."

"You be Jhesta Tu."

Bransen shook his head, and the warrior snickered.

"You give me the sword."

Bransen shook his head again.

"You give me the sword now, and you go."

"And if I do not?"

"Then I take the sword from your body, yes." As he finished, the warrior sent his nun'chu'ku into sudden motion, spinning the bottom length in a fast rotation at his side, then snapping it across his chest so that it wrapped under his upraised arm and slapped flat against his back. It came back in front of him and to his right for another spinning display before going under his upraised arm and around his back. When he brought the wooden pole humming before him once more, he set it into a furious reverse spin before him, then worked it back and up beside his right ear. He slapped his left wrist across his vertical right forearm and caught the flying pole in his grasp, immediately tugging it across back to his left while letting go with his right hand so that the other pole now flew freely.

Back and forth he worked the amazing weapon, changing hands and perfectly moving the momentum from one pole, through the leather tie to the other pole, reversing the spins.

It ended as suddenly as it had begun, the man somehow turning the nun'chu'ku so that its spin tucked it neatly under his right arm.

"Awful lot of bluster for so few words," Jameston quietly remarked.

"Give me de sword now," the warrior said.

Bransen drew his blade in a fluid and powerful movement, snapping the sword before him, angled diagonally to the sky. He slowly folded his elbow, bringing the back of the sword blade in against his forehead. After only a very short pause he snapped the blade down and to the side with such speed that it cracked through the air. He ended, as the practice demanded, with the tip of his blade a hair's breadth from the dirt, angled down and slightly away from him.

Bransen kept his expression purposely grim, although he was beaming inside in confidence, bolstered by the Behr warrior's expression, which confirmed to him that he had executed the sword salute perfectly.

"I think not," he said, taking a slow and deliberate step forward. Jameston faded away from him a couple of short shuffles to the side, bow in his left hand, right hand positioned to grab an arrow from the quiver strapped diagonally across his back.

The warrior paid no heed to Jameston, his dangerous gaze locked on Bransen. He moved his right arm just a bit, the nun'chu'ku dropped free of his hold and unwound to its full length at the end of his grasp. He slid into a crouch, left hand coming up before his chest in a blocking position, his right arm sliding back just a bit. He gave a brief shout and stood from his pose. He never blinked and never stopped staring at Bransen as he took a couple of steps farther to the left and fell once more into that ready posture.

"What's that about?" Jameston asked.

"He is showing me that he is unafraid," Bransen explained.

"Should I just shoot him?"

"You wouldn't hit him."

"Hmm," was Jameston's doubtful response.

The warrior's eyes narrowed, and his lip twitched into a snarl as if the chatter was an insult to him, which Bransen realized it probably was.

The Highwayman saluted crisply with his sword again then slowly walked his left foot forward toward the warrior, falling into a wide-stance, forward-diagonal crouch. He crooked his right elbow and turned his right wrist so that his arm looked like a serpent as he brought it back up high, his sword pointing forward past his head. He gracefully lifted his left hand before him, palm out. The warrior from Behr sent his weapon into a spin and strode forward a step.

The Highwayman dropped his arm, stabbing his sword forward in an underhand movement as he stepped closer to his opponent. He came up fast, handing the blade to his left hand and striking a mirror-image of the pose from which he had started.

They were barely three strides apart and then only two as the warrior from Behr gave a shout and came forward, his weapon working a dizzying blur of spins before he caught it in both hands. He turned them so the poles snapped vertically, the leather tie drawing a horizontal line before his face.

The Highwayman tried to sort out a counter. His next movement would likely end the posturing and begin the actual fighting. He tried to remember everything he had read about nun'chu'ku and the techniques involved, tried to somehow link that book knowledge against the minimal display he had witnessed from the Behrenese warrior.

He simply wasn't sure of what he was up against here, of the limitations and strengths of this exotic weapon. A mischievous grin came to his lips and he thought himself very clever as he began to shift again very slowly.

Suddenly, thrusting his blade, turning it over so that its razor edge pointed skyward Bransen poked toward the warrior's face but pulled up short and slashed the sword for the sky, thinking to sever the leather tie of the nun'chu'ku. The warrior didn't try to pull the exotic weapon away; the Highwayman thought he had scored a clean hit.

But the man from Behr lifted his hands as the sword came up, absorbing most of the strike's energy. As the blade connected with the leather but without any momentum to cut through, the warrior crossed his hands before his chest then thrust upward with his right and pulled downward with his left, the resulting turn of leather and wood nearly tearing the sword from the Highwayman's grasp!

The warrior drove the weapons higher and stepped through, turning right-to-left suddenly as he went, his trailing left foot snapping out to kick the Highwayman squarely in the gut. Bransen had to grab his sword with both hands to prevent it from being torn from his grasp.

The Highwayman threw his hips back, absorbing the brunt of the sharp blow. As the warrior turned about before him, now driving the sword's blade back down, Bransen went forward a short step and leaped into a twisting somersault, still holding fast with both hands and now tucking his elbows in tight to try to gain control of the movements of the weapons. He thought he could tear his sword free with the momentum of the twist and take the leather tie apart in the process, but the Behrenese warrior, again one step ahead of him, simply disengaged as Bransen tumbled past. The sudden freedom of his blade nearly toppled Bransen as he came around to his feet.

The Highwayman moved instinctively, knowing that his opponent would expect an overbalance. Taking his sword in his left hand alone, he pivoted onto the ball of his right foot, spinning around and dropping a downward backhand parry perfectly in line with the flying end of the nun'chu'ku. The metal rang out in vibration from the heavy hit as Bransen came up square with his opponent, falling immediately into a defensive crouch, hands joining on the hilt of his sword before him.

Not an instant too soon. The Behrenese warrior, offering no opportunity for Bransen to move to an offensive posture, launched a sudden and furious routine, the nun'chu'ku whipping before him in a sidelong swipe, then going into a spin above his head, where he cleverly changed hands and came in from the other side.

Bransen barely blocked.

Again and again and again the wooden poles hummed through the air up high, down low, behind the warrior's back. He came in left and down, right across, right and down from on high.

The Highwayman was purely reacting, trying hard to follow the man's dizzying movements to get his sword out to block. Somehow he kept up, but he felt as if he were drowning, as if the water were rising too fast for him to stay above it.

He tried to block another swing from the right, but the warrior shortened the strike and the nun'chu'ku whipped past. The Highwayman understood as the man dropped low before him, still rotating. Instinct alone had Bransen leaping and tucking his legs, narrowly avoiding a cunning leg sweep that would have put him to the ground.

He couldn't leap fast enough, though, and he had to put all his weight to his right leg and lift his left, turning it to absorb the blow as the nun'chu'ku came around and smashed him hard against the side of his shin.

Bransen gritted through the hit and stabbed down hard. With no momentum left in the nun'chu'ku, the warrior let it go and caught it quickly with a reverse grip, then slapped the pole against the descending sword blade. Again he loosened his grip and shoved, pushing Bransen's sword away, turning his hand over as he went, using that sword as a fulcrum to throw the bulk of the nun'chu'ku beneath it. His left hand crossed under his thrusting right elbow, catching the free pole as he sprang from the crouch before Bransen. Momentum regained as he lifted his left hand up high and over then down and back across, the descending warrior got past Bransen's desperate defensive turn enough to send the flying nun'chu'ku pole hard against Bransen's right shoulder.

The Highwayman gasped at the explosion of pain and

stumbled to his left, stunned by the sheer weight of the blow.

J ameston had seen more than enough. He had long ago taken a measure of the Highwayman as the finest young warrior he had ever seen, but he already knew that Bransen was ill-prepared to battle this fierce warrior. In a single fluid movement, Jameston's right hand snapped up and grasped an arrow, pulling it from the quiver, drawing it down over his right shoulder, and setting it expertly to the bow. Still moving in the same beautiful line, the scout drew back and lifted the bow, string coming against the side of his nose. He didn't have much space between Bransen and the strange warrior, but he didn't need much.

A form, a leaping and spinning, black-clothed warrior, flew in from the side and behind, just above Jameston. His bowstring lost all tension, the top of his bow snapping forward suddenly and awkwardly, arrow falling to the ground.

The scout cried out in surprise but kept his wits enough to grab his bow in both hands like a stave and swing to his left where the assailant had gone.

Had gone and was now coming back ferociously. Jameston turned that way. Smaller than the other opponent, a woman warrior came at him with clenched fists. She opened her left as she thrust it forward. Instinct alone prompted Jameston to pull his bow in close defensively. The small knife she had used to cut his bowstring stabbed into the bow and stuck fast.

At the last moment Jameston leveled his bow like a spear to fend the charging warrior. She did stop but slapped at the bow left and right, grabbing at the wood.

Jameston retracted and stabbed ahead repeatedly, trying to keep her at bay. He began rotating the staff's end in

small, fast circles; when he had her attention there he
cleverly charged and thrust forward. He thought he had
her, would have scored a solid hit, but a second stave entered the fray, chopping hard from the side, turning down
Jameston's bow-staff.

"What?" he cried, noting another black-clothed warrior to his left. He let go of his bow with his right hand and
lifted it to block. Too late, for the warrior ran the staff up
the angled wood above his lifting hand.

Jameston managed to turn so that he only took a glancing blow across his jaw, but when he looked back he saw
the woman flying through the air at him, spinning a forward somersault. She straightened as she came over, her
legs snapping forward, her black silk slippers poking
from under the wide cut of her silken pants.

That's going to hurt, Jameston thought, as one foot
crunched against his cheek and nose; the other slammed
him hard in the collarbone. He went flying backward,
arms and legs akimbo, and landed on his back, his breath
blasted away. Before he could begin to even think about
rising, the other warrior was above him, the tip of a staff
in tight against the bottom of his chin, ready to drive
through his throat.

Jameston lifted his hands in surrender.

The Highwayman tried to block out Jameston's troubles. He couldn't afford even to glance at his friend's
precarious position while battling a man of such talent
and speed. He was still reminding himself of that when
the Behrenese warrior faked high and swept low with his
legs, sending Bransen tumbling to the ground.

Even as he fell Bransen sought the malachite, lessen-
ing his weight. He landed lightly on his back, turned his
legs under him and tightened his stomach, hoisting his
shoulders with such force that he propelled himself right

back to his feet with a suddenness that took his opponent by surprise.

The Highwayman went for the win, thinking to wound this warrior fast and spring away to help his fallen friend. He thrust out, a certain hit on the warrior's hip, but he shortened the strike, both because he had no desire to kill this man and because he was anxious, too anxious, to get to Jameston. And because the Highwayman simply wasn't used to fighting someone this quick and trained in the Jhesta Tu manner.

So when he expected his blade to penetrate flesh, he found instead a nun'chu'ku spinning an underhand block, pushing the angle of the cut wide. Worse, the exotic weapon wrapped up and around and the warrior grabbed both ends, locking the sword in place. The Highwayman reacted in time to prevent the sudden twist from snapping his blade in half by turning with the angle change, but the movement had him and his opponent in an awkward alignment, slightly askew of each other and both leaning away.

The warrior from Behr fell even lower, dropping his back, left leg into a deep crouch. Then he began kicking with his right leg, hitting the Highwayman in the shin and side of his knee, and then again in rapid succession.

The Highwayman fell into a similar crouch and responded with his own kicks, but his opponent had the advantage, the momentum, and the initiative. Feet circled and kicked forward and back, slapping and bruising as the two held tight to their entangled weapons.

For a few heartbeats, the Highwayman took two blows for every one he delivered. He gradually moved to more even footing and even managed a solid hit against the back of his opponent's outstretched thigh, his toes jabbing hard into the man's hamstring.

But that leg came up higher suddenly and clipped Bransen's chin, nearly sending him tumbling away. He moved in closer, and kicks became jabbing knees. Again the Highwayman took the worst of it. He knew the style of fighting well from his readings, but he had never engaged in it, had never even sparred with this technique, and he was up against a master.

A knee came in hard against the side of his thigh, bruising him sorely. He shifted away from the assault. The warrior from Behr promptly straightened his leg in a snap kick that left Bransen's left arm numb.

He wanted to retreat and regroup, but he couldn't pull his sword free, and he surely couldn't surrender it.

So the Highwayman went the other way, crouch-walking even closer to his opponent. He let go of his sword with his left hand, punching at the warrior, who easily shifted back enough so that, even if the punch landed, it could do no real harm.

But the Highwayman wasn't trying to punch the warrior. Instead, he grabbed the man by the front of his silken shirt and with a yell, threw himself forward so that they were tight together.

The warrior from Behr laughed—exactly the response Bransen had hoped to elicit, for it told him that the warrior had believed his move to be a desperate attempt to drive the trapped sword in for the kill. The warrior then snapped his head backward and forward viciously, his forehead crunching against the Highwayman's nose.

Bransen accepted the powerful hit, for he was already deep into the graphite of his brooch, bringing forth its powers. As the warrior from Behr snapped his head back again for another butt, the mighty jolt of lightning power kept him moving backward, had him flying backward, arms and legs flailing. He hit the ground and jerked about wildly.

The Highwayman stood and with a flip of his wrist sent the nun'chu'ku into the air where he caught it with his free hand. He hid well his grimace of pain as he straightened, for his knee, thigh, and hip were beyond bruised.

"Drop the weapons!" the woman shouted.

Bransen glanced to the side, where the man holding the stave on Jameston retracted it just an inch and popped it down hard against the underside of Jameston's chin, drawing a pitiful gurgle from the prostrate man.

In front of the Highwayman, the fallen warrior finally managed to stand—or tried to, at least, but his legs wobbled uncontrollably and he staggered back down to one knee. He cried out through chattering teeth in the tongue of the southern kingdom. Bransen understood enough of the words to recognize that he was calling for his friends to back away from Jameston.

In the common tongue of Honce, the Behr warrior added, "This one is worthy to wield that sword!"

Sweeter words Bransen Garibond had never heard.

TWENTY-SIX

A Shiver of Sharks

He's a madman!" Laird Panlamaris roared, storming about and crushing the parchment in his powerful hand.

The courier from Delaval City shrank back from the wild man, eyeing the door of the tavern's common room as if searching for an escape route. He wasn't the only one; of the thirty men and women in the room, all seemed more than a bit unsettled by the powerful man's outburst. All save one dressed in monk's robes and sitting calmly at the same table Panlamaris had occupied when he had been handed the note—before he had leaped up, fuming.

"A madman!" Panlamaris said again and he kicked a chair across the room.

"He is the King of Honce," Father De Guilbe remarked. When the Laird of Palmaristown fixed him with a severe glare, he merely shrugged.

"Read it!" Panlamaris said, throwing the parchment De Guilbe's way.

De Guilbe didn't catch it, but rather, deflected it to the floor. "He demands that you attack Chapel Abelle," he said.

"Yes," Panlamaris replied. "He wants me to throw all that I have against those walls, with the monks hurling fire and lightning at us from on high."

"And with your finest warriors off rampaging in the far east," said De Guilbe.

"It is madness!" Panlamaris declared.

"Foolishness, at least," De Guilbe agreed. "King Yeslnik is a man who does not yet understand battle."

"Am I to write his lesson in the blood of Palmaristown's garrison?"

"Are you?"

"No!" Laird Panlamaris yelled. He took a deep breath and seemed to relax a bit. He even managed to grab a chair from a nearby table and take his seat across from De Guilbe. "We cannot go against such a fortress as Chapel Abelle. Not with their magical powers and with my ships getting sunk by powries behind them. Powries! Of all the ill times to have powries in the gulf!"

"A remarkable coincidence, you believe?" asked De Guilbe, and in a tone that suggested that he thought it no such thing.

"Is it not?"

"Among those who did battle against Ancient Badden were a pair of powries," De Guilbe explained.

Laird Panlamaris and many others looked at the monk incredulously.

"It is true," De Guilbe insisted. "When the Highwayman dropped Ancient Badden's head at Dame Gwydre's feet, he was accompanied by the man Cormack, who betrayed me, by a barbarian woman, and by a pair of bloody-cap dwarves. He introduced those powries to Dame Gwydre as friends, and the powries wintered in Castle Pellinor."

"This cannot be," said Panlamaris, giving voice to what almost everyone in the room was thinking.

"But it is, I tell you," said De Guilbe. "They wintered

in Castle Pellinor and were given free passage from the city as soon as the snows had calmed."

"Powries?"

"Ugliest little creatures I have ever seen."

Laird Panlamaris stroked his beard and stared through the tavern door and up the hill to the distant outline of Chapel Abelle. "You believe Dame Gwydre enlisted the little beasts?"

"I know that Dame Gwydre did not kill the two who came to Pellinor," De Guilbe replied. "I know that she released them, and that the one called the Highwayman named them as friends. Friends help friends, do they not?"

Laird Panlamaris stared off into nothingness for a long while, his eyes narrow, his nostrils flared. His defeat at the wall of Chapel Abelle had stung him profoundly, but the loss of three warships had positively infuriated him. Panlamaris had been a sailor throughout his youth, when his father had ruled the port city, and he had traced the Honce coast from Delaval City to Ethelbert dos Entel and from the Vanguard coast all the way to southern Alpinador. He had battled powries before, as well, out on the open Mirianic and in fact had been instrumental in devising ways to cripple the dreaded barrel boats, using ballista-launched weighted nets to drag the low-riding craft under the waves.

As with almost every sailor in Honce, Laird Panlamaris hated powries most of all.

And now—was it possible? The notion that these wretched little beasts had joined in with his enemies boiled his blood.

He slammed his fist down on the table so hard that the nearest leg creaked in protest, cracked, and nearly buckled.

"We attack, my laird?" one commander standing nearby asked with great enthusiasm.

"Shut up," Panlamaris said, then to De Guilbe added,

"I will confront Dame Gwydre in parlay. If she is in league with these beasts, then one day soon Vanguard will bow to the rule of Laird Panlamaris."

He stood up powerfully, his chair flying behind him, and called for a scribe. "Soon," he repeated grimly to De Guilbe.

Pedal faster, ye mutts, or we're to miss all the dippin'!" Shiknickel cried out to his crew. Up in the squat tower, the powrie watched as a pair of barrel boats closed fast on a warship, another flying the colors of Palmaristown.

Below and behind him, the tough dwarves picked up their pace, the barrel boat leaping away across the dark waters. Shiknickel grinned but didn't openly applaud their efforts, preferring instead the inspiring, "Yah, but ye call that fast? Ye mutts, me dead mum could swim past ye!"

He was smiling wider as he finished, but his grin disappeared a moment later when the Palmaristown warship attacked. Deck-mounted ballistae, giant spear throwers, let fly at the nearest barrel boat, launching thick, weighted netting. Their shots weren't true but didn't have to be, for just putting the spears near to the boat, which was no more than twenty yards from the warship's broadside, sent the net over its tower, hooking fast and draping over the back half of the boat. The drag slowed the craft immediately, and, worse, the netting hooked the barrel boat's single propeller. Instead of charging in now at high speed to ram the warship, the barrel boat was suddenly adrift and tilting as the heavy weights pulled at her.

Spotters ran along the warship's deck, pointing out the second approaching barrel boat while the ballista crews reloaded. A host of archers appeared at the rail and began raking the trapped barrel boat even as some of her crew tried to climb to cut the netting free.

"They was ready for us," Shiknickel whispered. "Bah! Stop yer pedaling!" he shouted down to the dwarves. "Stop, I'm tellin' ye!"

Mcwigik came to the base of the ladder. "Gwydre's boat?" he asked.

Shiknickel motioned for him to climb up. "Palmaristown, still," he explained. "But they're coming out ready."

Mcwigik grimaced as he considered the scene. The trapped barrel boat was listing now, water splashing in through her tower. Dwarves tried to come up, and arrows cut them down.

The second boat had turned, but the warship, too, was tacking to give chase.

"They ain't seen us yet," Mcwigik remarked, and Shiknickel nodded grimly.

"We got to be quick and hard."

Mcwigik smiled at him and punched a fist into his open palm.

Shiknickel lifted his signaling mirror and turned it behind the boat, where he knew three other barrel boats to be on the prowl.

"Lay quiet," he ordered Mcwigik. "They'll go by us chasing our friends. Almost." He ended with an exaggerated wink.

"They're turnin' inside us, are they?" Mcwigik asked.

Shiknickel smiled.

"Swing out wider?"

"Slowly," ordered Shiknickel. "They're lookin' th'other way, so keep our spray down and keep them looking th'other way."

Mcwigik went back into the hold and motioned for silence. Facing the crew, he held up his right hand while slowly turning circles with his left, and the right hand crew began a slow pedal, executing a left turn.

"Quarter," Shiknickel called down.

Mcwigik began a slow cadence of patting both hands and the crew began to pedal in unison at the easy pace.

As the Palmaristown warship continued its turn and gained speed, obviously unaware of Shiknickel's boat or those trailing, the captain called for a turn back to the right. When the angle was right he shouted down, "Full and fast, and get ready for a jolt!"

A powrie barrel boat was built for head-on collision, with a devilish ram leading its charge just below the waterline. Many buffers had been engineered around that ram, and, even without them, the thin planking of a typical surface sailing ship would have proven no match for the concentrated pounding of a barrel boat's solid ram. Slammed against a stopped ship, with only the power of pedaling dwarves, that ram would still break through to some degree. In this case, with the barrel boat coming in at an angle before a fast-sailing ship, the explosion knocked every dwarf from his seat and sent Mcwigik flying against the front inside wall.

But the dwarves were laughing, for they knew that their unsettling bounce had been nothing compared to what the unprepared crew of the sailing ship had just felt.

Indeed, the powrie ram drove a gaping hole in the starboard bow of the warship, and the momentum had lengthened that hole considerably, splintering planks near to midship. A man plummeted from the rigging, dislodged by the sudden and unexpected impact. Several others went flying over the rail, and all on the deck were tumbling, caught completely by surprise.

Without even being told, the powries rushed back to their seats and began pedaling in reverse. Wood creaked in protest, for the ram was fairly stuck, and the heavier warship dragged the barrel boat along as its momentum played out.

"Forward! Back!" Mcwigik shouted in succession, the

reversals rocking the barrel boat and tearing apart more of the sailing ship's planking in the process. From above, they could all hear the Palmaristown sailors crying out, "Powrie boat!" and calling for nets and arrows.

That brought more laughter than anything else, for every powrie on Shiknickel's boat understood the damage they had inflicted on the warship, and all knew that the blustering sailors would very quickly be far more concerned with the fact that their ship was sinking than with the powries.

The barrel boat finally slid free.

"Put her back a dozen and watch the show," said Mcwigik.

"Can't see a thing," one dwarf remarked to the giggles of the others.

"Listen, then," Mcwigik replied. "Sure to be a song sweet to me ears."

They heard but didn't feel another loud crash.

"Tikminnik's boat," Shiknickel called down. "Get yer caps ready, boys, for she'll list over soon enough!"

Much cheering and rubbing of hands ensued.

Within a very short time, the Palmaristown warship lay on her side, most of her underwater. Men bobbed and splashed or hung on desperately to the rigging while the powrie boats circled like sharks.

Shiknickel led the way onto the deck, calling for gaff hooks as he went. Heartbeats later, the first third of the crew in rotation had climbed from the tower, long hooked poles in hand. The remaining dwarves pedaled slowly and turned to Shiknickel's call, bringing the barrel boat beside one floundering sailor after another.

"Please, sir, no!" one man cried desperately. "I've a wife and little girl!"

"And ye should've stayed home with them, eh?" a powrie replied. He slapped his gaff hook down hard, catching the man by the shoulder, and hauled him to the side of the rounded deck.

Other dwarves were fast to the spot, serrated knives in hand. They expertly opened up the best areas for a long and thick bloodletting. And so it went throughout the rest of the day, until the sharks arrived. The boats went to the aid of their netted kin then, helping them finish cutting away the pesky ropes and then holding tight to the listing craft, keeping back the sharks while the crew powries bailed her.

The next morning the seas were calm, the Palmaristown ship and all her crew gone from sight, with not even flotsam to be seen.

The powrie captains and their top advisors all sat atop their respective decks.

"Where to, then?" one asked. "Getting tired o' waiting for them fools to come out here in the open waters."

"From the west, always," another observed.

"Palmaristown," Shiknickel explained. "West and at the mouth of the river."

"And with most of her fleet down? And most of her men out fighting on the field?" Mcwigik asked slyly.

Half a dozen barrel boats started out to the west, a shiver of sharks.

Hungry sharks.

They were in range of Palmaristown's archers, but in range, too, of the monks on St. Mere Abelle's wall with their devastating gemstones.

Dame Gwydre and Laird Panlamaris rode from their respective ranks simultaneously, meeting on the field at a tent Panlamaris's men had set up. Beside Gwydre rode Father Premujon and Brother Pinower, and a pair accompanied Panlamaris, as well, including Father De Guilbe.

The sight of the large and imposing monk distressed Gwydre, but not as much as it unsettled poor Premujon. She felt naked out here without Dawson beside her. Reports magically collected by the brothers had reached her of his escape from the Palmaristown ships in the gulf. She was beside herself with relief but sorely missed the man she had leaned upon for so many years.

Given the events in the gulf, where Palmaristown warships had somehow been defeated, Gwydre eagerly accepted the invitation to parlay with her opponents, hoping against reason that the impasse might be at an end. As she neared the tent and noted the expression on Laird Panlamaris's face, her doubts overwhelmed her optimism.

A table had been set inside the tent, three chairs on each side. Gwydre took hers in the middle, directly opposite Panlamaris.

"Lady, it is good to see that some among you have a bit of honor, at least," Laird Panlamaris began. "A very tiny bit."

"Good tidings to you, too, Laird Panlamaris," Gwydre retorted, "who came unbidden with his army to the gates of a chapel and stained the field before her with the blood of innocent men."

"Innocent?" Father De Guilbe growled, but Panlamaris silenced him with an upraised hand.

"You know Father De Guilbe," Panlamaris said. "And this is Captain Dunlevin Brosh, who commands the Palmaristown fleet."

"Father Premujon of Chapel Pellinor," Gwydre replied. "And this is Brother Pinower, who speaks for St. Mere Abelle."

"What?" De Guilbe noted, his brow furrowing. "Saint?"

"St. Mere Abelle," Dame Gwydre said again. "Until recently known as Chapel Abelle."

De Guilbe gave a wicked chuckle. "The fool Artolivan. Does he think that his symbolic gestures will help him against the inevitable fall? Will he hide behind a name—a name he dishonors with every treasonous action he takes?"

His voice grew louder with each question, his outrage bubbling over. "We will return to our mission when I am installed as the proper head of the Order of Abelle!" He slammed his fist on the table, trembling.

Gwydre and the two monks accompanying her looked to one another helplessly, incredulously. The dame turned to Laird Panlamaris. "You support this subversion?"

"Subversion?" the old warrior repeated. When De Guilbe began to bellow in protest again Panlamaris reached out and forcibly pushed the man back into his chair.

"Subversion?" he said again. "You would say that to me after what happened in the gulf?"

Dame Gwydre eyed him with confusion. "Your ships tried to attack—"

"You sent powries against my warships!" Now Panlamaris's voice began to tremble and rise with righteous outrage. "Powries! Bloody-cap dwarves working in concert with the ships of Vanguard!"

"My men plucked from the water and cut open so that the vicious beasts could brighten their berets!" Captain Dunlevin Brosh cried.

"You are mad to think I would—"

But Panlamaris cut her off. "It's a coincidence, then, that the ships of Vanguard were allowed to sail free while the ships of Palmaristown were sent to the bottom, all hands slaughtered? Am I to believe that a cruel trick of fate, Dame Gwydre? Or am I to call it what it is? You, and your church"—he added, poking his finger at both Premujon and Pinower—"have allied with powries against the men of Honce!"

"That is a lie!" Father Premujon leaped from his chair as did Brother Pinower, shouting with rage. For a moment it looked as if negotiations might turn physical.

But Gwydre calmed it all, standing tall between the

brothers and her opponents. "Enough!" She turned a withering eye on Laird Panlamaris. "You requested a parlay. For no better reason than to offer this slander?"

Laird Panlamaris forced both De Guilbe and Brosh to sit quiet. "Is it slander, Dame of Vanguard?"

"I know nothing of any powries in the gulf. I know only that your warships gave chase to my ships, unlawfully and without provocation."

"Without provocation?" Panlamaris howled, his voice thick with incredulity. "You have come here and stolen Honce land."

"I have offered support to the autonomous Abellican Church, which chooses secession before giving in to the heinous demands of the one who calls himself king. To murder men taken honestly in honorable battle! Shame on him, and shame on you if you agree with such a thing! Laird Panlamaris was known throughout Vanguard as a man of honor, but I wonder if that is still true, if you would agree with this vile edict of King Yeslnik!"

She accompanied her strong words with a wary eye on Panlamaris's every move. She'd clearly pricked his vanity when she mentioned his reputation throughout Vanguard, which was hardly true, given that few in Vanguard had ever heard the name before.

Panlamaris sat for many heartbeats in silence, never blinking as he looked across the table at his adversary.

"Reconsider your course," he finally said. "Come back into the fold of a unified Honce. And you as well," he added, addressing the monks. "Your Father Artolivan's time is passed, but we can salvage the remnants of your order. All can be forgiven—even Father Artolivan's reputation can be protected when he quietly retires—but only if you act quickly and wisely."

"And if we do not, you will storm the walls of St. Mere Abelle once more?" Dame Gwydre asked with obvious sarcasm.

"Or perhaps I will cede Chapel Abelle to you," he said, and beside him, Father De Guilbe winced. "And lock you in your walled prison. The waters of the gulf will be mine in short order despite your evil alliance with the dwarves."

"There is no such alliance!" Gwydre insisted.

Panlamaris snorted derisively. "Whatever the case may be," he said, "I will own the gulf. The Palmaristown fleet will find allies from Delaval City soon enough, and we will chase the vile dwarves from our waters. I will hold you in this prison of your making, your own little kingdom, while the armies of King Yeslnik debark in Port Vanguard and sweep your holding out from under you. How inviting will Chapel Abelle's walls seem then, good lady?"

Dame Gwydre didn't blink, though Panlamaris's words had indeed shaken her, for she saw their prediction as a quite likely prospect. Suddenly, it was a staring contest between the two, across the table, and it became apparent quickly that Laird Panlamaris wasn't nearly as confident as he sounded.

Still Dame Gwydre didn't blink.

The six rode away soon in opposite directions.

"So now we know how Dawson escaped," Brother Pinower dared say, walking his mount beside Gwydre's on the way back. "Powries. Powries! I cannot declare them god-sent, though I surely am glad that they chose their targets well!"

"It is a minor victory," Dame Gwydre warned. "As was our victory when we turned back Laird Panlamaris's charge. Neither offer far-reaching consequences or relief if the outcome across Honce continues in favor of King Yeslnik and his brutal lairds."

"And Father De Guilbe," Father Premujon said grimly. "He will fight us to the death, and more than a few brothers, I fear, will follow his angry call."

"It is going to be a long, dark summer," said Dame Gwydre.

* * *

Send out couriers to my son," Laird Panlamaris instructed Captain Dunlevin Brosh. "Runners across the land and a battle group of your fastest warships to run the coast in the hopes that he is near enough to see their pennants. Together Milwellis and I will drive the traitorous witch from her castle and right into the sea! And then we will win the waters of the gulf, as I promised, and will bring Vanguard under the rule of Palmaristown."

"Palmaristown?" Dunlevin Brosh echoed with surprise. He immediately swallowed hard, tipping his hand that he did not mean to blurt out his thoughts so freely.

"King Yeslnik will be so grateful to us for putting the Order of Blessed Abelle back into his fold under the fine Father De Guilbe, so grateful that we crushed the insurgent Gwydre, that he will allow me to expand my holding to the north all the way to the borders of Alpinador."

"Yes, my laird," Brosh replied.

"And even if he does not," Laird Panlamaris said with a snicker. "Simply killing Gwydre and Artolivan will be worth the war."

TWENTY-SEVEN

By Their Rules

H e felt naked before her. She was slight of build, with dark hair and brown skin and dark, darting eyes full of energy and life that scrutinized and drank in every inch of Bransen. She moved with incredible grace, as if her slippers weren't even disturbing the grass as she circled him. He wondered if she looked like his mother. Certainly she appeared similar to how Garibond had described Sen Wi. And her clothes were just like his, and thus, just like his mother's.

Had she known his mother? Bransen's eyes sparkled at the thought, but his smile didn't last more than a moment as he realized that Affwin Wi could not be much older than he, perhaps not even as old.

Perhaps, then, he wondered, Affwin Wi had heard of his mother. How he wanted to ask her, but her command had been uncompromising: Stand still and stand straight, look straight ahead only and say nothing.

This went on for what seemed like ages. It occurred to Bransen that Affwin Wi was testing his patience. A true Jhesta Tu, in tune with his surroundings and comfortable in his own contemplations, could stand silently and unmoving for hours.

"You carry sword of Jhesta Tu," Affwin Wi said suddenly from the side, just out of his line of sight and so somewhat startling him. Her heavy southern accent bit off every syllable, so it took Bransen a few moments simply to decipher her sentence.

"I do," he answered, taking her extended silence as a prompt for him to finally speak.

"You dress in clothes of mystic warrior."

"Yes," said Bransen.

"You are Jhesta Tu?"

Bransen turned his head to regard her—or started to before her widening eyes and upturning snarl warned him to look back ahead. "My mother, Sen Wi, was Jhesta Tu."

"Mother?" Affwin Wi echoed in surprise. Across the small clearing, Bransen saw the bald-headed warrior's apparent relief in his chuckle.

"Sen Wi of the Walk of Clouds," said Bransen.

"I do not know this name."

"She left many years ago, twenty-one years ago," Bransen explained. "She married my father and came to Honce with him."

"You do not look of Behr. Not full."

"My father was of Honce, a monk of a Honce church, who went to Behr and the Walk of Clouds, where he learned from the . . . from your masters."

"And they taught you?"

"I never knew my father. My mother died the day I was born."

"But you know!" There was no missing the accusation in her tone.

"From the Book of Jhest. My father penned a copy of the Book of Jhest."

"You taught yourself?" the bald-headed warrior called out incredulously from across the way.

From the corner of his eye, Bransen saw Affwin Wi thrust her hand to silence him. She stormed around to stand before Bransen.

"I did," he answered. "From the book."

Affwin Wi stared at him for a moment then laughed.

"Merwal Yahna"—she indicated the bald-headed man—"says you are worthy of the sword."

Bransen gave a slight bow, which he knew to be the proper acceptance of such a compliment.

"Why are you here?" Affwin Wi asked.

"I came to find the warrior who broke a sword in the chest of King Delaval," Bransen admitted, and the woman stiffened at the apparent threat.

"I came to find the Jhesta Tu to honor my mother and to learn," Bransen quickly explained.

"You were friends with this Delaval?"

Bransen snorted. "Hardly. His successor wants me dead."

Affwin Wi waited a few moments, even glancing back at Merwal Yahna, who offered a slight nod in reply. "You came to learn?" she asked.

"To confirm that I am correct in how I follow the Book of Jhest," said Bransen. "And to learn, yes. To learn more about this philosophy that has so guided my life. I have seen the broken end of your sword, and I knew it to be Jhesta Tu. So I came to find you."

Affwin Wi began to pace back and forth before him, occasionally glancing at him, deep in contemplation. "You are worthy," she decided. "You may join with me."

Bransen felt as if his heart would pound right through the front of his chest as he considered the implications, the great step forward he had just taken.

"Your friend will leave now," Affwin Wi stated.

The shock of that jolted Bransen from his whirling thoughts. Despite the orders placed upon him, he glanced back to the far edge of the clearing, where Jameston stood between the pair who had captured him.

"Begone," Affwin Wi ordered.

Jameston eyed Bransen.

"I care not where, but far from us," Affwin Wi said. "Now. Begone."

"I am supposed to watch over the boy," said Jameston.

"He is not a boy, he is a man," said Affwin Wi. "He follows Jhesta Tu. How are you, who are not Jhesta Tu, to watch over him?"

"I was—"

"You are not," Affwin Wi barked. "Only one more time I tell you, begone."

The threat in her voice clear to hear, Jameston looked in question at Bransen again. The young warrior took a deep breath and nodded.

Jameston met Bransen's eyes for a long moment before returning that nod in farewell and slipping off into the forest.

Leaving Bransen nervous and very alone and very naked indeed under the withering gaze of Affwin Wi.

H e is powerful with your stones. Are you not interested in protecting your Laird Ethelbert?" Affwin Wi asked succinctly and directly when Father Destros of Chapel Entel balked at arming his monks with sunstones in Laird Ethelbert's hall for the meeting with the strange Highwayman.

Father Destros swallowed hard. "Are you not confident of your abilities to protect my laird?" he asked. As soon as the words left his mouth he knew that calling out Affwin Wi on such a matter might be unwise.

The woman's hand snapped up quicker than Destros

could react, her poking finger right before his eye, meaning that she could have jabbed that finger right through his eye had she chosen to do so.

"He uses your stones, priest," she warned. "And he fights as Jhesta Tu. You will protect your leader, and my people will protect him." She backed away but didn't take her eyes off the man until she was out in the hallway.

Father Destros had to remind himself to breathe. She was right, of course. This wasn't about their growing personal rivalry but about the safety of Laird Ethelbert. He went to his desk and retrieved a sunstone, pocketing several others as well. When he entered Laird Ethelbert's audience chamber a short while later, he had the sunstone firmly in his grasp. Not only would the gem allow him to counter any use of magic, it would allow for detection of magic as well. Destros figured that he might learn more than a bit about this mysterious Highwayman; he only wished that Affwin Wi hadn't been the one to deliver the suggestion.

And certainly not the command.

J ameston Sequin picked up his pace. He knew that he had already been seen and was being followed, so moving stealthily really didn't help him much.

Perhaps they were just ensuring that he continued far from Ethelbert's holding.

Jameston wasn't one to leave things to chance, however, so instead of trying to find a way to hide or outrun them, which he almost certainly could not do, he sought instead a place to face them.

These were fine warriors, he knew from bitter experience, fast and deceptive. Unlike his usual confrontations, Jameston didn't believe that the chaos of a forest favored him. He needed something solid to narrow the field of battle.

He had passed this way the previous night, knew the lay of the area. So he moved quickly to a cluster of abandoned, mostly ruined cottages. Jameston picked a fairly concealed course and stealthily gained the door and slipped inside. He went fast to the far corner and put his back against the solid wooden wall, watching the door.

He hadn't long to wait. Within moments a black-clothed figure entered the dimly illuminated, one-room cottage.

Jameston smiled, thinking it the same woman he had battled earlier that day.

"You should relax and tell me why you're following me," the scout said.

Caught by surprise, the woman froze in place, slowly swiveling her head to regard the man and his leveled and ready bow.

She stood straight and turned to face Jameston squarely.

"Don't even think about trying to get back out that door," Jameston said. "You're leaving in front of me, in case your friends are about and curious. Now, tell me why you're following me."

The woman narrowed her eyes and took a deep breath as if contemplating her options.

"You won't get to me, and you won't get out that door," Jameston promised. "And you won't get a dagger or some other bolt into the air before I let fly. I don't miss. So start explaining why you followed me."

"You are to be gone," she said in a halting command of the language.

"I was going. Do better."

The woman lifted her chin defiantly.

Jameston pulled back on his bowstring just a bit more. He hated the thought of killing a woman, or anyone for that matter. But he had done so before and would do so again if he had to. Saving his skin was an acceptable reason.

And saving Bransen's, he realized. If this woman had come out to kill him, what did that portend for Bransen?

Jameston's face tightened, and he drew back his bow-string further. "I'm going to ask you just one more time," he said grimly.

Bransen was not wearing his mask across his eyes as he paced into Laird Ethelbert's audience hall beside Affwin Wi, instead letting it hang loosely about his neck. They strode right up to the large chair on which sat the aging laird, a disarming smile on his face.

"So this is the Highwayman," Ethelbert began. "Yes, young warrior, I have heard of you even here. I was quite sorry to learn of the death of Laird Prydae."

Bransen took the jab calmly. "He was killed of his own actions by his own champion."

"Yes, yes, I know the sad tale."

"Do you know that he was trying to rape my wife when Bannagran's axe found his chest?" Bransen asked.

Affwin Wi's hand flicked out at Bransen's side, jabbing his thigh hard. He looked at her; she glared her reply. "Proper respect," she whispered.

"That is quite all right, my huntress," Laird Ethelbert said with a lighthearted laugh. "Better that this one speak the truth in his heart so I may better come to know the truth of him, yes?"

Affwin Wi gave a curt bow.

"And I do know enough of Prydae to acknowledge what you claim. Well, let us just say that he was not capable of such an act," Ethelbert said to Bransen.

"That did not stop him from trying," Bransen replied. "Or from falsely condemning her mother"—he glanced to the monk wearing the robes of a father and standing at Ethelbert's side as he finished—"to the Samhaists."

"I surrender, I surrender," Ethelbert said with a jovial

laugh. "I will not replay those events and will not argue with one who was there when I was not. I was saddened by the death of Prydae, a man I had known as an ally in battle. Whether he deserved it or not. . . ." He let it go at that with a shrug.

Bransen accepted that reasoning with a bow.

"And you are an interesting mutt, are you not?" Ethelbert said. "You wear on your forehead the gemstones of an Abellican monk, yet you fight with the techniques— and clothing—of the southern mystics."

"My father was of the Order of Blessed Abelle, my mother a Jhesta Tu," said Bransen.

"I know that," Ethelbert said. "I met your father and your mother on their return from Behr. They came through my city two decades ago, and I granted them an audience. It did not end well for them, I assume."

Bransen's face went from a sudden brightening to a dark cloud at the grim reminder of Bran and Sen Wi's respective fates.

"I warned your father that the brothers would not be as tolerant as he hoped," Ethelbert said.

Bransen felt as if the ground were shifting under his feet. He had come in here full of confidence and determination, and now Laird Ethelbert had maneuvered the conversation to a place that clearly had Bransen on edge. He wanted to hear more of Ethelbert's encounter with his parents, and he knew that such desire ensured that he would not.

Ethelbert read him perfectly and quickly deflected the conversation yet again.

"You know of my struggle with Laird Yeslnik?" he asked.

"I thought he called himself King Yeslnik," Bransen replied with enough obvious disdain to draw a large smile from Ethelbert.

"He can call himself God Yeslnik if it pleases him,"

Ethelbert replied. "Because when I kill him it will matter not at all."

Bransen didn't react.

"So I have met him as you desired," Ethelbert said to Affwin Wi, suddenly sounding very bored with it all. "What is the purpose? Is he friend, or is he foe?"

"He states that he is Jhesta Tu," the woman replied. "He will pledge loyalty to Laird Ethelbert."

Bransen looked at her in surprise.

"Because I am his superior," Affwin Wi clarified boldly. "And the decision is not his to make." She turned to regard Bransen directly. "Is that not true?" she asked, invoking a clear test of his loyalty.

Bransen paused, but only for a moment, before answering, "Yes."

"Is there anything more?" asked Ethelbert.

Affwin Wi studied Bransen for a few moments then said, "Speak your mind freely. This is your last chance to do so."

Bransen didn't know exactly what that might mean. "I am Jhesta Tu," he explained. "In part. But because of my heritage and my experience, I am more. I have found the promise of my father, the joining—"

Affwin Wi hit him so hard across the face that he was sitting on the floor before he had even registered the pain of the blow.

"You are Jhesta Tu, or you are not," she said while Ethelbert laughed. "Which are you?"

"I am Jhesta Tu," Bransen said, lowering his gaze to the floor.

My arm's getting tired and I just might let go," Jameston warned.

"You must be gone," the woman replied.

"I was going—" Jameston started to say, but he bit it

off, suddenly realizing what she really meant. He had tracked them and had found them. He had fought this very woman and believed he was beating her when her friend had intervened.

He knew of them, which made him an intolerable threat.

"So that's what it is, is it?" he said. "You can't have me wandering on my way knowing what I know." He gave a little laugh. "Well, I know a lot more now, I expect. . . ."

He heard the pop behind him, a sharp bang and the splintering of wood, followed by what he thought was a hard punch in his back just behind his right hip.

Jameston instinctively glanced down, and then he knew. For the nun'chu'ku had blown right through the wall behind him and into his back with such force that Jameston's leather jerkin was pushed out in the front.

"Oh, now," Jameston muttered, realizing that the pole had gone right through him. Already the feeling was leaving his legs, and he was having a hard time drawing breath.

He looked up at the woman, who stood easily now, smiling at him.

Jameston managed a nod. Growling, he drew back and sent his arrow at her. She got her arm up with amazing speed, but the arrow bored right through her forearm and into her forehead. She was still smiling when she fell dead to the floor.

Jameston shuddered, a thousand fires exploding within him as the warrior with the shaven head—it had to be that one, Jameston knew—tugged the nun'chu'ku out of him and back through the wall.

Jameston was sitting when the fierce warrior came around the front and entered through the door. The scout wanted to put his bow up for one last shot, for one chance to kill this vicious man, but when he lifted his left arm, he only then realized that he wasn't even holding the bow anymore, that it was on the floor at his feet.

Merwal Yahna crouched over the dead woman, then

rose and glanced at Jameston. He would come over and finish the job, Jameston figured, but surprisingly the man just snorted and turned away.

Jameston watched as the warrior cradled his fallen friend, then carried her out of the house.

And as he left, the darkness began to close in on Jameston Sequin.

TWENTY-EIGHT

Bloodletting

Mcwigik leaned his elbows on the top of the small barrel boat tower, staring at the distant fires and candles twinkling in windows. So many lights. More than Mcwigik had ever seen, more than he had ever imagined possible. For a hundred years he had looked across the waters of Mithranidoon, where even a single firelight was an oddity. For many years of life before that, the largest collection of people together he had ever seen was the town of Hard Rocks on the Weathered Isles.

But even that place, once thought impressive, couldn't have been one-twentieth the size of this!

"Got to be Palmaristown," Bikelbrin said, coming up beside him. "We're at the mouth o' the river, and that's where Shiknickel said it'd be."

"We get ten of us boys together, and we call it a town," Mcwigik replied, shaking his hairy head. "Thirty and we call it a city, a hundred and it's a kingdom."

"Lot o' people in there," Bikelbrin agreed.

"Lot o' blood," his friend reminded.

"We get killed to death in there, and there's none to be burying our hearts."

"Bah, but we won't be knowin' that anyway!" Mcwigik said with a laugh, and he and Bikelbrin clapped each other on the shoulders.

The powrie shiver stayed offshore as the lights went down in the city, and only then did the eager dwarves resume their pedaling, moving very slowly and quietly. With a hundred thirty warriors among all the boats, they figured they'd find themselves outnumbered a hundred to one or more.

Dreams of berets shining brightly enough to light up the night carried them on their way.

Bransen sat on the roof of the inn in Ethelbert dos Entel, his legs tightly crossed before him, his hands on his bent knees and his eyes skyward, basking in the contemplative light of a million stars. His thoughts were out there and within himself all at once, a meditative state of serenity in the face of the great questions of purpose and being. To face the many questions of his future meant that he needed the cleansing experience of being fully in the present, of recognizing his mind-body connection and putting that in context with his greater connection to the universe around him. He needed to find that moment of perfect, unfettered clarity, that complete sensation of peace.

But the stunning revelations and twists of the last day stayed with him, nagging him with doubts, particularly on where Cadayle might fit into his new allegiance to Affwin Wi. She had dismissed Jameston out of hand; what might that portend for Cadayle?

Bransen took a deep breath and threw away that unsettling thought. He forced himself back inside his *ki-chi-kree,* his line of life energy, and then sent that line spiritually up into the dark and starry sky.

A different sensation tugged at him, though, and

suddenly and unexpectedly, a feeling that something, somehow, was amiss.

Bransen interrupted his meditative journey to refocus on this disturbance, this ill feeling. It had direction, like a cry of pain, out in the dark night.

Bransen let his soul slide through the soul stone of the brooch and escape his corporeal form. He started away spiritually, but hesitantly, until he felt again that strange sensation that something was terribly wrong.

Then he moved with purpose, willing his noncorporeal form over the city's wall and out across the empty fields to the edge of a forest he had traversed that very morning.

The docks were quiet, those few guards on duty either asleep or gambling, throwing bones against a warehouse wall. One or another would occasionally glance at the harbor to check the masts of the few ships in port.

Barrel boats didn't have masts.

The powrie craft came in slowly, their underwater rams prodding the sand below the wharves so that even as the dwarves climbed from their craft and slowly walked across the top arc of those rams, they remained out of sight to the distracted guards up on the boardwalk.

"Beat that point!" one gambling sentry shouted triumphantly as the bones rolled a strong number.

The words had barely left his mouth when a mallet cracked down atop his head, breaking his skull and shattering every bone in his neck.

"As ye asked!" a dwarf explained.

How the other four guards started to scramble! Started, but never even made their feet, as a score of powries, weapons flashing and swung with bloodlust, fell over them. They cried out for their companions on the docks but those sleeping or inattentive men and women were already dead, powries already wetting their berets in freshly spilled blood.

The dwarves methodically formed into six units, each crew as a battle group. They used the very bones the men had been rolling to determine which of the six would stay behind and watch the boats for the first forays.

"Not to worry," many told the losers. "Plenty to kill."

Five battle groups moved up into sleeping, unwitting Palmaristown, a hundred weapons, a hundred serrated knives to open veins.

Like a plague of hungry rats they roved through the town, sweeping through houses and tenements, at one point overwhelming a group still drinking and shouting in one of the nearby taverns.

They came in, and they killed. They dipped their bloody caps, and they moved on.

After a very brief while, the crew still on the docks realized that their companions were into powrie bloodlust now and would not be coming back, so they, too, went up into the city. As their friends had assured them, there were plenty still to kill.

It took nearly an hour, with hundreds and hundreds murdered, before Palmaristown even began to organize any semblance of defense against the intruders. Many, many more people died to powrie blades before the dwarves faced any real resistance. Even then, with armies of both Prince Milwellis and Laird Panlamaris out of the city fighting in the war, the fierce powries pressed on.

With Laird Ethelbert on the run in the south and his own mighty warships securing the gulf, Laird Panlamaris had never imagined such an attack.

The bloodbath went on throughout the night, a night that would be known in the region for decades hence as "the dark of long murder," and, when the powries finally did retreat, they set fire to every structure they passed so that, by the time their barrel boats pushed back out into the river, a quarter of the great city was ablaze.

By the time those fires finally died away days later, two of every three structures in the great city—the second largest in Honce—lay in ruins. One in every three residents within the city was dead.

Warships sailed fast for home as the word of the tragedy spread, but the powries, with their shining berets, slipped past them unnoticed into the open waters of the gulf.

Using the cat's-eye gemstone set in his brooch, Bransen had no trouble navigating the darkness beyond the wall of Ethelbert dos Entel. He ran on light feet, falling into the malachite as well as the soul stone to provide added lift and distance to each desperate step.

Soldiers walking perimeter outside the wall called to him, but he ignored them and sprinted on. They couldn't hope to catch him with his magically enhanced speed, and even the few spears they threw out at him fell far short of the mark.

Bransen didn't look back, his focus squarely ahead as he tried to recall the exact route his spirit had taken as he tried to hear again the disturbance that had sounded so clear in his state of meditation.

His heart beat even faster when he entered the small forest. He nearly fell over with fear as he skidded to a stop before the small cluster of ruined houses. Behind him in the east the sky was still dark, still hours before the dawn.

Bransen tried to hear again the psychic cry, but all was silent. He summoned his courage and ran into the house, to find Jameston crumpled on the floor, blood pooled about him.

"No!" Bransen fell over him, reaching into the soul stone, bringing forth mighty waves of healing magic.

But Jameston was already cold.

Bransen dug deeper, seeking any flicker of life energy, any notion that the man's soul had not yet fled, seeking resurrection itself, something even the greatest of gemstone users had always believed impossible, something Abelle himself had never managed.

Because it was not possible. Jameston, this man he had come to know as a friend, as a teacher and mentor, as a father, even, was lost to him.

TWENTY-NINE

Darkness Rising

Astorm?" Brother Pinower asked. He stood on the wall with Brother Giavno, looking out to the west. The sun was not yet halfway down from its zenith to the horizon, but a dull pall had already settled on the land, a premature twilight.

Brother Giavno was shaking his head before Pinower even asked the obvious question. "No. Not a storm, not clouds."

Pinower looked at him curiously, and the man's grim expression, horrified even, had the young monk even more perplexed.

"Smoke," Brother Giavno explained.

"Smoke?" Pinower echoed, turning fast to regard again the strange phenomenon. "But that is too far . . . I see no flames. It is out to the horizon and more. . . ."

Brother Giavno didn't bother to respond. It was smoke, he knew. Somewhere far to the west something big was burning.

More monks came to the wall over the next few hours as the daylight waned and the gigantic cloud in the west grew darker and more ominous. Across the field the army of Palmaristown seemed equally engaged by the spectacle.

Many brothers stayed on the wall after night fell to view the sky three-quarters full of stars and one quarter, the western edge, an eerie combination of blackness built on the foundation of an ominous orange glow.

Dawn's light showed the cloud expanding still, and that morning everyone in St. Mere Abelle moved to the towers and the walls to view the spectacle, even Dame Gwydre and Father Artolivan.

The old father groaned at the site.

"What could it be?" Brother Pinower asked from behind him.

"Palmaristown," the old monk said with certainty.

"The Highwayman is still out there," King Yeslnik said to his perfumed wife.

"And you think he is coming to slay you?" Lady Olym asked.

"Do not be flippant with me, wife!"

"He didn't kill your Uncle Delaval."

"You know nothing!" Yeslnik scolded. "We found his sword. . . ."

"There are many swords."

"Not like his!"

Lady Olym sighed and waved him away. "Perhaps he dropped it or someone took it from him."

"Plundered his corpse, perhaps?" said Yeslnik in a sneering tone that struck hard. "That would not please you, would it?"

"I do not know of what you are speaking," she said, but the possibility worded by Yeslnik had clearly knocked her off-balance here, and there was little conviction in her assertion.

King Yeslnik slapped her hard across the face. It was the first time he had ever done anything remotely like that. When she lifted her hands to try to deflect him, he punched her squarely in the nose. She staggered back and fell on her backside, staring at him in wonder.

"I will hear no more of the Highwayman from you. Ever," Yeslnik warned.

"You spoke of him first!"

"Ever!" he repeated threateningly. Wailing, Olym curled into a fetal position.

"Ever," King Yeslnik said again, leaning over close. "Bannagran will kill him. Kill him!" he shouted suddenly, and the startled Lady Olym jerked and wailed. Yeslnik whirled away from the pitiful woman and plopped into the chair at his desk, dropping an elbow on the arm and chewing at his nails.

Had he failed in fleeing the field before Ethelbert dos Entel? Should he have accepted the losses and pressed Ethelbert to the edge of the sea to be done with this foolishness quickly? But Ethelbert's assassins would have killed him!

He lurched to his feet and began pacing nervously. "Panlamaris will deal with those traitors at Chapel Abelle," he said to himself. "Why is this so hard? Why won't these fools just concede to the inevitable?"

"You are king," came an unexpectedly supportive voice. Yeslnik spun about to see his wife sitting up. He looked at her curiously, then more closely.

"You are the King of Honce," she said again. "Only the prideful laird of that miserable city in the south and the traitorous fools at Chapel Abelle refuse to see it. All the rest is yours."

Yeslnik continued to stare at her, but he felt compelled to move over to her. He fell to his knees, very close, and stared into her eyes, one swelling from his punch.

"Gather the lairds who follow you," Olym suggested.

"The dozens who love you. Lend them warriors to extend their holdings to engulf all of those flattened by you in your glorious march and by Prince Milwellis. Take the Inner Coast and the Mantis Arm. Take all those communities along the Belt-and-Buckle. Take them all, and let Ethelbert in his city and the monks in their chapel watch from their walls as the world, as King Yeslnik's Honce, goes along without them."

Yeslnik's jaw hung open, for never had he heard such advice from this source. He was amazed that Lady Olym even knew about the march of Milwellis in the east or of the many communities he had run across and run over to Ethelbert dos Entel and back. He continued staring for just a few heartbeats. Slowly shaking his head with disbelief, he pulled her close and kissed her more passionately than he had in a long, long while.

Lady Olym pushed him back after a few more heartbeats. "They cannot come out against you, or you will destroy them," she said.

"Delaval warships will blockade Ethelbert dos Entel," King Yeslnik proclaimed.

"Yes!" Olym squealed.

"And Chapel Abelle!" said Yeslnik. "A prison of their own making!"

"Yes! Oh, yes!"

"And I will send Panlamaris by land and by sea into Vanguard, and Dame Gwydre will know her folly!"

"Lead them yourself! You are the King of Honce!"

Yeslnik tackled her, showering her with kisses all over her face.

"Take me, my king!" she cried. "Ravish me!"

Yeslnik nearly swooned, overwhelmed, for he had never seen his wife in such a state of passion aimed at him before. His confidence grew with every kiss and every caress.

It was good to be the king.

* * *

Panlamaris," said the whispers across the wall as the lone rider stormed across the field toward St. Mere Abelle. "That is Laird Panlamaris himself!"

Some calls went out for archers or for gemstone assaults as the large and imposing Laird of Palmaristown drew closer to the wall, but those were few and without conviction.

That cloud of smoke rising in the west, that sign of Palmaristown burning, served as a white flag of temporary truce in the stunned sensibilities of all who glimpsed it. Although Palmaristown had come against St. Mere Abelle, even in the face of the executions of Fatuus and the other brothers, the image of certain horror occurring in the west allowed Panlamaris to make this ride unhindered, right to the base of St. Mere Abelle's high wall.

Behind him on the field a few other riders halfheartedly followed, but it was obvious that the laird's seemingly reckless ride had caught his own soldiers by surprise.

"To eternal flames with you, damned witch!" the man called when he came in sight of the Dame of Vanguard. "The blood of thousands, of mothers and children, stains your pretty hands. How will you wash it away?"

Dame Gwydre rocked back on her heels.

"She is here, as are those in support of her!" Father Premujon yelled down at Panlamaris. "Whatever ill has befallen your city—"

"Powries!" the fiery old laird interrupted. "Powries by the score. Powries set loose by the witch of Vanguard. What horror have you set upon the folk of Honce, wicked Gwydre?"

"I did no such thing," Gwydre managed to reply.

"As in the harbor with my ships!" Panlamaris yelled. "And now a cowardly assault on a sleeping city, to cut the throats of children and burn the buildings to ash! Eternal fires for you, I say! And, oh, but do not doubt that your precious Vanguard will feel the wrath of Palmaristown, of Panlamaris and Milwellis, of King Yeslnik and all the goodly folk of Honce! They will know you, powrie friend, and they will loathe you! I await the day when Dame Gwydre is dragged through the streets of Palmaristown that all may spit upon she who invited the powries back to Honce!"

He whirled his mount around and thundered away, and not an arrow or bolt of gemstone lightning reached out after him.

The siege of St. Mere Abelle ended within the hour, Laird Panlamaris and his army moving with all haste back to the west.

Later that same day Prince Milwellis's army appeared in the distant south, moving with great speed to the west, to home, to the ruins and the dead.

THIRTY

No!

How had this happened? How was it possible that this man, so competent, so formidable, so seasoned, had been taken down? What manner of foe had come against Jameston to corner him and defeat such a warrior? Jameston had successfully battled trolls and powries and barbarians, even giants for decades. Who could possibly have brought him down?

There was only one answer. Jhesta Tu.

Bransen knelt over Jameston for a long while, cradling the man's head, trying to come to terms with his loss. The minutes continued to slide past and still Bransen sat, recalling his first meeting with Jameston in the wilds of southern Alpinador, when the scout had joined in a fight against a company of Ancient Badden's trolls. He remembered the look on the face of Crazy Vaughna when she realized that it was Jameston Sequin, *the* Jameston Sequin, who had joined in their cause.

Walking with Jameston these last weeks, Bransen had come to appreciate that awestruck expression of Vaughna's all the more, for truly this man more than matched his impressive reputation.

Now Jameston was gone.

How alone Bransen felt at that terrible, terrible moment. Not just alone but confused, consumed by the unsettling notion that he had played a role in this, that he had allowed Affwin Wi to dismiss Jameston and send him away. All those thoughts swirled and coalesced, first reducing Bransen into a battered and defeated shell, weak in the knees and unable to hold back his tears.

But the stretch of pity and self-pity and hopelessness lasted only a few heartbeats, replaced by a bubbling rage that turned Bransen's churning gut into a pit of pure acid. He gently laid Jameston's head back and jumped up to his feet, seeking focus, seeking an outlet.

He considered the hole in the wooden wall, punched through with tremendous force. He turned Jameston's body over a bit and noted that the same blunt force had hit him with enough power to skewer him. An image of Merwal Yahna and his exotic weapon flashed in Bransen's mind.

Jameston had been near the wall, his back to it when slain. Bransen turned to see what his friend might have witnessed at that moment and noted blood on the floor by the door. He went to it, following the clear trail of blood droplets to the back of the cottage, a short distance into the forest, where he found the remains of a makeshift pyre and the charred and shrunken remains of a person. He saw a black silk slipper and knew beyond any doubt. No simple soldier had taken down Jameston Sequin.

"Jhesta Tu," Bransen mouthed as he regarded that slipper, and knew from its size that it had been worn by the woman who had battled Jameston while Bransen had fought Merwal Yahna in their first meeting with Laird Ethelbert's assassins. At least those two Jhesta Tu had hunted Jameston Sequin. They could not have done so without the permission, indeed the command, of Affwin Wi.

Bransen felt his jaw go tight, the muscles in his arms and legs twitching in anticipation. It took him a long time to slow and steady his breathing, to find his center and his mind-body connection. He couldn't hold that connection for long.

Too overwhelmed was he, too betrayed and confused. And too angry. Only once in his young life had Bransen Garibond felt such rage: on that terrible day when Laird Prydae had abducted Cadayle for his sexual pleasure and given Callen to Bernivvigar to be murdered. That same terrible time when he had learned of the murder of his father, Garibond Womak. That rage had allowed him to sit within the branches of a bonfire and feel no heat. That moment had incensed him to kill.

Bransen turned to the east, toward Ethelbert dos Entel. Toward Affwin Wi. Sprinting nearly the entire way, Bransen reached the wall of Ethelbert dos Entel before dawn. The sky over the Mirianic glowed in predawn light, but stars remained clear in the west. The city was only beginning to awaken. The Highwayman used that slumber to his advantage. He could have walked in through the gate; Affwin Wi had introduced him to the guards there, and she carried great weight in the city, but something deep within, his Highwayman instincts, told him that stealth was his ally here.

He moved along the wall, listening carefully, until he came to an out-of-the-way corner where he could climb and keep the still-dark western sky at his back. There, he fell into the powers of the malachite and used his strength and training to easily scale the twelve-foot barrier. He peered over the wall, the cat's-eye allowing him to see as clearly as if the sun was up in the east, with complete confidence that the guard he then viewed a dozen strides away could not see him.

The Highwayman went over silently, the dark sky behind him presenting no silhouette for the half-aware sentry to observe. He could have killed that sentry—it would have been an easier course than slipping across the wall top and down the other side—but he dismissed that notion out of hand. Still utilizing the powers of the malachite to lighten his step, Bransen crossed over quickly, allowing himself to drop to the ground in near silence because of heightened balance.

Though he could see Castle Ethelbert, it took him a few moments to get his bearings and determine the best way to navigate the crowded city, time he didn't have to spare as more sounds of the city awakening filled his ears and the sky brightened a bit more. He started at a trot, quickly a run, letting that low but imposing castle guide him. Affwin Wi and her group were in a wing of the castle. In short order he could see the balcony from which his spirit had answered Jameston's dying call.

He could just go back in the room. It was unlikely the others knew he had left or had learned their terrible secret. Prudence called him to that plan, but anger prevented it.

"No," he said, shaking his head. This was no time for secrecy and plotting, for deception and caution. Or perhaps it was just such a time. Bransen, so consumed, didn't care. "No." He walked in the front door of the castle's far western wing, the complex afforded Affwin Wi's group.

"When did you go out?" Pactset Va greeted him immediately. "How did you get out?" Va shook his head, his topknot dancing with the movement as he called across the way to his companion Moh Li, noting Bransen's dark expression.

Moh Li responded quickly to the call, stepping through a hanging curtain to look curiously from Pactset Va to Bransen.

"You did not tell me that this one left," Pactset Va reprimanded.

"He did not," Moh Li replied. "Not while I guarded." Both men turned suspicious stares upon Bransen.

"I left from my balcony."

Pactset Va waved a finger at him immediately, the man's face screwing up into a stern look. "You cannot do this!"

The Highwayman smiled slyly and walked right up to that poking finger.

"You leave only on the command of—"

"Shut up," the Highwayman cut him off.

Pactset Va's eyes popped wide.

"Shut. Up." the Highwayman said again, biting off each word through his gritted smile.

Pactset Va slapped him hard across the face.

"Shut up now," the Highwayman clarified, smiling wider and staring at him, oblivious to the sting of the slap or his red face.

The man moved to slap him again, but this time the Highwayman used Pactset Va's incredulity to get inside the man's defenses. He opened up a sudden and furious barrage of punches, left and right, into the face of the man. Five short punches sent Pactset Va back hard into the wall. Va brought both his arms up high to block, but the Highwayman leaped and spun a complete circuit, kicking expertly right below the man's blocking elbows, scoring a hard kick into Pactset Va's belly.

The Highwayman landed softly and leaped and spun again immediately, bringing his foot around to connect solidly on the side of his lurching opponent's face, launching Pactset Va into a sidelong somersault. He landed hard on the floor, semiconscious and groaning.

"You will pay the price!" Moh Li cried.

Without even a glance at him, the Highwayman strode up to tower over Pactset Va. Still not looking at Li, the Highwayman drove his foot down hard on Pactset Va's throat.

Moh Li gave a cry that told the Highwayman the man was charging at his back. At the last possible moment, the Highwayman reached down and grabbed the sword on his left hip with a backhand grip so that he easily pulled it free and snapped it back out under his right arm, blade stabbing behind him.

Just as Moh Li leaped for him.

The man collided with the Highwayman, but not hard, for he was scrambling desperately to avoid impalement. The Highwayman's sword angled down, and Moh Li crumpled to the floor. The Highwayman pulled the blade free and spun to see him writhing in agony. Moh Li had come in with a flying kick and had taken the sword into the back of his thigh, a deep, deep wound. Screaming, he flailed around now, trying to stem the blood flow.

"Shut up," the Highwayman said to Moh Li, kicking him in the face, silencing him. Perhaps he would bleed out, perhaps not. The Highwayman didn't care. Perhaps Pactset Va would choke from the throat kick, perhaps not. Images of dead Jameston filled Bransen's mind, and he did not care about these men's suffering.

He stalked through the room and kicked open the opposite door into the small anteroom before Affwin Wi's large chamber entryway. That second door swung wide before Bransen crossed to it. There stood Merwal Yahna staring at him, staring at his bloody sword. No look of revulsion showed on Merwal Yahna's face, though. Indeed, the man's smile widened wickedly.

The Highwayman reacted with anger, leaping ahead, but Merwal Yahna anticipated the charge, for he was moving even as Bransen did. The warrior from Behr leaped backward and to the side, and the Highwayman went through the door in a rush, skidding to an abrupt stop, acutely aware that Merwal Yahna was not alone in the room.

"You act rashly, warrior," said Affwin Wi, standing in a corner of the room. "Jhesta Tu do not act in such a manner."

"But they murder without cause," Bransen replied through clenched teeth.

"He found his friend," reasoned Merwal Yahna.

Bransen turned sharply to Affwin Wi and started to ask why, but he bit it back. It didn't matter; he didn't even want to know. He presented his sword toward Merwal Yahna, inviting him to battle.

The warrior snapped out his nun'chu'ku in a dizzying, spinning blur, ending his fast movement with a battle shout. He held the poles straight before him, leather cord taut, the muscles on his arms tight under the black silk sleeves of his shirt.

At the back of the room, Affwin Wi similarly exploded into sudden motion, whirling her arms in wide circles as she leaped into a wide-legged, ready crouch.

"A'shin ti!" Merwal Yahna shouted at her. "Abidu a'shin ti!"

Bransen didn't know the exact translation of the phrase, but he recognized it as plea from the warrior that Affwin Wi allow him to fight this battle alone. From the corner of his eye, he watched Affwin Wi relax and stand up straight, bringing her hands together before her chest and offering a slight bow before stepping back.

Bransen's gaze shifted back to Merwal Yahna. The Behrenese's face was locked in a stare of absolute concentration and simmering eagerness. The man went into another flourish, releasing the nun'chu'ku with his right hand and sending it into a violent spin with his left, around and up, over his head and around, and around the back of his head, where he caught it in his right hand and continued the flow around the other side.

The Highwayman didn't let him continue his display. Bransen rushed forward with a sudden and ferocious stab, retraction, and slash of his blade. Neither came close to hitting the agile Merwal Yahna, who deftly reversed the spin of his own weapon to send it snapping out to intercept.

But Bransen leaped to his right, using the malachite to enhance the great jump and turning his hips to keep his shoulders squared to the warrior from Behr as he sailed past. He bent his legs as he came over a chair, planting one foot on the arm, the other on the back and riding it to the ground as it tipped over.

Merwal Yahna came in fast pursuit, but Bransen hooked his foot under the arm of the chair as it and he descended. He kicked out, launching the chair Merwal Yahna's way.

Merwal Yahna blocked the spinning chair with a straightened leg, then battered it aside with his nun'chu'ku, breaking off pieces with the mighty blows.

The Highwayman seized the moment and leaped at him, kicking and stabbing. Up came the nun'chu'ku, spinning and snapping. Bransen blocked with his foot, then with his blade, then again to the left and back to the right. He stabbed ahead and Merwal Yahna's weapon was there, wood slapping the side of the sword, and again a second time.

There was no thinking here, no movements other than instinct as the two warriors let loose tremendous volleys and counters, wood hitting metal, sword slapping nun'chu'ku, a leg thrusting forward to steal momentum from a swinging pole and absorb the blow, an open palm slapping flat against the side of the sword, turning the thrust harmlessly aside.

It went on for a long while, a furious explosion that rolled and rolled from one end of the room to the other. Only Affwin Wi, so trained in the ways of battle, witnessed it. To her, it was a thing of beauty, a dance of precision and discipline.

To any other onlookers, it would have seemed a thing of chaos, a blur of movement and a cacophony of discordant sounds. Untrained onlookers would have gasped through every heartbeat, thinking a kill to be had.

Affwin Wi just smiled, pleased that her lover was

showing himself so well here and excited by the possibilities of this stranger who had taught himself the ways of the warrior.

Bransen stepped quickly back against a sudden burst of snapping nun'chu'ku thrusts, the pole popping forward in the air before him in rapid succession. He felt the broken chair behind his heels and jumped backward reflexively, landing lightly.

Over the chair came Merwal Yahna, leaping high in a spin. He landed with his right side facing Bransen and unrolled his right arm out at the Highwayman, the nun'chu'ku lashing out like an extension of his arm.

But Bransen had seen the movement in his mind before it had happened. As soon as Merwal Yahna had leaped the chair, Bransen had known the end of the play. More importantly, he knew that his opponent could not easily alter the ending.

Instead of backing away, the Highwayman went forward and leaped high above the swing of the nun'chu'ku. He threw his sword up past Merwal Yahna, a daring distraction. Bransen turned as he sailed and kicked out, scoring a stunning blow to Merwal Yahna's face, snapping the man's head back viciously. He landed close to the warrior, his chest against Merwal Yahna's outstretched hand. Without slowing, Bransen punched his right arm under Merwal Yahna's elbow, then stabbed it out across the man's back, planting his hand firmly against Merwal Yahna's opposite shoulder blade. At the same time, with his left hand he grabbed Merwal Yahna's weapon hand. As soon as he had executed this locking hold, Bransen drove forward and upward hard, throwing all his weight into the move. Merwal Yahna, dazed by the kick, still stuck in the momentum of his initial attack, couldn't begin to turn about appropriately to respond.

Bransen heard the pop of the man's shoulder coming out of joint, and he drove ahead again to accentuate the move and the pain. He released fast, unafraid of the nun'chu'ku at that point, and spun backward, lifting his foot in a circle kick that caught Merwal Yahna square in the chest, knocking him back several steps. To his credit the tough warrior didn't fall, but the Highwayman pursued, jabbing hard with a left-right combination, avoiding Merwal Yahna's attempt to block with his right arm and hitting him squarely in the face.

The Highwayman faked his next punch, half throwing a right before retracting with enough force to drive himself into a backward lean. From there he lifted his left leg up high, so high, straight over his head!

His leg came down hard, outstretched and atop the dislocated shoulder with tremendous force. For all his toughness, Merwal Yahna blanched and lurched to the side. Bransen waded in with another combination of heavy blows, positioning his opponent perfectly to drive his knee into Merwal Yahna's gut.

The Highwayman sprang back then leaped up in a spin, his flying foot catching the doubling-over Merwal Yahna on the side of the head with such power that it sent him into a sidelong somersault. He landed hard and awkwardly, growling with agony, and grasped his torn shoulder in a mighty grip, groaning through gritted teeth. He was tense and curled, but he couldn't hold it, and gradually, he melted back to the floor, his growl receding with his strength.

Bransen leaped over him in a crouch, left hand extended against Merwal Yahna's face, lining up a surely fatal blow from his cocked, right arm.

And a blow did fall, a hard one, but it fell against Bransen before he could finish Merwal Yahna. Affwin Wi's kick staggered him to the side, and he had to fall over into a roll and then come back to his feet, spinning to face this newest opponent.

"You murdered Jameston!" he accused.

"He attacked those sent to make certain he had left."

"No!" Bransen retorted. "Never! Not unless he were forced to defend himself!"

Affwin Wi settled back easily and began to laugh. "Foolish young man," she said.

"I came here as a fellow traveler in the way of Jhesta Tu!" Bransen shouted, and Affwin Wi laughed louder.

"I am not Jhesta Tu!" she shouted back, and the words hit Bransen much harder than her kick ever could have. "Hou-lei!"

Hou-lei? The title rolled around Bransen's head for few moments until he connected it to his reading of the Book of Jhest. Hou-lei, the tradition that had inspired Jhesta Tu, an old mercenary warrior class, a tradition of divorcing fighting skill from moral judgment, of preparing for battle under the will of whatever sheik or king paid most handsomely. A Hou-lei warrior was an instrument, a weapon, and nothing more.

Bransen stood there blinking in disbelief, but everything suddenly made sense. "You are paid assassins," he said.

Affwin Wi shrugged as if that fact should have been apparent long before. She came forward suddenly and viciously, her arms waving alternating circles before her, her hands set in hooklike fashion, thumbs tucked, fingers tightly bent at the knuckles.

The Highwayman dropped his left leg back and fell lower, his own arms up before him.

As they closed, Affwin Wi kept spinning her arms, occasionally jabbing forward. Bransen blocked those first few stabs easily or turned aside from them, eventually coming to the same rhythm as Affwin Wi.

She picked up the pace. He stabbed with his hands. Back and forth they circled and slapped, hands stabbing like striking snakes, hands striking hands. They went faster, more furiously. Affwin Wi dodged one of the Highwayman's punches and kicked her leg out right before her. Bransen's shin came up to meet it. They hopped about, each keeping a leg in the air, waving, kicking, punching, slapping like a pair of cranes battling over a frog in a crowded pond.

Unused to this style of fighting, Bransen could not keep up. He was hit by more blows than he landed. Every strike the expert Affwin Wi delivered was in perfect balance, her weight behind the blow, her angle precise.

Bransen knew he couldn't win this kind of fight. He suddenly threw himself to the side and into a roll, coming up with Merwal Yahna's nun'chu'ku in his hands. He put the weapon into motion—it had looked so easy in Merwal Yahna's hands—and nearly clipped himself in the head. Affwin Wi laughed at him and charged.

Bransen dropped the exotic weapon, reached into his brooch, and met her flying form with a lightning discharge that sent her flying back the way she came. She landed and stumbled, fell over and rolled, came back to her feet and stumbled again, her teeth chattering, her black hair jumping wildly.

The Highwayman focused on the image of Jameston, focused on his brooch, focused on the power of Abellican gemstones. He enacted a serpentine shield and became a living torch, using the malachite and his fury to hurl himself at the Hou-lei warrior.

She shrieked and tried to dodge, and Bransen knew he had her. He crashed into her, bringing both to the floor. Bransen closed his eyes, not wanting to watch the flames curl her flesh.

She laughed at him, punched him in the face, and wriggled away.

Bransen looked down to see that his flames were no more. He looked up at Affwin Wi to see her smiling smugly, her hand extended, a gemstone in her open palm. A sunstone. The stone of antimagic.

"I know your secret, Highwayman," she said.

Bransen tried to yell his fury, but his words came out garbled, indecipherable, Storklike. His thoughts rushed back to the moment on the trail in the fight with the trolls, when a blow to the head had dislodged his gemstone and left him stumbling and helpless.

No, he decided. This was not akin to that. This was a gemstone countering his own. Damn it! He would be the stronger! He reached more deeply into the brooch and this time felt the connection through the static of the sunstone. Bransen leaped to his feet with a growl and charged. Another furious exchange brought him around to the side. Still, he couldn't keep up with the speed of Affwin Wi, so he focused his blocks and counters to his right side.

Predictably, the Hou-lei warrior seized the opening and launched a left hook Bransen could not block.

He didn't try to, taking the hit and using the force of the blow along with his own sudden retreat to open the ground between them enough to scramble to the side and grab his sword where he'd dropped it. But the incredibly fast Affwin Wi was there to stomp on the blade. Bransen had to let go of the hilt and throw his arm up to block. To his credit, he did deflect her short left jab, but her right hand swept in from behind and above, slashing down and across. The Highwayman fell back and tried to turn his head to make the hit a glancing one, and indeed, he was nearly out of Affwin Wi's reach.

But she wasn't trying to strike him. Her slender fingers caught the edge of Bransen's magical brooch and wrenched it with her as he fell away, tearing the skin, tearing away the magic.

He was the Stork again, so suddenly, so helplessly, blood running freely from his torn forehead. He somehow got one leg under himself and stumbled halfway to standing, but Affwin Wi was there, dropping a series of heavy and strategic blows, more to taunt and hurt him than to finish him.

Bransen felt himself falling. Affwin Wi caught him by the shirt and hauled him to his feet. Before he could determine if he had the stability to stand, she punched him in the face. He fell away, Affwin Wi leaping a circle kick that snapped his head to the side violently.

All the world was spinning. Bransen hit the floor face-down and helpless. Affwin Wi could finish him with a stomp to the back of his neck. He tried to turn and nearly got to his side when her foot slammed him in the gut, doubling him up. Then she kicked him in the face, straightening him out again.

With a sudden burst of energy, Bransen pushed up to his hands and knees and scrabbled away, Affwin Wi laughing behind him. He thought of Jameston, dead Jameston, and of Cadayle, whom he would never see again. He thought of all the promises of his road and his life, of his brooch and his consistent strength, of the hopes and dreams he had dared entertain. Of his unborn child.

"No!" Bransen heard himself cry from somewhere deep within, from a primal place of pure rage and denial.

"No!" to Jameston's murder.

"No!" to his failure.

"No!" to the sudden end of his road.

"No!" to his loss of Cadayle.

"No!" to the thought of never seeing his child.

"No!" to the return of the Stork.

Just "no!" A wall of utter denial, of utter refusal.

Affwin Wi walked up to him.

The Highwayman, with all the grace of a Jhesta Tu warrior, kicked his leg out behind him and hit her in the knee, locking her leg painfully. The Highwayman leaped up, spun about, and launched a barrage of punches and kicks that had the Hou-lei warrior backing desperately, her arms working in a blur to try to slow the onslaught.

Where had he found this power and coordination? He had no soul stone, but his line of life energy ran strong and ran straight. He charged as she backed, his barrage did not slow, and all momentum fell to him, to the Highwayman, the Jhesta Tu, the angry warrior.

Fury guided but did not consume him. He punched and kicked with rage but with all his strength and speed in complete control. He focused on the sheer wall of denial that drove him but never lost sight of his surroundings or of his opponent.

Thus, when Affwin Wi feigned a block and fell to the floor, rolling in to take him out at the legs, the Highwayman reacted by leaping straight up into the air so high and gracefully that it felt as if he remained connected to the malachite. He landed in perfect balance, so lightly and perfectly, now towering over Affwin Wi, who had to work doubly hard and at an awkward angle to try to fend him off.

The Highwayman stayed focused enough to detect movement to the side and to get his arm up just in time to block the sliver of silver flying at him through the air. Holding his torn guts with one hand, Moh Li lifted another missile with the other. The spinning, many-toothed disk flashed past the crouching Highwayman. He had to finish Moh Li quickly, he realized.

He glanced at Affwin Wi, thinking that he might have to fend her off fast and then make the run to her companion. She stood with his sword in hand.

Another disk, another *shur'a'tu'wikin*, a "sword hidden in the hand," as the clever weapon was known, flashed out at him. He couldn't dodge and had to block again, this time the disk slicing hard as it deflected off his hand, all but severing his little finger. His digit fell limply to the side, hanging by nothing more than a strand of bloody skin.

Bransen made a decision. He swung his hand around gingerly as he brought it in close, catching the swinging finger in his grasp and tucking his fist tight against his ribs. He broke into a run. With a great leap to the side, he crashed through the grated window.

He dropped to the courtyard on his feet and kept on running. Never looking back, blinded by pain and confusion and a profound sense of despair, the Highwayman ran through the Entel morning. He smashed his way through the market, upsetting carts, and rushed down an alley. He found the strength to lessen his weight and make a great leap to a low roof, then scrambled from there to the city wall.

Sentries and commoners alike yelled at him as he went right over, sprinting away, the bright morning light dazzling through the tears that filled his eyes.

To his surprise he found no pursuit, but he kept running because to stop was to face the awfulness that had found his life.

And he feared, too, that, as soon as he settled and took a full measure, his moment of clarity, of escape from the Stork, would be at its end, and he would become helpless once more.

EPILOGUE

Exhaustion finally caught up to Bransen on a rocky hill several leagues north of Ethelbert dos Entel. He stared at the crashing waves of the Mirianic for a short while, his mind racing every which way. His anger was gone, stolen by remorse, shaken by disappointment as profound as anything he had ever known. All that he wanted at that terrible time was to get back to Cadayle, to sleep in her arms, to forget the wider world.

He had lost everything.

But he knew that he would never forget Jameston Sequin. He was surprised by the magnitude of that loss. This man he had known only a few months, whom he had come to know only in the last short weeks, had become so important to him. A friend, a mentor, almost a father. And in his excitement in thinking that he had found Jhesta Tu, he had sent Jameston away.

It had been there all along, Bransen realized, as he slumped to the dark sand beside a ridge of black rock. He hadn't needed any tutelage from the Jhesta Tu. Was there anything they could teach him greater than the wisdom that Jameston had shown him along the road? Truly?

Because most of all, Jameston Sequin had reminded Bransen to look within himself, honestly and openly. Jameston had nudged him to consider the truth of the many roads before him and to come to terms with the responsibilities of his training and skill and that gemstone brooch.

The brooch!

Bransen's hand went up to the dried blood on his forehead, the torn skin where the brooch had been set. He tucked his legs back under him and stood up suddenly, then sprang to the ridge of lava stone, a leap of several vertical feet.

He had no soul stone.

No fury drove him.

What was this transformation? Had the gemstone's magic, so closely attuned to his line of life energy, cured him of his malady? Was the Stork lost to him forever and without need of a magical crutch? Or was it a temporary fix?

The thought haunted Bransen suddenly. He looked away from the dark waters of the Mirianic to the north and west, toward Chapel Abelle, where he believed Cadayle to be. He had to get there, to her and to Father Artolivan. He had to be near to a cache of soul stones in case this confusing clarity could not hold.

More than that, even without the stones, even if he became the Stork again forever and evermore—particularly if he became the Stork evermore—Bransen needed Cadayle's warm embrace.

He didn't know if the clarity would last.

He didn't know that King Yeslnik was even then summoning the lairds of Honce to begin a new and more determined offensive, to wipe the world of Ethelbert and Artolivan and Gwydre.

He didn't know that Palmaristown had burned and that the rage of much of Honce was even then refocusing against Dame Gwydre.

All that he knew was that he needed Cadayle, and fast.

He started away and didn't look back, so he didn't see the sails of *Lady Dreamer* gliding above the dark water behind him, nearing Ethelbert dos Entel and the meeting of desperate men that would become the last, best hope for the land of Honce.

Turn the page for a preview of

THE BEAR

R. A. SALVATORE

Available in August 2010
from Tom Doherty Associates

TOR®   A TOR HARDCOVER   ISBN 978-0-7653-1791-9

ONE

Coward, You!

E very now and then he glanced at the rising sun just to ensure he was going north, though most of the time he would discover that he was not. He meandered aimlessly, not sure of where he was or who he was or, worst of all, why he was.

Bransen still wore his black silk pants, but he had taken off the distinctive shirt, replacing it with a simple shift he had found in an abandoned house. Gone, too, was his mask, the signature of the Highwayman. Soon after being chased out of Ethelbert dos Entel without his prized sword and gemstone brooch, Bransen had pulled the mask from his head and thrown it to the ground, thinking to be done with it, to be done with that persona forever. Almost immediately he angrily retrieved it. Fashioned from the one sleeve he had torn from the black silk shirt, that headband, like the rest of the outfit, had been the uniform of his Jhesta Tu mother, though he wasn't exactly certain of what that might mean anymore, given the beating Affwin Wi and Merwal Yahna had inflicted upon him.

However deep Bransen's despair, however lost he might be, he would not dishonor the memory of his mother.

He wandered throughout that first day after fleeing, finding water at a small stream. By late afternoon his stomach began to growl. He'd need a way to hunt, and so he started out, halfheartedly, to find implements—a stick he might fashion into a spear, perhaps. He got distracted rather quickly, though, as the smell of stew cooking wafted past on the breeze.

Bransen had no interest in meeting anyone, but his stomach wouldn't let him ignore the aroma that led him to lie on a knoll outside a small cluster of houses. In the center of the village burned a roaring cook fire with a large cauldron set atop it tended by a pair of old women. Bransen noted well the many inhabitants of the town milling about. Most were very old or very young; the only people near his age were women, many pregnant, probably from when the press-gangs came hunting. Like so many villages of Honce, this one radiated the unbearable pain of the protracted war.

The ridiculous, horrid reality of a world gone insane stung the young man anew, but it was, after all, just another in a long string of profound disappointments. He surveyed the area, looking for a way to sneak in, preferring to remain unseen and unnoticed. He glanced to the western sky, estimating another hour of daylight. The villagers were gathering to enjoy their meal. More and more would likely come out of those small cabins, and Bransen wondered how much of the meal would be left for him to pilfer.

He sighed and mocked his foolishness with a derisive snort, stood up, brushed himself off, and walked down into the village. Bransen was met by many curious stares. More than one person yelped in surprise, more than one mother pulled her children aside. Bransen understood their fear; he and Jameston had come upon several towns that had been ravaged by rogue bands of soldiers. He held his open hands before him unthreateningly.

"Far enough!" one old man said to him, brandishing a pitchfork Bransen's way. "Ye got no business here, so turn yerself about and be gone!"

"I am hungry and tired," Bransen replied. "I hoped that I might share some of your food."

"So ye think we've enough to be handing out?" the old man asked.

"I will work for it," Bransen promised. "Repair a roof, repair a wall, or gather wood. Whatever you need, but I could surely use a meal, friend."

"Which army are ye running from?" asked an old woman whose long nose hooked so profoundly that it nearly touched her chin, which hooked upward from her lack of teeth. She looked him over. "Yer voice sounds like Yeslnik, but yer clothes're more akin to Ethelbert. So which?"

"I found these clothes, as my own were too worn," Bransen explained, not wanting his distinctive pants to link him with Affwin Wi and her murderous band. Such a misconception might prove valuable to him in these parts, but still, the thought of anyone confusing him as a member of that Hou-lei troupe disgusted Bransen.

"Yeslnik, then," pronounced the old man. His snarl and the way he then gripped the pitchfork made Bransen know that he didn't think it a good thing.

"I serve no army."

"But ye did!" said the woman.

Bransen shook his head. "No. Not Yeslnik or Laird Ethelbert. I have come from distant Vanguard."

"Never heard of it," said the old man.

"Far to the north across the Gulf of Corona where Dame Gwydre rules with great compassion and love."

"Never heard of it," the old man said again. Those around him nodded their agreement.

It occurred to Bransen then just how parochial this and most communities of Honce truly were and how worldly he had become in so short a time. He thought back to his humble beginnings in Pryd Town, in the days when he could barely stumble the distance across Chapel Pryd's muddy courtyard. Never could he have imagined the road he had journeyed! The enormity of his travels only then began to become clear to him.

"I am no part of this awful war," he said.

The old woman's eyes narrowed. "I'm not for believing ye."

"And how'd ye get that tear on yer head, then?" asked the old man.

Bransen lifted his hand to touch the wound in the middle of his forehead where Affwin Wi had ripped the magical brooch from his flesh. "I . . . I ran into a low branch," he said.

"I'm still not for believing ye!" the old woman said with a hiss. "Now, ye turn about and be gone from here, or me old fellow here'll stick ye hard with four points o' pain."

"Aye," the old man said, prodding the pitchfork toward Bransen.

Bransen didn't flinch.

"Go on!" the old man insisted, thrusting the fork closer.

Unconsciously, the Highwayman reacted. As the pitchfork stabbed in, Bransen went forward and only slightly to the side, just enough so that the old man couldn't shift the weapon's angle to catch up to him. Once past the dangerous end of the pitchfork, the Highwayman moved with brutal efficiency, grabbing the shaft just below its head with his right hand, then knifing down his left hand with a swift and powerful chop. The handle shattered beneath that blow, leaving the old man with a short staff and Bransen holding the tined end of the pitchfork.

Bransen stepped back out of reach before those around him had even registered the move.

With a yelp of surprise, the old man took the stump of

the staff and lifted it above his head like a club, stumblingly rushing at Bransen with something between terror and outrage.

Bransen dropped the broken end of the pitchfork and brought his arms up above his head in a diagonal cross just as the old man chopped down at his head. The Highwayman caught the club easily in the crook of his blocking arms and, with a sudden uncrossing, tugged the piece of wood from the old man's grasp. Bransen caught it immediately and sent it into a furious spin, twirling it in one hand, working it expertly behind his back and out the other side as he handed it off to his other hand. The old man fell back, throwing his arms up before his face and whining pitifully. No one else made a sound, transfixed by the dazzling maneuvers of this stranger.

Up over his head went the broken handle, spinning furiously. The Highwayman brought it down before him and around his right hip, then back out from behind his left hip. Bransen fell into the rhythm of his display; he used the moment of physical concentration to temporarily block out the darkness that filled his mind. Around and around went the staff, then Bransen planted one end solidly on the ground before him. One hand went atop that planted staff. The Highwayman leaped into the air, inverting into a handstand that brought his kicking feet up level with the eyes of any would-be opponents. He landed gracefully in a spin and used that to launch the staff once more into a whirlwind all about him.

Bransen's eyes weren't even open any longer, as he fell deeper into the trance of physical perfection, deeper into the martial teaching he had devoured in the Book of Jhesi his father had penned. What started as a show for the villagers—a clear warning that Bransen hoped would prevent any rash actions leading to injury—had become something more profound and important to the troubled young man, a method of blocking out the ugly world.

Bransen's display went on for many heartbeats, spinning staff, leaping and twisting warrior, swift shifts and breaks in the momentum where Bransen transferred all of his energy into a sudden and brutal stab or swing.

When it finally played out, Bransen came up straight, took a deep breath, and opened his eyes—to stare into two-score incredulous faces.

"By the gods," one woman mouthed.

"Power," a young boy whispered, only because he could find no louder voice than that.

"Who are ye?" the old woman with the hooked nose asked after catching her breath.

"No one who matters, and no one who cares," Bransen answered, throwing the staff to the ground. "A hungry man begging food and willing to work for it. Nothing more."

"Begging?" a younger woman asked skeptically. She clutched a toddler tight in her arms. "Or threatening to take it if it's not given?"

Bransen looked at her closely, reading the anger on her dirty face. She might have been a pretty girl, once, an attractive young woman with blue eyes and wheat-colored hair. Perhaps once soft and inviting like a place to hide from the world, her hair now lay matted and scraggly, unkempt and uncut. The war had played hard on her; the only sparkle in her eyes was one of hatred, reflected in bloodshot lines and weary bags. There remained no soft lines there, just a sharp and hardened person who had seen and borne too much and eaten too little.

Bransen had no answers for her. He gave a helpless little shrug. With a slight bow he turned and started away.

"Now where are ye going?" the old man asked behind him.

"As far as I need to pass beyond this war."

"But ye ain't going away hungry!" the old woman declared. Bransen stopped and turned to face her. "No one's to say that we folk o' Hooplin Downs let a stranger walk away hungry! Get back here and eat yer stew, and we'll find some work for ye to pay for it."

"Might start by cutting me a new handle for me fork," the old man said, and several of the others laughed at that.

Not the young woman with the toddler, though. Obviously displeased by the turn of events, she held her young child close and glared at Bransen. He looked back at her curiously, trying to convey a sense of calm, but the glower did not relent.

Repairing the pitchfork proved no difficult task, for there were other implements about whose handles had long outlived their specialized heads. With that chore completed quickly, Bransen moved to help where he could, determined to pay back the folk equitably and more for their generosity in these dire times.

In truth, it wasn't much of a stew they shared that night, just a few rotten fish in a cauldron of water with a paltry mix of root vegetables. But to Bransen it tasted like hope itself, a quiet little reminder that many people—perhaps most—were possessed of a kind and generous nature, the one flickering candle in a dark, dark world. Reflecting on that point of light, Bransen silently chastised himself for his gloom and despair. For a moment, just a brief moment, he thought his decision to return to his wife and run away with her incredibly selfish and even petulant.

The people of Hooplin Downs didn't talk while they ate. They all sat solemnly, most staring into the distance as if seeing another, better time. Like so many in Honce, they seemed to be a haunted bunch. Their silence bespoke of great loss and sacrifice, and the manner in which each of

them tried to savor every pitiful bite revealed a level of
destitution that only reinforced to Bransen how generous
they had been in allowing him to share their pittance.

Darkness fell and supper ended. The villagers worked
together to clean up the common area about the large
cook fire. As the meager and downtrodden folk of Hooplin Downs moved about the sputtering flames, Bransen
felt he was witnessing the walk of the dead, shambling
out of the graveyards and the battlefields toward an uncertain eternity. His heart ached as he considered the
condition of the land and the folk, of the misery two
selfish lairds had willingly inflicted upon so many undeserving victims. His heart ached the most when he
considered how futile his flickering optimism had been.
Two men could destroy the world, it seemed, much
more easily than an army of well-meaning folk could
save or repair it.

Bransen sat before the fire for a long while, long past
when the others had wandered back to their cabins, staring into the flames as they consumed the twigs and logs.
He envisioned the smoke streaming from the logs as the
escape of life itself, the inexorable journey toward the
realm of death. He took the dark image one step further,
seeing the flame as his own hopes and dreams, diminish-
ing to glowing embers and fading fast into the dark reality
of a smoky-black night.

"I don't think I have ever seen a man sit so still and
quiet for so long," said a woman, interrupting his com-
munion with the dancing flickers. The edge in that voice,
not complimentary, drew him out of his introspection
even more than the words themselves. He looked up to
see the young mother who had questioned him sharply
when he had first entered Hooplin Downs. The toddler
stood now in the shadows behind her, which seemed to
relieve some of her vulnerability, as was evident in her
aggressive stance.

"All the work is done," he answered.

"And so is the meal you begged, uh, worked for," she added, her words dripping in sarcasm.

His eyes narrowed. "I did what I could."

The woman snorted. "A young man, very strong and quick, who can fight well . . . and here you sit, staring into the fire."

That description of his fighting ability tipped her hand.

"Your husband is off fighting in the war," Bransen said softly.

She snorted again, helplessly, angrily, pitifully, and looked to the side. "My husband got stuck to the ground by a Palmaristown spear," she said, chewing every word with outrage. "He'd likely be there still if the animals hadn't dragged him away to fill their bellies. Too many to bury, you know."

"I know."

"And here you sit, because your work is done," she retorted. "Here you sit, all whole and breathing and eating the food of folk who don't have enough to give, while men and women fall to the spear and the sword and the axe."

Bransen stared at her hard. She shifted and put her hands on her hips, returning his look without blinking. He wanted to tell her about Ancient Badden, how he had fought a more just war in the northland of Vanguard, how he and Jameston had saved a village from marauding rogue soldiers. He wanted to blurt it all out, to stand and stomp his feet, to scream about the futility of it all. But he couldn't.

Her posture, her expression, the power forged by pain in her voice, denied him his indignation, even mocked his self-pity. He had his life and his wife, after all.

"What side are you on, stranger?"

"Doesn't matter." Bransen dared to stand up straight before her. "Both sides are wrong."

He saw it coming but didn't try to stop it. She slapped him across the face.

"My husband's dead," she said. "Dead! The man I love is gone."

Bransen didn't say that he was sorry, but his expression surely conveyed that sentiment. Not that it mattered.

"They are both wrong?" The woman gave a little help-less laugh. "You're saying there's no reason we eat mud and go to cold beds? That's your answer? That's the an-swer of the brave warrior who can dodge a pitchfork and snap its head from its handle with ease?"

Bransen softened. "Do you wish that I had fought and saved your husband?" He was trying to send a note of ap-peasement and understanding, but the question sounded ridiculous even to his own ears. His face stung when she slapped him again.

"I wish you had got stuck to the ground and not him!" She spun away from him, and only then did Bransen realize all the village folk had gathered again to hear the exchange. They looked on with horror, a few with embar-rassment, perhaps, but Bransen noted that many heads were nodding in agreement with the woman.

"It's all a matter of chance!" The woman stomped back and forth before the onlookers. "That's what it is, yes? A hundred men go out, and twenty die! A thousand men go out, and more die." She turned on him sharply. "But the more that go, the more that come home, don't they? A thousand targets to spread the bite of Yeslnik's spears mean that each has more of a chance to miss that bite. So why weren't you there?" She launched herself at him. "Why are you here instead of showing yourself as a tar-get to the archers and the spearmen?"

This time Bransen didn't let her strike him because he knew the situation could escalate quickly and danger-ously for everyone. He caught her wrists, left and right as she punched, pinning them back to her sides. She began to wail openly, keening against the injustice of it all. He instinctively tried to pull her closer to comfort her, but she tore away, spinning about so forcefully and quickly that she lost her balance and tumbled to the dirt, where she half sat, half lay on one elbow, her other forearm slapped across her eyes.

Bransen's instincts again told him to go to her, but he didn't dare. He looked up at the many faces staring at him, judging him. He held his hands out questioningly, starting to back away.

A trio of women went to their fallen friend, one pausing just long enough to look up at Bransen and mutter, "Get ye gone from here." Her words sparked more calls. The woman's rant had touched a deep nerve here.

They weren't interested in his truth. All that mattered to them was the injustice that a young, obviously capable man was sitting here, seemingly untouched by the devastating reality that had visited upon all their homes.

Bransen took another step back from the outraged woman and held his hands up again, a helpless and ultimately sad look upon his face as he walked away.

Back in the empty forest, wandering the dark trails, Bransen's encounter in the village only reinforced his growing belief that he did not belong here . . . and perhaps not anywhere. He thought of Cadayle, the one warm spot in his bleak existence, and of their unborn child. Was he damning them both to a life of misery by his mere presence? Should he, after all, go the way of the younger Jameston Sequin, the way of the recluse, and not the way of the Jameston who had made the fateful and errant decision to come back into the wider civilized world?

What kind of husband would drag Cadayle and their babe into such an existence?

That question nearly drove Bransen to his knees. The implications were too harsh for him to even entertain their possibility.

Where would he fit in? How would he ever fit in?

And most important of all, why would he want to?

TOR

Award-winning authors
Compelling stories

Please join us at the website
below for more information
about this author and other great
Tor selections, and to sign up for
our monthly newsletter!